Tricia Sullivan was born in New ~~~~
pioneering Music Program Zerc ~~~~
received a Master's in Educati ~~~~
taught in Manhattan and New ~~~~
1995. Her novel *Dreaming in Smoke* won the Arthur C. Clarke award.

Find out more about Tricia Sullivan and other Orbit authors by
registering for the free monthly newletter at www.orbitbooks.co.uk

By Tricia Sullivan

MAUL

DOUBLE VISION

SOUND MIND

soundmind

TRICIA SULLIVAN

www.orbitbooks.co.uk

ORBIT

First published in Great Britain in 2006 by Orbit

Epigraph
Quote by Benjamin Boretz, copyright © 2000 by Benjamin Boretz,
reprinted by permission. Quote by Stephen Wolfram, copyright ©
2002 by Stephen Wolfram, LLC, reprinted by permission of
Wolfram Media, Inc. www.wolfram-media.com

A CIP catalogue record for this book
is available from the British Library.

ISBN-13: 978-1-84149-405-0
ISBN-10: 1-84149-405-4

Typeset in Palatino by M Rules
Printed and bound in Great Britain by
Mackays of Chatham plc

Orbit
An imprint of
Little, Brown Book Group
Brettenham House
Lancaster Place
London WC2E 7EN

A Member of the Hachette Livre Group of Companies

www.orbitbooks.co.uk

For Sean

There is no such thing as 'structure' outside the sound of a piece, not the sound of the piece indicates the presence of something called structure: a metaphysical fiction, ontologically obnoxious, as far as I am concerned.
– *Benjamin Boretz*

While we might have imagined that science would eventually show us how to rise above all our human details what we now see is that in fact these details are in effect the only important thing about us.
– *Stephen Wolfram*

part one
the rending

October, 1987

Annandale, NY

What Happens After

I made it to 199 and stuck out my thumb.

Normally I wouldn't hitchhike but I couldn't have walked much further on that leg. I had already come four miles. I'd ditched all my books, so all I had in my backpack were a couple of sticks of gum, my Pro Walkman with some recent recordings, a notebook and the bra I'd taken off while Craig and I were messing around in his room. For some reason, when IT happened I'd had the presence of mind to put on my sweater and stuff the bra in my backpack before climbing out the window. Saving your bra isn't a very practical use of a precious five seconds; but then, climbing out the window wasn't too bright, either.

Craig lived in one of the Ravine Houses, which are these wooden dorms built on stilts out over the wooded ravine. They look like treehouses, and they sway like treehouses, so when the place first started shaking we didn't think anything much about it. We were sitting on the floor and Craig was sharing his Captain Beefheart LP collection with me. This was maybe less kinky than it sounds, and I complained that I was bored.

'OK, Cassidy-the-Real-Musician,' said Craig, and reached into my backpack. 'Let's find out how *your* stuff compares, then.'

He pulled out a white plastic bag with *Staples Office Supplies* printed on it. He took out a cassette and held it up over my head.

'That's not mine!' I cried. It wasn't; I'd found it near the dead guy the other night. I tried to get it off Craig but he wrestled me away and stuck it in the deck. I tackled him, things got kind of horny, and I wasn't really paying attention to the music.

I didn't yet know that I was hearing the first approach of IT, right there in Craig's tape deck. Still, I tried to get him to turn the music off, because I didn't like it, but he wouldn't let me near the deck. That was how the bra came off.

I was laughing so hard that at first I didn't hear the screaming. But we both heard the first explosion, so Craig told me to stay put and went to check things out.

I took the tape out of the deck and put it in my backpack. A minute later there was more screaming and a lot of demolition-site noises, and I smelled smoke. I opened the door and the hallway was on fire. So I grabbed my sneakers and went out the window.

Got banged up pretty bad when the building went down. I was still clinging to a strut and ended up jumping clear just in time. I scraped one leg on a protruding nail and twisted the other ankle when I landed. I also bit my lip so hard that I was sure it would be detached, but it only swelled.

I clapped my hands over my ears. The sound of IT was all around: in the air, in the ground, in the trembling branches with their ragged autumn leaves. I started running. Away from IT, into IT, through IT.

A pickup whizzed past me and my thumb on 199. I blinked away grit, feeling embarrassed. I had never hitched before. I wasn't prepared for the feeling of rejection.

There were some pieces of concrete on the highway, and a

fallen tree blocked Annandale Road on the other side. The traffic light was out. I could hear, but not see, a helicopter somewhere over the river. When a green Pathfinder stopped at the fallen tree I limped over and banged on the window.

There was a blonde woman inside. She was wearing a Mets cap and sunglasses, and she had put her head and arms on the steering wheel like she was asleep or crying. When I banged, she jumped and then shrank back away from me, reaching for the glove compartment with her right hand, using jerky, panicked movements.

'What do you want? Get back!' she yelled. Behind her back, her hand closed on a king-sized Milky Way and I saw the knuckles go white as she gripped it, bringing the candy bar forward with a defensive jerk; then she seemed to realize what it was and chucked it into the back seat. She groped some more in the glove compartment.

I wanted to laugh, but by this time I was pretty tired because I'd come about three miles from campus on the bad leg, and the initial burn of adrenalin was gone, leaving me sort of in a daze. My whole body was starting to ache and feel heavy. I guess I didn't look too good, either.

'Whoa,' I said slowly. 'Chill out. I was only going to ask for a ride.'

A Volkswagen hurtled past us, spraying me with gravel. I had to lean against the side of the Pathfinder. The woman had finally grabbed what she was looking for: a sharpened screwdriver. But once she had it she just kind of looked at it, then at me.

'You're hurt,' she observed. She sounded suspicious. I shrugged. I could hear the helicopter approaching from the direction of Rhinebeck, fast. The woman frowned at the screwdriver.

'I don't know what . . .' she said. 'I'm a little . . . look, it's shaking in my hand. Look at my hand shake!'

I wasn't so sure that I wanted to get in the car with her after all. If she was this nervous, she might crash. But now she glued me with a blue-eyed stare and said, 'Come on. Get in.'

As I climbed up into the passenger seat I had, like, a muscle insurrection. As in none of them would work. I had to lean out to pull the door shut, and the helicopter dove at us and swooped past as I fought with the door and the wind. It was a military aircraft and I could see a guy with some kind of big gun leaning out the side. He didn't point it at me. He didn't have to – I freaked out anyway.

'Jesus!' I screamed, and the woman threw the Pathfinder into reverse and then into first gear, weaving it around the fallen tree with a roar and a squeal. I grabbed the door with both hands and threw my whole body weight backward into the car. The air pressure shifted and I was thrown against the driver as the door slammed. She kept accelerating: by the time we hit fifty I was back in my own seat, apologizing and cursing at the same time.

The helicopter lifted and went haring off towards Bard. I leaned on the dashboard, wide-eyed, and watched the road hurtling toward us. We were lucky that nobody seemed to be coming the other way, because this woman was kind of all over the place, side-of-the-road-wise.

'It's OK.' I kept saying it over and over, hoping she would slow down but she didn't. 'It's OK, we'll be OK.'

The woman glanced at me, braking and looking left and right as she got ready to take the Red Hook turn.

'You got blood on your face. Were you at the bridge?'

I checked out my face in the vanity mirror and wished I hadn't.

'Bridge? No. What happened at the bridge?'

She glanced at me again, then stepped hard on the gas. She gave a little laugh. 'You don't want to know. I'm Michelle, by the way.'

'I'm Cassidy. Nice to meet you.'

I felt like a jerk when I said that, but Michelle didn't even seem to listen. She swerved around an eighteen-wheeler coming the other way, even though she had plenty of room and didn't have to. As a result she clipped the edge of Kurt's Truck Stop parking lot and the Pathfinder rocked from side to side like a boat. An electronic chime sounded to warn her that we were about to tip over.

'Oops,' she said. 'Sorry about that. Should you be going to the hospital? Because I'm going to Red Hook and that isn't really the right way if you're going to the hospital, now that I think about it.'

'Doesn't matter,' I said. 'I don't care. I'll go anywhere as long as it isn't Bard.'

'Bard?'

'Yeah, Bard College, you know? That's where I just was, when . . . well, if you don't want to talk about it . . .'

I stopped talking. I didn't want to provoke Michelle. She was awfully antsy. Her face twitched.

'Was it really Soviet? I talked to a guy who saw it take out the bridge. He said something big hit the water half a mile south.' She shook her head like she was arguing with herself. 'They set up a roadblock and they got boats out there looking for survivors. Cars got swept off the bridge and everything. I wanted to stay and help the divers – they could've used the back of my car, and I got ropes and stuff, I got a first-aid kit. But the police made me go back. One army chopper, is that the best they can do after two hours?'

I steadied myself on the dash again as we hurtled around a bend. The bridge was down. What the hell.

'So were you on the bridge?'

'No, I was at Bard.'

'Who's Bart?'

The suspicious look came back again. My right leg was

throbbing and my left ankle was so swollen I doubted I'd be able to walk on it at all.

'Bard,' I said. 'Where I go to college.'

Michelle took her eyes off the road a little too long and the Pathfinder drifted right, brushing against some overhanging bushes. She corrected just in time.

I saw her shake her head to herself. People can be funny about Bard students. The locals seem to hate us.

'Where is this college?'

'Oh, it's just a couple miles from where you picked me up. I'm surprised you didn't see the sign.'

'Never heard of it,' she said in a clipped tone. 'And I lived in Red Hook all my life. The Moonies live up by there, though.'

I didn't say anything for a minute. There was indeed a Moonie complex in Barrytown, just down the road from Bard. Did she seriously think I was a Moonie? There had to be something wrong with this woman.

'I really appreciate the ride,' I said finally. 'If you could drop me anywhere in town, that'd be great.'

There were no police in Red Hook ('Diverted to Poughkeepsie, big surprise,' snorted Michelle) but there were enough guys with CBs and megaphones to cover each of the four roads. Everybody and his lesbian aunt were trying to fill up at the crossroads Shell gas station where Michelle dropped me. I was uneasy about the proximity of all that gasoline, especially after what had happened at Bard. I started to cross the street with some vague intention of getting a ride to the hospital from there when I noticed the crowd lined up at the payphones that were fixed to the brick wall between the Shell station and the Tivoli Gardens restaurant.

I stopped. It was crazy to go to the hospital if the emergency room was going to be overrun. It was a long line for the phones but I decided to call my mom and try to get home. I stood in line, trying to ignore the weird looks people were giving me. Instead, I pictured my mom in my mind. It would be lunchtime: she'd be in the staff room having coffee with Ethel or reading a magazine and eating a tuna sandwich. If I was lucky, I could just catch her before her afternoon sculpture class started. She'd go into a panic when she heard my news. Maybe she already knew, if it was on TV. Anyway, she'd panic. Then she'd tell me not to panic. Then she'd call Dad and he'd drive up and pick me up at the hospital. Maybe he was even on his way already. Yeah, that would be good.

The sun shone on my face, making me want to close my eyes. I was really tired. I took a half-melted Nestlé crunch out of my backpack and ate it slowly, taking deep breaths of gasoline-smelling air. My tongue felt exhausted when I ran it over my gums to clean up the chocolate. Of all the muscles in my body my tongue had been the least used, and it still went on strike. My eyelids drooped and I shut my eyes for a little while. I swayed on my feet.

At the nearest pump a whole pickup-load of construction workers had the radio tuned to an emergency broadcast, but the announcer kept getting blotted out by the sound of IT. I shuddered, wanting to hear the news but cringing every time the sound of IT overpowered the radio ... *Route 9 closed south of Poughkeepsie, Route 84 closed at the New Paltz bridge ... IT ... governor's office issued ... IT ... Mike in our helicopter over ... IT ... not to stockpile ... IT ... emergency generators ... IT IT IT IT—*

I put my hands over my ears and glared at the men. They listened with focused intent. How could they do that? How could they stand the sound of IT? Were they hearing something that I wasn't? Or was it the other way around?

I had a bad feeling. Maybe *I* was the one hearing things.

So maybe I was just paranoid, but stuff can happen to your head when you see things other people don't see. Or when invisible people put staples in you while you're inside the piano. Not that I wanted to think about that.

Back at Bard I can remember jamming my feet into my sneakers and running across the dirt track that passed for a road-cum-parking lot in front of the Ravine Houses, squeezing between the bumpers of cars that were piling up in the rush to get out. One of the dorm proctors was trying to get his jeep across the big field between the Ravine Houses and Tewksbury and bypass the road entirely, but the field was soaking wet and he'd gotten stuck. Some guy called Shawn who lived in Bluecher House went jogging over in his Doc Martens and ripped jeans and Butthole Surfers T-shirt, dragging his girlfriend Pru who was wearing only panties and a leather jacket. They started trying to move the car.

I made it out into the field; then I first heard IT. The sound was coming at me from all directions. I was awestruck. The sound opened up rooms in my mind that I'd never known existed. I seemed to remember places and ideas that I knew hadn't happened to me. I wondered if it was like tripping – which I've never done but you hear enough about it at Bard to feel as though you have.

For a few seconds – and I'm guessing how long it was, but I'd say it was really only a few seconds even though they were stretched-out, long, intense ones – I was in balance with the sound and it filled me and I felt empty at the same time. I felt like a guitar string that's been tuned to its neighbors, tightrope-taut and in perfect resonance. But then IT kept going. ITs sound kept mounting and increasing and taking strange turns, and in a flash I lost it. Lost my scrambled eggs and OJ, lost my composure, lost myself for a little while at least.

When I got up off my knees and wiped the puke off my chin, Shawn and Co. had managed to push the jeep back onto the road. I saw Craig then, standing in front of the burning Hirsch

House with his T-shirt pulled up over his face because of the smoke, looking from side to side. I thought maybe he was looking for me. Where Craig's dorm had been there was now just a ragged chunk of the front porch, framed by bright light and trees beyond. Craig's blond hair was gray with ash. I wanted to go to him. But the sound made that impossible. IT was getting more and more intense. I had the horrible feeling that the sound was actually drilling its way outwards from inside my body.

Then a shadow passed over everything. At the same time, the fire jumped from Hirsch to the line of cars, and I threw my arms over my head and eyes and flattened myself to the ground like a rabbit in a strong wind. I looked up and saw Craig get in a VW Bug.

'No, stupid!' I cried, but I couldn't hear myself. I was panting and I could smell my armpits and my groin in the sheltered air between my clothes and my body. Something big was passing overhead. It wasn't a bird and it wasn't a plane and it wasn't Superman. My first thought was that it was a UFO, but the way the air was moving I could swear I heard the beating of wings so big that I wouldn't want to see them. I was totally cowed. I squeezed my eyes shut and waited. I don't even know what I thought I was waiting for. I wasn't thinking. I was just reacting.

The shadow moved off me. I got to my feet, but I didn't look up at the sky. I didn't want to see IT. ITs sound continued at the same intensity, but the volume abated so that now IT was all mixed up with people yelling and the explosions of gas tanks as cars caught fire. I saw flames running along the hood of the VW. I must have seen the explosion, too, but I don't remember that part. I know that I pointed my butt at whatever happened and ran from it, slipping on the wet grass. I felt gangling and useless and the leg wasn't cooperating, but I dragged myself forward anyway.

Ahead loomed the white bulk of Tewksbury, the ugliest building on campus and the only dorm that looks and feels like a dorm. Everything about it screams Institution. Under normal circumstances I would never go there, and even under these circumstances, it seemed a stupid place to be. Everybody else was running *out* of the building and I had to stand aside in the stairwell to let hysterical freshmen get loose.

I went in. I had to get away from the sound.

Tewks has a laundry room in the basement, and piano practice rooms with soundproof walls. I went into a practice room and sat under a battered old spinet, but I could still hear IT. I tried another room; same thing. Finally I went into the laundry room, where somebody's jeans were slushing around in one of the machines and somebody's colors were spinning in the dryer, and all that white noise took away the thing I didn't want to hear. I crouched next to the warm dryer and tried not to see the Volkswagen containing my boyfriend going *boom* on my mental projection screen, over and over and over.

Somebody was tapping me on the shoulder. I was in Red Hook and it was almost my turn to use the phone.

I turned around and took my hands off my ears. The pickup truck was gone and I couldn't hear IT on the radio anymore. A round bearded face with glasses confronted me.

'Jeremy!' I heard myself exclaim. I sounded overjoyed, like some popular chick at a party fakely greeting a guy she doesn't really like. 'Hey, what's up? Are you OK?'

It was hard to read his expression through his beard and glasses, which I was sure he used to cultivate his overall air of faintly superior detachment. Jeremy is the kind of person who knows everything about everything and always wants to tell you. If he sees you drinking an Anchor Steam he'll lecture you about the politics of independent breweries. He has a thick voice, the kind that always sounds like he's got some mucus or something way down in his throat, or like he's talking through a mouthful of peanut butter.

He said, 'Yeah. I'm OK. You look like shit.'

I was kind of surprised he even remembered who I was. He was my friend Anitra's former boyfriend, and I'd seen him around the music department – he even took a computer-music class last year. I sat in on it but it was too dry for me. So was he. The last time I'd run into him, I'd asked him the standard, 'How was your summer?' question and he'd said, 'I spent it calculating pi as far as I could. Got about seventeen pages.'

Now I snorted. 'I guess you weren't there, then. I look *good* compared to . . .'

I halted. The first few people that you see on fire, running and then falling down and not getting up, you don't really take in the information. By the time your brain has gotten around to figuring out what it is you're seeing you're practically inured to it – or something has happened, anyway, to make you numb and unfeeling. Or just sick-headed – because I had this tremendous urge to make flip remarks about human torches. I realized I was probably skating on the edge of sounding nuts.

'I wasn't where?' said Jeremy.

I shook my head. I didn't want to start crying; not in front of him.

I tried not saying anything for a minute. It was my turn for the phone. I dialed my mom's work number but I got one of those annoying beeps and an uptight female recording telling me to check the number and dial again. I did, and it was the same thing. I tried calling home; I could leave a message on the machine, anyway. The exact same thing happened.

'That's weird,' I said to Jeremy. 'The phone's not going through.'

'Let me try,' he said. 'Maybe it's this phone.'

I stood back and he dialed, had a brief conversation, and hung up. He shrugged.

'I just called the house. Got the machine. Seems OK.'

I tried again, with him watching me. It still didn't work.

'Shit,' I said. 'How am I supposed to get home? I can't take a bus all the way to New Jersey.'

I tried calling Ben's office, but that phone didn't work either. I called his home number. Machine, of course. I stammered some kind of message and hung up. Ben would know what to do, wouldn't he? I mean, he hadn't known what to make of the stapling thing but maybe he would know what IT was all about. Music-wise.

I followed Jeremy into the gas-station office. There were a few racks of groceries and some magazines, and a lot of people talking semi-hysterically. The TV was showing rack and ruin in Poughkeepsie, but I couldn't hear the reporter's voice over the din of the real people. I thought I heard a faint hum of IT starting to come through, like fire starts to ignite paper with a spreading black stain before it bursts into flame. I tried to ignore it.

'I don't think you're going to get to Jersey,' Jeremy said. 'The highways are all blocked. I'm supposed to be in Albany. I had to turn around and come back.'

He opened his wallet and took out an Amex gold card. A lot of Bard students had them. Mom and Dad paid the bill. I started working my way through the crowd that was jammed into the tiny station, looking for something to eat.

Then this girl Leona from my dorm walked in. I dodged behind the Hostess rack for a minute to try to compose myself. Leona always made me nervous. She reminded me of the younger sister of this guy Paul I really really liked in high school. The younger sister, Diane, was a gymnast but not built like a typical anorexic gymnast, no: she was compact and muscular and, as my friend Janie once cattily remarked, 'She has the same legs as Paul,' who had really solid legs from skiing. But of course that kind of bulk looks nice on a guy but not on a girl. Especially a short girl. Anyway, due to this resemblance I'd always found myself staring at Leona and feeling a weird mixture of being intimidated by her and jealous of her and attracted to her. But we'd never been friends. When I talked to her on the first night of freshman orientation our conversation went something like this.

Me: 'Where you from?'

Her: 'New York.'

Me: 'Yeah, what part?'

Her: 'Manhattan' – i.e., the real New York, *stupid*.

Her: 'Where are you from?'

Me: 'Um . . . Jersey.'

Silence.

Still, I found myself drawn to Leona and I'd even wondered if it meant I was a lesbian or bisexual or something and I ended up avoiding her for this reason and also because I suspected she was stupid and – worse yet – that *she* thought *I* was stupid.

Hence me hiding behind the Hostess rack. But she must have spotted me because she came around the corner and said, 'Hey. What's up?'

I blurted, 'How'd you get here?'

She looked at me pityingly and I could tell it was going to be another one of those conversations.

'I got a ride?' she said, raising the pitch of her voice at the end like she was asking a question: her way of letting me know she did indeed believe I was an idiot.

I grabbed her shoulders and shook her.

'Where from? From the city?'

Leona pulled away, aghast. 'No. From work. What's the matter with you? You didn't even show up this morning. I heard Dominic just disappeared and Hannah locked herself in the house. Sally can't pay anybody.'

I stopped shaking her and tried to pull myself together. She was talking about my job. How did she know about my job?

'You work at Moonshadow.' I said it like a statement, but of course it wasn't true.

'Duh. Cassidy, what's with you? Come on, you can't let this disaster stuff get you down. Everything's going to be OK.'

Leona had never worked at Moonshadow that I could remember. It was hard to picture her shoveling shit. I wondered if she rode the racehorses or something and that was why I hadn't known about it.

'I came to buy chocolate,' I said irrelevantly. 'I don't know where to go or what to do. I can't go back to Bard.'

'Who?'

Oh, here we go again.

'Never mind,' I said.

It must have been then that I started to adopt the shut-up-and-wait-for-the-authorities-to-arrive game plan. Not that it was a real strategy, more like a default response to terror. And it does seem to be something people do. Pass the buck, I mean. I know why I did it. When you grow up in the suburbs you don't tend to think of yourself as responsible for the world as such. You don't even consider yourself as *living* in the world: you occupy this semi-abstract realm of TV and shopping and school, waiting for your life to start. You get a fuck-this attitude by the time you're fourteen. Well, *I* did, anyway. When I got to Bard and everything was chilled and there were no cliques and being different was better than being in fashion and everybody hung out getting stoned with everybody else and the professors expected you to actually *think* and credited you with some intelligence and you were allowed to try new things – well, I admit I did suddenly turn sincere. Or, at least, the edge of my cynicism about the world got blunted a little.

But that change must have been only superficial, because as soon as IT swooped down on campus and drove me out of Annandale and into redneck Red Hook, I reverted to my original nature. I became suburban again. I wanted somebody else to fix it. I wanted to call the monster-exterminators and charge the whole thing on my mom's credit card. I didn't want to deal at all.

'We're going to get out of here,' Leona said. 'We got space in the back. You could come.'

She said it reluctantly, like she'd half-thought better of it.

'Jeremy said the roads were blocked.'

'Preston has a four-wheel drive. We can go over the fields.'

'Where?'

'The city. Preston's paying for the diesel right now. He's got a credit card. Do you have any money?'

I shrugged. 'Like, ten bucks,' I said.

Now I could hear Preston arguing with the girl behind the counter and I guess she didn't want to honor the card on account of the phone lines being down. I don't know where Jeremy had disappeared to, but he was gone and so was his Infiniti. There was a line of about fifty cars backed up on the 199 waiting for gas, and the shelves of the minimart were looking pretty bare with everybody stocking up.

We went outside to wait, me with a Diet 7-Up which was all I could get hold of in the crush, Leona with a pack of Winstons and a bag of M&Ms. With my paint-stained Dr Scholls I scuffed at oil spots on the pavement in time to 'Timebomb' on Preston's car stereo. Preston was a cornfed Iowa boy with blond hair who said 'yup' and 'nope' and 'maybay,' but he took his Public Enemy seriously. 'I'm studying their angle on syncopation and space-time architecture,' he said earnestly when he brought a tape into Ben's class once. Preston's roommate Cliff called them Pubic Enema. Relentlessly.

It was all very thin and bland; just life. Just pavement and cloudy late-summer sky and the taste of M&Ms because that was the kind of thing we bought when we were hungry, like kids let out of mom's sight, just because we could. I was bored and, underneath that, anxious.

All these people lining up to get out of town, they were just responding to what they heard on the CB, or to word-of-mouth rumors, or maybe to the TV reports that had cropped up thick and fast on local news. Evidently we were cut off from the rest of the state. How, exactly, nobody could or would say; but you couldn't cross the Kingston Bridge to get to the Thruway, you couldn't get to the Taconic, you couldn't take a train. The only media stations that worked were the local ones. No one knew what was going on. Was it nuclear war? A seismic event? Invasion by aliens?

'An unexplained atmospheric disturbance,' the news people were saying. The correspondents had a glassy, vague look. I probably looked like that, too. I don't think anyone else in Red Hook had seen IT, because they were all acting pretty normal and none of them were the walking wounded like me. Nobody else from Bard seemed to have made it out yet. The only Bard students I could see had been off-campus at the time of the attack. None of them wanted to hear the word 'Bard' and they looked at me like I was deranged when I referred to it.

But I was scared, and I wanted to get out of here in case this thing wasn't over.

I bit my lip. 'What's taking so lo—'

Over Leona's shoulder I saw the first crack. It wasn't obvious: just a displaced cornice on the old building catty-corner to the gas station on 199 and 9G. The building had been painted dark red at ground level and white from the first floor to the roof. On the corner at the point where the white paint started there was a raised molding in a scalloped design. A section of this was black. Not black like black paint, and not black like there were missing bricks and you could see a hole, because there was no discernible edge. It was black as in void – just not there.

I stared at it, mouth still half-open with my unfinished complaint. There was a florist's shop in the store below, and the staff must have planted some decorative flowers along the edge of the molding, because there was a lilac-colored lace of blooms to either side of the black space. The missing area was C-shaped, a crescent moon. I thought that the proximity of the flowers, their petals stirring in the breeze off the road, made the black spot all the more menacing. And it was beginning to grow, like the wall was a piece of paper and there were flames on the other side beginning to stain it, beginning to break through . . .

No one else had noticed it. I thought: *Fuck, what do I do?*

Preston had succeeded in paying; he came out of the shop waving his credit card and smiling. The card flashed in the sun. On the clean new pavement of the forecourt there was a web of cracks, some of them sprouting grass. I could see tendrils of black there, too, and they shook like a dance floor. IT was coming faster this time. They didn't know, but IT was almost upon us.

I made an inarticulate noise. I wanted to warn them but I couldn't find the words. I turned to Leona, who was leaning on the hood. There was a black spot on the hood.

'The car!' I said, pointing idiotically. 'See? Shit, we better get going *now*.'

Leona wasn't reading me at all. Half a smile started up the side of her face. Then the wind knocked her flat against the diesel pump as IT came on.

I threw myself downwind, rolled, ran, fell, crawled.

The sound went through my body like a fat blunt spike. Again.

I took it personally. How could I not? As sound, it was a transliteration of terror. It was the sound I'd been looking for all semester, the sound I'd made a fool of myself for, and now that I was hearing it for real I wished I could crawl back in the womb and start everything over.

I'd been working on this collage of found sounds. I called it 'Nuclear Day Dream' and it was about nuclear war. I find it really hard to believe there won't be one. Ever since I was a kid and I found out the whole planet could get wiped out I find it hard to make, like, plans of any kind. I guess it's just a realization of death, but the nuclear shit makes it all seem so absolute. Some people would say what does it matter if the whole world blows up because if you get killed, you get killed and you're not there to appreciate what's left anyway. But I'd like to think of there still being trees and stuff; the idea that everything would be wasted is pretty hard to take.

Anyway, I played a tape of my piece in Ben's class and he didn't think the total-noise part was anything much. Which was kind of embarrassing because I went all-out hell-for-leather on chaos and I was hoping to get some kind of rise that I was daring enough to trash the world in this way.

Ben said, 'I think the thing that would be really interesting is what happens *after* the big explosion.'

'After?' I said incredulously. 'There isn't anything *after*. That's the whole point.'

'OK, so there isn't anything after, but it would be interesting to hear what there would be *if* there was something after.'

I didn't say anything. I was disappointed. He didn't get it.

All of this is my way of not talking about exactly what happened next. I'd rather not spell it out. I'm not even sure I could.

All I really know is that when the second attack ended I found that I'd fetched up against the lattice covering the crawl space under the front porch of a Victorian house, where the foundation would otherwise have been exposed. Smoke was coming from the direction of the Shell station a few blocks away. I didn't know how I'd gotten from there to here. I felt giddy, and after IT faded a silent lacuna lay in my head where IT had been. In the silence there seemed to be no time. I couldn't hear my own heartbeat or anything.

I drew a couple of breaths. Cars were stopping or had stopped; people were getting out and walking – or running – in various directions.

*

At Bard, when I had finally crept out of the Tewks laundry room it had been a little like this. The sky had been blotted out by clouds of smoke. Kline Commons seemed to have imploded, or been crushed. The library was burning, but it didn't generate enough smoke to explain the color of the sky, which was a luminous sepia dragging to black at the horizons. I stood outside Tewksbury looking across the wet soccer field, wondering if I could flag down a car on the road to North Campus. There was a spicy smell in the air. I started walking toward the chapel – and that was when I saw the footprint.

It was a star-shaped depression in the low part of the field between Tewksbury and the Proctor art center, and it had collected muddy water. I guess the main part of it was about the size of a small car, with long claw marks protruding for several feet in five directions. It looked more like a hand than a foot.

From the surface of the water came the sound of IT, only softer. The identity of the sound was the same; but this version was almost tolerable – like the fingerprint of a psychopath, it was only scary because I knew what it implied.

I whipped out my Pro Walkman and pressed *Rec*. I had to get this on tape.

IT sounded like a zillion different radio stations all playing really loud and the sound was like *packed*, it was like multi-level, it was so thick like at once really loud and outside and also really tiny and close inside your ears.

I recorded it for a few minutes. I was unable to hear much of anything else, actually. I could see cars and people and the flashing lights that meant there must be sirens, but I couldn't hear anything but IT. I thought maybe the blast of sound had done something to my ears, you know how like after going to see a band you hear the jungle in your ears for the whole next day, and people sound like they're coming to you underwater.

I held the Walkman in position until I saw something move in the air above me – a helicopter, a cloud, a wing, I don't know – and this seemed to set my legs in motion whether I wanted to go or not. I started running south on Annandale Road, and then walking, and then limping.

And as I got farther and farther from IT my head got emptier and emptier. This draining sensation was almost pleasant. Then, for a few seconds, I found myself walking in dead silence. This happened near the crossroads leading to Barrytown. I took four or five steps, and there was no sound. Anywhere. Not even inside me. Not even my heart. And I had the sense of some visual presence just on the borders of my peripheral vision: when I tried to look, there was nothing there. Faint impression of something architectural. Maybe white stone; maybe a distant skyline. Maybe creeping numbers like insects. But only maybe. Nothing definite.

When the sound came back I realized I was whimpering a little with each breath. They were small rodent noises, frightened, self-pitying noises, and all the way along Annandale Road I didn't stop making them until the Pathfinder pulled up.

Now I was in Red Hook. I had to keep reminding myself about this. I was losing my moorings, and I kept flashing back to Bard. My brain must have believed I was about to relive what I had just been through. I had the feeling it was prodding me into action, coaching me to do something differently next time – but I didn't know what. And I didn't want to think about the possibility that there could be a next time.

I did what they tell you to do under stress: focused on breathing slowly and deeply. I could still feel the residue of IT echoing in my head. I could hear it coming out of the CBs of tractor-trailers. I could hear it, faintly, coming from the diner across Route 9. In fact, IT seemed to be my personal soundtrack.

'Well, Cass,' I said to myself, getting painfully to my feet. 'You got your sound.' And I patted the Walkman in my bag with what I hoped was ironic satisfaction, but I wanted to cry. I started walking again, slowly. I didn't know where I was going. Away from the exploded gas station, that was all I knew.

I was thinking about my so-called 'piece' 'Nuclear Day Dream' and how butt-ass stupid it was, after all. And here I thought it was so important, so revolutionary, so fuck-you. It was only ever lame, and now that I'd seen the real thing – heard the real thing – I knew I'd gotten it wrong.

I stopped.

'You're walking north, stupid,' I informed myself. 'The hospital is south.'

'Cassidy? Are you OK?'

I turned around and there was Anitra on a decrepit old three-speed, just catching up with me. She wobbled as she slowed down and had to put a foot out to the curb to stop herself.

'Hey, Anitra,' I said wearily.

'Are you OK?' she repeated. Her forehead was furrowed, drawing her thick black eyebrows together. Anitra is big and solid; she has the most gorgeous dark green eyes and skin the color of whole-wheat toast. I met her in a figure-drawing class I took last semester: she was the model for several of the sessions. Her body is like a piece of ripe fruit. She doesn't shave her legs, either. This gives her an ancient, primal quality as a model.

She was shaking her head at me and looking really worried.

'Jeremy said you looked all beat up, but he didn't mention the blood. You better come back to the house and get cleaned up.'

'OK,' I said.

'Can you walk?'

'I was walking. I've been walking. I walked.' I recited the phrases successively and then gave a small smile, because I reminded myself of eighth-grade Latin classes. Anitra was checking me out like she was pretty sure I wasn't all there.

'You've just been standing here,' she said gently. 'I could see you from back at the diner. I was having a Reuben and I saw you standing under this tree, doing nothing. Then I ran into Jeremy and he told me he saw you at the gas station this afternoon.'

This afternoon? 'Yeah, a couple minutes ago,' I said. Then I took in the fact that the neighborhood was looking pretty gray and dim, and there were yellow lights in the windows of the nearest houses, and the street lights had come on over by the diner.

Anitra pulled the bike off the road and propped it against my sycamore. She took my elbow like I was an old lady she was going to help across the street.

'I'm fine,' I said. 'I can walk.'

But when I tried to move my leg it felt like a piece of dead wood.

'I was afraid of something like this,' she said. 'When you didn't come home last night, and then when all this . . . stuff . . . started happening, I was afraid you were mixed up in it.'

'What do you mean, I didn't come home last night?' I said, hobbling along beside her. 'You're not my roommate.'

I could feel her tense slightly when I said that, and I had the feeling she was going to disagree. But instead she said, 'OK, OK, let's just get you back to the house.'

'What about your bike?'

'I'll come back for it.'

'Does all that smoke back there mean Preston and Leona are dead?'

Anitra looked like she'd been punched in the mouth. She gripped my arm and said, 'Shh . . .'

Model Panzer Tanks and Popsicle Sticks

Anitra took me to a place she called The House, and she treated me as if I'd lived there forever. The House was a huge white Victorian farmhouse with a wraparound porch and an attic, and I learned that although it was rented by Jeremy's parents it was shared by five to eight people, depending on the day of the week and who was together with who and who'd just broken up or flipped out and gone home to Atlanta. It smelled of incense and patchouli and cat pee. There were three bedrooms upstairs; 'my room' turned out to be the former dining room.

There was some kind of misunderstanding going on here, because Anitra claimed the dining room *was* my room, and *had been* my room since last summer. There was some stuff there that could have been mine, I guess: some tapes, some books, some clothes that I didn't particularly recognize but which were my size. But no musical instruments.

The fact that I had saved my bra and not my guitar really sucked, actually. I went into 'my' room, sat down on the mattress covered with Indian batik spreads and faced a stump of candle, and the thing I wanted most was to have a guitar in my hands. But my guitar was gone. So was all my other stuff.

Not that I'd have the courage to play, now. Yeah, on second thought maybe it was better that I didn't have the guitar. Still, without music, what was I going to do?

I had come to Bard because their music department included rock, jazz, classical, and a smattering of Everything Else in what looked from the outside like a carefree do-your-thing mix. It was the only place in the world where I could remotely imagine fitting in, considering that my musical skill level was practically zero. I mean, I had a certain facility for the guitar and the extra finger didn't hurt, but I was no Yngwy Malmsteen. I just wrote songs. Kind of weird songs, apparently. I am pretty much tone-deaf (at least since the *Golden Dragon*; apparently before then I had an ear) so the idea that I would be a musician was a kind of gauntlet thrown down from me to the logic of the world. I needed it badly, that was all.

I probably wouldn't have lasted very long had it not been for the fact that at Bard there was this teacher called Ben. He was a famous guy in music-theory circles, but he reminded me more of a farmer when I met him because he had a bullshit-free air about him that doesn't crop up often in academia, and he didn't talk like an academic. He also had these blunt hands. There was a practical air about him.

Ben's courses had once been part of the music curriculum but lately he'd been forced out of the music department by the conservatory types and he effectively had his own department, which he called Music Program Zero. He was allowed this because he was a highly respected music theorist of impeccable pedigree – and he had tenure. Otherwise he'd have been out on his ass, I'm pretty sure. The powers that be at the college treated him like a pariah, probably because he didn't respect the titles, degrees, and formalities that they so deeply treasured and clung to for dear life. And he treated the students as equals – maybe even better than that, because he genuinely tried to help us and used all his abilities to do so. Until you encounter a teacher who does this, you just don't realize the degree to which most teachers really don't work for your benefit but for the goals of the Institution.

Ben had us making music from the very first day, listening to kinds of music I never even knew existed and talking about music in terms that were unconventional, to say the least. For the first time, somebody was talking about music in a way I could relate to, and I was riveted because every word he said seemed to open up new possibilities for me, sparking my imagination and making me think in wholly new terms. Ben also made it clear that music was mine for the making – not something I had to apply to the gods to receive.

I started thinking there might be hope for me after all. I stopped being afraid of instruments. I got a flute and a violin, I changed the tuning on my guitar, I started experimenting with vocals. Songs and other oddments poured out of me effortlessly. There was no longer any separation between 'schoolwork' and what I did to please myself, probably because Ben's assignments were always really expansive and sparky.

Create an environment in which to listen to a particular stretch of sound.

Make a piece of music entirely composed of parts of recordings of other music.

Do a close reading of a piece of music, examining it through any medium you like.

People sometimes laughed when they first heard what Ben considered 'work': they thought that the assignments were gimmicky and cute. But they turned out to be the only real work I'd ever done in school. They were rigorous. Compared with Ben's projects, traditional assignments only resembled real work the way that cardboard cutouts resemble living movie stars. The usual assignments were all surface, whereas Ben's threw you right in over your depth. And in my own composition I loved having permission to be authentic instead of just imitating some 'style' or other.

Beyond all this we had improvisation sessions – group music-making with no rules, no preconceptions, no limits, so that a group of people would be playing together like fish in an ocean, everybody floating in this big collective, protean sound. But a session wasn't noise; it wasn't just a bunch of different individual outputs washing into neutrality. On the contrary. The collective 'noise' could pick itself up and go in all kinds of surprising directions, when it had a mind – and it often did.

That's the thing about music. It lives at this crossroads between intellect/intention and body/emotion and if you take away the imposed structure of tradition, which is the hard part for most people, you get a clear window into someone's inner state as it's changing. Well, you get a window: maybe it's not such a clear one because our inner states are so noisy and because it takes work to hear and interpret a music whose structure is pure bootstraps, no premeditation. Being in a room with some-one playing a session isn't like being with them in any other way.

Every Friday night was Open Space: a few hours of sound-making where anybody could come and do anything they wanted in the communal space. At the first one, I remember there was this tall filthy guy in a black turtleneck called Aurelio. He waved his big puppy-like hands and said, 'Wait a minute, wait a minute – I can do *anything*? You mean I can piss on the floor if I want?'

Everyone laughed but Ben just looked at him and said, 'If that's the most interesting contribution you can think of to make.'

The Open Space end of it was foreign to me. I tried to get into it – I didn't want to be uncool or repressed or unimaginative or unable to go the final mile cerebrally speaking. But it always came off so amorphous, and we'd sit around afterward listening to the tape and then talking about it. Ben always had a lot of ideas about what had happened and what the implications of that were, but I always felt clueless. And most of the discussion seemed to be about people disagreeing over what had actually gone down.

I guess you could say I should have seen the foreshadowing – you know, girl's first brush with nonconsensual reality leads to tears in the fabric of space-time, it sounds like *Star Trek TNG* – but I kept feeling that there was something in the sessions that I was missing and that if I could just check my preconceptions at the door and really listen, I'd understand what it was.

I think Ben was trying to get at people under the skin of their preconditioned behaviors. I think he was trying to get past all the bullshit we all carry. But that's not so easy. And paradoxically, maybe Open Space was too open, because hardly anybody even came. Where were the dancers, the painters, the poets? They were all getting stoned on a Friday night. Nobody was interested in being creative after hours. I don't think they knew what to do with that kind of freedom. People took classes and left it at that – this *was* school, right? They didn't want to really put themselves on the line.

But I needed it. I needed MPZ like I needed oxygen. I already knew music was some kind of lifeline for me, the only link I had with my pre-*Golden Dragon* self, and I felt like I was digging for something whenever I composed. Trying to get at something that I knew was there but couldn't see, much less articulate.

My piano version of 'Nuclear Day Dream' hadn't rung Ben's bells, so at Trinity's suggestion I started recording nature sounds. Trinity always had way-out ideas.

I took the Pro Walkman everywhere. I was looking for something that I'd never heard before in music, some sound that I'd only know when I heard it.

But found sound was tedious. Progress was disheartening.

'Things don't sound the same on tape,' I said to Trinity. 'They don't sound like you think they will.'

'Yeah, that's the cool part,' she responded. 'When I was about nine I tried photographing Captain Kirk and Spock action figures riding on my Breyer horses in the backyard. I thought it would look really cool and since the shots were still I thought they'd look totally real. I forgot to take into account the fact that the grass was as tall as Spock's chest. And everything was plastic, after all, even Spock's hair.'

Trinity laughed.

'My imagination had been filling in the gaps, but the camera couldn't do that for me. I was really bummed to discover that. Context is such a bitch. But now? I take that and run with it.'

I grimaced. I wasn't looking for effect. I was looking for a reality ... of some kind. But *real* reality couldn't give me enough. I mean, you could record a volcano erupting and it would just sound like a bunch of white noise. You've robbed it of its context, and so it falls flat. Things only start to get interesting in the place where reality meets itself head-on inside you, and that's just not the same as straight reality.

I didn't know that then. I just knew I wanted something, and the officially sanctioned version of reality wasn't it. So I was always racing for the edges of things, wanting to find the limits of the known world so I could more quickly throw myself off its edge.

Stupid. Stupid, stupid, stupid. Well, I had my sound now. Or it had me.

'Cassidy? Do you want to take a shower first, or do you want me to look at your leg?' Anitra was frowning. 'You ought to get off that ankle and get some ice. You might need an X-ray.'

I jerked out of my reverie. My whole body hurt.

'I'll take a shower,' I said. And screamed when the water hit the cuts.

While I was in there, leaning awkwardly on the wall to keep the nail-torn leg clear of the shower massager, I took a look at my butt in the steaming mirror. There was still a mark where the stapler had gone in. That much had really happened, and I could prove it.

Anitra made me drink a lot of vodka before she cleaned up my leg and bandaged it.

'This ankle could be broken,' she said. 'I think it's just twisted, though. Elevate it and ice it, and we'll see.'

'What if Ben's dead, Anitra? What if they're all dead? I mean, I finally found my place here, and now it's all fucked up and I think it's my fault.'

'Shh,' said Anitra. 'It's not your fault. That's a crazy way to talk.'

But she didn't know. 'Nuclear Day Dream' had been one huge destructive fantasy, and when I was composing it, things had started happening to me. I'd started finding . . . things.

Objects.

I'd started doing a lot of improvising, solo and otherwise, and while the weather was good I often played outdoors. My solo improvs had started as efforts to find chords, melodies, ideas to make songs out of. But after a whole year's exposure to Ben and his students they had become more genuinely meditative and exploratory. I'd take my instrument of choice out into a wood or field, turn on the Pro Walkman, and start playing. I'd look inside my own sound for something to follow, like a wildlife photographer. If I heard something I'd hunt it, pursue it, otherwise I'd just wander around looking. It was all very inaccurate but that didn't really matter because the act of my trying took me into a state of mind that was non-rational and non-verbal. The sound was a wilderness of possible outcomes, out of which I'd make a trail.

I thought I was creating something, but sometimes it seemed

like I was expressing something that was already there, some latent sound-meaning. And early one morning, during a solo violin session behind Woods Studio, my playing turned into something less like creating and more like making a brass rubbing. I played, and in front of my eyes I saw something come into being that must have already existed, elsewhere or elsewhen. But it was my sound that brought it up before my eyes.

It was cold, and I'd changed the tuning of the violin to make things more interesting, but I was having some trouble because the cold air was affecting the strings. The violin isn't easy to play at the best of times and when you have an extra finger, like I do, that just gets in the way. In the fog the tone sounded mournful and dull. The sound seemed to die as soon as it left the instrument's body. My nose was running and I had to keep sniffing. But I kept at it, because I was feeling something in the sound and I wanted to find out about it.

As the ground mist cleared, a shape resolved in front of me in the underbrush. At first I thought it was the foundation of an old building, half-obscured by vines, dead leaves and mushrooms. I could see hints of rectangular structure that stood out against the natural lines of the forest. I played to it. The sound-path I was following grew stronger. I had very little control over the instrument, but I'd fallen into a kind of trance state where everything I did felt right.

As I played I saw more and more of this hidden building. It seemed to take shape before my eyes, never forming directly within my focus of attention but somehow growing peripherally so that I couldn't quite witness the change. Details resolved.

By the time the sound had run down to nothing the place surrounded me. The walls were about three feet high in places, and if there had been rooms they must have been very small ones. The scale of the thing seemed off. But it most definitely hadn't been there when I started.

I turned off the Pro Walkman and put my violin in its case. I neither accepted nor rejected what I saw. I did spend a little time exploring it. When I brushed away the leaves and pulled back the vines, I saw that the walls were made not of stone or wood but of tightly packed Maybelline wands, rolled-up cardboard Tyco racing-car boxes, styrofoam packing, and plastic Coke bottles.

It must have been somebody's idea of an art project. But it had been here awhile, judging by the vines, and it had not decayed.

Which was impossible because I had no recollection of climbing over anything to get to the rock where I'd sat to play the session.

I felt my forehead. I told myself I should be freaking. But I wasn't.

I walked up to Kline Commons to have breakfast, thinking. I wasn't sure what to tell people, if anything. Halloween was coming up and there was a lot of LSD on campus. People would assume. Also, the stories of hauntings at Blithewood Manor on the south side of campus were proliferating, even though no one was living at Blithewood this year and the place had been turned into a construction site for the new Economics Institute. So what was I going to tell my friends? 'I found a ruined miniature building made of broken plastic model panzer tanks and popsicle sticks! And I think it *constructed itself* out of my sound. Wanna see?'

I kept my mouth shut. I was already taking a certain amount of ridicule from Craig and his friends over my role in the Open Space sessions and for hanging out with 'that weird cult in the music department'. People seemed to equate sound sessions with orgies.

A few days later I returned to the spot with my guitar. My fairy building was still there, but you had to be practically on top of it before it was visible in the undergrowth. I played for about ten minutes. I couldn't get anywhere, I was boring myself, and I felt self-conscious. So I stopped. I left. I'd been hoping for more magic, but it didn't come.

Frustrated, I went back to my room. I sat on my mattress on the floor, shoving aside the notes on Aristotle that I was supposed to be converting into a term paper. I dug around until I found the tape I'd made of the popsicle-stick violin session, then banged it into the Walkman with unnecessary force. I shoved gum in my mouth, chewed aggressively, and prepared to listen to myself noodling away making no sense on the violin I'd deliberately tuned wrong.

But there was no violin on the tape.

There was something else. It wasn't even an instrument. It was just *something else*.

I was scared, but only by inference. Like seeing the instrument bag of a surgeon, with all the scalpels revealed, gleaming; the forceps; the sponges meant to soak up your blood. The sound on the tape was itself oddly neutral – without malice, yet no less destructive for all that.

And I'm not talking about Beat Fascism either, by the way. This thing was destructive like a physical force. It was blowing free in the wind of its own coming. It didn't contain or even obey a clock. It was tying time in knots, marching, slithering, flying. And though the sound could be separated into registers, patterns of articulation, timbres, it was all one sound, one skeleton of crackling bones and stumbling progress, blundering and falling and shrieking in . . . *triumph*, I guess.

I switched it off after only a couple of minutes.

I didn't like what it was doing to my head.

I could not have made this sound. No way.

I checked the tape, thinking that I'd grabbed the wrong one. But it was labelled with my own handwriting, dated, the works.

Maybe I'd mixed up the tapes and this was some piece of computer music from that class I took last semester. Maybe I hadn't pressed REC the other day in the woods, and I was hearing some scrap of something that was already on there.

So I took out the more recent tape, the guitar tape I'd made that very morning.

It was different, but no less weird.

It sounded like something breathing.

'That's about all I can do,' Anitra said. She took the vodka bottle away and cleaned up the bloody cotton wool. She made camomile tea. I was feeling distinctly ill.

'Should I stick my finger down my throat?' I said.

'No. You should eat something and go to bed.'

I couldn't eat. I got up and reeled across the kitchen on one leg before Nina caught me and helped me into 'my' room, where I crashed. Disappointingly, it took me a long time to get to sleep, and when I did sleep I dreamed in murmuring voices, just out of earshot; sometimes I came half-awake and heard other denizens of the House talking in the kitchen, playing Cat Stevens records, or softly crying. Then I went down again into the murk and blur, the oppression of something terrible just beyond my reach.

After that for three days I did nothing but get stoned in the kitchen, and eat. I developed a fever and a hacking cough, and Anitra injected me with antibiotics that she said she'd filched from work.

I didn't remember Anitra having had a job. But she kept talking about Ferncliff Nursing Home and how bad she felt about not being able to get there to help out.

I grabbed her hand when she said that.

'Stay here,' I said. 'Don't go to Ferncliff.'

On the second night Jeremy came home and announced that cash was worthless for getting stuff.

'Some gang broke into Hudson City Savings and now there's so much money on the streets you could use it for toilet paper.'

'Speaking of which,' Anitra said cheerfully, 'the toilet's still broken. When's Tom going to get a snake? It's stinky in there.'

Jeremy ignored her. 'People, this is serious. The social order is breaking down.'

'Gang?' said Mary. 'Do we have gangs in rural Dutchess County?'

'They were caught on Route 9 on their way from New York to Boston. Got a BMW and everything. They're real pissed off about being stuck here, so they did the bank just for a laugh. Barry said they were driving down River Road throwing money out the car windows.'

There were a lot of conversations that happened on this level, but I have to say I just didn't care that much. It must have been the pot, which I wasn't used to. I had the feeling that everybody else wanted to talk about What To Do but they didn't even know what had happened. All I wanted to know was what had happened, and nobody could or would talk about that.

The pot made me chatty, I admit it. I spilled a lot of the stuff that was bothering me. I talked and talked about the shit I'd seen until eventually even Anitra told me I might as well shut up about fires and exploding cars and shadows in the sky and deep sounds – whatever they were – because all this talking didn't seem to be making me feel any better.

I said, 'You don't understand what this means to me. All my life I've been looking for something like, you know, *outside* the boundaries. I wanted there to be magic. I didn't want to live in a reductionist reality.'

'Yeah, that reductionism is a real drag,' said Tom in his gorgeous French accent. He happened to be passing through the kitchen, carrying a bucket. The smell of piss and shit came with him powerfully. 'By the way, the toilet's not broken, we just have no water and people have been using it without flushing.'

Mary tried to stand up but she must have forgotten she was

high, because she moved too fast. As she tried to get her balance she looked like seaweed in a current.

'Omigod, Tom, that *sucks*,' she said intensely.

'Yes, tell me about it.' Tom went out the back, leaving us holding our noses. 'I am going to dig a hole and we'll use the garden. Meanwhile, if you have to go, don't do it in the toilet. I am not going to clean it again.'

Anitra turned on the faucet. There was a small spurt of water, then nothing.

'No shit,' she said. 'Why didn't we notice this before?'

Tom came back in. 'Because you are all wasted. Get yourselves together.'

We watched him go. His bad mood spoiled our warm and filthy kitchen confab.

'You see?' I said. 'He's right. What have I been doing all my life? I can't fix a toilet. I can't splint somebody's leg if it's broken. I'm not even sure I could change a tire. I can't even cook! All my skills are useless.'

'That's negative thinking,' said Mary. 'And I can teach you how to cook. Or I could if we had some fresh food. Or water.'

I waved her idea away. 'What about the world? What are we going to do?'

Anitra sang some of that R.E.M. song about the end of the world.

I laughed then. I couldn't help it; I was stoned.

'I'm sorry,' I gurgled after a while. 'I just wish I could get back to Bard.'

Mary and Anitra looked at each other as if to say, 'She's doing it again.'

Anitra said, 'I bet the Dalai Lama wishes he could go back to Tibet but meanwhile he just has to deal, right?'

'Yeah, and Mork from Ork would like to get back home, too,' Mary added. Anitra punched her.

My eyes filled with tears. I nodded, feeling my lips mush

together and my chin bunching up. 'You guys are making fun of me,' I managed to say.

'No, we're not, sweetie,' Anitra said. 'Have some Rescue Remedy.'

She spritzed me with one of those plant misters and the flowery smell came into the room – a major improvement on raw sewage and marijuana.

Rabbits and Burrows

I hid the most recent tape of IT in a pair of boots purported to be mine; they certainly smelled horsy enough, but I couldn't remember ever wearing them. I hid IT from myself. I felt guilty for not listening to it. I had tried to call Ben at home lots of times, but I kept getting his machine and knowing that the fact that he'd probably been in the coffee shop when IT came meant that he might not have gotten out of Bard.

But why not?

I had walked out. There had been nothing to stop me. Yet not one other Bardian survivor had turned up in Red Hook. It couldn't be that everyone at Bard was dead. That was just statistically impossible. So what was going on? None of the campus phone numbers worked. No one around me would acknowledge the existence of Bard, not even Anitra, who stoutly maintained that she worked full time at Ferncliff Nursing Home as a nurse's aide.

I tried to take this in good temper, but it was hard. Hence the incessant stonage.

Jeremy wasn't around much, but when he was he kept playing the same Emerson, Lake and Palmer album at elephant-felling volume from his stereo in the attic, over and over again.

When I challenged him about the soundtrack he blandly said it was his house and *Brain Salad Surgery* was his favorite record.

'But no matter how much you like it, how can you stand listening to it all the time?' I said, frustrated. 'Don't you get sick of it?'

He shrugged. 'It's like wallpaper,' he said. 'I like it. Why should I get tired of it?'

Really listening, I guess, is too much like hard work. We want to have our buttons pushed; want the music to skillfully stimulate us with all our favorite moves, altered just enough to make them seem novel. We want to be safe and still think we're having an adventure.

I wanted to say this or something like it. I wanted to say:

That would be OK if that was all music was there to do. But there's more, isn't there? A lot more. Music can take us out of the straitjacket of linearlanguagelogic, out of the dominion of the visual cortex, and into a mode of feelthinking that is at once rising from the body and reaching beyond it. In academia we feel the tyranny of words, explanations, discourses when they are used to corral something whose essence is free; abstract jargon persists to the point of parody, but the true meaning has long ago fled or been murdered.

But what would be the point of saying it, even if I could pull words like this out of thin air? I would just become entangled in yet another verbal argument in which I couldn't articulate the coiled feeling that lived in my guts and wanted to strike out because it was always being made to beg for what should have been freely given; to defend what should have been unassailable; to explain what shouldn't need explaining, or so much of it.

Plus, I would come across like a dufus.

'Oh, what' s the point?' I said, and scuffed away to get another roach.

I was no longer convinced by my own rhetoric. And what I used to think were big problems didn't seem like that anymore –

because all of my musical philosophy had been built before IT came. The scale of what constitutes a problem got rewritten after that.

Even back then I had a feeling, though. I had a feeling all fall, while I played and while I listened. Like: *something's coming.* You notice it when you wake up in the morning. There's an anticipation, of what you don't know. The days gleam, and you're nervous.

The second weirdness went down while I was working on a metacomposition in the library basement. Metacomposition is the remix. It's how you get more from stuff that's already been composed. And you don't need new instruments because you can make an instrument out of a stretch of recorded sound. Or you can build it from scratch with a computer. Or both. So you don't need to have a fascistic structure like an orchestra anymore. You can make whatever sound you want, thanks to the technology.

Preston said rap was already doing this. He played us some. Ben talked about Beat Fascism. How the beat makes everything in the sound slave to it.

'Public Enemy is *all beat*. It's really aggressive,' Preston said. 'And really playful at the same time. I don't get how it's fascistic, though.'

I tried listening to it. I thought it was bizarre. There was big emptiness where you'd expect melody. It sounded like people having a party inside a giant meat-grinder. It was everything happening at once, shit coming at you out of windows and passing cars and somebody laughing in your ear and anything that came to hand being co-opted and used, and it made no sense to me.

Actually, it bothered me a lot. I thought: if you could do all this stuff with recordings, wouldn't it be better to do something that stretched the new medium more?

That was the reason why, on the night of the second weird-ness, I was down in the library basement alone. I had a pair of thick plastic headphones that ruined the spikes in my hair and a stack of albums that I'd chosen from the college archives on the basis of wanting things that didn't belong together. I was trying to get a remix of some spoken-voice recording by Edward Teller in which he asserted, in a thick goofy accent, 'the Earth sits on the back of a giant turtle with sleepy eyes,' or words to that effect. I was going to work this in with some Yugoslavian female choral singers and a little bit of James Brown, and I was wishing I could use the Debussy *Sur La Mer* record I'd found but Debussy wasn't really up to the challenge.

Anyway, I was having a great time and in my own mind my creativity bordered on genius. *Eat your heart out, rap music*, I thought.

Down in the basement next to the LP collection were the shelves housing the Senior Projects of Bard alumni/ae. These were bound in black notebooks and organized according to some schema of topic, year, and author, and in between bouts of musical thinking I'd sometimes pull one down at random and see what was in it. They were mostly academic papers but occasionally you'd find a poetry collection or a novel, or sometimes an art portfolio or a film script. I was always struck by the fact that although the lifestyle of the average Bard student was far from conventional their academic work was often stultifyingly dull if this collection of projects was anything to go by.

I finished a six-minute chunk of tape, which had taken almost two hours to compile. I was trying to decide whether to continue or go home, and I reached up to pull down a thesis.

I grabbed a spine and tugged. It didn't budge. I pulled again and the entire shelf of projects moved. I tried to separate the book in my hand from its neighbors, but they seemed to be stuck together. After a minute I managed to angle the row of

books out from the shelf so that I could see around the backs of
the first few. I had been afraid to pull too hard and tear or break
something; but I needn't have been. At first I thought somebody
had taken Scotch tape and attached all the books. I gave the end
book a hard tug and it snapped free, and then I saw that instead
of tape holding the books together there was a mesh or web of
very fine plastic. I broke a piece off. It was like a sheet of plastic
food-wrap that had been rolled onto itself and then stretched:
originally it had been a thin membrane but it had become
twisted and tugged into a stringlike shape, yet it still clung to
the books with what felt like static attraction.

I unrolled one of these sheets and saw that it was packaging
for something, with warnings in English and Spanish to keep
the plastic away from babies and small children.

Now, there was nothing scary about this. Except maybe that
it was strange, purposeless, making no sense. I went up and
told the work-study librarian about it and she said she'd report
the vandalism to Security and Buildings & Grounds. I went
home.

I didn't go back to the library, or finish that piece. I don't
know why. I made excuses to avoid it. I also slowed down on
the composition front, although I didn't admit this to myself. I
started doing more social music. I played in the Improvisers'
Ensemble and I started going regularly to Open Space evenings,
even though this annoyed Craig who was too cool for that stuff.

I must have thought that it would be safer to be in a group.
That way, if something happened, I wouldn't be the only one to
witness it. That must be what I thought. If I thought anything.

On the fourth day after I'd moved into the House, someone
banged on the screen door to the kitchen and I looked up
blearily to see this kid called Ray who worked weekends at
Moonshadow. Anitra asked him what he wanted and he peered
in through the mesh and said that I'd better go to work because

nobody was feeding the horses or bringing them in at night and they couldn't live on hay chucked over the fence forever.

'She can't go,' Anitra said. She moved to the door in a chunky dance among stacks of dirty plates and piles of books and tapes, a coffee cup gripped backwards in her left hand with the handle sticking out. The stub of a lit roach just protruded from between her first and second fingers. 'Cassidy is traumatized. You can't expect her to work.'

Mesmerized, I watched her; she was always doing something in the kitchen but it was never clear what, except that at the moment she was humming along to a David Sylvian tape as she did it. I hardly noticed that I was the topic of conversation. I hadn't brushed my teeth or showered, and I'd been sleeping in the Lay-Z-Boy in front of the dead TV because I was afraid of the cassette in the boot by my bed. My lungs felt furry from the pot.

'Cassidy, come on,' Ray urged. 'Sally's missing. You're the only one who actually cares about the horses, and we gotta think about the foals.'

'No!' said Anitra, stepping over a pot of old spaghetti to block Ray from coming through the screen door. Ray started looking pissed off.

'Get out of the way – nobody asked you to interfere.'

'Speaking of *get out*, you can get out of my house,' Anitra began.

'It's OK,' I said, finally catching on to what they were saying. 'Don't fight. I'll go.'

There was a moment of quiet.

David Sylvian sang something about rabbits and burrows.

I got to my feet. 'Mary, can I borrow some jeans?'

'Yeah, if you want, but your purple work jeans are in the clean laundry pile.'

I didn't think I owned any purple jeans. I hesitated. Anitra was giving me a complicated look. Assessing, somehow, and worried.

'OK,' I said. 'Where's the clean laundry pile?'

'Closet under the stairs,' Anitra said quickly. Mary looked puzzled and gave a little laugh. She was still insisting that I had lived here for a year, not four days. Anitra added, 'Cassidy, you don't have to go.'

I found the purple jeans, size seven. I pulled them on over my boxer shorts. They were loose. I had dropped weight. I could hear Mary and Anitra conferring in whispers.

'. . . Might be good for her . . .'

'A chance . . . out of the house . . .'

'. . . Jeremy says . . . pills . . .'

I came back to the kitchen.

'I'm ready,' I said.

Moonshadow Farm in Livingston was a thoroughbred-race-horse outfit. They bred their own stock and prepared them for the track. For the past year I had worked part-time as a yard hand in the breeding division. There were about thirty mares, their yearling foals, and two stallions. The mares were all pregnant: they'd have their foals throughout the winter and spring.

The job was basic: minimum wage, hard, dirty physical work with none of the romance people usually associate with horses. There was no riding. Up at the track everybody rode, and they thought they were better than us because of it. We thought we were better because we were involved in breeding and birthing foals. Either way, everybody smelled bad by the end of the day.

When Ray and I drove up on his moped the horses were out in the dead fields. They were shaggy and listless, except for the yearlings, which were just skinny. On the way Ray had told me that there was enough feed to last the pregnant mares another month, provided we gave all the other horses hay only.

'The stallions are easier to handle if you don't feed 'em too much,' he said. 'I keep trying to get Hannah to come out and help. She used to ride. But she locked herself in the house and won't come out. I think she's . . .' He whirled his finger next to his temple and whistled.

I was a little alarmed at this. Hannah, Dominic's wife, did the administration for the outfit. She was a bitch, but she wasn't the type to go nuts. I was feeling a sliding sensation. Didn't seem like I could trust anything or anybody.

'What about after the month?' I said.

'It ain't going to be like that,' Ray said, laughing. 'We only been cut off a few days.'

'But what if? What if we're still cut off after several weeks?'

Ray shrugged. 'When you put it like that I guess we're pretty much screwed. Three due to foal in January. They need extra feed. We'll run out by then. I went over to Les's Feeds yesterday and bought out the last of their stock.'

'People will want to shoot them,' I said. 'One of my house-mates is French. They eat horses.'

'We might have to put them down if things get really bad,' Ray said. 'They're a liability, I figure that's why Dominic left 'em. They can't make money, all they do is eat.'

'Then why are we doing this?'

'Sally left me in charge,' said Ray. 'Until I hear otherwise from her, I'm doing my job.'

Ray was only fifteen. I didn't know if he made me feel ashamed or if I thought he was just stupid. But I picked up a fork and started mucking out Badger's stall. There's nothing like several days' worth of stallion urine for clearing your sinuses. And your brain.

'What else is going on? What have you heard?'

He told me there was an old lady in Red Hook who had shacked up with a bunch of black guys from the city because she figured they'd protect her. He told me about some local liquor store owner called Sweeney and his plot to take over the police station. Sweeney had armed guards controlling all the gas stations, and he controlled the fuel rations. Ray said even the Moonies had emerged from their complex in Barrytown to get news of what was going on, but went back quick enough when some truckers confronted them.

The state police and the Army were arguing over who had authority, but since neither agency could get hold of its higher-ups it seemed that this Sweeney character had taken control of a bunch of stuff while they squabbled. And some low-level mob guys had done a bank in Millbrook. They'd been spotted on foot in the woods near the Omega Institute, carrying sacks of money.

'It's really cool!' Ray kept saying. 'It used to be so boring around here. I been waiting my whole life for something to happen!'

I didn't say anything.

At night I went home and stripped off outside so as not to bring the stink of horses inside. Couldn't get the smell off my hands, though, and my hair reeked like a pony show.

Over the weekend Jeremy called a House meeting.

'The social order is changing big time,' he said. 'Money doesn't mean anything here. So we have to think about how we're going to get by.'

The women looked at him with a watchfulness that I suspected he was taking as acceptance.

'We agree we don't want to get sucked into the redneck thing, right?' he continued. 'So, we have to get out of here.'

Tom kicked back from the table, his cigarette ash balancing like half a drawbridge.

'Jeremy, you're a fool if you think we can get out,' he said. 'No one else can do it.'

'We have to try!'

Tom shrugged. 'You try. Let us know what happens, OK?'

All kinds of talk broke out at once. Everyone had heard stories about the boundaries that couldn't be crossed, the places that we couldn't pass out of and, apparently, that no one from outside could pass into. The shorthand for these boundaries had become 'the mist' or, more recently, 'the blur'. Because evidently you couldn't see the edge of the world clearly. It was hard to look at. And you were unable to cross the blur. Just unable, like unable to fly.

But there were other stories. A pet dog had chased a ball into the blur, never to be seen again. Objects thrown into it just disappeared. A helicopter pilot had tried to ascend far enough to see what might be on the other side, but he couldn't get over the top of it.

In the middle of this talk Anitra got up and changed the tape from Meredith Monk to Tracy Chapman. Tom told Jeremy he was full of shit. Jeremy ignored Tom. Neither of them had any interest in what any of the women said unless it happened to support either of their respective arguments. Anitra and I exchanged bored glances.

Jeremy drummed on the table with his palms. 'Well, it's the only real solution that I can see. What do you suggest we do, Tom?'

Tom shrugged again. It must be a French thing. 'It's simple. We barter, yes? No problem for us. But we must be careful of that idiot Sweeney. He wants to set up his own government, with himself as dictator.'

Jeremy made a face. 'He can sit in his gas station all he wants pretending he's in control, but the gas will run out and then where is he?'

'That's why Cassidy is important,' Tom said. Everybody's gaze rolled toward me in synchrony.

'Me?' I blurted. Tom snorted and rolled his eyes, presumably amazed at my stupidity.

'Oh, I get it now. What is this, a cowboy movie?' scoffed Jeremy.

'It's reality,' said Tom. 'If this only goes on a few more days or a week, then we can survive. But if it lasts any longer we will need transportation. None of the roads get us out. We don't know what we'll find on the other side of the mist, anyway. Now, if Cassidy could get some horses—'

I shook my head. 'We don't even have enough feed to last the winter. And thoroughbreds aren't easy to ride. Half of them aren't even really broken. It's just not that simple.'

'We'll have to train them,' Tom said. 'At worst, they are meat.'

'Oh, God!' Mary exclaimed. 'That's sick!'

Everybody started arguing again.

I got up.

'I'm going to take a shower,' I said.

'There's no hot water, sweetie,' Anitra reminded me.

I washed with a sliver of soap and a bucket. I checked for the staple mark. It had already healed.

This made me uneasy.

The Ghost Hand of Peter Sellers Strikes Again

I'd gotten the staple during last Friday night's Open Space. I was there even though Craig wanted me to go with him to see a film about twin gynecologist murderers. I was struggling to find a way into the sound: the session had rapidly become loud and macho and I didn't know how to deal with it. Ford was heavily engaged in what Ben would call Beat Fascism and everybody else would call drumming; Aurelio was jamming with him on electric guitar while Justin made a stand against both of them by sharply syncopating against Ford on his electric bass. Elizabeth had stopped even trying to sing and was instead walking solemnly around the room tossing her pre-Raphaelite red tresses and occasionally striking a small gong that she held over her head like some wannabe Druid priestess. Gretchen lay on the floor under the ruined piano, yelping. I abandoned my guitar and crawled inside the piano as if to seek refuge. I found the second to lowest unbroken string and twanged it, as hard and loud as I could. Out of the corner of my eye I saw Trinity go to the blackboard and start writing words on it, very small, in pink chalk. Preston was playing an African finger-piano but no one could hear him. He had a look of intense seriousness on his face. I wondered what he was thinking.

It was fairly dark and I had to strain to see the words, which read **sound the faultline the cracking point where the beak comes through egg U on this persistence OF habit OF cookie cutter behaviors just do what you know how to do DON'T bother i said DON'T bland suffering U this remember** Trinity arranged them in a peculiar way and I started playing to her words. I could hear Gretchen sculpt her yelping to reflect the emerging words, too. Elizabeth dropped the gong and fell to the floor where she lay, face obscured by her hair, doing nothing much. Justin went over and handed her a kazoo.

Aurelio and Ford finished their jam; both were sweating and they exchanged congratulatory grins with each other, then seemed at a loss as they realized everybody else was still in the session. Ford actually chucked his drumsticks over his shoulder and Aurelio said something about boy he could go for a cold drink and then sort of realized everyone else was still playing. He looked pained. Then he put down his guitar and took huge steps across the room to where Trinity was writing. He picked up some green chalk and at the bottom of the blackboard he drew a little stick figure and wrote, 'Hi.' Preston came over with a spool of thread and started winding it around Aurelio and Trinity.

Trinity wrote: **deafening squeal i want your name is a place-holder but zero is real**.

Gretchen came out from under the piano and picked up the gong that Elizabeth had abandoned. She started to strike it and walk around the room in what seemed to be random spirals. She was doing what looked like that Zen walking, where you hardly move, but she hit the gong with great energy.

All this while Ben was sitting on the floor playing this

ancient Krumar synthesizer with a cheesy pseudo-string sound, very very softly, but persistent. Every so often through a gap in the rest of the sound you could hear him. What he was playing sounded remarkably musical: it reminded me of Beethoven or something. Which is sort of unfair because he *can*. Do that stuff. Whereas the rest of us can only grunt, metaphorically speaking.

Suddenly a bunch of things happened in fairly quick succession. Elizabeth, who had been crouched in a puddle of Handknit In Ireland shawls in the middle of the floor, sighing into her kazoo, sprang up and gave a scream.

The sound stopped. Elizabeth clapped her hands over her face and strode across the room, still screaming. Then she opened a window and climbed out. We could hear her shuffling through the woods, wailing like a banshee in a Disney movie.

Ben was frowning. It was pretty obvious this was just Elizabeth's idea of drama, but I think I picked up the collective sense that jumping out the window was not really cool. Personally I thought it was kind of funny.

Aurelio snapped his amplifier on and came jangling in with some nasty guitar chord, which Ford took as license to jam again. I got inside the piano and started beating on the strings against the time of what they were doing, trying to make an impression on their self-satisfied mutual masturbation. Trinity began singing in a high voice.

Then something hot pressed up against my butt and pinched me. Really hard. I whipped my head around and banged it on the inside of the piano lid. Nobody was there.

My head banging on the piano set Gretchen to stringing her string around Aurelio's guitar, which he really seemed to like. Whatever feeling of hostility there had been started to give way to playfulness. I rubbed my butt and carried on.

After about half an hour, the sound died down and the session slowly petered out. There was a long silence. Ben quietly got up and turned off the tape, rewound it. People went to the bathroom, made coffee, stretched.

My butt was still stinging. Maybe it wasn't a person after all. Maybe I'd been stung by a bee or something . . . I went into the bathroom and took a look.

There was a staple in my butt.

I came out of the bathroom and everybody was settling into chairs and couches, getting ready to listen to the tape. The atmosphere was relaxed, although I could hear Trinity and Gretchen quietly discussing the histrionics of Elizabeth.

'. . . Lady Macbeth,' I heard Trinity murmur.

'Georgette Heyer on a bad-hair day,' replied Gretchen.

I knew I had to say something. But what?

'Um . . . before we play the tape back . . .'

Everybody looked at me. Ben said softly, 'You need to say something, Cassidy?'

I wasn't sure how to put it.

'I guess it's just . . . there are some funky energies in the room that I could do without.'

Everybody was still looking at me. There was no sense that they'd understood. 'Uh . . . could you elaborate on that?' said Trinity.

'Well, somebody was out of line with me and I'd like to know what it was all about.'

Ben nodded, looking into his coffee cup, and then glanced around at the others. Nobody looked guilty or even nervous. Only puzzled. I didn't myself know whose hand it had been so I didn't know who to watch. My money was half on Aurelio the carpet-pisser – but then he looked too stoned to be getting jiggy – and half on Ford the drummer, but he had pretty strong B.O. and I think I would have smelled him. While I was trying to decide where to look now that everybody had their eyes on me Ben was saying something to the effect of, did I want to be more specific so we could talk about it? And I realized that nobody had the faintest idea what I was talking about. I took a deep breath.

'Somebody grabbed my ass,' I said. 'While I was in the piano. And then they pinched me, or I thought they pinched me, but I pulled down my pants just now and there's a *staple* in my butt.'

It took a lot for me to say that. The effect was spoiled by the fact that Elizabeth now reappeared via the door, sweeping into the room in a pseudo-Celtic swirl of long red hair and shawl and hiking boots. She went into the bathroom without talking to anyone and a few seconds later we could hear her puking.

'Whoa, *Cass*idy,' said Aurelio, swaying like a tree in a windstorm. 'Is there really a staple? Like, what kind of staple, you mean like a staple staple or . . .' He was really excited, showing yellow teeth and a childlike light in his eyes behind their black-rimmed glasses.

I displayed the staple, which was a little shiny with blood. My butt was still throbbing.

'Does anybody have anything to say about this?' Ben said, looking paternal and really angry for the first time since I'd met him.

'OK, where's the stapler from Ben's office?' Gretchen said, jumping up. 'Let's find it and then we can take fingerprints.'

'What about the video?' Ford said.

'Doesn't show the piano.'

'It wasn't me, people,' Aurelio announced, spreading his hands as if to show how clean they were, even though they were filthy. 'Cassidy, dude, I swear it wasn't me.'

'Well, it wasn't me, either,' Ford said, looking at Gretchen. 'And you can take my fingerprints any day.'

'Whoa, this is cool,' Aurelio added, then looked at me and hastily amended it to, 'I mean, sorry, Cassidy, it's not cool for you but it's like Agatha Christie night at Open Space, so nobody can leave until we find out who stapled Cassidy's . . . uh . . . butt.'

Ben, frowning, said, 'I can only communicate my deep distress that anybody should use Open Space as an opportunity to exercise their sick freakout attention-seeking behavior in this way—'

Before he could continue, the others started chorusing that they didn't do it, they swore, etc., etc., etc.

'Well, somebody did it!' I said angrily. 'It wasn't Gretchen because she was at the keyboard of the piano I was in, and it wasn't Ben because he was on the other side of the room behind the drum kit, and I don't think it was Elizabeth because she already jumped out the window. But I assure you, I didn't do it myself!'

Aurelio looked a little disappointed, like he'd been hoping maybe I *had* done it myself. Then he perked up. 'Maybe one of us has a split personality,' he said. He started pacing up and down the room, taking huge strides and flapping his hands. 'You know, like in that movie where the guy in the wheelchair has this hand and it keeps doing these weird things he can't control, and he spends the whole movie fighting with it, and then at the end he says, "I can valk!"'

'Seems like a long shot,' said Ben drily. 'Unless that's meant to be a confession.'

'What? You think *I* – ? *No!*'

'What movie was that again, anyway?' said Trinity.

'*Dr Zhivago*,' Ford said. 'With Peter Sellers.'

Ben started to make a negating gesture as if he disagreed, but he changed his mind and put his hand over his eyes. He looked like an Excedrin commercial.

'But he's dead. Poor guy.'

'The ghost hand of Peter Sellers,' Gretchen murmured.

'*The Pink Panther Strikes Again*. That's one of my favorite movies of all time.'

'Oh, I like the one where he ends up as the back end of a zebra at this embassy party, and he's running around – hey, Elizabeth, what's the matter?'

Dramatic exits weren't Elizabeth's only specialty, as it turned out. She came staggering out of the bathroom, quaking like Lucille Ball in the episode where Lucy and Ethel get locked in the deep freeze and emerge with icicles hanging from their noses. She leaned on the harp and waited until finally Gretchen asked her if she was OK. Then, in a rasping voice, she said, 'Can somebody call the police? There's a dead body in the woods.'

The Golden Dragon

When I was fourteen, something happened to me. I lost my memory. All of it. Apparently I was in Lodi with my mother. We were getting a Chinese takeout. My mother says she went back to get the spring rolls they'd left out of the bag and left me standing outside. And when she got back I didn't recognize her.

I don't even remember that part. I remember being in the hospital and not being able to answer the nurse's questions. I found out afterward that I had had what they called a 'psychotic episode'. I refused to get in the car with my mother. I ran away from her and had to be picked up by police several hours later. They took me to the hospital and that's where my memory starts.

The funny thing about it isn't that I can't remember. Because I know lots of stuff. I know Michelangelo painted the Sistine Chapel. I know the Pythagorean Theorem. I know where Bolivia is, sort of. The funny thing is that I don't have specific memories organized into the story of myself. I'm not a story. I'm just a collection. And it strikes me that most of the stuff I know probably doesn't come from 'experience'. It comes from TV, or reading, or people telling it to me and me

buying into it. Because I've never been to Bolivia. Is it like driving a car without being able to build one? Or is that a false
analogy? Yeah, probably.

After the welfare people satisfied themselves that I hadn't
been abused, they let me go home with these two strange
people. The strangers – my parents – took me to a bunch of different therapists. They started with hypnotists – regression
therapy – but I was a terrible subject. Can't be hypnotized,
apparently. So they moved on to the fringes of the psychiatric
profession. I saw a lot of weirdos. My favorite was Dr P – he
had a long unpronounceable name so everybody called him Dr
P. He was a little Indian guy with a caste mark on his forehead.
He kept cats even though he was allergic to them. He sneezed a
lot as he exhorted me to live in the moment.

'Living in the moment sucks,' I said quietly. 'Living in the
moment is what happens when you have no memory. When
you reach down inside yourself and there's nothing. Just a well.
Just a hole. The moment is nothing. I don't want to live in the
moment. I want to be someone.'

And Dr P. said, 'The thing about humans is, we're just like a
great big ball of tangled-up string. You pull any thread and it
will unravel us all. You exist in everything you do. You don't
need a history, Cassidy. You're inside yourself. History, the past,
that's just a way of packaging yourself to make yourself neat
and clean. Take any memory, any object, any word, any image,
that you know. And you'll find all of yourself as you start to
define it.'

'I don't believe you,' I said.

'Try me. One hundred per cent money-back guarantee.'

'It's not my money,' I said.

And he said, 'Your money or your life.'

Then he sneezed.

My parents didn't think much of Dr P, and because I felt
guilty about all the money they were spending, all the worries

they had on my account, I didn't press to keep seeing him. Besides, what was the point? It wasn't like I was remembering.

I only had one thing to go on, and that was music. The first time I walked into my room and was confronted by the evidence of myself it was disconcerting. There were posters on the wall. Pat Benatar. Joan Jett. The Doors. There were clothes in the closet. And at the foot of the bed there was a guitar.

When I picked it up I found I knew how to play it. If I didn't think about it. If I thought about it I froze up.

I remembered lots of songs. But Dr P was wrong. Nothing else came of it. Nothing unravelled.

Still: music was the only thing between me and the void.

So when I played my recording of 'Nuclear Day Dream' and Ben said, 'I wonder what would happen after?' the truth was, I didn't know. I didn't know, because after was really before. And before the *Golden Dragon* I might as well have not been alive.

It's strange, isn't it, how sanguine we are about the time before we were alive. It doesn't scare us. The idea of our prior absence from the world seems perfectly acceptable. Yet we live every day in subconscious fear of being removed from the world when we die. I guess most people have a handful of conscious memories and a whole lot of unconscious ones that sort of ease them into existence. The mind building itself in the womb and thereafter.

I wonder if it's like the sound of a piano played backwards. You have this long buildup of messy drawn-out sound that pulls itself together out of nothingness and then, abruptly, cuts off. Is the sound of a piano played backwards the same as the ontology of being human, in time? This great building-up of a person, only to snatch everything away.

Well, I don't have that. I just have a cardboard box of noodles warm in my hand, and the neon *Golden Dragon* sign, and a strange woman walking toward me with a bag of spring rolls. She seemed to think she was my mother.

So anyway. All this by way of offering a possible explanation for why the dead body behind Woods Studio didn't upset me as much as it seemed to upset everybody else. I'd come to expect the unexpected. So I didn't feel freaked so much as usurped. Nobody even remembered about the butt-stapling incident after that; in fact, I'd have accused Elizabeth of making the whole thing up just to get attention, except that when we all went trooping outside we found that there was indeed a dead guy behind Woods Studio.

The guy had to be about forty. He was clean-shaven, wearing what looked like an old-fashioned woolen Army uniform. He had a horrible wound in his midsection. Knife or axe or something. The leaves all around were black with his blood.

'No gun,' said Ford, lifting the edge of his jacket. 'Just a Swiss Army knife.'

'Shouldn't you, like, leave that alone?' said Trinity.

Ford shrugged and let the jacket fall back.

Ben had called Security but by the time they arrived a small crowd had gathered. Everyone working late in Woods Studio came out. A few metalworkers and a photographer stood around the beam of a flashlight that Ford had found somewhere, speculating in low voices and smoking.

'Isn't this, like, a crime scene?' said Aurelio. 'Shouldn't we, like, stay away so we don't destroy evidence?'

'Crime? You think he was murdered?' the photographer said, shivering.

'Could be seppuku,' said Ford sagely. 'Japanese ritual suicide. I saw it in *Shogun*.'

'Yeah, he looks real Japanese. Anybody know him?'

Everybody shook their head. We all started acting extra jumpy, like we'd just collectively realized there could be a mad axe murderer still on the loose, watching us from behind a nearby tree.

'Let's leave it to the police,' said Ben, returning to the scene with Elizabeth, who was making the most of it.

'I t-tripped over him,' she croaked, teeth chattering.

'Gretchen?' said Ben. He meant for Gretchen to take Elizabeth away, which she and Trinity did. I started to go with them, but lagged behind. We were only a stone's throw from my popsicle-stick house, and I wanted to see if I could find it in the dark.

It was still there, almost invisible in the ferns. My eye caught something white shining in the fallen leaves. I bent and picked up a small plastic bag from Staples, the office-supply store. The bag hadn't been there long; it was completely clean and dry. I opened it and inside was a cassette tape. Maxell XLIIS. The same kind I used.

It was labeled: *Wellspring Process – Induction*.

I slid the bag into the pocket of my jeans jacket and went back to the group. And we spent the rest of the night sitting around drinking coffee and speculating about the dead guy.

The man had no ID on him and his clothes weren't even labeled, except for the jacket which was US Army issue from about the time of the Korean War. Rumor got out that the clothes were 'weird' because they were made all of wool, and the guy's boots were real old, handmade, and had felt stuffed in them. He was a hippie from Bearsville, some said. Others thought he was a Soviet spy. There were plenty of communists at Bard, after all. I even heard somebody speculate that he was the long-lost father of this girl Katje in the art department, come to check on his daughter after all these estranged years.

Well, back at the House the staple was gone and whatever evidence I might have had that anything weird had happened that night had gone with it.

The rug had been pulled out from under me and I didn't like it. There had to be an explanation of some kind. You just don't get your butt stapled, like, out of the blue.

*

At the House, I still had the tape I'd found in the Staples bag. The pun wasn't lost on me.

The Wellspring Process: Induction.

I remembered what it sounded like. It had not been nice. And then things had started blowing up . . .

From the kitchen I could hear Tom shouting in French. Something like:

'You aren't even a real intellectual, you're just a computer nerd with more money than education. You torture us with Karn Evil 9 and then expect us to like you. You don't even know the taste of a good mature cheese!'

'Yeah, yeah, fuck you too,' Jeremy muttered. 'At least I don't put aspirin up my butt.'

Mary was crying.

I put on the headphones.

IT. ITITITITITITITIT –

I ripped the cassette out of the deck and threw it at the wall, shaking.

Where had the fucking thing come from? And why had it turned up so close to my fortress of popsicle sticks and Tyco model car boxes?

I should have handed it in to the police. Now there were no police, not in any real sense. I wondered where the guy's body was. In a morgue in Rhinebeck?

Ugh . . .

But. Important to be rigorous here. Important to use our head. There had been weird shit going on all fall. Every time I played, it seemed, stuff was turning up. What about those other session tapes?

That horrible one with the breathing . . .

I got them out of my backpack. I played the popsicle-stick session and then the guitar session.

Both now sounded like IT.

I also took out my library composition.

IT again.

I was feeling sick to my stomach . . .

There was a knock on the wall and I jumped in my own skin. Jeremy poked his head around the curtain.

'Where you been? We're still having a meeting. You can't just bail.'

I looked at his smug, knowing face and snapped,

'This is all bullshit, Jeremy, and you know it.'

He pushed his glasses higher up the bridge of his nose.

'What's bullshit?'

'Let's not be weird,' I said. 'I don't even live here. I go to Bard. So does Anitra.'

'Bard? Isn't that a beer?' He was laughing. 'Oh, no, that's Harper.'

'You've even got a sweatshirt! You wear it all the time, Jeremy.'

'You must be mixing me up with somebody else,' he said. But he let me storm past him and into the hallway. He followed me upstairs to his room, where I opened up the closet to reveal a forest of pot plants basking in the glow of a battery-powered lamp. The whole closet was lined with tin foil.

'Where's the sweatshirt?' I said. He shrugged and threw himself on the bed. He started saying snide little things like did you forget your medication. I couldn't find the damn sweat-shirt.

'OK, maybe it's in the laundry,' I said finally. The hair on the nape of my neck was still damp from my strip-wash and I shiv-ered. My leg hurt so I held it off the ground a little.

'Look,' Jeremy said, 'Anitra isn't a college student, all right? Anitra works at the nursing home. I dropped out of MIT. You know that. But it's cool. Cassidy, whatever, you know? Just . . . whatever.'

There had to be some way I could catch him out. Some gap . . .

'You said you were going to Albany.'

'What?'

'When I ran into you at the gas station. You said you were going to Albany. Why?'

'Oh, that. Yeah, I was. To meet my supplier. What's it got to do with you?'

'Your supplier?'

'Where do you think the money comes from? My parents don't pay for everything. I have to supplement my income.'

'But Jeremy! Who do you sell to if not Bard students?'

'You look really tired,' he said. 'Why don't you get something to eat and go to bed?'

'I don't think it's very funny. After what happened there. You didn't see it. I saw it, Jeremy.' I let a few tears go and then got a hold of myself. 'It's not very funny to play these mind games with somebody who's been through what I've been through.'

'I can see that. Do you have like a doctor or anything? Because, I mean, I'm not qualified to really talk to you about it.'

I turned my back on him. I went into the kitchen where Anitra's spaghetti squashes were sitting on the counter among a bunch of empty beer cans. I picked up a knife and hacked through one of them with three savage strokes. I wanted to pretend it was Jeremy's head but I'd seen a few things that made me not pretend that it was anybody's head. The cutting sensation was not as satisfying as I'd hoped. I put the squash in the oven and sprawled over the counter.

Jeremy put his hand on my shoulder.

'You OK?'

'No,' I said against the cold fiberglass. 'I am not OK. I walked out of Bard, Jeremy. I was there when IT happened. I saw the whole fucking thing. You all think I'm crazy but I'm not.'

Jeremy sat down opposite me.

'Maybe you're not crazy,' he said. 'Maybe you did walk out

of somewhere, and into here. Maybe we just don't remember that place you walked out of.'

'Your sweatshirt,' I said. 'If I could find it, I could prove it.'

'Never mind that,' said Jeremy. 'Cassidy. Did you at any point walk through the blur?'

I shook my head. 'No blur. Just silence. Total silence. And maybe . . .' I was trying to remember what I'd seen in my peripheral vision as I neared the Barrytown crossroads. Whatever it was, it had been shadowy. I couldn't pull it together into an image. 'No, it was definitely not a blur.'

'*Maybe*,' said Jeremy, 'you should try crossing the blur, say over at the bridge. See if you can find help and bring it back here. Maybe *you* could do that.'

'You *asshole*,' said Tom from the doorway. 'What are you trying to do to her? If you want to go out through the blur so badly, do it yourself.'

'I *can't* do it,' said Jeremy. 'Nobody can, but maybe Cassidy is different. I saw her before the blast at the gas station. She was already injured. Something had happened to her. Maybe she knows something.'

They went on arguing over my head. I pressed my nose to the counter. Every muscle in my body ached from working all day. I was hungry. I was cold. I wanted to sleep.

Jeremy started talking about hypnotic regression. Tom got progressively more furious.

Fuck, I thought. *Why am I always in this situation?*

But, in truth, this situation was the opposite of amnesia. This time everyone else had forgotten; but I remembered.

The way people treated me was almost the same.

My parents had tried so hard to make me remember. Didn't say much to me directly; they weren't pushy like that. No: they thought they were sneaky. But I'd hear their whispered conversations in snatches. I hardly caught any words, but I knew they were talking about me.

. . . Don't pressure her . . .
. . . You never know . . . might trigger . . .
. . . What she saw? Erickson . . .
. . . Trauma . . .
. . . Defense mechanism . . .
. . . Normal routines . . .
. . . Reassure . . .

Everyone was convinced that in those five minutes that my mother had been inside getting spring rolls, something profoundly shocking had happened to me to make me lose my memory. Everyone was obsessed with the supposed trauma I had suffered.

What they didn't understand was that my real problem was like a wall of water, the underside of a curling wave, hard as stone and soft as skin, that constituted my lack of a past. I didn't know my parents at all. I didn't know their house, or my clothes or my bed. I didn't even know my own body except in a dream-like, constantly shifting way.

Sometimes a small event would trigger a feeling of déjà vu, and I would think that something was coming back to me, and I would get excited. But these were only flashes, and they seemed to be comprised of pure recognition with no actual context. Like, once, while walking in some empty fields behind the railway line I saw some black kite-string tangled up in the top of a tree. And I swore I'd dreamed it. Or seen it before. As my gaze followed the black thread across the sky to a stand of sumac that grew on the wasteland in choking profusion I was gripped with the sense that I knew what was going to happen before it had happened. That each moment was unfolding with my perfect prior knowledge of it. That it had been all laid out and now was merely revealing itself to me.

But the black thread led nowhere. It led to no other memory. I didn't know how I could have seen it before, or even if I had. And after a few moments, the feeling of déjà vu faded.

I also had this feeling sometimes on waking. I'd hear the alarm clock going off. And as I came to consciousness I could have sworn I remembered thinking that the alarm clock was about to go off in the moment before it did. It was as if the thought of the alarm clock going off had hit my awareness before it actually hit my ears in a kind of reverse echo. This happened a lot. I used to believe it had something to do with my amnesia. But again, nothing ever came of it.

And I'd felt like a long-distance swimmer. There were so many stretches of empty time, time in which I was unaware of myself. No interior world: everything was outside. I got to know people and places around me. I had no idea what I thought of them or me. This, evidently, was not how it was supposed to be. Every person I saw, whether real or on TV, had an identity. But I was just a monkey, and I mimicked whatever was said around me because I didn't know what else was expected.

My mother kept saying, 'Why don't you find something to do?' and she would suggest projects for me. Macramé. Pottery. Redecorating my room (hopeless). Or, 'Let's go shopping. School will be starting soon.'

I knew what school was, but only in the abstract. The week before it started, my mother invited three of my friends over. I didn't recognize any of them.

'It's cool, Cassy,' said the small redhead, whose name was Kate and who seemed to be the leader. 'Don't worry about it. Stick with us, you'll be fine.'

They came into my room and dragged out last year's yearbook. Within half an hour they'd told me more than I ever wanted to know about everyone in it. And when school started, I did start to feel better. All I had to do was go through the motions.

I worked hard to create myself. I took cues from my parents: what they believed I had been, I tried to become. I studied myself: read my own books, listened to my own record collection, and read what few diary entries I could find. In general I found myself disappointing, but I tried to keep my chin up. I tried to see all this as an opportunity to become what I wanted to be.

So that by the time I got to Bard, I had mocked up a convincing facsimile of myself. And I'd found out something else, too: when I was playing music, the memory problem just wasn't a problem.

In the end, music was the only thing I felt really sure of. OK, I couldn't sing a note, I had a sense of rhythm that was pretty much totally randomized and/or spastic, but it didn't matter. When I was listening, or playing, I entered a world that was complete. No omissions. No dead ends. Music flowed. It made sense. And I understood it without knowing how.

They say that after someone you love is gone you search for words to hold them with, images to lasso their spirit, sounds to reinvoke them because you have nothing more direct. Or maybe you sit among their possessions, breathing in the lingering scent of them and weeping.

But what if you don't know who or what you're grieving for? Because it's all gone now but if I could only find something besides a gaping wound when I grope around in memory. I feel like a bad surgeon who's looking for the sponge he lost while removing somebody's spleen.

Must have fallen asleep. I woke in the House's kitchen to the smell of burning. The others had left me there, dozing on the kitchen counter in a little puddle of my own drool.

And now my squash was on fire.

Mutineers

Ray was supposed to pick me up for work before dawn on his moped, but the morning after the House meeting he was late. This gave Tom time to follow me outside and ask if he could come with me.

'I want to see this farm,' he said.

'There's no room for you on the bike,' I said, starting to walk away as Ray came puttering up in the gloaming. He had wound a long stripy football scarf around his neck and it kept blowing across his eyes.

'Tonight, then, we talk. You and me. I'll meet you outside the diner at half past four, OK? It's important, Cassidy, believe me.'

I shrugged and got on the bike behind Ray. I just wanted to go back to bed.

Ray was so happy not to be in school that he worked twice as hard as me. He showed me how to measure Bute and went over the milk feed stocks with me. The horses were restive and stupid, and we both got dragged across the ice a couple of times by unhappy mares trying to get to the feed room while we were walking to the paddock.

We mucked out side by side. Ray told me that Sweeney

had now taken over the CB channels and claimed to be keeping order. Sweeney's guys had commandeered supermarkets as well as gas stations, where they operated a rationing system based on a combination of urgent need and bribery. They were using Rhinebeck Elementary as a prison for anyone who got out of line. But darker rumors had it that anyone who questioned their authority got shot or thrown into the river. Ray took a certain glee in recounting this. It annoyed me but I didn't say anything.

'And get this,' he added, tossing a forkful of manure into a wheelbarrow. 'I heard the blur doesn't lead to "outside". It leads back to another point on the – what do they call it? The perimeter? So, like, say you walk out east, well, the next thing you know you're just walking back *in* west. That's what happened to this one guy – my brother told me about it. He only just found out about it because the guy was wandering around out in the woods all this time, he didn't know where he was. For, like, days.'

'I thought nobody could go through.'

'Not on the roads,' Ray said. 'Some kids got through the woods down by Montgomery. And they ended up in Tivoli. That was, like, a south/north jump, I guess.'

'That's one way to cut down on gas,' I said, digging my fork into a dark, damp patch of shavings to dislodge it. I'd hit a patch of stallion pee that was particularly rich in ammonia. I put my scarf over my face and stopped talking.

After work I stopped at the House to change into non-smelly clothes. Well, to change into less-smelly clothes. We hadn't been able to do any laundry other than underwear, which we washed in Palmolive and creek water in the bathroom sink and then hung to dry over the kerosene heaters. I brushed my hair and grabbed somebody's coat, and then Jeremy waylaid me in the hallway.

'If you're going to meet Tom,' he said, 'don't. He's trouble.'

'How do you figure that?' I said.

'He's got a bug up his ass because I won't go along with his plan.'

'I didn't know he had a plan,' I said.

'Ah, that's because you flaked out of our meeting. He wants us to start a business here. He wants us to settle for this situation instead of looking for a way out. But I'm not going to give up looking for a way out. Are *you*, Cassidy?'

I didn't like his pushiness.

'What do you mean?'

'You said you came "out" of somewhere. You've obviously been through something. If we work together, maybe we can get to the bottom of things.'

'If I was going to do anything, I'd go back to Bard,' I said. 'And I'm afraid to do that because IT might still be there. IT probably is. And anyway, Jeremy, I think you just want to use me. Tom is right – why don't you put yourself on the line sometime?'

'Use you? I'm trying to help you,' Jeremy said. 'You know more about what's going on here than you're saying.'

'Every time I say something, people laugh at me.'

He looked away. He couldn't deny it was true.

'Anyway, what's the point?' I added. 'Ray told me that people who walk out one side walk back in the other.'

'People, yeah. But you're different. Right?'

'Maybe I don't want to,' I said. 'I told you I'm not going back to Bard.'

'Fuck Bard. What about the world that's abandoned us? What about the whole rest of the planet? Where are they? On the other side of some barrier. You could try to go through it.'

'Leave me alone,' I snarled, and left. I was in tears as I went down the front path. I stopped a block away from the diner and tried to collect myself. I could see Tom waiting for me, walking up and down, hands in the pockets of his sheepskin jacket. His dreads were swinging. I gulped a few times and went up to him.

'Hey.'

'Are you all right?'

I nodded, not trusting myself to speak. Then I shrugged. 'Jeremy still wants me to go into the blur,' I said in a clipped voice.

Tom laughed. 'Dickhead,' he said, and it sounded very funny in his accent. 'They are idiots at the House. None of them does any work. They have no practical skills. Jeremy thinks he is a genius because he has a large vocabulary and knows about computers. What good is he to us now?'

I had to agree.

'You don't belong there,' Tom said. 'I don't think I belong there either. I know everybody says that I live here, but I can't remember anything about the place. Maybe I was drunk when I signed the lease, you know?'

We laughed.

'I wish I was drunk now,' I said.

Tom beamed. 'Come with me!' he said. 'I have the cure to all things! Come, come, don't be afraid!'

He led me down an alley to the back entrance of the IGA.

'Sweeney's men are making a drop here tomorrow,' he told me. 'There will be supplies. No one else knows. You and I, we'll camp out and be first in line.'

'How do you know this?'

'I fixed the pump at the police station. Sweeney has got hot water now, he is happy. One of his associates gave me the information. And he gave me this, too . . .'

He pulled a fifth of vodka from inside his jacket. We settled on some crates and set to it.

'I think you must have been a Bard student, like me,' I said. 'I don't recognize you, but then I don't know everybody in the school personally. And what else would a young Frenchman be doing in rural New York? How old are you, anyway?'

'Nineteen. I took a year off when I finished my schooling in Nice, to travel the world. I was supposed to study law in Versailles. But . . . here I am.'

'Maybe you're just an innocent tourist, caught up in this mess. But I think you were an exchange student and you happened to be off-campus when IT happened. You really can't remember why you settled here?'

He made a flowery Gallic gesture that I guess was supposed to mean, 'What does it matter now?' or some such. Passed me the bottle.

'Everyone's memory is fucked-up,' I said. 'Except mine, of course.' And I slapped my knee in an excess of humor. 'Or maybe mine most of all, depending on how you look at it. Not that it fucking matters.'

'You say "fuck" a lot – are you always so crude?'

'I'm fucking upset,' I said. 'Why the fucking fuck shouldn't I say "fuck"? If ever there was a situation that fucking called for it, this is fucking it.'

I gave him the bottle back.

'Fuck, yes,' he said, eyeing it.

It took us some time to finish the bottle. I don't have much of a head for liquor and we didn't have anything to mix it with. I tried to take it slow so that I wouldn't puke.

'So, what's your big plan?' I said. 'Why did you want to come to Moonshadow this morning?'

'The horses will be valuable,' he said. 'I want to get there before Sweeney thinks of it.'

I shook my head. 'You can't just expect people to go from the twentieth century to *Little House on the Prairie* in a matter of weeks. I mean, the idea that people are going to start riding horses and growing their own vegetables . . . it's romantic, but that's about all it is.'

I couldn't see Tom's face very well in the dark. 'It could be all we have,' he said. 'That's a fact we have to face.'

We drank more. Fell asleep propped against some cardboard boxes, and woke to the sound of a truck engine. Headlights.

'Here they are!' said Tom, staggering to his feet. Blearily I copied him. I was stiffening up from the physical work at the farm, and I was still pretty drunk. I felt seasick.

Tom went and talked to the driver. When he came back he said, 'We're first in the line for supplies. Now, we need to think carefully about what we get. I brought some things to trade.' He opened his backpack and showed me cigarettes and dirty magazines and chocolate bars.

'Where'd you get all this?'

'When the gas station blew up the front window of the stationery store crashed in. Everything was there to be taken.'

'Tom, are you an anarchist?' I said.

He shrugged and smiled. 'I am a survivor,' he said.

This sounded very impressive. But we were just standing there like a couple of idiots. A crowd began to form as word of the distribution got out. A couple of four-wheel drives pulled up and parked. Men got out and walked away. Other men arrived later, conspicuously armed, and stood around while the truck was unloaded. An officious-looking woman had also come along and she started taping up signs on the outside of the IGA. We had to form lines. There was a separate line for baby formula, and she guarded this like a gargoyle. She also started handing out numbers. A handwritten sign read:

NO PLACEHOLDING.
NO STOCKPILING.
NO RESELLING.
The diaper line was almost as bad.

We took our numbers for food and duly waited. The atmosphere was tense, and I got the impression that people were cutting in line and cheating in other ways. It wasn't exactly a spirit of cooperation.

We huddled together and stamped our feet to keep warm. A group of rednecks had gathered nearby and had started up a hibachi. They were joking loudly about storming the place and getting hold of all the beer. The sun came up.

'Who is your favourite philosopher?' said Tom. 'Mine is Buckminster Fuller.'

'Uh . . .?' Was this a trick question?

The rednecks were giving us looks. There was a skinny, freckled dark-haired one in a plaid hunting jacket who seemed particularly offended by us. He kept nudging the others and pointing to us, and saying stuff.

Tom was oblivious.

'A lot of people assume that, being French, I am going to have a sympathy with Sartre, Camus, but—'

'Tom,' I said out of the side of my mouth. 'This might not be the best time to advertise the fact that you're not American.'

He followed my gaze and gave a haughty sniff. The dark-haired redneck took it as an invitation to come over, with his buddies hard on his heels.

'Hey!' sneered Tom to the rednecks. 'You want to fight me?'

The skinny one hit Tom before Tom knew what was happening. He fell against me and I fell down.

'Whoa,' I said. 'Whoa, easy, this is my cousin from Canada – give him a break, all right?'

'You got a nigger cousin?' A fat unshaven face leered down at me.

'Just take it easy, OK?' I said. 'We're sorry. We won't be bothering you. Come on, could you give me a break?'

'Yeah, she's fucking her nigger cousin from Canada. See,

honey, you're not supposed to screw your relatives. Your kids will end up nigger retards.'

I fumed but said nothing. They wandered off, chuckling. Tom sat there with his sleeve pressed to his bleeding nose, saying something in French.

'Keep your head back,' I said. 'And keep your mouth shut.'

'Your country is foul,' he hissed. 'I am no stranger to racism but this is deplorable.'

Then a police car pulled up. Some black guys in puffy ski jackets jumped out, jogged into the IGA and came out seconds later carrying a cigarette machine. The rednecks pretended not to notice as the black guys loaded the whole machine into the back of a police car and then broke into a silly little kung fu demonstration, making high-pitched Bruce Lee noises all the while.

The rednecks seemed to melt into the crowd. The black guys were laughing among themselves. In all, there were five of them.

'Are *they* police?' said Tom.

'I think we should go,' I said.

But there really wasn't anywhere to go *to*. The crowd blocked the entrance to the parking lot, and the store was guarded by militia. Walls of adjacent buildings hemmed us in. Nobody in the waiting crowd seemed to know what to do. You just don't see this kind of thing in Red Hook. People here don't even see Eddie Murphy movies, by and large. But Tom was just European enough to perceive all this as a huge curiosity, and he refused to budge from his spot at the head of the line.

The rednecks were now conspicuously absent. They were presumably shitting in the bushes. But after the police car pulled out in a blast of bass and shouted words, they reappeared from the crowd.

'You niggers is all alike,' said the skinny kid who had hit Tom. He was clearly drunk, whereas we were just hung-over. 'You helping your friends steal stuff? Hey, honey, you don't got to go with this greasy ape.'

I felt like I was living inside a TV movie.

'I told you, he's my cousin,' I said. 'He's from Canada. We don't want any trouble. We were just leaving, OK?'

'You can go, but Cousin Nigger better stay right here where we can keep a eye on him.'

I started to walk away, beckoning to Tom to follow me.

'Don't listen to these idiots,' I said.

'We waited all night,' Tom said. 'We are first in line and we are going to stay here.'

I sighed. 'It's not worth it, Tom.'

He wouldn't listen, so in the end I walked away. But I hadn't gone very far when they set upon him, punching and kicking. I turned to the crowd waiting in line.

'Somebody do something!' I shouted. 'Help us! My friend hasn't done anything!'

People shook their heads at me. They looked disapproving. Like it was *our* fault.

'Better stay out of it, honey,' said an old lady. She had bleach-blonde hair and a Bronx accent.

I pushed past them and into the street. The rap-music cop car was pulled up halfway on the sidewalk with the doors open. A dreadlocked kid of about sixteen was sitting on the hood with some kind of automatic rifle leaning between his legs. He was blowing pink gum bubbles. He looked at me scornfully as I ran up to the car, shrieking. My voice disappeared in the noise of the music.

'Hey!' I banged on the hood and leaned in. 'There's a guy getting the shit kicked out of him over there because you guys took a cigarette machine.'

The driver was another young kid, skinny and nervous and hostile. In the passenger seat was a mature man in his twenties, a big guy. He turned down the stereo and cupped his hand to his ear. I repeated what I'd said.

'Come on,' I added. 'There's an innocent black man getting

beat up right over there. You guys have a police car. You guys have guns. Can't you do something about it?'

'What black man?' said the big guy. 'Around here? Who is he?'

'He's a goddamned plumber!' I said, idiotically.

The guy in the passenger seat opened his door and stood up. He was tall enough to play for the NBA. He grabbed the rifle from the kid on the hood and loped on foot toward the IGA, motioning the driver to follow him. The sirens went on and the crowd parted for the police car.

I saw the rednecks scatter. The tall guy went over to Tom, who was curled up on the ground in the fetal position, and gave him a shake. After a moment, Tom struggled to his feet and followed the tall guy to the car.

The tall guy said to the crowd, 'Y'all are real neighborly around here.'

No one said anything. I could see the muscles on the guy's arm flexing where he gripped the big gun. He made it look like a toy.

We all squeezed in the car, with the tall guy driving. This involved me being jammed in the back seat cage between the kid who'd been on the hood (Jason) and a muscleman who used way too much cologne. Fortunately the gun had been put in the trunk. The muscleman grinned at me and introduced himself as Chester.

'I'm Cassidy,' I said.

'Nice to meet you, Jenny,' he answered. He had a lot of gold teeth. 'Hey, Alvin, where we going now?'

'That depends,' said Alvin from behind the wheel. He glanced sideways at Tom. 'You a plumber or not?'

Tom made 'comme ci, comme ça' gestures.

'Well, this could be your lucky day, homeboy. I got a little plumbing problem. Maybe you can help me with it.'

'That would be entirely my pleasure,' said Tom. 'Are you from around here?'

Alvin was smoking a cigarette and the smoke burst from his nostrils. He shook his head.

'I'm from Yonkers,' he said. 'Where the hell are you from? England?'

Tom made a face. 'France. My family came from Algeria before that.'

'Oh, *France*,' said Alvin, flashing a white smile and sucking in more smoke. He offered Tom the pack and Tom took one. 'Did I offend you, man? The English are your historical enemies, aren't they?'

Tom shrugged. 'No problem. So where is Yonkers?'

'Yonkers, you know. Just outside the Bronx. We on our way up to Albany when this shit start going down. I got a job up there, that's why all they's with me.' He gestured to the others. 'Plus my little brother, he goes to college up there and I was planning on checking up on him, too.'

Job? I thought suspiciously. *What job? Bank job?*

Alvin eyed me in the rearview mirror. He raised his voice and added,

'I work in security. Got my own company. We do concerts, sports events, plus a little bodyguard work sometimes. We're like private police.'

Tom laughed. 'Is this your car? It looks like the real thing.'

'It *is* real, man. The cops got into a firefight with some of Sweeney's guys out at some gun store in Hyde Park. We got caught in the crossfire and the cops shot out the tires of my car, so we took theirs. Don't think they'll be needing cars where they're going, you know what I'm saying?'

'There's no gas around here anyway,' Tom said. 'We have one station in Red Hook and it got blown up on the first day. That's why you won't see many cars on the road here.'

'Won't see 'em anywhere at all if we don't find a way out of this mess soon,' Alvin replied. He turned along a driveway. The place was a Victorian farmhouse only a quarter-mile from the House. The sign hanging from the front porch had been amended from 'Antiques For Sale' to 'Antiques For Food'.

And somebody had scribbled graffiti on the American flag.

'OK, here's the deal,' said Alvin. 'We got a generator, we got a well, an actual well in the backyard, and we got fuel. But the pump's busted. Take a look at it – if you need parts, let me know, and I'll get you the part you need. You got tools in the garage. You got a flashlight over there in that shed. All right? No problem. What's your friend's name again?'

'Cassidy,' I said.

'Cassidy, come on in. I want you to talk to the old lady for me – she's giving me, like, a big headache.'

Alvin led me into the kitchen at the back of the house. Like the House, the place was an old Victorian farmhouse, and the kitchen ran all along the back wall. The place had been thoroughly trashed by people living in it without cleaning up after themselves, but there were still clumps of garlic hanging from the ceiling in net bags, and a set of expensive copper pots and pans on display. There were little magnetized religious poems on the fridge.

Mrs Hoffman was in a small room downstairs, a sewing room I guess. She was sitting with a cat on her lap doing needlework. She must have been at least eighty.

'Oh, Alvin,' she said. 'Did you find out about my magazine subscriptions yet?'

'Cassy here is gonna help you with that,' said Alvin sweetly. 'Anything you need, you just ask Cassy.'

'Come in, dear. Sit down.'

I did so. I wondered if it was obvious that I was still somewhat drunk.

I told Mrs Hoffman about events at the IGA. She received word of the chaos with equanimity.

'I'm too old to be afraid of anybody or anything,' she told me. 'These homeboys understand that. I told them they can stay here as long as they need to; they won't get any racial prejudice from me. They're city kids, you know. They don't know anything about pumping water or chopping wood, but they might have to learn if this thing goes on any longer.'

I tried to smile. She had a puzzle spread out on a card table near the window. She'd done only a few bits of it; there must have been a thousand pieces. It was some kind of Austrian castle or something, with wildflowers in the foreground. Escapism for the older generation, I guess.

'I suppose I picked the wrong trade,' Mrs Hoffman said. 'Alvin's going to chop up my armoire for firewood when we run out. After you get the magazine subscriptions, do you think you could find some wood somewhere? I'd hate to see that armoire go. When this is all over I'd like to have it to sell. Who knows? What if the social security payments don't get through?'

'Try not to worry,' I said. 'This can't go on forever. I'll see what I can do about your magazines.'

'Oh, thank you, honey,' she said.

I went to find Tom. He was sawing two-by-fours outside the shed.

'What's she like?' he said.

I laughed. 'Old people!' I said. 'She's just got to have her *Wooden Dollhouse* and *Coin Collectors' Monthly* or life isn't worth living. If I ever get like that when I'm old, I hope somebody puts a sock in my mouth.'

Tom stopped sawing.

'We'll be lucky to make it through the winter,' he said. 'Never mind growing old.'

'Thanks, Tom. Thanks. A lot.'

'She should offer to let us eat her,' he added. 'Are you really going to look for those magazines?'

'Alvin told me to get them if I have to write them myself.'

Tom shook his head. 'Americans,' he muttered cryptically.

Later, inside the farmhouse, we ate Spam and Ritz crackers. Jason, Chester and a boy called Trinidad all moaned about the cuisine. Tom tried to bring up his survival ideas with Alvin, who was uninterested.

'You just get the water,' said Alvin. 'I want that pump running so I can take my shower. I hate being dirty.'

He looked at me.

'Do I smell?' I said.

His forehead wrinkled. 'What you so uptight about? All I did was look at you.'

'Yeah, and his eyes be hurting now,' chimed in Jason.

'She a dog, Alvin,' said Trinidad, giggling.

'Yo, they all dogs around here,' said the one whose name I couldn't remember. The other two went *ooh*. Alvin grabbed his ear.

'Kerlee? Remember we talked about giving people respect?'

'Sorry, no offense,' said Kerlee.

I felt my face heat up. Alvin told me, 'It's all right, baby. Why don't you go upstairs and lay down? You look tired.'

Kerlee and Trinidad giggled some more. Jason's face was a study in self-discipline.

I was trembling.

Somebody put a mug in my hand. It was the biggest of them, Chester, a mountain of a guy made of muscle and fat, smelling strongly now of armpit.

'Have a cup of coffee,' he said. 'They only playing.'

I sipped.

Tom went out to the garage to look for a piece of wire. Alvin followed him. When they came back they were deep in conversation. They disappeared into the dining room.

Chester kept moaning, 'We got no TV. I missing *Alf the Alien*.'

'My kid watches that!' said Jason. I stared at him.

'How old is your kid?' I asked. Jason couldn't be more than sixteen.

'Three and a half.' He pulled out a picture of a boy so cute it took my breath away.

Kerlee was looking out through a crack in the drapes.

'Do you think a axe murderer could be loose in the woods? I don't like it here. It's too quiet, it's like one of them movies with Jason . . .'

This kind of thing seemed to go on and on. I didn't know how to relate. I had never hung out with black people before. I mean, I had hung out with individual black people but I'd never been outnumbered like this, and these guys weren't the Cosbys. It felt weird. Probably this was as good a time as any, because the giant slithering sensation of the world turning into something unexpected out from under my own butt was oddly dampened by the black/white thing. I was afraid and trying not to show it. And at the same time I felt myself going to pains to be respectful so that I wouldn't come across like a racist. But I had a bad feeling that this came off like condescension.

I had always thought race wasn't supposed to matter. That you should treat everybody the same. But these guys were so different from me, and they didn't for one single second seem to aspire to being like me or my culture. It was as if they'd existed in parallel to my world for all this time, and I'd never known this. You never saw many black people where I'd grown up, and Red Hook and Rhinebeck were whiter than white. I felt tongue-tied. I realized that on some subconscious level I'd gone around believing that black people didn't eat the same food or wear the same clothes.

Having this realization about myself right up in my face made me feel totally lame and stupid. I didn't know what to do. I said 'please' and 'thank you' a lot and this made Chester guffaw.

Alvin was just confusing. He could shift so easily from one personality to the other that I just yielded to everything he said. He was like a magician. He was fast, and he kept you distracted, and when he was done with his act you wanted to clap, whether or not you liked him. I retreated deeper and deeper inside myself. I became ever more timid the more Jason and Kerlee made fun of me. I hated them for it but tried not to show it in case that was racist, too.

It never once occurred to me that the racism thing could cut both ways. I was that far up my own butt.

I slept on the floor in Mrs Hoffman's room. She snored like a longshoreman. In the morning I felt even more exhausted. I went into the kitchen to do some cleaning up, but there wasn't much I could do with dry paper towels against crusted food. I could see Alvin and Tom in the backyard, looking at the pump and doing the male-bonding thing.

They had left the dining-room door open. Somebody had set up a whiteboard and it was covered with notes and diagrams in colored marker. I recognized Tom's handwriting.

Basic needs were listed. *Resources. Essentiel* (sic) *Tools.*

Also: *Enemies.*

Tom came in while I was studying it.

'Tom, what the fuck are you doing?' I whispered, shutting the door.

'I'm helping them, what do you think? They have guns, Cassidy. They are street-smart. They are survivors. If anybody is going to get through this crisis, it's these guys. I'd rather be on their side than against them. All they need is some help getting organized.'

'I think you've lost the plot,' I said.

'What?' hissed Tom, waving his cigarette. 'Do you want to go back to the House and wait to be rescued? They will have run out of pot by now and they will run out of cookies and then what? Do you want to freeze to death?'

'All right, all right,' I said. Chester had come in the room behind me; what else could I say? But this felt like a kind of giving up. I kept feeling I ought to be solving something.

'Why can't life be like Agatha Christie?' I moaned. 'Why can't there be a design to it all?'

Tom snorted. 'Design? The world is ruled by thugs – don't you understand that?'

'Someone must be masterminding something.'

'Yeah?' said Chester. 'Try God. You got to have faith in God.'

Another wordless noise of French derision. 'Don't you know that every problem is defined by the lowest common denominator? That is why all experiments in social justice end in failure. Thuggery will always win out.'

'What is civilization all about, then?'

'Organized thuggery,' Tom said.

'You got a real chip on your shoulder for somebody so young,' said Chester. 'Whatever happened to you that's so terrible?'

'*Cassidy!*'

It was Alvin's voice, carrying down the hallway. I went.

'Cassidy!' Alvin sang again from the bathroom. 'You there?'

'Is something the matter?' I said warily.

'I just remembered I need you to get some tranquilizers for the old lady. She having trouble with her insomnia, you know what I'm saying? She got a prescription under one of them religious magnets on the fridge. There's a little gold necklace in my jacket pocket – take it down to Sweeney's and tell them I sent you. Get her some Halcyon, too, will you? But you watch your butt with Sweeney's dudes.'

He paused, grunted a little with an effort I'd have preferred not to have to visualize. I made a face. He couldn't see me, of course, but he barked with laughter as though he could.

'Do you know what this is, Cassidy?' he said in a fake English accent. 'This is what they used to call, in Elizabethan times, a privy council.'

I didn't answer. I wasn't sure if he was insane or just smart.

'The queen, she used to linger on the pot and take advice on matters of state.'

There was a splashing sound.

'What's up with toilets, anyway?' said Alvin in an exaggeratedly ghetto voice, 'Who designed this shit? Why they gots to make the water level in the toilet so high? Cuz when I sit down my equipment keep dangling in and it's *unhygienic*.'

He flushed. The door opened and he came out with the water bucket dangling from his forearm, wiping his hands on Luvs.

'You still there? I thought I was talking to myself.'

Such was my reality for some days. All this time I kept working up at Moonshadow. It was almost sane up there, with only me and Ray and the horses and cats. I felt solid and safe in some undescribable way, just by virtue of being outside in the air and working hard all day. We kept busy, bringing hay down from the hay barn and emptying the spreader. The physical exertion was a great antidote to thinking; so much so that one time, when I went up to the hay barn to get a few extra bales of straw for Northern's foaling stall, I actually fell asleep on a stack of bales.

When I woke up, shivering, it was dark.

'Holy crud,' I heard myself say, unfolding myself with a creaking sensation. My neck was killing me. The barn was half-empty, and my voice echoed; so did all of my movements.

'Brrrrr!' I shrieked in a high voice, rolling my r's like a Spanish speaker.

The echo of that made me laugh. Then I couldn't resist and like a little kid, I started shouting to hear the echoes of my own voice. This evolved after a little while into something more purposive. And before I knew it I was vocalizing just as if I was in a session.

I'd never been big on singing. It felt too naked. But I was alone here, and I had no instrument, and now it seemed that I was articulating everything I had been feeling and thinking and sensing all this time. All at once, I was singing back at what had happened to me. To the world. And it felt good.

I'd been singing for some time when the sound of my own voice began to change. Gradually I noticed that there was more than just an echo in the barn. My voice had been multiplied, like with a digital chorus. It sounded as though there were several of me, all singing the same thing.

At almost the same time, my eyes picked up something shining out of the darkness near the rafters. The images resolved into a collection of luminous bubbles drifting down from the ceiling. Shining, fragile bubbles with little miniature worlds in them. There must have been seven or eight of them. They settled on the hay, wavering a little. And there could be no doubt: they were singing back to me in my own voice.

I completely freaked out. Turned tail and ran for the tractor. The sound of the engine obliterated my voice, and I bounced back to the barn as fast as the machine would take me.

I didn't go back to Moonshadow the next day. I told Ray that I had a fever, and then found excuses to make myself useful at Antiques for Food instead. I reorganized Mrs Hoffman's sewing basket. Important stuff like that.

I didn't play the tapes from Bard. I thought about burning them, but didn't.

I didn't sing. I didn't even hum.

That night over baked beans and saltines Alvin said, 'Tomorrow we got new arrivals on Gilligan's Island. I met them down at the hospital. They need someplace to sleep – so Cassidy, you go upstairs and set something up.'

'Who are they?' said Tom.

'A engineer and two radio guys. We got to get working on communications.'

Tom shook his head.

Alvin said, 'Yo, you want to go back to the days of the horse and carriage, that's fine. But this radio guy seems to think we might be able to get a signal out *over* the edge of the mist. And it's worth the gamble.'

Tom shrugged. 'If that is the case, why are there no planes flying overhead?'

Alvin must have retorted to this, but I wasn't listening. I went upstairs to do as Alvin had told me. The old lady had a whole room devoted to dolls. Most of them were in glass cases. There were no beds. I stood there trying to figure out where to start.

Chester was standing right behind me. I hadn't heard him following me.

'That some weird shit – look at all this. Don't you feel like they looking at you?'

China eyes, gingham dresses.

'They're kind of spooky,' I agreed.

Chester picked up one of the dolls, some Swiss-looking thing with flaxen hair and a frilly dress, stupid pouting lips. He turned it over in his big hands. I was thinking of something sarcastic to say about the doll when he began to shake.

I held my breath. Why was he shaking? Was he on drugs?

Droplets fell on the doll's cornflower-blue dress. Shoulders bowed, head down, he was *crying*.

'Chester, you OK?'

He rubbed his eyes, babyish. Sniffed loudly.

'I don't want to be here,' he said. 'It too quiet here. I miss the people in my block I miss my kids I miss my girlfriend. What's happening to them right now? Are we the only ones left? Are they OK out there or do you think they worse off than us?'

'I don't know.'

Chester wiped his eyes a little more, sighed heavily. 'Jenny, ain't you scared?'

'Not really.'

'No? Because if you was scared, I could protect you.'

'That's OK.'

'Yeah? You that brave?'

I didn't say anything.

'See, you got to humor me a little. Act more *feminine*. Men, we like that. We like to feel we powerful, you know?'

'Oh,' I said, because he was watching me expectantly.

Chester laughed like a bear.

'Now a girl like you, just talking to you and I'm getting excited. See, I'd really like to touch you, baby.'

'Um . . . Chester, please don't do this . . . you just told me you have a girlfriend. Kids. And . . . and . . . I have a boyfriend, too.'

'Forget him. I'll make you forget him.'

I heard myself laughing nervously. I said,

'Um . . . OK, well, there's no bed in here, let's try another room.'

Chester went out the door like a shot. I slammed it and snapped the lock. He pounded on it, but I was already pushing a display case over to block it. There was a crash, and dolls went flying.

I dove for the window. Unlocked it. Jerked it up and was halfway out when I heard him push his way into the room.

It was about a twelve-foot drop into the bushes. I swung over the sill and let myself hang. My shoulders felt like they were going to pop out of their sockets. My fingers were weak.

'What the fuck you doing, you going to break your neck—'

I let go. Hit the mountain laurels. Rolled.

All the wind went out of me. This was incredibly unpleasant. I lay there for several seconds making fishy movements with my lips, unable to get any air into me. Above, in a husky panicked voice, Chester was calling:

'You all right? You alive or dead Jenny?'

I heard the air going into my lungs, high-pitched and pathetic.

Chester said, 'Man oh man, talk about rejection. I been turned down, but I never had nobody jump out a window on me before.'

The Bridge

I started to crawl away. The grass was covered with a slick layer of wet maple leaves, and I couldn't get much purchase.

I was embarrassed more than anything. I had panicked, and now I was embarrassed, and that made me panic even more. I didn't go back inside, I didn't talk to anyone, I just took off, crawling and then stumbling and finally running.

The people in the house next door had been avoiding us. They had a sheet hanging over the front door with a big cross crudely painted on it. The place was lit with candles.

I went to the back and looked into the kitchen.

There was a bunch of kids sitting on the floor, playing with toys. Two women were cooking over a camp stove and washing dishes, respectively. Little baby suits hung drying from a clothesline over the sink.

I slunk away.

I thought about going back to the farmhouse. But then I would have to deal with Chester. And Alvin. And Kerlee, Jason, Trinidad. And Tom. And now the radio guys . . .

The truth was, I didn't want to deal with anybody.

It was cold out there. I doubled back on myself and went up the driveway of Mrs Hoffman's house under cover of darkness. The police car was parked in the driveway. They never locked it. I opened the passenger door and grabbed a big puffy jacket belonging to either Jason or Kerlee and slid it on. Then I dashed off.

Red Hook was eerily quiet. Without electricity, the town was just a series of dark lumps. The sky above dominated the scene, the Milky Way streaking across the firmament and stars scattered like wildflowers in the black. I set off up the 199 towards Bard.

I only had to go a few miles but it took me about two hours to get to the intersection with River Road, which would ultimately turn into Annandale Road. This was the place where the Pathfinder had picked me up. I wondered what had become of Michelle.

The traffic light had been moved out of the way and the wires were clear of the road, but the fallen tree was still there. Beyond, where the road rose toward the Kingston Bridge, I could see the darker bulk of the Catskills, the faint glisten of the river under starlight, and the partial outline of the suspension stanchions of the bridge. There wasn't enough light to see the cables, except at the foot of the bridge, where several campfires had been lit.

No sign of any blurring, as far as I could tell. I mean, there were the Catskills. There was the bridge.

Maybe we weren't cut off anymore? Had something changed? A miracle . . .

A group of people were standing around in the vicinity of the fires. Several vehicles were parked on the lower part of the bridge, making a roadblock. One of them was a white limousine. As I approached, a couple of big guys in jackets and boots came to meet me, their breath flying sideways in the night breeze.

'Bridge is out. Name's Red – what's yours?'

'Cassidy,' I mumbled dutifully. I was preoccupied with

looking at the bridge, which was, as far as I could tell, not 'out' at all.

'Come on, Cassidy. We got coffee.' The guy had a thick red mustache and the beginnings of a beard. He turned and I followed him toward the fires. I looked up the slope of the bridge but still I could see no evidence of damage.

'I wish you people would stay home and keep out of trouble,' he said. 'Ain't nothing to see here. Now, Cassidy, here's a cup of coffee. You drink that up, then go home and tell all your friends there ain't no point in coming out here, all right?'

I accepted the coffee gratefully. It was lukewarm.

'I heard the whole bridge got blasted out,' I said. 'It doesn't look so bad from here.'

Red guffawed. 'Depends on what you mean by bad. Look at that friggin' blur, would ya?'

I squinted. 'You know what?' I said. 'I have a kind of eye problem. And I lost my glasses. I can't even see it.'

'You better be all the more careful,' Red said.

'What does it look like? Is it really a blur? Can you see where the bridge is broken?'

'No, no. It's just like a black smudge. No more bridge. Just an end, out there not quite midpoint. No more river, either. Just nothing. Big smudge. It looks like the end of the world. Them Moonies loved it. But we had to clear them out of here. This ain't no place to camp. See? That's their limousine. Them being here wasn't doing nobody no good.'

I nodded. 'You work for that guy Sweeney?' I said.

'You could say we got an understanding. What you want out here, anyway? I told you, go home where you're safe.'

'OK. Thanks for the coffee.' I drained the cup. I walked back up the road until I was sure I was out of sight and Red had gone back to warming his hands with the others. Then I crept back, keeping to the rough grass verge and crouching down until I got past the campfires. I waited until no one was looking my way before climbing over the metal fence and then running up the bridge.

'Hey!' somebody yelled. I sprinted full-out, aware of the pain in my leg but determined to ignore it. I pumped my arms and drew great gulps of air as I pelted up the bridge. I could hear them running behind me, shouting at me to stop, but I had a good head start.

I had almost reached the midpoint and the men were closing. Something wasn't quite right up ahead. There was a kind of disjunction, a gap, like when you stick a pencil in a bathtub and the light refracts and displaces the image of the pencil. The bridge looked like it had been cut and stuck back together in not quite the right proportions.

I slowed. I didn't know if I dared throw myself at the gap. It hadn't been like this, leaving Bard. I hadn't had to do anything special. Now, out above the roiling Hudson, I needed courage.

Men were shouting, '*Don't do it!*' Red was close on my heels. He reached me as I hesitated. He grabbed at my jacket, tackling me, and I went sprawling. Broke free for a second, long enough to throw myself forward several feet—

I hung in silence. I was breathing, but soundlessly. I could feel myself hurtling through space, and rushing past me I glimpsed the edges and forms of strange buildings, improbable shapes. Numbers rushing past my eyes, dim, watery, and fleeting; then—

—into a rush of warm air, tumbling until I was stopped by a rack of jeans. I leaned on my hands and knees, inhaling factory-new smells and staring at a pale green carpet. I was in bright fluorescent light and it was very warm. I started to stand up but bumped my head on a chrome clothing rack. Finally I struggled to my feet.

Strains of 'Do You Want to Ride in My Mercedes, Boy?' drifted through the air.

I was in a store. A woman in a navy blazer was coming toward me, an expression of distaste and fear souring her face.

'Where is this place?' I said loudly. I was still gasping for breath. Sweat sprang out all over my body.

Other shoppers were looking at me. It was a department store. Downmarket. Maybe Sears.

'I'm going to have to ask you to leave,' said the woman. She was gesturing to her colleague at a nearby sales desk. The colleague was already on her phone, nodding.

'*Security to Young Men's*,' said the loudspeaker.

'Oh my God,' I heard myself say. 'Am I on the other side?'

The woman didn't answer me. She looked uncomfortable. I craned my neck and saw out of the Sears and into the mall. I was pretty sure this was the mall at Lake Katrine, on the other side of the bridge. Well, that could explain the gap in the bridge – I must have 'jumped' to a location a few miles away.

I hadn't expected anything like this. I'd had no time to think. What to say, how to explain . . . ?

'But don't you know what's happened? People are in trouble. They need help . . .'

I could feel my eyes widening as I tried to impress my sense of urgency on her. My heart was still pounding from running, and my cheeks were still cold. I could see that she was scared of me – not physically scared but scared of what I was. Of what was inside my head. I knew the look.

I shut my eyes. I was only making things worse for myself. They thought I was drunk. Or on drugs. Or just nuts.

My parents came to get me. My father stayed in the mall to deal with the people at Sears and the police, while my mother walked me to the car. I found that I couldn't walk very fast, and she kept trying to take my arm. I kept shaking her off, like a child.

She had been crying, for which she had compensated by

putting on too much makeup. This was especially obvious in the natural light of the parking lot, where I noticed that the car was different. It was still a Toyota, but a different model and color than our old car.

'What happened to your hair?' I demanded.

My mother's hair was red. Normally it was dark brown, but now it was red. She had lost weight.

She touched her hair and tried to make a diffident gesture. Her hand was shaking.

'It's henna. It doesn't matter. Come on, put your seat belt on.'

I stared at her. *Seat belt?* A bark of laughter escaped from my throat. My mother frowned.

'When was the last time you took a shower?' she said.

I shook my head.

'I don't believe this. You have no idea what I've been through. It's terrible back there. People have died. There's no electricity or water. When was the last time I took a shower? Like, who cares? I'm glad to be alive.'

My mother was frowning. She had turned halfway around in her seat to look at me. She reached out and took my hands.

'Shhh,' she said. 'You're not yourself. Just relax and we'll go home. Your dad got you some burgers if you're hungry. You must be hungry.'

I sat there while my father got in the car and started the engine. The car was spotless. There was a box of tissues in the back window. My mother offered me Tic Tacs. I was aware of my own smell against the leather smell of the car. My chin started to shake.

'Can I see a map?' I said after a while.

My mother gave me an odd look but didn't ask any questions. She was afraid I'd start talking weird in front of my dad again. And they're funny, my parents. They protect each other from stuff. As if each thinks the other is somehow fragile.

My mother opened the glove compartment and handed me a map of New York State.

There was no Poughkeepsie. No Kingston Bridge. No Rhinebeck. Lake Katrine was right on the edge of the Hudson.

I scrutinized the map for other changes. I couldn't be sure, but everything else seemed OK.

I leaned back and stared out the window. I ached all over. I was hungry. I could smell the McDonald's burgers in the bag next to me. Trembling, I opened it.

'Anybody else hungry?'

My mother said no, too brightly.

My father guffawed.

I took out a cheeseburger and plugged my mouth with it. It was cool and greasy and it tasted like a dead animal. My father nodded approvingly in the rearview mirror.

The naked trees flashed by. The sky was cobalt. My mother turned on WHN for my father, who sang along with Dolly Parton.

Snow Globe

I was home. The world was frightening in its beauty and easiness. It heaved like the deck of a ship because I did not believe in it. But it was wonderful. Hot water, buses, 24-hour diners. MTV. The phone. Shopping.

I learned that I had gone missing three weeks ago. Prior to that I had been a student at Rutgers. Molecular biology. My friends had gotten worried that I hadn't shown up for an organic-chemistry lecture, or for dinner, or for a party. My parents reported me missing the next day.

At least they were the same parents. As last time, I mean. And at least I could remember something. Because I could still remember remembering nothing, if you know what I mean, and that had been about as bad as it could get. Or so I'd always believed. Now I was not so sure.

My parents looked small and pinched. They'd always worried about me anyway. About my 'problem'. Now they took me to a succession of doctors for a succession of tests. Brain scans. Questionnaires. Interviews. Art therapy.

I didn't crack. I wasn't stupid. Life in a mental ward didn't appeal to me.

I claimed that I remembered nothing of the latest 'episode'.

The dining-room table was covered with scientific journals and spiral notebooks and file folders. My parents did nothing by halves.

My father got on to the police. I must have been kidnapped, he said. Possibly tortured. Weren't they going to do anything about it?

He initiated a campaign to find and punish my abductors. Bizarrely, he urged all my 'friends' at Rutgers to go on a 'Take Back the Night' march in my honor. And they did. They came to see me, too. I didn't recognize a single one of them. That was awkward. I tried to downplay it.

I felt sorry for my folks. They wanted their ordered world back. They wanted their daughter. They would do anything to restore these things.

What was I supposed to do?

It's hard to go against the grain. Much harder than you'd think, if you've never done it. There are tacit pressures all the time, to think like them, be like them. It's much easier.

And so, in time, a kind of shift started to happen in me.

I began to trust the verity of my parents' world.

I began to believe them.

After all, the garbage was collected every Tuesday. The eleven o'clock news reported on events in the Soviet Union. Stern's had a sale on boots.

I began to relax.

I was sorry about what had happened to Bard and Red Hook, but what could I do?

The only sane thing to do was to forget it and move on.

A part of me knew that I should still be in mourning. But that didn't seem fair. Hadn't I been through enough? Here was my chance to start over. I was going to take it.

Every so often I flashed on Craig. Or on one of my friends that I'd never see again. Or campus. Or Ben and the crew. Or the House. And I thought: I should pack toilet paper and go back. But I didn't. I was afraid. I was a coward. I felt guilty and in my guilt I made no effort to act better but in fact the opposite. I pretended it had nothing to do with me. Not my problem.

And this world had a lot going for it that I'd never even noticed. Running water – hot, running water – is a pretty decent thing when you haven't had it. So is TV.

I figured that even working in the worst job I could get a roof over my head and a cable subscription. And I thought I could do better than that in time. My mother was hinting about how I should go back to Rutgers.

Molecular biology – what did I know about that? I'd be faking it. On the other hand, this was an opportunity to study something lucrative. I wouldn't mind that, now. I'd seen what could become of studying something philosophically deep. Lucrative was fine. I'd sit in an office, drive a car, watch TV, and if the toilet broke I could pay a plumber. Hell, I'd have gladly trained as a plumber, for that matter.

It was going to be so good, this real world, now that I was back.

If only I could trust it.

But I was afraid. I was too afraid to do anything much. I watched TV. If you knew how to look at it right, everything was great. I could even grow to love the commercials.

If I was very careful I could navigate my way between the TV and the bathroom and the fridge without getting into trouble. I tried not to look out the window. The sight of the cars going by on the highway made me nervous. Where were they getting their gas? Should I have brought a horse with me? And at night I sat up looking out, waiting for IT to attack.

My parents said a lot of idiotic things. They disapproved of me being home, but tried hard to hide it. My mother developed a strained smile. She had always had a habit of throwing out food that was even a little bit old, and I found it really hard to watch her do this now. She had bought a treadmill that she called the Love-Handle Eradicator and she spent a lot of time on that. This also freaked me. It made me think of everyone in the House, going out to shoot dinner. Digging holes to bury our shit. Putting on layer after layer of clothes to stay warm.

I watched Save the Children commercials with tears streaming down my cheeks.

I didn't know what to do.

I wondered if the pregnant mares had enough to eat.

A few weeks before Christmas, my mother arranged for me to take a temporary job at the Florence Shop in Bergenfield. At first I was shaky but after a week or so I started to get in a routine and then I found the job helped me escape from my own thoughts. In bed at night I saw little green numbers marching across the inside of my eyelids: merchandise codes and prices from the register. And endless repetitions of 'Walking in a Winter Wonderland' played in my ears instead of the echoes of IT that I usually fell asleep to.

On a Tuesday afternoon a week before Christmas I was typing in the merchandise code for a pair of sunglasses when IT came sauntering down Main Street, a great big bright melody embedded with distant screams and the occasional fire siren. IT was trailing sloppy, faltering scraps of sour harmony like seaweed, and lagging behind were flabby drumskin poundings whose echoes pooled out dark and liquid.

IT took hold of me at once. More so than any other sound I'd ever heard, IT presented in the form of an entity, not a texture. And ITs aggression was indisputable.

I slammed the cash register shut and bolted for the door.

I was supposed to be waiting on a Hispanic woman reeking

of perfume and with dozens of rings on her fingers. I heard her calling after me in a brass-knuckles voice, making a big fuss, but I didn't look back.

Wet snow was falling. The town was crowded; everyone was shopping. IT was there, in the street, rippling like a river of sound. Cars were moving through IT like ghosts: I thought of all those gas tanks and what IT had done at Bard, and I began to shiver. My teeth chattered. My eyeballs felt stripped, peeled back to white, when I tried to look at IT.

I couldn't actually see IT. There was pavement and then IT intruded, a non-sequitur, unprocessable and, in its refusal to comply with my understanding of the world, complete. Impenetrable. Antagonistic.

A few things crossed my mind in sequence:

1. ITs sound had changed. IT was becoming, to some degree, comprehensible.

2. I could hear voices inside IT.

3. Female voices.

4. My voice.

I clamped my lips shut. I could still hear myself: singing, but singing in no way I'd ever sung in my life. No such tones, no such manner: not me.

I started to walk towards the bus stop, head down against the force of ITs noise. In my peripheral vision I was beginning to get flashes of what IT looked like: wires; numerical figures; blue-veined treelike structures like exotic corals you sometimes see in tropical fishtanks; eyes; orifices; lightning in a castle made of cloud. Black eggs hatching skeletons

I strained to understand what my voice was singing, within IT. I think there were words. I couldn't make them out, but the fact that there were words had to be significant. Even a word is a reproduction, isn't it? The duplication of an experience – and a duplicity, because the word pretends to be the thing, for that moment. Words are how we summon the other world, the world of thought – and also how we send it back again. Words are, after all, only utterances.

But IT was more than an utterance. And I didn't know how to send IT back.

A heavyset woman bumped into me with her shopping bags, said 'Excuse me,' and stepped around me. As my eyes focused on her I glimpsed the split ends of her spiral perm and the tiny stitches in the seam of her lavender ski jacket, and in that same brief impression I saw something else.

Numbers. Symbols.

She was made of them. They were crawling out of her, or she was becoming them..

I half-turned to stare after her, stopping in my tracks. I wasn't sure if I was seeing things, or hearing things. There were symbols under my feet and in the passing cars. I could perceive these symbols, even as I could perceive the metal curves and winter boots and clouds of steamy breath and snowflakes, even though the symbols and the objects were identical. It was like looking at two versions of the truth at the same time; it was like an optical illusion. My mind kept toggling back and forth between one reality and the other, unable to settle.

I felt disoriented and sick. All around me, people carried their Christmas presents unknowing of the fact that they were being changed to integers and fractions and placeholders that resonated with the sound of IT. And they didn't suspect a thing.

I could hear it in the sound of IT. In a fall of needles, in a cascade of sonic events coupling mind to mind to IT, in a wash of self-reflective other-swallowing ichor, IT could be heard to be performing the rendering.

No more, no less: IT was rendering us all into ITs own terms. IT was, quite simply, thinking about us. And we were becoming what it thought.

So that, it seemed to me, soon there would be nothing in the 'real world' outside of the mind and thought of IT.

And the real world didn't mind, not at all.
But I did.

I looked down at myself. I was still flesh; hadn't been zapped into numbers or computer language or whatever was happening to the others. This was good.

What was not good:

IT was crouched on the road in front of me, a sonic monster of no physical dimension other than by implication: e.g. the crushed and burned cars snapping beneath ITs legs. People moved around IT as if avoiding a cloud of gas. Some people ran toward IT, and others ran away. They behaved as if IT were a car crash.

My body was not cooperating. I couldn't seem to move. I was no longer certain of where or when I was. Bergenfield at Christmas – or Ravine Road in October? There was smoke and ruin, and the hint of a dragon's presence, but never a long enough glimpse to be sure. Yet I could feel ITs regard of me. IT sent a hook of sound towards me, personally, as if IT were calling my name. Calling my name with my own voice.

The town around me was getting further and further away, as though it were coming apart, and I was left standing in some middle void where Bergenfield had been. As Bergenfield receded from me in all directions, paradoxically it shrank smaller and smaller. Its edges blurred to darkness and sound and, as I stood there inert, Bergenfield was snatched away from me and I was left alone. I felt like I was standing in the bottom of a well watching a bucket go up the shaft toward light.

The sound of IT ended in a thunderclap. Silence. All light vanished. Globules of luminous color tumbled across my field of vision, but they were just phantom patterns stamped on my retinas: I couldn't see my hand in front of my face.

Now my own voices began to creep up all around me like vines. They wanted inside my skin. They wanted inside my eyes and the home of me.

I was angry. What right had IT to come after me this way? I had not played music. I had not solicited IT.

'Leave me alone,' I whispered. 'Get away from me. I don't want anything to do with you.'

The sound of my own voice, multiplied, only grew stronger.

I put my hands over my ears but it did no good.

I squeezed my eyes shut, but that was worse.

When I opened them there was an object in front of me. I was standing in a patch of asphalt amid utter darkness, and with me was a small gleaming thing. It looked like a snow globe. One of those glass things filled with clear liquid, with a miniature village inside, and when you shook it white flakes swirled around and fell.

I was holding Bergenfield, NJ, in my hand.

I ran. IT let me go. IT didn't have to, but it did. I ran uphill, still gripped in a darkness; then I came to crumbling buildings and twisting streets that looked like the set of a disaster movie. Crows called from darkened windows but did not appear. The sound of IT faded.

Then there was traffic. Gray people, unseeing people, performing their algorithms all unknowing, like ants on a scent. There was a street with stores and cars and bus stops. Numbers began to reassemble into objects. Like an optical illusion where you can see either a vase or two facial profiles, I found I could see either object or representation.

A storefront sign read *Tenafly Hardwear*.

I boarded a bus and rode through Tenafly. I checked road signs to try and figure out where we were going, but it was hard to see the real letters through the teeming symbols that were still being flung before my eyes. The longer I was on the bus, the stronger the physical world became, until finally I could be sure where I was.

I got off in Hackensack. The cold was bitter. I remembered this street; remembered the last time I was here. Supposedly I had gone with my mother to this check-cashing place, because she had gotten some kind of wire transfer from a guy in Sweden who had ordered one of her cast-bronze cat statues. We had walked up Main Street and then headed over to the *Golden Dragon*, where my mother had gone inside and I had stayed in the parking lot.

I hadn't been back here since my therapists made me recreate that day. I had remembered nothing then, and I remembered nothing now. But this time I noticed a small newspaper store, and I went in and bought a map of Bergen County. I opened it outside, in a stiff wind, and snowflakes lingered momentarily on the surfaces of Cresskill and Dumont before melting into the paper.

No big surprise.

Bergenfield didn't exist.

Crying, I put the snow globe in my coat pocket.

Post-IT Bard

When I got home my father was watching *Wheel of Fortune*.
My mother had left my dinner on a plate in the microwave
before going out Christmas shopping.

'Where'd she go?' I asked my dad, trying not to sound pan-
icky.

'Paramus, I think,' he muttered, his nose buried in the
Bergen Record.

'Are you sure? She didn't go to Bergenfield?'

'She said she was going to Riverside Square. Nothing is
open late in Bergenfield.'

I bit back the words, 'Nothing is open at all.'

Dinner was chicken with pasta. I ate slowly, while from the
living room came tinny cries of *'Come on! Big money! Big
money!'*

I knew this could be the last real food I got for some time,
but it was still hard to swallow.

'I'd like to buy a vowel, Chuck.'

I felt complicit, again. IT had trashed and then sucked up a
whole town, and used my voice in the process.

And, as before, IT had let me out. I had walked away
unscathed.

'I'd like to solve the puzzle. HOME IS WHERE THE HEART IS.'
Wild cheers.

Home is.

There were tears dripping down my face as I shook the snow globe and set it on the kitchen table, and a Lemon Pledge commercial came on TV.

I had to go back to Bard.

I got up from the table. Scraped my plate and put it in the dishwasher. All the while feeling the certainty of what I had to do coming over me like a chill. I had to do it. I had to do it *now*. I leaned around the corner of the kitchen and the living room, trying to look casual.

'Dad,' I said, 'can I borrow your car? I need to pick up a few things for Christmas.'

He handed over the keys and said something unkind about Vanna White. I pretended to laugh.

I packed my backpack with supplies and an old Instamatic camera. My plan – such as it was – was to take pictures of Bard and bring them out into this world. Then people would have to come to their senses and get with me.

I drove up the Thruway and slept in the back of the car under a sleeping bag.

I knew from my parents' map that there was no Kingston Bridge, so I had to use the bridge at New Paltz. I made it as far as Rhinecliff in the car, and after that I had to walk.

Walking was good. It took the edge off me, and with every step in the crusty snow I felt more real. The road had a tired look: the snowbanks all had mustaches from truck exhaust, but there hadn't been much traffic here lately, and I didn't pass one car in seven miles.

After I'd passed through the outskirts of Rhinebeck I started getting nervous again. The air bit my nose and throat. Squirrels chattered as I passed. I crossed the 199 at the broken light where Michelle had picked me up in her Pathfinder, but I didn't even look in the direction of the bridge. Instead I followed my own footsteps back north on River Road, towards Bard.

Now that I knew what to look for, I started to see the telltale signs of the boundary: bald tree branches against the sky, their shapes bending and dividing and finally yielding to tiny scraps of number/symbol combinations.

Fields of cut hay, repeating decimals and ragged stalks of half-formed integer arrays.

Look too close, and you'd miss it. Like in that Pink Floyd song – you could only see it out of the corner of your eye. But it was there.

I thought of Jeremy spending his summer calculating pi. What would a math-head make of what I was seeing? I wished I had someone to talk to.

When I had last seen Bard, autumn had been at its climax. There had been so many maples that the campus had looked like a bonfire in the fall. The leaves flew radiant through the air, and the cold blue sky would hold the auras of the trees like Kirlian photography, and with the grass lying underfoot in some billiard-table perfection your eye could start to go a little insane. It was all so Kodachrome. Where you could see the river there would be a block of declarative color, too: a hard, dark cobalt lifting into whitecaps, and the geese passing over, mournful and prescient – just when you'd swear the days couldn't get any better – of winter.

That was the Bard I remembered. But what would I find now?

I was sore from walking. The road deteriorated as I got closer to campus. There were layers of fallen leaves on Annandale Road as I came past the former Adolph's coffee shop, years' worth of mucky oak and maple leaves so that the road looked more like a trail through the woods. The houses on the riverbank were dilapidated and seemed abandoned. One of the

Victorian farmhouses on the Annandale triangle had a collapsed porch, and the white modern tower-house built over the
river had broken windows. I kept walking. The first dorm I hit
was Sands on the left, near where the road to Blithewood and
the theater center split off. There was a rusted Schwinn leaning
against the pine tree outside the dorm, but ivy had grown over
it and the tires were flat.

It looked like a lot more than a couple of months had passed.

Tewksbury looked ugly but nothing new there. Beyond, the
Ravine Houses all seemed to have collapsed, except for a part of
Hirsch that still hung on gamely, its insides exposed in a way
that gave it an Escherian beauty. I steeled myself and went off
toward Leonard, across the field where I had seen whatever it
was I had seen of IT.

In the field I found the first clue that I hadn't been hallucin-
ating that day. There was a pond in a star shape that could have
been a dinosaur's footprint. This was where I had first made a
recording of the sound of IT

I stood there for a while. The spot was not far from where I'd
thrown myself down in terror while IT passed overhead. Now
there were flocks of blackbirds in the trees around Proctor Arts
Center, and in what was left of the trees surrounding the Ravine
Houses.

The blasted-out cars were still there. Black stained the dirt
road in front of the Ravines. The scene had a stale look. The
place had been languishing like this for a while.

I thought of Craig. His fingers. His laugh. The smell of his
bed.

I wanted to cry but I felt watched. There was a creeping,
prickling sensation at the back of my neck and across my shoulders. Wariness. I stood there to one side of myself, unable to cry
or anything and knowing this was not good. Deep in my teeth
I could still hear IT. And IT would always be here. If there were
radioactivity here, you wouldn't be able to see that either, but it

would be no less deadly for being invisible. IT was not nuclear but it had left some other poison, some indeterminate and malevolent influence.

So far I had seen no people. I realized that unconsciously I was heading toward Brook House. When I saw that it was still there, that was when I started to tremble and leak tears. I walked past the window that Elizabeth had jumped out of during the Dead Guy Session. I tried the front door; it was unlocked. It let out a long, shrieking protest when I opened it.

Inside was cold and damp. There were some shoes and sweaters strewn around on the floor, and I braced myself to see bodies. But no one was there. I went to the stereo and popped the tape out.

Philip Glass, a copy of *Einstein on the Beach* labeled in feminine handwriting

Ugh, I thought, and for a moment I was back in MPZ and the whole mindset of myself then. I had never understood the allure of Philip Glass. Sound to bore you into submission. Sound to make you less than you were. Resignation. Stagnation. Submission. Sound of the walking dead. Know-it-all, smug, capitalizing on the bafflement of us all when faced with the big howling unknown: like selling tickets to sit in a dark closet in case of tornadoes.

There was a nylon tape case next to the stereo. The contents had had their labels inked out in Ben's hand. It was probably sound for his Close Readings of Music class, which would have been meeting here the day that IT descended.

Ben. He was so unlike every other professor in the college. Everyone else did the Western Canon. Ben had played us Mississippi delta blues and Korean court music, the Ramayana Monkey Chant and Mahler. With Gretchen he talked about Elias Canetti's *Crowds and Power*. He referred to the Austro-Hungarian Empire as easily as he talked about Coltrane. None of it was for effect. He was just like that: interested in a lot of stuff, but not interested in the status systems that academia used to categorize the world. You got the sense that, wherever he was coming from, not too many people had the chops to stand there with him and engage him on every level. Maybe nobody did. But – and this is the Major But – he was happy to engage with the students as if what we did and thought and felt was as valid as what Some Professor thought. He absolutely refused to set himself apart from us.

That had been very, very cool.

My chin wobbled.

Where was he?

I climbed the hill, past the blasted-out commons with the burned library beyond, toward Stone Row where the post office and bookstore had been. The feeling of desertion deepened. Bard had never been a populous school, but there had been over eight hundred students, not to mention faculty and staff and miscellaneous visitors on campus every day. Surely they hadn't all been wiped out?

The administration building stood at the end of Stone Row and I thought that probably if anything were left of the infrastructure of Bard it would be here. At the top of the steps near Stone Row there were some people standing around an oil barrel with a fire in it, warming their hands. Suddenly hesitant, I sidled over. Among them I recognized a girl with pink-framed glasses as a friend of Craig's from the film department . . . groped for her name . . . *Wei*? Anyhow, we nodded at each other. She didn't seem surprised to see me. I did a double take when I looked at the guy standing next to her: it was forty-something Seth who worked in Buildings & Grounds. He had lost thirty or forty pounds and was barely recognizable.

'What I wouldn't give for a plate of fried mozzarella,' Seth was saying.

'A hot bath,' someone else said.

'Teresa had a hot bath last week,' said a tall bearded guy. Well, he was wearing a beard but he sounded distinctly gay. 'We found some dry wood behind the theater and made a fire on the stage. She looked to die for. You should have been there.'

It went on like this. I felt impatient with the chit-chat, but I was afraid to ask the wrong question, say the wrong thing. Then, over Wei's shoulder, I saw Ben! He was walking toward Stone Row. I broke away from the group. He was moving with a long, loping stride, head down, purposeful, and I had to jog to catch up with him.

'Ben?' I called.

'Hey,' Ben said, stopping. 'Good to see you.'

Like we'd just met up after Spring Break or something. No biggie. I checked him out for signs of madness but there was genuine warmth in his eyes. He ventured a smile. He hadn't shaved for a couple of days and this made him look older and also vulnerable, which doesn't make sense when beards are supposed to be socially and physically protective. But there you go.

'I'm so glad I found you,' I blurted. 'I wasn't sure—' and I caught myself. His gaze shifted away and he let my remark slide. I later realized that somewhere in those first moments when we encountered each other it had been decided that we wouldn't talk about IT. I'm not sure, but I think Ben proposed this and I went along with it. The agreement was subliminal, communicated in body language and the occasional retreat of eye contact on my part or on his. I could be wrong about the causal order of the decision, though. It's possible that he would have talked about it if I hadn't been so scared. I think what happened was that I saw that if we talked about IT I was going to find out things I didn't want to know and he was going to say things he didn't know what they might bring up and I was really needing him to be older and wiser and stronger but I had a bad feeling that if we talked about it he wouldn't be, so we just didn't talk about it.

Not one word.

It sounds crazy to say this. I'd had my experiences all bottled up, and for so long I'd been praying to find somebody I could corner to talk to about IT. To compare notes. To share whatever it was I was feeling – grief? Something prior to grief? I did't even know, *because I hadn't talked to anyone*. Then I find somebody mature and sensitive and articulate and I don't say anything.

I can't explain it. Maybe I just wasn't ready to have the conversation on the deep level that I knew Ben would engage me on. Maybe I saw how fragile he was and was afraid for what would happen to him if we spoke. Even after everything that had happened to me, to him, to this place, I was still more afraid of the unknown than of anything else. And I still didn't know what IT was.

My bones were quaking. Everything started coming on instinct again. I asked Ben what he'd been doing to pass the time and he said that today he'd been listening to session tapes and reading an Elmore Leonard novel from the bookstore.

'How is it?' I said.

'Not really my thing. But it beats Kierkegaard for laughs.'

We snorted together at his joke. Now we were in collusion: standing amid the wreckage of Bard, talking about everything but IT. The grace with which we avoided the subject was pretty amazing.

I went with Ben to the bookstore, where there were a lot of people standing around talking and holding books. I was surprised. I hadn't been sure some of my classmates could even *read*. There was a nervous air about the place, and it took me a little while to figure out that nobody was smoking.

'Did people run out of cigarettes?' I asked Ben softly.

'Nearly,' he said. 'A carton of cigarettes is priceless around here. I wish I had some to trade. We got some stuff set up at the Field Station,' he said. 'Been living on coffee and potato chips from the bookstore. I'm just going to see if I can get anything now.'

'Wait!' I said. 'I've got some . . .' I lowered my voice to a whisper. 'I've got some supplies with me. Is this where everybody comes to trade stuff?'

'That's right.' He looked at me like I was beyond ignorant.

'Not here,' I said. 'Let's go back to the Field Station. I don't want to start a stampede.'

The Field Station was all the way down at the end of the stream where it let out on the Hudson. They had canoes down there and various kinds of weather-predicting equipment. There were also radios (useless) and camping equipment (useful).

Just before we reached the bottom of the waterfall, Ben led me down to the bank of the river. There were two wizened women who I recognized as kitchen staff from the commons. They were washing clothes and dishes and stuff. They had a little campfire going just up the hillside, amid the bracken. They greeted Ben warmly. He took a fishing rod down from the branches of a birch tree and dragged a plastic yogurt container up from the shallows; it was full of worms. He baited a hook.

We sat down. We didn't talk. I wanted to, but it was hard to know where to begin.

I had expected Ben to have some kind of grip on things. But here he was with his fishing rod, staring at the water. And I realized I had assumed that he would solve the problem for me.

Sometimes when you're talking about weird things like time and space and the meaning of life you hit this thing. It's like a patch of black ice, a feeling of lubrication that means you think you're into some truth. You think with your fingers – like a blind person reading someone's features – that you are exploring and discovering the shape of a true concept: a reality. And your language skates around on the black ice, unable to settle, until in the end you're going 'you know' and 'like' to fill in the gaps of the unsayable. But the taste of truth hangs in the air like bread baking, a promise of something substantial, and it's shared by everybody in the conversation. 'Yeah, yeah, yeah' you say to each other. The ideas follow each other too fast and instinctively to be grasped. Language can't carry it. It's more than language.

This *black ice breadbaking lubricated aha!* feeling is something I've been wondering about a lot lately. With Ben it used to happen all the time. He'd put into words what I felt. He'd hear the undercurrents in my music. The ones I didn't even know were there. He'd give a form to the vague shapes that I could feel but couldn't articulate.

But here's the thing: a lot of the stuff is abstract. You grasp it like a handful of water. You can't stand on it. It can't save you.

So when I watched Ben with his fishing line in the river and the two ladies put away their washing and started peeling hard-boiled eggs and dropping them in a big mayonnaise jar, I got an awful swooping sense of ice beneath me, cracking.

'Salt,' said one of the kitchen ladies to me in a heavy Bronx accent, sagely. 'You put salt in the water and it makes them easy to peel.'

I nodded my appreciation for this tip.

I asked Ben, 'Have you seen any of the other MPZ folks?'

Ben looked at me sidelong. His eyes were just a little bit Oriental, a hint of some epicanthic thingie there in his sidelong glances and I'd always wonder what he was thinking. He was the smartest person I'd ever met and at the same time he never foisted that on you, but those little glances of his always made me feel like I was looking into a maze.

He said, 'The spray from the waterfall's not so good for the recording equipment.'

I wondered if this was like *Mission: Impossible* and we had to talk in code.

But after a minute he added, 'Gretchen's OK. Ford. Trinity . . . I'm not sure about Trinity. She seems a little fragile.'

Abruptly, he stood up. 'You want to go down to the Field Station? I don't think we're going to catch anything this time of day.'

The Field Station was a wooden building with a rustic, Western look to it. A couple of dead does were hanging from the frame of the porch, glassy-eyed. A handful of survivors had gathered within, including the MPZites Ben had just mentioned. After we'd greeted each other in the same weird way that didn't quite admit to the fact that really strange things had been happening to all of us, I opened my backpack and took out the stuff I'd brought.

They pounced on it like a pack of wolves.

'I'm sorry there isn't more,' I said. 'I didn't know what I was going to find when I got here. And I didn't know what would be most needed . . .'

'Do you have any tampons?' said Gretchen, and I had to shake my head. The things you don't think of.

Even so, they looked at me like I was Santa Claus.

There was a little party of sorts. As it got dark, Trinity lit tea lights and Ford made popcorn and dusted it with pepper and cumin. We all reminisced about MPZ.

Trinity said, 'Hey, remember the time in Close Readings of Music when Chris made us listen to Ravel with a cheese score?'

'Oh, yeah . . .' Ford tilted his head back, eyes closed. 'He wrote the cheese into the score. We had to eat a different cheese every time the score said so. It was like, Brie, Camembert . . . what was that other one? Gouda?'

'I don't know, I'm allergic to dairy.'

'I don't know about Gouda, but there was definitely Swiss.'

'You want cheese?' said Ben. 'Caerphilly – now there's a cheese.'

'Never heard of it. Would it go with Ravel?'

That was about how the conversation went. I began to give up on anything meaningful ever being said. I went out into the woods to pee and when I came back Ben was standing in the doorway of the Field Station with his hands in his pockets. As I came up the steps he said, 'You figure anybody else is on their way? With you, or after you?'

I shook my head. I thought about saying more but I was afraid the news would be too shitty for him right now. Instead, I said, 'You gotta come with me.'

'No rescue efforts? Nothing?' He looked worried, like the whole world had been wiped out or something.

'It's not like that,' I said. 'They don't know anybody's here.'

Ben came out on the porch and shut the door behind him. It was freezing. The Hudson flowed dark and serene. I pointed.

'What do you see out there?'

'Can't you see it?'

'I don't think I can see the same as you. That's why I want to know.'

'Halfway across, the world vanishes. The sky above the water is cut in jigsaw patterns. Some of them are starry sky. Some of them are utterly black. That's what I see. I hear other people see mist.'

'Oh,' I said.

'Hey, so – what do you see?'

I looked at my feet. 'I see the other side of the river. The Catskills. I see lights. It looks pretty much like it always did.'

I felt guilty saying it. Ben kind of stuck his lower lip out and nodded, hands in pockets, rocking back and forth.

'It was kind of hellish around here for a while,' Ben said. 'There were a lot of bodies. Big mass grave out near the theater.' He nodded towards the hanging deer. 'I used to feed them, outside my house.'

'So now they're feeding you.'

Ben shook his head. 'Winter's here. I don't think very many of us are going to make it. If there's no rescue.'

I had to force myself to keep my voice down; I was upset, but I didn't want to be overheard.

'Is anyone trying to do anything? It still seems really . . . Bard.'

'Well, my take on that is that everybody's had a different experience of what actually went down that day. There's no kind of consensus as to what the problem is, and I've just been watching the different factions play out their ideas. There's been a lot of talk, you know . . .' He laughed. 'Well, you can picture it. Not too many people here have experience of dealing with a crisis. It's a lot of headless chickens. Hard to say how it will shake down, but it doesn't look pretty.'

'It's the same in Red Hook,' I said. 'Everything's about who can play the best bully, or who's in with a church.'

'Yeah, well. Maybe there are a few more nuances here but it boils down pretty much the same. I tried everything I could think of to get out, but you know when you're working on just surviving day to day, it's hard to make plans.'

'You have to come with me,' I said again. 'You have to try again.'

Ben gave me a pitying sort of look. It was as if I'd said, 'You should try playing Lotto, I hear it's a great way to make a living.'

'You know what I think is the strangest part of all this?' Ben said. 'It's how everybody seems to process what happened differently. Everybody seems to have their own framework about what happened, and what is happening right now. Like, you have your conventional visions of the event – people thinking somebody spiked them some bad acid or something. And you have your UFO/alien-invasion theories. People talk about maybe it was an earthquake or a meteor falling, but then when they see there's no evidence of that, they can't think in those terms either. So then the talk turns to what *caused* it to happen, whatever it was. And on top of the alien invasions and everything, now you have your garden-variety government-conspiracy theories, you know, that we're part of some secret experiment. But the strange part about it is, nobody can really talk about *what actually happened.*'

'Like a session,' I muttered.

'It's like, you try to talk specifically about what was seen, what was heard, what was felt, and what was done, when the whole thing was going down. And the more specific you try to get, it seems like the further away you go from being able to describe anything. The sense of the thing breaks down on inspection. I've found this again and again. For example, you're the first person who has asked me to describe what I see when I look out over the river. Now that I've told you, I'm not even sure I got it right.'

I realized that I was shivering, but my mind was working away and I didn't want to move.

'What you're describing sounds a little like the feeling I got when I crossed the border to come back in here,' I said. 'And I've had this feeling since I got here . . . well, time doesn't seem to be running the same. And there's a general feeling of decay, there's a feeling that whatever happened that day, it isn't over. Things are still changing. Yeah, I think that's what I'm getting. It's not over yet, not here.'

'You shouldn't be here, Cassidy,' Ben said. 'If you can get out, then get out.'

I didn't look at him. How was I going to explain Bergenfield? And how was I going to explain that this was all my fault, somehow – all connected to me? I didn't have the guts to tell him that.

'I'm looking for some kind of answer,' I said. 'And now that I'm here, I can't just leave you guys . . .' I had been about to say *to die.* But I checked myself and said, '. . . behind.'

'I guess we all have our reasons for what we do. From the little you told me, I'd been thinking maybe you came back here so you wouldn't be the only crazy person out there.'

I reeled a little. 'OK, maybe that could be it, too.'

'Come on, let's go in. Eat popcorn, for tomorrow we die.' And Ben smiled as if to show that he still liked me, even if I was an idiot.

In the morning, rummaging around the makeshift kitchen looking for baker's yeast, I found Trinity's notes from Professor Schiff's 'History of Science' course, known colloquially as 'Science For Idiots'. Schiff was famous for his against-the-grain thinking, which featured various conspiracy theories about the politics of science as well as a passion for unconventional cosmogonies. Trinity had highlighted some lines relating to something called string theory and superstrings. Then she had crossed them out. She had also scrawled notes in green pen inside the cover of a worn paperback called *The Case of the Midwife Toad*.

Topological legerdemain: what if worlds could nest inside one another? As an egg is released, penetrated, attaches to womb, turns itself inside out and is ultimately ejected. Reproduction a metaphor for these offspring realities.

Calabi Yau spaces. String theory. Sound waves/vibrations. Music?

A problem of scale. All that cool quantum stuff happens too small to matter.

I went to find Trinity. She and Gretchen and Ford were hanging out on the front porch of the Field Station. Trinity was holding a sketchbook, drawing a tree stump in charcoal.

'Hey,' I said. 'Have you been trying to relate physics to our . . . um, problems? Do you know something I don't?'

Trinity had arrow-straight dark brown hair cut unfashionably in bangs. She wore bifocals and her lips were chapped almost to the point of bleeding. She used to be plump but now she had sculpted cheekbones; they gave her a haunted appearance. Now she looked at me as if I'd asked her about her kitten-torturing habit.

'Those notes were all wrong. I couldn't make any of it hold water. I don't even know the math.'

'Can you at least explain the idea you had?'

'Does it matter?' she said. 'There isn't much point in trying to figure it out if we can't do anything about it.'

Stung, I started to turn away. Then Trinity said, 'It was just an idea about abstract structures and how they might reproduce. Nothing to do with string theory at all, really, it's just looking at these Calabi Yau spaces and thinking about topology and how one shape can become another, I was thinking that you could have these offspring bubbles of dimensions. And I was interested in string theory because everybody talks about the vibrations of these tiny folded dimensions, but it's not really the same thing. It's only that the words we have to talk about it are so limited. You can't get there with language.'

'The idea of worlds nesting inside worlds sounds about right to me,' I said.

'Like I said, what difference does it make?'

I tried a different tack.

'Ben told me that everybody saw something different the day it happened. Mind if I ask what *you* saw?'

Trinity shot me a suspicious glance, like it was a trick question.

'We were in Close Readings of Music. I got up to put on my tape and I saw these flashing lights from over by Proctor. I thought it was a fire engine or something. There were explosions. Then . . . the sky overhead cracked open. There was just this darkness behind, but there was sound coming out of it. The sky started to crack in all directions like glass, or like an egg. Yeah, like an egg. That was what gave me the idea about reproduction.'

'And then what? What happened after that?'

'Oh, everybody started running around. There were fires all over the place. I thought we'd been bombed. Cars were exploding. Buildings were going up in flames. Trees. You can see the worst of the fire damage by the New Gym, between there and the Robbins Gatehouse. And then . . . it stopped. Sky closed up. People acting nuts. People hurt. People dead. Phones down. You know.'

I said, 'That's a pretty wild idea you got, about eggs and stuff.'

'Yeah, I know. That's why I didn't tell anybody. It just sounds too stupid. I didn't think anyone would be snooping around my notes.'

'I'm sorry,' I said. 'I was only looking for the yeast. See, I really don't know what I'm dealing with. The different . . . worlds . . . seem to be locked inside each other. Bard inside this Red Hook, but invisible to them. And Red Hook inside the outside world, but also invisible to it. And Bergenfield seems to have been sucked into a snow globe . . . the whole thing's sick. And if there's another world outside that . . .'

Trinity turned the page of her sketch pad and scribbled a little doodle in charcoal. She said, 'Nested patterns and repetition. That's about as complex as humans can go when it comes to spotting the hidden order of nature.'

'What's a nested pattern?'

She drew me a little picture. 'It's a pattern inside a pattern – it keeps repeating. Like a fractal.'

'Hey,' said Ford. 'If you can walk across boundaries, then maybe we could give you some kind of message, something that would act as proof that we exist. Signatures. Photographs.'

'It won't matter,' I said. 'The people outside, they can't get in. And this thing – this IT – follows me wherever I go. As long as it's around, the world will keep fracturing.'

'Do you know what a Calabi Yau space is?' Trinity asked.

'Ooh, I know!' Ford beamed. 'That's in *Star Trek II* where Kirk talks about this test he took at Starfleet Academy and how he changed the parameters so he could win.'

'That's Kobiashi Maru,' Trinity said in a scathing tone. 'A Calabi Yau space is how dimensions are folded over on each other, mathematically speaking. There's a shitload of other dimensions but they're really tiny and they're curled up in these weird configurations. But people tend to mix up chaos theory and string theory, they think anything goes. It doesn't. They're two different kinds of abstraction. It's like when people use the new physics as just a big opt-out clause. They think because the observer is significant on a quantum level that it means you can just throw objectivity out the window. The Tao of this and the Tao of that. That's why I don't like talking about it. I don't know the math. I don't really understand it.'

The talk turned to other things. Eventually I headed up to Security to see if somebody was, like, in charge of the scene in an official way. Security was based at the Old Gym, which was itself a stone's throw from Route 9G at the edge of campus. I decided to first walk over and see whether any of 9G was included in Bard's chunk of reality. If it was, there might be non-Bardians trapped there. And there might be cars.

I walked past Stone Row and across the visitors' parking lot, through a thin strip of wood and on to 9G. A blue Subaru had run off the road and crashed into a tree: one headlight was out and the front quarter-panel was damaged. The skid marks were still visible. Nothing moved on the road now. I started to walk up toward the North Campus entrance. After a while I came to the border. I knew how to recognize it now: everything went out of focus somehow, and I felt dizzy. The seethe of numbers flickered just beneath the surfaces of things. I saw Persian tile floors and compound leaves, and surf and protractors. And more numbers. A few more steps and I'd be out of Bard and back in Red Hook.

I felt myself frowning. I started to walk back toward Security.

'Hey!'

It was a tenor shout. Out of the trees ahead of me strode a lanky young guy with a mop of reddish hair.

'Justin!' I cried.

He shaded his eyes. 'Cassidy? What are you doing out here?'

I pointed back the way I'd come.

'Is that the edge?'

Justin closed the gap between us and started to steer me back toward the main campus.

'You shouldn't do that,' he said. 'I'll get in trouble.'

'Shouldn't do what?'

'You just appeared out of nowhere. I'm supposed to write up stuff like that, but I won't since it's you. But still. Come away from all that.'

'You saw me cross over?'

Justin put his head down and made for the dispatch desk. He left me standing on the visitors' side of the counter while he lifted the hatch and let himself through. He got out a clipboard. He scratched his head.

'Does the radio work?' I asked, seeing the mike across the desk.

He shook his head.

'I've been in Red Hook,' I blurted. 'No one from out there knows about Bard. It's totally weird. People have like different lives . . . the maps don't even include the campus. No one remembers it.'

'Uh-huh,' said Justin. 'Um . . . did you do the weekend rota or were you going to leave it to Alice?'

Here we go. He thinks I work here. He has no idea what I'm talking about. He's seen me step across the boundary but he hasn't seen it . . .

Carefully, I said, 'I had to leave it to . . . Alice.'

'Okey-dokey.' He stuck a pencil behind his ear and put a Cat

Stevens tape in the boombox. He pressed 'play' but of course nothing happened. He tapped his fingers on the counter and hummed. I tried to play it straight.

'Justin?'

'Yup?'

'What's on the other side of Route 9?'

He chuckled.

'Kid, you OK?'

'I'm OK, Justin. Could you just humor me?'

'Seriously?'

'Seriously.'

He pushed his glasses up the bridge of his nose.

'A peanut butter and jelly sandwich.'

'What?'

'You just asked me what my mom used to put in my lunch box on Fridays. And I'm telling you, all right?'

'No, I asked what's on the other side of Route 9.'

'I just *said*. C'mon, now, I got stuff to do.'

'OK – Justin – where'd she get the peanut butter? You can't grow that here. Can't even grow wheat. Where did you actually *live* as a kid, Justin?'

'Whoa, did you take a pedantic pill this morning?' laughed Justin. 'I lived in a house. Or an apartment. No, a house.'

I nodded. Persisted, although I guess I wasn't sounding vastly logical. 'What about when the toilet paper runs out?'

'I don't know – ask Jerry.'

'Who's Jerry?'

'He runs the physical plant.'

'Did Jerry dig the graves? Do you have a hospital? Who put out the fire at the library?'

'Library burned down years ago,' he said. 'Alexandria and stuff.'

I turned away.

*

On my way back to the Field Station I came across Gretchen at the waterfall. She had a plastic crate of dishes from the Kline Commons dishwasher, and she was cleaning them in the running water. She had a bottle of generic dishwashing liquid and one of those horrible fluorescent orange plastic scrubbies you use in the galleys of boats. Her boots were soaking wet from the spray.

'Hey,' I said. 'Are you sure this is a good location for washing stuff?'

Gretchen looked up at me. She took off her glasses, which were wet, and gave a few owlish blinks.

'Do you know of a hot river?' she answered, chucking the plastic thing to one side in frustration and scrubbing at the coffee cup with her bare fingers.

'That's not what I meant!' I exclaimed. 'Think! Where does this river come from?'

'Oh.' She smiled. 'You're going to ask me a deep philosophical question and I haven't even had coffee in days.'

I stared at her. 'Deep philosophical question?' I said.

'Let me think. I read something about this once. I can't remember all the theories.'

'Theories? Gretchen, this river picks up runoff from the sewage treatment plant. You can't wash coffee cups in it. You'll get dysentery or something.'

As I said it, I had a crumbling-ground feeling. I wasn't too sure what dysentery actually was. I knew it had something to do with children dying in Third World countries, and dirty water, but I didn't know what it actually *was*. But Gretchen just smiled as if I were talking about the weather.

'I like the river,' she said. 'It's so white. Nice.'

I looked away, embarrassed. Gretchen might have been many things, but idiotic she was not. What was happening here?

'OK, I'm going up to Blithewood to see if any of their phones work,' I said.

'Blithewood . . .?' Blinking incomprehension.

'Gretchen, you lived there. Before they started turning it into the Levy Economics Whatchamacallit. Remember? Crazy Mary used to ride her bike down the hallway?'

Everyone knew Blithewood. White manor house. Women's dorm, long skirts and black-rimmed spectacles, formal dress parties in the ballroom with Butthole Surfers and Dead Kennedys on the speakers, giant bathtubs with clawed feet. Seances and an obligatory ghost. Sliding down the back lawn on cafeteria trays in the snow . . .

'The construction guys are gone,' said Gretchen softly.

'Gone? Gone where?'

She scrubbed.

'Attrition.'

'What does that mean?'

'Attrition.' Gretchen looked angry, like I was making her talk about something she shouldn't have to talk about because it was so obvious. 'When people go.'

'Die?'

'No, just go.'

'Go where?'

'You know – go!' She lowered her voice to a whisper. 'They just disappear.'

Now we were on to something.

'The thing is – and it took me a while to figure this out but I think I've got a handle on it – after they go, we can't remember them. Isn't that weird?'

'Yeah . . . um if you can't remember them, how do you know they're gone?'

'By inference!' Gretchen was excited. 'Like dark matter. I read about that, too. Negative space. We know where they are by where they aren't.'

I am supposed to pursue problems with rigor. I learned that term in Symbolic Logic when I wasn't doodling in back of the class and giggling over the recent loss of my virginity. Rigor. A rigorous proof left no turn unstoned. Rigor was about taking the world seriously.

So I went up to the construction site that had been Blithewood Manor. It was all fenced. They might have their own generator but I didn't know how to use that stuff. I stood on the lawn and looked out to the Hudson. I could see the other shore. At least I still had that much.

'What about the boats?' I said aloud. 'Are they skipping over us like we're not even here?'

Then I saw someone coming towards me across the leaf-strewn lawn. It was Justin again. He waved.

'Feeling better now?' he asked when he reached me. Mute, I nodded.

'That's cool. Gretchen said you freaked and came up here. It happens to everyone, you know. Come on – let's go see where everybody else is. I want to talk to Ben about something.'

Down at the Field Station, Ben and Gretchen were having an argument. She was half-smiling in frustration. He was pursing his lips and shaking his head, looking at his shoes while with splayed fingers he dramatized his points.

'*Not this again,*' Justin muttered to me out of the side of his mouth.

'*What?*' I whispered back.

Justin leaned over and said, 'They're talking about *The Bride Stripped Bare by her Bachelors, Even.*'

'Oh,' I said. I didn't know what that was, but I didn't want to have another one of those non-sequitur chats with Justin. Anyway, the argument seemed to be peaking. Gretchen looked like she wanted to get out of it, but Ben was persisting in trying to make himself understood.

'Hey,' he said finally, standing up and coming toward us, 'but if you want to sell yourself down the river that's your business, not mine.'

I winced. Ben greeted us with a forced smile. We all sat down on scruffy deck chairs on the chilly porch.

'How's it going?' I asked, sincerely.

He indicated the mug he was carrying with a pained expression. 'Tea,' he said, and he might as well have said 'Cyanide.'

I gave my head a questioning tilt.

'We ran out of coffee. I got a headache most of the afternoon – withdrawal, I guess. We ran out of Tylenol, too.'

'I can get you coffee and aspirin,' I said. 'But I'd rather you came with me. I don't think this is a good place to be. It's unstable. And the resources are running down.'

Ben moved his hands over the mug in a considered way.

And then he said something. Whatever it was he said, it must have been something sad. It had nothing in particular to do with what I had said. At least, not in a way that I can remember as being pin-downable.

Strange how I have so much trouble remembering what Ben said.

As if his words, thoughts, music, all fled from my mind just as those people and places eluded Gretchen and the others.

Whole qualities of experience carved away from the sheer face of memory.

Odd how it's only the words that are missing. My memory won't fetch them up. I can see Ben there so clearly, his elbows on his knees as he leans forward holding a coffee cup, lower lip out-thrust, comb-over falling across his glasses. Brown corduroy pants and black Reebok sneakers and a black corduroy shirt. His body stumpy and earthen, significant. His eyes shifty, and that elfin grin; his accent that could never make up its mind whether it was Brooklyn, British or Black from Downsouth. These things are before me in my senses as true as the memory of an old song or smell. But his actual words have fled. Every witticism, every unique and tangy turn of phrase – gone. My recollection substitutes vague likenesses, like bananas instead of butter in a low-fat cake recipe. Never the real thing. Never alive, pungent, specific as a trowel of good spring black earth dug to birdsong.

I'm shoveling shit against the tide.

That's the one thing I can remember him saying for sure.

He said that a lot.

We spent a fair amount of time sitting around smelling the food cooking at the Field Station. There was one meal a day, and usually it was simmering for some hours. Occasionally one of us broke down and opened the big tin of cookies that Gretchen had baked during the first week of the crisis: there had been butter and fresh eggs then, and although some of the cookies had gotten fur mixed up in them from Gretchen's now-feral cat they still tasted pretty good.

'Ben,' I said. 'If someone took something essential away from the world, but at the same time you didn't know it was gone, would you miss it? Do lobotomized people know they aren't all there? Or would you just watch the slow death of reality and never understand?'

'In medieval times hell was real,' he said. 'People took the Bible literally.'

'Hell was on Earth,' Trinity said. 'Judging by what you read about the way people lived and died.'

'What?' Justin quipped. 'No indoor plumbing and it's automatically hell?'

'In a pastoral society people become sheep,' Trinity said, ignoring Justin. 'And shepherds. It's only natural.'

'So what are we now? The information age? Are we just binary? And can you whack away chunks of logic and still get the program to run?'

'It'll run,' Ford said helpfully, twirling his chopsticks like drumsticks. He 'knew about' computers. 'But you know what they say: garbage in, garbage out.'

'What about the missing stuff? What about the folded stuff? You don't know it's there. Does your brain somehow compensate?'

'Your eyes do it,' said Trinity, angrily. 'Your ears do it. Why not your thought? Fill in the blanks.'

Ben said, 'It could be some variation on hysterical blindness. A self-protective mechanism.'

'Protection from what?' I said. 'I'm trying to be rigorous. I'm really trying. But I just keep thinking about clean clothes and hot food. Even cold food. Any food.'

'That seems pretty normal in the circumstances,' said Justin. 'Some people are, like, this is the worst thing that's ever happened to me, boo-hoo. And other people kind of rise to it. They seem to switch on.'

'Really?' I said. 'Which one am I?'

'I don't know. You just keep asking questions.'

There was a knock on the door and a guy in a parka came in.

'Hi. I'm Lenny. Somebody here want their deer butchered?' he said. Ben sprang to his feet.

'That'd be great,' he said, and followed the guy outside. 'Thanks for stopping by.'

So much for that conversation.

The thing about Ben was, you always got the feeling he was just visiting from some other place. And I don't mean that in a funky, spaced-out way. It was, like, his mind could work on this whole other level, and he'd share stuff with you, but you could never really get where he was because he was just *too friggin' smart*. To me he was a world-opener, a rewriter of my programming, someone who unlocked all the doors. Maybe too many doors. So that I felt like a little kid, ringing the bell and then running away – I was afraid of what he'd bring out in me.

I was afraid of Ben's need, too. The howlingness of the mismatch he felt with most of the world, the isolation; and how small I'd be, measured against all that.

I was afraid what I'd be and what he'd be too would turn out to be sameold sameold, that I'd disappoint myself and so would he.

I never wanted to be ordinary, you see. In the years when I was looking for myself in the vacuum of memory I was most afraid that the 'lost me' hadn't been somebody I would want to find.

I didn't want to open the Gothic sub-basement mystery trap-door and step down into darkness and find nothing but dirt and spiders.

I didn't want to admit I was just a child.

I wanted to be a visionary.

I wanted to graduate to some other, more enlightened level of being.

What a crock of shit.

And it was too late now, because everything was rended, rendered, rent. Call it Calabi Yau or whatever they did with particle accelerators, it wasn't important. My ontology was shot full of holes and I was eating cat-fur cookies like that was a solution.

I vowed that if I I got out of this shit, I'd never question reality again. And I'd become a plumber.

Beat Fascism

It was Friday night according to somebody's calculations, and that meant Open Space. I dragged myself along, feeling depressed and confused.

But it didn't turn out like I thought.

Strange: playing in the gray light of Brook House, in the angles of four walls, speakers, window moldings, bare trees. Strange: the gritty old carpet, worn and cigarette-scarred, and the objects (instruments and otherwise) belonging to the participants that lay on it, and the slightly damp furniture dividing this simple room in simple ways.

Strange, because of the sound. The sound picked us up and carried us. It came from inside but billowed out and around to include us, as if the waters of our bodies could communicate with the ocean and *this* ocean, a musical ocean, now took us both toward and away from our selves. Because it was *our selves* and not only my self and their selves; there was a genuine mingling going on, and by that mingling it was clear if only in the shape and form of that music that there was more to us than previously suspected. We were, without question, great lumpy sacks of hang-ups and contradictions, and this was all too evident. We were also something under ourselves. We were something more basic, and in tapping that basis we flowed with it. We moved within and in and of sound, ourselves.

Or so it seemed to me.

Rituals always feel this way, don't they? That's why we have them. Rituals take us into that older place, that more connected place. But this was ritual-no-ritual, because its express purpose was to get beyond itself. Its goal was to go beyond habit. Its goal was to undermine itself.

Was that happening?

Was that express purpose being fulfilled?

What is my *express porpoise?* I thought, looking out the window with the recorder between my lips. You couldn't do much with a recorder – well, I couldn't. I wanted to climb into the ruined old Steinway but I also didn't want to risk another stapling.

The sound, increasingly anarchic as Justin thundered on his bass and Gretchen steadfastly made tiny tinny string sounds from the corner most distant from the microphone. Ben was weaving a slow narration of stacked chords on the old Krumar, and I, frustrated with the squeaking – porpoise again! – of my recorder, got to my feet and began to walk around the room, noodling.

And I knew that I wanted to feel safe. That was my purpose. I wanted the sound to come and enfold me like an old blanket that is more pills than weave. That smells a bit doggy. But it wasn't happening; not here. The sound was developing qualities of being Bigger and More Complex, not through loudness or anything so obvious, but through the way everyone in the room was connecting to everyone else, or not.

And as I walked around the room looking out each of the many windows, I could see the jigsaw sky that Ben had told me about. I could see it now, beginning to reassemble. The black gouges were moving, shuffling with the pale clouds, until the sky had begun to organize itself into something close to a real sky.

Except for the howling gaps.

What had felt like a dispute between Justin and Gretchen had turned into a cat-and-mouse pursuit that had all our ears standing up. Trinity was struggling with something on the grand piano, trying to enter but not sure how to do so without toe-stepping; she knocked on the door of their dialogue.

Trinity went up to the microphone and whispered something. None of us could hear it – but it would come out on the tape. The idea of that seemed to create a gorgeous conceptual friction, and it elicited a chorus of Meredith Monk-y vocalizations from Gretchen, eventually supported by Ben's Krumar sound.

Suddenly the top of the baby grand dropped off its support stick and hit the frame. The sound that resulted brought silence from the freaked players. The piano-smash sound decayed slowly, with a lot of wah-wah because the thing was out of tune. We let it die. Afterward it was so quiet you could hear the tape spooling. Eyes down, inward, we waited for the session to be over. Must have stood, or sat, right where we were for ten minutes before Ben got up and switched off the tape. Justin went to the bathroom.

I realized I was shivering.

Everybody sat down on the moldy furniture or the floor. We talked in soft voices about nothing much. The toilet flushed and Justin came back. He tossed his hair back as he sat down.

'Are we playing the tape?' he said.

I don't remember who said what. I just remember listening to the sound of the water rushing in the cistern. I mean, you can flush a toilet with a bucket of water, but afterward it won't fill up again unless you have pressure from the mains. But Bard hadn't had any mains pressure since IT came. Still, the high pale steady hum of the cistern refilling hung in the air for several seconds before cutting off.

'Oh my God,' I said, half to myself.

'Cassidy?'

'Nothing,' I said. I got up. 'I'll be right back. Go ahead, don't wait for me.'

I ran into the bathroom. Turned on the tap. There was *hot water*.

When I came back, everybody glanced at me and then away, as if embarrassed by me.

'D-d-did you know?' I said, addressing the group at large. 'Is this to do with the session? It's like magic. There's hot water in there.'

Here was the test. Would they be surprised? Or would they pretend there had *always been* hot water?

Ben said mildly, 'Why do you think we're playing? It's not the kind of thing you do just for kicks.'

That sinks in: slow stone, deep lake.

Now maybe I understand.

The sound is all that's holding this place together. Bard is, like, the epicenter of IT. The whole place is a living boundary. Stuff is going in and out of existence all the time, and the sound of the sessions is the only sensemaking they have available to them. Question these post-IT Bardians in terms of what I take for logic, and they don't even react: I'm already off the edge of their map. The only way I can get with them is in the sound.

Justin plays the tape back. I'm listening. I'm listening. This is what the session sounds like.

Any kind of being is better than being dead. Crawling might not be walking but it still beats being dead, you know what I'm saying? As and when this sound moves off into the past, into memory's vanishing act, we'll know a lot more than we know now. Now what we know is the tension of things not being done yet. Things not able to be put in their right, or even wrong, or even irrelevant, boxes. Fully stackable realities, of course, are the space-saving ideal, but hey. You can't have it all and eat your cake. What we want here is to make a point, as big and sense-referent as possible, of the fact that we're not dead yet.

And I was thinking: could I rescue them? Could I, say for starters, kidnap Ben and take him out of here in a sack? Drug him and remove him and get him into my world? Would that even be possible? Should I attempt it with a small animal first, as a trial? But small animals didn't seem to be bothered with these petty distinctions of consciousness.

There had to be rules. If there were no rules I was fucked. So there had to be rules, because even if there were no rules and I was fucked, I didn't want to know about it. I needed it to be that if I could just find out what the rules were, however crazy, I could survive. Right?

Afterward, I stayed behind to talk to Ben. The others headed off toward the Field Station, subdued and somehow replete. I saw through the back window that there was a street lamp shining in the woods. Magic.

'So, what's up, Cassidy?' Ben was giving me his full attention. The full attention of somebody that deep who doesn't play games of any kind isn't something you take lightly. I knew I had to say this carefully.

'People aren't thinking straight. It seems to me. Sometimes I say something to someone and they answer me as if I'd said something else.'

Ben nodded.

'That could be about survival,' he said.

'But some of the things that people believe are so . . . hard for me to believe. Impossible for me to believe.'

'Trees do it,' said Ben. 'They warp and bend in the wind. You can't see the wind, but you can see the result.'

I looked up the hill toward Stone Row. Crows were diving in and out of broken windows on the third floor, fighting over something. I shivered.

I said: 'I know what caused this whole thing.'

Ben didn't say anything. He was waiting.

'Well,' I amended, 'I know something about it.'

Ben's eyes flicked to one side and back, very fast. I knew he'd thought volumes in that flicker. He's like that.

'You wanna talk about it?' he said.

I told Ben what had been happening all semester when I'd been playing. How things seemed to appear out of nowhere. Nonsensical things with no content: just packaging, like in the library. Or structure plus packaging, like in the miniature city near the dead guy. I told him how my sessions didn't sound right when I played them back. And I told him about the Staples tape I'd found the night my butt got stapled.

'It's just too much coincidence,' I said. 'The guy turns up dead, practically on top of a miniature city of gum wrappers that I swear wasn't there when I started playing. And you can look at me funny all you want, I saw it happen. And I picked up this bag with the tape in it, and Craig plays it and *bang*. We're all in the middle of a catastrophe. And I just keep thinking how I was working on this piece about annihilation, how badly I wanted a sound that reflects the end of everything. And I got IT. Now I can't get rid of IT.'

'Only it's *not* the destruction of everything. We're still here.'

'What happens after?' I said. 'That's what you asked me.'

'I wondered if you were OK, that night,' Ben said. 'That whole thing about the staple. I didn't know how to handle that one.'

'But I can't just keep crossing over,' I said. 'Every time I cross, IT gets closer to me. IT hasn't followed me here yet, I don't think, but every time I cross one of the boundaries, I can hear IT.'

'It's pretty traumatic,' Ben said. 'Finding a dead body. I think we were all shook up. Elizabeth went home to Georgia – did you know that?'

'Good for her,' I said. 'But I'm not traumatized about the dead guy. It's this tape I found. All the tapes I've been making lately have been screwed up. And then I find this tape and Craig plays it and everything's fucked up.'

'You're saying it's the sound.'

'I *know* it's the sound.'

He twisted his lips, looked down.

'I know I sound crazy,' I said.

Ben chuckled. 'Hey, who doesn't, these days? OK, I'll give you this. Why not try and find out if you're the only one who can leave and come back?'

I frowned. 'Why would you want to come back, if you could really leave?'

'Well, we know people can leave. Because they disappear. Attrition, right – and I don't mean freshman attrition! But if we could get in and out freely, then we might stand a chance of getting something back together.'

I shook my head. 'I don't think anybody should stay here. I think it's like a fault line. I think Bard is dangerous, unstable. I want to get people out.'

Ben shrugged.

'I don't think you'll find any shortage of volunteers for that.'

The thing took a day to organize. Despite Ben's optimism, there were only six people for starters: Gretchen, Trinity, Justin, and Ben (who was clearly participating because he felt sorry for me that no one else believed me), and two others I didn't know. One of these was a B&G worker called Anna whose daughter had been in the hospital in Poughkeepsie at the time of ITs attack – she would have scaled Everest to get out of Bard. The other was an Art History professor who said very little and stood back a pace from the rest.

'OK,' I said. 'We're going through the same spot you saw me go through the other day. It's easy. If you're freaked by what you see, then don't look. Just close your eyes and let me guide you. I'll let you know as soon as I'm sure we're across. OK?'

Everybody nodded.

'Who's first?'

Justin volunteered. I took hold of his red ski jacket and walked with him toward the road. It was bitterly cold and my ears stung. I counted steps. I looked at him periodically to gauge his reaction.

I could hear IT now, clearer and clearer, ever more intrusive. Justin seemed oblivious.

When would we be across? A step, another step, our boots crunching in the old snow . . . I hesitated.

We were into the borderland. Things didn't look right. I had the feeling you get when you're about to faint, where your senses recede but you can still think: you know you're losing consciousness but there's nothing you can do.

With my senses lost in this borderland, it seemed that the sound of IT was turning trees to numbers. Light turned to patterns of lines, snake dancing; colour turned to tiny blocks like fabric swatches all lined up in a giant game of *Concentration*, only to change places with each other, rapidly, unpredictably.

But then the number trees started to dissolve, too.

There was something else, behind them. Something that was not IT.

And now I could see a city skyline below a glowing, vaporous cloudscape. It flashed at me, in and out, teasing. Between me and the city was darkness, an indeterminate space. Still holding on to Justin, I started forward.

But he was dragging like a dead weight. I couldn't pull him. I turned and in the darkness and noise of IT I perceived that he was not with me. Somehow, in some split version of events, he had slipped into deep, cold water.

'What the hell – help!' he yelled, and kicked mightily. He was fully dressed and sinking. 'Get me out of here!'

He lost his voice after that: he was breathing too hard with the effort to keep afloat. At the same time that I could also see the cityscape, I could see the Hudson River. It was pulling him away from me. I was there, yet I wasn't actually in the water. I was standing in some in-between place.

I turned and, still gripping the puffy sleeves of Justin's ski jacket, threw myself back across the border.

Everyone gaped at us. We sprawled on the ground, Justin rolling over and curling up, shivering uncontrollably, coughing, gasping, yelling. There was confusion as he had to be picked up and taken into Security where a propane heater kept the building above freezing. Gretchen went running to find dry clothes for him. The others avoided looking at me.

'I'm sorry,' I whispered. 'I didn't know. It's just like in Red Hook. We walked out east and Justin ended up coming back in west. I don't know why that happens.'

No one said much. I said it as many times as I could before the lack of response made me shut up altogether.

Justin didn't say much to me. I was not popular, and I found myself at a loose end. I spent the next day wandering around campus hoping I'd discover more people that I knew. I ended up outside Kline, drawn by the smell of singed bread floating on the air. There was a small crowd gathered outside the coffee shop. A fire was burning. But there was no party. People were gathered around the fire, listening to a voice I thought I knew.

'You see, most people when they consider their own musical expression rely on other people to do it for them. They express themselves in terms of what they listen to. They elect heroes. They "appreciate". But they don't dare take it further than that. They don't dare use the medium themselves. Because music education is so fascistic and structured and nose-down-looking that they could never make it by the official route. And if they are talented enough to make it by the official route, that route

brands them with its own fascistic structured nose-down-looking ways. And if they do it in jazz, then they're lucky because
maybe they have a shot although what the odds are of making
a living as a jazz musician I don't know. And if they go for anything post-1960 in origin like rock or soul or rap then their
whole aspiration becomes getting a record contract and you're
right back into the System again, under the yoke of commerce.
Not to mention under the musical yoke of an increasingly con-
ventionalized form.'

I got close enough to confirm with my eyes that the speaker
was Justin. I'd recognized his voice, but the quality of his ora-
tory came as a surprise to me.

'So here's music, universally lauded as the deepest expression of cosmic humanity or whatever you want to call all that
music-of-the-spheres stuff. Here's music, making the screaming
hordes move like one organism at a big concert. Here's a
mother singing her baby a lullaby, here's music and we're
totally cut off from it except as consumers.'

Some freshman women nodded and said '*Mmm.*'

'Bring back Bob Dylan!' somebody said.

'No, don't you get it – that's just the point. Bob Dylan is just
a guy. Hey, we wouldn't dare make sound in our own right. If
we did, we'd feel compelled to judge our sound on the basis of
the commercial stuff. Somewhere along the line, listening
became the whip hand of judgment instead of a tool for understanding.'

'You know, that's kind of true,' said a small black guy I recognized as a psychology professor.

Justin said: 'Now we're stuck. We're trapped in a small world
and we can't get out of it. And the whole thing is in our own
heads.'

'In our heads?' A woman's voice, loud, New York.

'Yeah, this whole thing with us being trapped here is like a
metaphor,' Justin said. 'It's just taking what was already true

and making it more obvious. Thinking in music means that the sounds you make are limited by what you are able to think. And vice versa. We're sitting ducks. We can't make shit. Unless—'

And everybody sort of leaned forward.

'Unless we start stretching ourselves.'

People came to the next Open Space in droves. The windows threw light across the forest; you could see the place from far away, because the rest of the campus was so dark. At first I was afraid to go in, but when I finally did Justin smiled at me.

'I'm bummed I didn't get out,' he said. 'But I feel like I've got more of a grip now. I think what we did, trying it, I think it was good.'

I smiled, nodded my thanks.

'Where's the power coming from?'

'Emergency generator. In the basement.' He smiled. 'Just for now. I'm sure we'll get a kickback from the session and then we won't need the generator.'

I took my hat off and spit on my hands to flatten my flyaway hair. The air was warm and dry, almost like old times. A kerosene heater stood in the middle of the soundspace, squat and radiant.

Someone had written notes on the blackboard, typical of *Forming* or *Open Space*. Cutely different-coloured chalks:

BEAT MEANS BEAT

MEANS DOMINATION.

HENCE: BEAT FASCISM.

BEAT IS PARCELING OUT TIME.

ORGANIZING AND THEREBY OBLITERATING

THAT WHICH DOES NOT FIT IN WITH

BEAT IS TYRANNY.

Trying to stay alive to the leading
edge of experience even as it's
decaying around you. That's music.
Spitting in the eye of entropy. It's an accumulation, a buildup of
moments that resonate upon one another and give each other
being. Music is world-building.

It isn't *about* anything.

It doesn't reference reality.

It *creates* reality.

I watched people read the messages on the board. I watched
people unpack their instruments and unwind their scarves.
There were so many people that the room was already getting
hot.

In the middle of the room there was a big box of instruments:
everything from African finger-pianos to rainmakers to an old
banjo. Some people brought their own instruments. A bearded
guy called Josh brought a sitar and made a production of running up and down his scales. He wanted everybody to know
that he was a real musician. As for the others: all the faces were
vaguely familiar. There were a couple of professors and several
students that I knew weren't musicians in any official capacity.
The rest must have been staff, or students I didn't really know.

'Why are there so many people here?' I whispered to Justin.
'Is this all about your speech?'

He ducked his head, grinning. 'Dunno. It's pretty weird, isn't
it? Ben always used to say music was about survival . . .'

Trinity was unrolling white butcher paper in a strip along the
back wall. She had pots of paint and brushes and rags. Justin
draped Indian cotton sheets over all but one window. I spotted
Ben, unobtrusive as usual, fiddling around with the recording
equipment. There was a rising hum of talking and whispering
as the room filled. The speakers popped and emitted a shriek of
feedback. Everybody laughed.

Then things settled.

The room quietened. Someone laid a soft chord, a low stack of seconds on the Steinway. And it began.

I watched their faces. They were intent, sincere. Did I dare enter their sound?

Ben had been urging me to 'ditch the instruments' over and over. But I don't like coming out from behind my guitar. I know the guitar. I am somebody when I play it. I have familiar things that I can do. They make me feel good, and they make me feel like me.

And I particularly do not like to sing.

But something both safer and riskier than performance is happening here. It's safe because it's risky for all: we're all in the same leaky boat with each other. We grope; we fumble; we look for the ways we can be ourselves with each other. We carry with us the resonances of all our histories. We carry in our sound all the sounds of the world, all of the crenellated interiors of our own individual selves, all the tendrils of known and unknown history that we collectively understand.

We carry everything we have ever heard. We carry our own cries as babies and the calls of birds and the wind and the dying sounds of tape recorders whose batteries have run down. We carry our fears and our self-consciousness and at the same time we carry nothing, because by carrying it we let it fly. And still we stay in this place and listen to the sound that we are making as it unfolds, talks to itself, colors itself, doubles back and stretches out like some crazy-ass elastic time-defying (non)sense.

And in the context of this sound I think I finally perceive IT. IT forms in the air of the room. IT is in no way solid. IT slithers over the old ruined piano and past the amplifier. IT is insistent. IT moves through every thing. IT moves through every one. At ITs best maybe IT is a desire for understanding. At its worst IT is a drive to capture the formula of things. Give me the magic beans. Swallow the pill. Make everything simple and use your knowledge like a plowshare to take what you want from the world.

Hey: I know! Let's motherfuck the wilderness of human reality and get it to carry and bring forth millions of identical books and records that everyone will love! Let's get them all addicted to McDonald's. It's OK because we're helping everybody out. We're just helping nature along. We're just finding out what people really like and giving them more. Gradually add nicotine to cigarettes until they're totally hooked. It's OK because they like it. And happiness is good, right? Isn't it better to be happy and not think?

IT isn't afraid of us musical thinkers. Not anymore. IT knows we're no threat. We never can be.

And IT's here, specifically, tonight, for me. IT throbs in the floor and shivers in the air. IT holds that which I love most under the shadow of ITs wings.

And I feel sick.

What the fuck do I do now?

The beat is starting. Despite the words on the board; or maybe because of them. The professors and cleaning ladies and art-history students are picking it up. Beat is easy; beat is natural; we all succumb to crowd politics. Thump, thump, thump. Heartbeat, clock, lock step, unison, everybody all together now. Gretchen and Justin drown in the beat. Ben persists, brow furrowed, shoveling shit against the tide on the Krumar, while IT comes to take everyone. The session sounds more and more like IT.

I shake, I quake, my stake in this is in ITs jaws and claws.

IT's turning Open Space into ITself.

I'm stunned to silence. I'm not Elizabeth; I won't jump out the window.

IT's got me beat. Pun intended. If I stay here, IT will destroy everything I ever cared about.

If Beat Fascism is real, how to coexist with it?

Can't obliterate it.

Won't join it.

Yet by definition BF makes everything that doesn't fall into line with it sound irrelevant. By definition BF negates or denies all that isn't part of BF.

Jazz guys agree to groove.

They play a limited game.

Still their sound tests the ear, mind, soul.

So what about groove-free 99.44% rule-free come-as-you-are let's-try-this do-you-dare-to-be-present check-in-&-be-account-able-for-yourself socially responsible process-sound?

What about Let's Make Something, Guys? Authentically gimmick-free?

Could THIS have cracked IT?

And if not . . . why NOT??

As in: how could this idea not change the world?

How could it be that no one really cares?

There I go again. Skewered on my own sincerity. And Bon Jovi sells another record.

The beat goes on.

I put my head in my hands and wait for it to be over.

After the session broke up I hung back to talk to Ben. He looked tired.

'I wish I could convince you to leave,' I said. 'I don't think Justin really tried.'

'I'm trying to get into reality,' Ben said. 'I'm not looking to escape. I'm not looking for a way out. I'm looking for a way in.'

This made me feel lame, but what could I do?

'You're going to think I'm bailing,' I said. 'But I have to leave.'

Whatever he thought, he didn't say it. 'I wouldn't dream of standing between you and what you need to do,' he said at last. 'So by all means, go ahead, and hey – good luck.'

'But it's not like that. See, I'm going to go get the tapes I told you about. I want you to hear them. I'll try and bring supplies, too.'

But I didn't know where I was going to find the supplies. Unless I went back to Lake Katrine and shoplifted . . .

'I'm not going to just stand by and let this happen,' I said. 'I'm going to try and help you, I swear to God – I'll do everything I can to make it right.'

Ben gave me a sad look.

'I don't think it's we who need your help,' he said, placing the gentlest emphasis on the pronouns. Then he said, 'You take care of yourself.'

part two
the rendered

June 1987

Wanaque, NJ

Donuts or Thorazine

After she had finished serving the prison sentence she had incurred by beating up her karate teacher, Cookie got her stuff out of storage and moved into a tiny apartment in Paterson. The only job she could find involved selling cable-TV subscriptions over the phone. She was supposed to stick to a script, but that was too boring, so she improvised.

'You could be in imminent danger from your TV,' she told her prospective customers.

All calls were taped for training purposes. When after four days she was called into the office of Kelly, her supervisor, Cookie expected to be fired. But Kelly couldn't have been listening in much because she only said, 'You haven't made any sales. But you have a nice phone manner, and you're always at your desk on time. I'd like to take you out of Sales.' Then she took Cookie off the sales floor and put her into 'Verifications', where her job was to call people back and verify that all the sales her colleagues had made were legit.

Cookie sat in a little room by herself with a stack of sales slips. It was an easy job, but the people she had to call often seemed pathetic. They liked to chat about nothing in particular. They volunteered intimate details about their lives, whether Cookie wanted to know or not. At first she found this disturbing. But after a while she came to the conclusion that people had bought their subscriptions because they were lonely and the telemarketers had managed to keep them on the line long enough to squeeze a sale out of them. People were effectively paying to talk to someone.

Out of a sense of sadness about this, Cookie chatted with the customers some more while making the verifications. If the person was old or house-bound, sometimes she chatted for twenty minutes or more, long-distance. She wanted them to get their money's worth.

Plus, she was half-hoping she'd get fired. But no one seemed to care. And she couldn't quit. It was hard to find a job, being an ex-con and all. At Dataplex she'd made enough that she never had to worry; but she couldn't go back there, and she couldn't really put that job on her résumé.

1981-1984: Act as remote-spy-plane organism on distant planet during war with suicidal flesh-golems in order to facilitate video advertising campaigns.

No. Probably not.

To make ends meet, Cookie worked an evening half-shift at DRS Controls in Wanaque. Bent over a brightly lit magnifying glass, she soldered circuit boards for armored all-terrain vehicles commissioned by the Army.

The twin ironies weren't lost on her. TV. The military.

Cookie just couldn't escape the Grid.

The good thing about the military job was that it kept Cookie away from home during prime-time TV. She had watched TV every day while in prison, but that had been a group activity. She didn't feel so secure about watching it alone. It was safer to be at work. The factory foreman played Z-100 on the radio and Cookie learned all the words to 'Sledgehammer' while the smoke from her soldering iron spiraled away into invisibility.

Sitting on the tall metal stool at the formica work table reminded her of Biology lab in high school, which in turn reminded her of the Grid.

The rest of the shift were all men. Two of them were fairly cute, but one was married and the other one was an idiot. In high school, both would have ignored her (at best) but here they were polite and friendly. Everyone was. Bob, the foreman, was easygoing about workers chatting to each other. He sat in his office doing more or less nothing, and Emilio the janitor came by and talked to Cookie every night. He was forty-five and had two kids that he only saw on weekends. He was shorter than Cookie and probably half her weight, but he didn't let that stop him from asking her out.

'Cookie, you want to go see *Terminator*?' he'd ask. Or, 'I got tickets for Gipsy Kings, you want to go?' Or, 'Feel like a pizza, after?'

When she declined, he'd say, 'That's OK, I understand. You don't want to go out with an old fart like me.'

Cookie let him think that, but the real reason was that she was afraid that if she touched him she'd inadvertently break him.

Then came the night when Miles called her at work. Bob motioned into his glass-fronted office adjacent to the shop floor and pointed to the phone. Then he walked back and forth outside the open door, whistling.

'How did you get this number?' Cookie said, feeling herself go hot.

'We have ways,' said Miles, trying to sound German.

'What are you, like, the CIA?'

'My dear, the Pimpernel had only to call the parole board and pretend to be your brother Darren.' Now he was trying to sound English. 'What choice did you leave me? You don't return my calls. You have been trying to elude the Pimpernel, but the elusive one knows every trick.'

'Sorry,' Cookie said. 'How are you, anyway?'

'I am my usual dashing self.' Then Miles's tone changed; he was too excited to keep up the accent. 'Hey, I did some digging on Gunther Stengel. Would you believe it? He's not a doctor. He's not even educated. The guy dropped out halfway through an associate's degree in psychology from Empire State College – ever heard of it?'

'No.'

'Precisely. The place isn't exactly a prime institution of higher learning.' Miles snorted with laughter. 'Can you believe the nerve of the guy? Gunther faked his résumé and managed to convince Dataplex that he could automate sales-prediction software for the entertainment industry. But he has no computer background to speak of. And he was doing psychotherapy illegally – remember LeRoy Jones? To put it delicately – the guy's a total con man.'

Cookie sighed. 'This is supposed to make me feel better? At least I wasn't the only one getting conned, something like that?'

'I just wanted you to know I took care of him for you. I thought it was the least I could do.'

'What do you mean, *you took care of him*?'

'Aw, shucks, it was no big deal.'

'Miles, I'm at work and I have to go. What are you saying?'

'You know that necromancer Justin who took on the purple worm that time in the *Destrier of Doom* campaign? His ex-girlfriend works as a stringer for the *Daily News* and I got her to get the skinny on Gunther. Then I went to Gunther's boss Hagler and told him what I found out.'

'Oh, Miles,' Cookie exclaimed, and then covered her mouth. She looked at Bob out of the corner of her eye (he was whistling along to 'Born in the USA' and tapping his foot). 'I don't know what to say.'

'You could say, Thanks, pal, and I now believe there are such things as paladins and I'm putting Monty back in circulation.'

Cookie swallowed. Tears welled in her eyes. 'Thanks, pal.

But, like you said, I have to learn to deal with reality. I guess you just proved that I'm easy to fool.'

Bob turned around, still whistling, and tapped his watch at Cookie.

'I have to go,' she said. 'I'm at work.'

'Well, I have to say I'm disappointed in you, Cookie,' Miles snapped. 'I thought you'd have more fight in you.'

'Sorry.'

'Are you taking your medication?'

'Yes, yes, I am, believe it or not.'

'Well, that's good. You want to know why I went after him? Because he was looking for you. He approaches me with some bogus job offer to help him fake some software, and then he starts dropping hints about how much he misses working with you and did I know where you were and all that.'

Cookie's stomach felt all swervy. 'And what did you tell him?'

'Nothing! You don't need that creep back in your life.'

'Thanks. Look, I really have to go now.'

'I told him not to come looking for you. I told him I'd call the regulatory board for psychotherapists in New Jersey and report him, based on what LeRoy Jones told us. So don't worry about it. Hey, why don't you come up and I'll take you on a tour of IBM. I want to introduce you to my girlfriend, too.'

Girlfriend? This was news.

'And I bought a great keyboard,' Miles added hastily, before she could ask about the girlfriend. 'It actually takes samples of sounds and lets you record sequences digitally. I'm going to use it in my next opera.'

After Cookie got off the phone, she felt shaky. She worked with exaggerated care, and she barely heard the radio because she was thinking about the Grid and how angry she felt at Miles. She knew the real person she should be angry with was Gunther, but it was easier to shoot the messenger.

She'd tried so hard to put the whole thing behind her. She had assumed that Gunther's little project would have fallen apart without her. Not that it mattered. Or did it? After what had happened with the Third Wave, where did that leave Gunther? Did he still have access to the Grid – the Synchronicity, even – without Cookie?

She ground her teeth and burned her finger on the soldering iron twice. She wished Miles hadn't told her. Miles just didn't know what he was stirring up.

Cookie clocked out of DRS at 11:08 and walked across the windy parking lot to her Rabbit. She could see the New York City skyline in the remote distance with the street lights of all the suburbs cast out like blurry citrines in between here and there. The trees were flailing their leaves at the sky.

Emilio the janitor had followed her to the factory door. He pressed a box of donuts on her and asked her out, like he did every week. As usual, she declined politely.

'Good night,' she called, and waved to him as he went back inside. She stood at the bottom of the stairs, breathing in the night, while the parking lot emptied. The rest of the people on her shift were already pulling out and turning on to Skyline Drive. It was like this every night: everyone moving in synchrony. Except Cookie. She stood watching while headlights cut the darkness, crossing lances. Then the last crunch of gravel sounded as Ricky's Nova turned left towards Ringwood. His stereo was playing 'Smoke on the Water' and the bass line gradually flattened as he drove off.

It was quiet. Cookie took another long breath. She was tired, but the cool darkness was refreshing. She started toward her Rabbit.

The new sound began overhead, in the rub of leaf on leaf. Out of this white rush that normally elicited no special attention, there slithered some other entity – or entities. The unexplained sounds were snakes of something darker: solid, localized beings that lived inside the pale shuss of leafwindsound. Cookie froze and tilted her head. The snaking sounds were coming simultaneously from far away and close in her ears. They began to blossom, multiply, blend again, so that she was aware of many interconnected sonic identities.

Some years ago Miles had bought a Walkman and had made Cookie listen to his favorite Jethro Tull album at the time: *The Broadsword and the Beast*. Cookie remembered the first song, 'Broadsword', and how it had opened up inside her head a huge flat space over which the initial guitar had seemed to approach like a messenger. The sound was a transliteration of a science-fiction paperback cover: she could see it. She had actually pulled the headphones away from her ears and looked at them as though expecting to see inside each of the ear pads a window into some vast expanse of red dust and roiling cloud.

'It's only reverb,' Miles had told her, as if she were stupid. But the big space of the sound hadn't been merely a result of an echo effect. The space had been internal, conceptual. And now, as she stood in the DRS Controls parking lot, she had that same feeling. But this was no red desert. It was something alive.

The sound was growing in her ears and hanging from the trees. It was looming in the sky. It was humming under the soles of her feet. Something was approaching.

Cookie's mouth worked. She had heard this kind of thing before: in the Grid, when Serge's nine neverborn six-fingered daughters were around. It was the sound of transformation. But the girls had been eaten by the Mfeel dragon. And the Grid existed only within TV. There was no TV in sight.

So what was happening?

In rising panic, Cookie turned on her heel and ran back to DRS. Emilio was still there, putting away his mops. His eyes lit up when she appeared.

'Ah, Cookie, you change your mind! I knew you would, I'll—'

'Emilio, what's with all that noise outside?'

'Noise? Where? Show me.'

She led him to the nearest fire door and pushed it open.

'There. You hear that? What the heck is that?'

'I don't hear nothing. You playing a joke on me?'

'No. No joke. I'm sorry. Never mind. I thought I heard . . .' She still *did* hear it. The sound was becoming increasingly animate. Emilio was looking kindly at her. He had an interesting face, all Central American sculpted bones and weathered skin. There was an inherent dignity in him.

'I don't hear it, sweetheart – you want me to walk you to your car? Come on, you scared? I walk you, no problem.'

'I'm not scared!' Cookie said.

'Then why you shaking?'

'OK, then.'

She went to her car with Emilio running to catch up with her.

'You sure you don't want to go for a drink? I'm leaving in a half-hour.'

'No, I better go home.'

'You feeling OK? Give me your keys.' He took them off her, unlocked her car, and ushered her inside. Then he handed the keys back and shut the door. 'Maybe you been working too hard. It's not good for your eyes, all that soldering.'

'I'm OK,' Cookie said weakly. 'Thanks, buddy.'

'OK, buddy,' he replied. Emilio stood back from the car and she started the engine. The Grid sound was muffled inside the Rabbit. For some reason this made her feel slightly better. She managed to find reverse and backed out of her parking spot. She crawled across the empty lot in first gear. The sound was fading now. The engine seemed to negate it.

Cookie drove to the end of the parking lot and stopped at Skyline Drive. She put on her right signal. In her rearview mirror she saw Emilio go back inside. She opened the window.

Tiny fragments of sound began to creep in, like a mist or insects.

'Goddamn you, Miles.'

Cookie rummaged in her bag. She took out her bottle of thorazine and threw it out the car window into the road. Then she opened the box of donuts and began to eat.

Suggestion

The haunted house appeared the following Monday morning, sandwiched between Cookie's building and the corner 7-11 convenience store. She saw it when she unlocked her car to go to work. It looked like a haunted house out of a cartoon, all top-heavy and crooked with a sagging front porch and black paint and a Gothic excess of chimney-pots. Naturally, no one else could see it.

Cookie got in her car and sat hyperventilating until she remembered to breathe into her cupped hands. The building where she lived overlooked the 7-11 with no gap whatsoever, not even an alley. So how there could be room to squeeze a whole house in between the two, she couldn't imagine.

This was all Miles's fault. Once, when they'd been playing D&D, Miles had created a spell that did things like this. He'd told her there were different layers of infinity and by drawing a diagonal line through a series of linear infinities stacked on top of each other you could get another level of infinite infinity. Or something. Cookie hadn't really understood it. She just knew that Miles's spell had enabled one of his evil-warlord NPCs to stick a whole castle inside a snuffbox. It had caused Monty the paladin no end of trouble then, and the whole idea of it was still causing her trouble now. Why had Miles had to go calling her up, disturbing her hard-won equilibrium?

She laid her head against the steering wheel.

'I take it back,' she said. 'God, whatever I said, I take it back. I don't want there to be real dragonriders. I don't want there to be more to life. I don't want to be a hero. I just want to be normal and go shopping and watch TV like everybody else.'

Either God wasn't listening, or there was no God – or maybe God thought this was all a good joke, because after that the music started following her around. And inevitably the intrusion of sound went hand in hand with more alarming intrusions: events that Cookie called Haunted House Sandwiches because they consisted of anomalous objects appearing where they shouldn't be. Most of them were small and quotidian intrusions: a bottle of Japanese nail polish appearing in her refrigerator; an extra aisle in her local supermarket devoted only to bicycle tires; etc. Some were horrific, like the bonus insert in her subscription copy of *The Dragon* magazine: it was a sample issue of something called *Grid Times*. It featured body parts in green-and-white photography; faces with glassy eyes and tongues swollen in dead mouths; schemata for machines she didn't recognize.

Cookie burned it and flushed the ashes down the toilet.

One Friday afternoon, Cookie came back to her desk from lunch yawning. She confronted her stack of sales slips with zero enthusiasm. The long hours were wearing on her, and she was looking forward to sleeping late tomorrow. With a sigh, she began punching in phone numbers.

Her third verification was with one Michael J. Borland of Pearl River, NY. She dialed his number and went into her spiel, finishing with, 'Can I just confirm with you that you ordered our Premium Movie Package including Showtime, HBO, The Movie Channel and fourteen other premier services including MTV and ESPN?'

'Oh,' Michael Borland said, sounding dejected. 'Um, is it too late to cancel that? I might have made a mistake.'

This was the first time this had happened to Cookie. 'That's all right, sir. So you don't want to order this package?'

'No,' he said darkly. He had an expressive voice: he could have been a radio personality, she thought. Maybe *he* should have been selling the subscriptions. He added, 'Look, I'm really sorry but it was just a moment of weakness. I don't think more TV would be a good idea for me. Can I just ask you, do you think . . . what did you say your name was?'

'Cookie.'

'Cookie, do you think there are any risks associated with long-term exposure to cable TV?'

'Risks, sir?'

'Please, please. Call me Mike.'

Cookie held the phone away from her head and let herself sigh. Another lonely soul. Another life story about to spill out to her over the long-distance wire. She pinched the bridge of her nose between her thumb and forefinger.

'Mike, I'm not aware of any risks associated with our service. But if you wanted to cancel it . . .'

'Well, you see, I know you're going to think this sounds silly, but sometimes when I watch certain programs on TV I find that I'm not seeing the same things as other people. Like, for the life of me I can never seem to follow the plot of *Knots Landing*. Do you watch that?'

Cookie began to tremble. 'No, I don't, but people tell me it's pretty complicated.'

He laughed. 'Yeah? You can't imagine how *complicated* it is when I play it on my TV. It's like watching something that happens on another planet. And I really feel like I'm there. And it's not the same actors, either. You know that blond guy who was in *Dallas*? He's not in my *Knots Landing*.'

Cookie had broken out into a light sweat.

'Some people do have problems with TV,' she ventured. 'But I don't think cable is any worse than your regular channels when it comes to . . . that kind of thing.'

'Really? Is that what you heard?'

She was beginning to tremble.

'That's been my experience, actually.'

'So you don't think I'm crazy.'

'Well, I don't know you, Mike, but let's just say you're probably not alone in terms of what you're experiencing.'

There was a long silence. 'Wow,' he said. 'You're the first person I've ever met who even knew what I was talking about.'

Cookie looked at the clock and did a double take. Could she really have been talking for twenty minutes? *No,* she thought. *Impossible. We've hardly had time to say anything. But better not risk getting caught.*

'I can't really get into this now, Mike,' she said. 'I'm at work, and . . .'

'Saynomore, saynomore! I understand. Hey, but . . . well, I don't mean to be pushy or anything, but it would be really great if we could talk about it a little more sometime. Is there any way you could, like, write down my number and call me back when you have more time? I could call you, but you probably shouldn't give out your number to someone you don't know.'

'Well, I'd like to help you, Mike, but it's long-distance and I don't know . . .'

'Call me collect. Anytime. Cookie, I'm not being creepy here, I just honestly wish I could talk to somebody who understands about the TV thing.'

'Well, I'll think about it. I've got your number.'

'Thanks! Thanks a lot! I'm really looking forward to talking with you, Cookie.'

She hung up. She canceled the order. Then she looked at the slip with Michael Borland's phone number on it. She copied the number onto a Post-it note and started to put it in her bag. But, without really knowing why, her hand crumpled the paper and chucked it across the room to the wastepaper basket. She picked up the phone to make her next call.

The dial tone sounded like a wall. Behind it, faintly, Cookie could hear a female voice singing, an odd and off-balance tune.

On Saturday Cookie went to Union City to help Karina Rodriguez paint her new apartment. Karina had been doing time for possession at the same time as Cookie had been in jail for assault, but she was out now and she'd moved into a new place with her boyfriend, a dealer. She had been accepted to study nursing at Trenton State at night, and she'd called Cookie in ecstasy.

'I think it's gonna be hard,' she said. 'It's gonna be so hard, but I got to do it. My mother's going to take the kids while I got classes.'

'Wow,' said Cookie, and meant it. 'So you and Charlie are still on?'

'Oh, him. Well, he's their dad, you know? At least he got money. I'm going to get my independence, though, Cookie. Like you. You'll see.'

Cookie couldn't get over the fact that Karina looked up to her. Karina was nineteen. She had two kids already. Cookie had two cats and a donut habit. What did she know about life?

They spent the afternoon dodging kids and putting down primer. Karina chattered away about the joys of being free, while Cookie worked with her back to the TV. The kids were watching an old Jacques Cousteau special about sharks.

'You know Rosa?' said Karina. 'She reoffended. She's back in. And Diana? She moved down to Florida and now I hear she's getting in trouble down there. That's why I wanted to call you. We didn't really belong in there, you and me. I want to be like you, not like them.'

Cookie laughed. 'That's nice of you to say. But you don't really know me.'

'Who does?' said Karina. 'Why you think everybody use to call you Easter? You're like a piece of stone.' She stopped rolling paint and turned to Cookie. She was wearing cutoffs and a tube top, and her long hair was pulled up into a topknot. 'You know, it's OK. We can paint this wall and it's cool.'

Cookie was embarrassed. Some people were just nice. There were horrible people like Gunther who seemed nice but weren't, but there were also people like Karina, who didn't have any ulterior motive and didn't mind if you were a little crazy and would still give you their favorite recipe for meatballs. It was difficult to know how to deal with people like that. If Karina knew what the inside of Cookie's head really looked like, would she be so friendly?

Karina was telling the story of learning to give injections by practicing on an orange and Cookie was laughing and cringing when Karina's son Juan grabbed the base of the ladder she was standing on and said, 'I want to help you. Let me try!'

'OK,' said Cookie. 'You can help me pour out the next tray of paint.'

'Oh man,' Karina said. 'I don't even want to look.'

She covered her eyes dramatically and turned away from Juan. Then, in a different tone, she squawked, 'What the hell is this?'

Cookie looked up and noticed that tiny Jennifer was standing two feet away from the TV watching a shark ripping into a chunk of bloody meat on the end of a spear. Karina changed the channel to MTV.

Cookie looked away and then back. Gunther had made her watch so many music videos that it was hard for her not to associate them with the Grid. Peter Gabriel was on, some kind of fancy computer-animation stuff, and Cookie couldn't seem to take her eyes off it.

But the sound itself was not Peter Gabriel. It was that weird singing again.

And then came the vertigo. The falling-without-falling. The loss of control.

The synchronicity.

I'm not sure. I'm just really not sure what this is. I'm on my way up an uneven flight of steps, wide and shallow, covered in brown carpet. They plot a wandering curve toward a swathe of cloudy sky. The clouds look mucky with yellow groundlight, and the buildings seem to crowd together overhead. It feels like they're going to come down on top of me at any minute. A hard rain smacks the brown carpet and bounces off; the stairs make squishing noises under my sandals.

I don't think this is right; something isn't right here. I don't know what's behind me and I'm not sure how to turn around. I'm moving up, but I'm not even sure how it is I'm doing that. My body's on automatic. I feel powerless.

In the free air above I can see there are so many antennae sprouting from the higher points of the buildings that they blend together into a fuzz. The buildings themselves look derelict. Plants bristle from broken windows. Only very high up are there any lights in the windows. As the rain falls into my face I feel like I'm at the bottom of a storm drain. Or a well.

I'd better keep moving. In the air, between the buildings, there are things at work. An endless mutter of engine noise searches for me, raking through the substance of this place with its vibrations. I can't see what these engines are, but I can hear them. I don't want them to find me. I mount the steps two, three at a time. Sometimes the flight becomes so narrow that I can barely pass between the buildings; sometimes my space widens and I feel like I'm climbing a set of bleachers.

I sweat, but the rain cools me. My heartbeat gets faster. My feet slip within the wet sandals so that the straps between my toes dig in, hard. I put my hand down for balance, touch the sodden brown carpet, and thoughts fly through me like arrows:

: *how could I be so stupid as to think Gunther wouldn't hunt me?*

: *what am I doing out here wearing only sandals?*

: *should I try to climb through a window, find safety in one of these ominous buildings?*

: *what's the deal with the carpet? I mean, who puts carpet outside?*

I come to a gap between buildings and pause to look through. I can see down into the alley beyond, and I realize that I'm already at a great height. Down there is some kind of airfield, only I can't see any planes. Hundreds of gray vans are parked there in neat rows. They are strange vans, segmented like those bugs you see underneath your garbage pail when you pick it up.

I don't want to be here. Gunther wants me here. How can he reach out like this and draw me in? I don't want to be here.

And I'm panting, freaking. I turn away from the sight of this air-field-with-no-planes so that I can climb higher. But the stairs have changed into a wall.

I'm being steered. And I can see something up there against the sky. I can see something transparent that moves in and out of buildings and cloud, clear and shining like Wonder Woman's airplane, and it has a head and eyes, and I think it's an Mfeel and it hasn't seen me yet but it's looking for something—

Voices were arguing in Spanish. Something slapped Cookie's cheek and a guy said,

'Hey! Baby, time to go.'

Cookie shook her head like a swimmer clearing water from her ears. She took an automatic step backward, away from the guy she could only assume was Charlie. He was small and neatly put-together, dressed in sweats; but when he smiled his mouth was mostly gold.

'What you on?' he said. 'I don't want you doing none of that stuff around my kids.'

Karina said something to him in Spanish, shooting Cookie a reassuring smile. Charlie stepped back from Cookie, head cocked to one side and tilted back as he took another look at her.

'Ohhh,' he said wisely.

Cookie found her voice. 'I have to go.' She located her bag under the edge of a drop cloth and slung it over her shoulder. 'Hey, Karina, good luck with everything. Give me a call some-time and let me know how it's going.'

'Don't go, Cookie!' Jennifer said, and threw her arms around Cookie's legs. Cookie fished around in her bag and found a roll of Lifesavers. Jennifer giggled when Cookie gave them to her.

Karina walked her downstairs.

'Sorry about Charlie,' she said. 'You OK?'

'I'm the one who should apologize,' Cookie said. 'This isn't supposed to happen to me anymore. I'm over it. I'm supposed to be over it.'

She stopped. Karina was looking at her curiously. There were things you just couldn't tell people. Cookie said, 'Good luck with everything, really. Take care, Karina.'

Then she put on her sunglasses and turned away.

When she got home, Cookie fed and brushed the cats and thought about calling Miles. She actually picked up the phone twice and started to dial, but then thought better of it. Miles had a life. He even had a girlfriend – miracle of miracles. What would the girlfriend think if Cookie called up out of the blue and started involving Miles in her problems? She'd think Cookie was after him, was what. And anyway, he worked at IBM now. Blue suits. Miles lived in a different world.

So she called Gloria.

'*OH*, my God,' Gloria said. 'Cookie!'

'Yeah, hi.' Rocky leaped into Cookie's lap and started dig-ging his claws into her thighs. She shooed him away.

'Well, we should get TOGETHER, it's been such a long time. Where are you?'

'Gloria, I don't want to put you in an awkward position . . .'

'No, no, of course not. Cookie, guess what? I got my black belt! Can you believe it? I have this heavyweight Tokkaido gi, you should hear it snap when I do my reverse punch, it's so awesome . . .'

'Yeah, um, so do you still work for Gunther?'

'Didn't you know? I'm in the executive offices now. I have an expense account. You know, you should come up. I do all the catering for the board meetings, I use the Market Basket in Franklin Lakes and they have the best bologna . . . you're not still on that weird diet, are you?'

'So what happened with Gunther, then?'

'Gunther?'

'You know. Your boss. My boss. Gunther Stengel?'

There was a small silence. Cookie wondered if he was dead. Nebbie and Rocky both jumped in her lap at once, hissed at each other, and sat wobbling on Cookie's legs.

'Uh, Cookie, I'm not sure what you mean. Hey, we should go for a drink or something. Give me your number and I'll call you tonight.'

'Gloria! Please, I have to know. Is it some kind of secret?'

'Is what some kind of secret? What's your number, anyway?'

This hide-and-seek went on for a minute and then Gloria said,

'Oh, my *previous* boss, you mean?'

'Yes,' said Cookie, feeling her blood pressure mounting. *'What happened to him?'*

There was a little silence. Then Gloria gave a snort. 'You know, I can't remember. Does it matter?'

'You seriously can't remember?'

'Seriously. Would I mess around with you, Cookie?'

Cookie stroked Nebbie's back. 'Maybe they told you not to talk to me about it. Or not to talk to anybody. And if that's the case, then I understand, you can just say so.'

'No, no, I'm not shitting you – I just can't remember.'

'But . . . don't you think that's weird?'

'Everything in media is weird, sweetie. But the money flies around like you wouldn't believe. Oh, you know what? I met Don Johnson. I went on the set of *Miami Vice*! And you know who is *really* sweet? I know you don't watch TV, but Don has this black sidekick and he's a *doll*, he's a real gentleman and I'd love to see you with somebody like that. I actually have his phone number, he gave it to me and he invited me to come down to the set again. So now that I have *your* number I'm gonna give it to him, is that OK?'

'Oh, uh, Gloria, please . . .' said Cookie. Nebbie head-butted her in the face and she spluttered to get the cat fur out of her mouth.

'I have to go. I'll call you when I have something set up. I mean the guy's a superstar, but what the hell, why not aim high?'

The dial tone sang in her ear again, that weird soprano interference. Cookie groaned and threw the phone away. Nebbie chased it.

After dark Cookie went up to the haunted house carrying a heavy flashlight and knocked on the front door. It was unlocked. Inside, the whole place was done in wood paneling and dark green baize, and there were large semicircular mouse-holes at regular intervals in all the walls. Just like in cartoons. A suit of armor stood in one corner.

'Hello?' said Cookie.

No one answered, but she fled anyway. It seemed to be called for, somehow. The tapping of her heels on the dusty parquet floor sounded exactly like men's dress shoes running over concrete as captured in the title credits for the *Pink Panther* movies.

But Cookie was still wearing sandals.

She reached the front door, which she'd left standing ajar by about a foot. Through this gap she could see the sign across the street: *Tony's Pizza Gyros Ice Cream.* She could smell the exhaust of passing cars and the kitchen of the pizza place. She turned slowly and looked back into the gloom of the haunted house.

The spider webs were overdone. The billiard table was too big. *And the ceiling . . .*

Cookie slapped her hand over her mouth and whispered, 'Help.'

The ceiling was Grid.

My bologna has a first name

Half an hour later, Cookie was sitting at an orange formica table in Tony's Pizza, looking at a gyro on a white plate, while the fans turned overhead and the fizz in her Coke slowly popped itself out. She dragged a piece of lettuce from beneath the bread and put it between her lips. Oil had made it dark, translucent, limp.

WNEW was giving away $1,000 to the lucky hundredth caller to know the answer to today's rock trivia quiz.

Tony's son, Tony Jr., was spinning pizza dough, kneading, stretching. Then he dipped his ladle into the sauce and spread it on each pizza with a flourish. She watched him sprinkle cheese and then slide the pizzas into the oven on a long-handled wooden platter. It was soothing. He whistled. He looked sure of himself.

'It *is* a Scooby Doo house,' Cookie murmured under her breath. 'It's not real. The Grid is punching through. I should have known this would happen. I *did* know this would happen. What am I going to do now?'

Lynyrd Skynyrd came on the radio. 'Free Bird.'

'Oh, dear,' sighed Cookie eventually, thinking of Gossamer. 'I can't hack this.'

She got up, tossed the food in the garbage can by the door, and went to her car. She went to see her mother's friend Agnes Perretti in Pompton Plains.

Agnes was home; Agnes always seemed to be home. And of course she wasn't surprised to see Cookie, because she'd 'had a feeling all day'. She welcomed Cookie warmly and took her straight into the therapy room.

'So how are you?' Without waiting for an answer, Agnes added, 'You're so bright, Cookie. You should go to college.'

'I'm pretty busy with my jobs.'

'I hear you. Hey, all I'm saying is, I think there's more for you in life than this. Put the prison thing behind you. Are you still going to counseling?'

'Yeah,' Cookie lied. 'But I'm seeing things. Hearing things. That's why I came to see you.'

'Are you taking your medication?'

'Yeah,' Cookie lied again. 'It doesn't do any good. And it makes me sleepy.'

Agnes squinted at her, clasping her hands together in her lap so that her many rings clicked against each other.

'I think your aura needs balancing. You should go see my friend Mindy, she'll do you for free. She used to take your mom's tarot class and she's heard all about you.'

'Oh, great.'

'Call her, Cookie. You're looking a little yellow around the edges. I think you have a hole in your aura. You don't want to get sick.'

Cookie went to Mindy. Mindy balanced her aura and sent her to Fred the iridology expert. Fred referred her to Jocelyn and Julie. They threw the I Ching and sent her to Pascal, who gave her copper bracelets and hung magnets over her body. He used tuning forks, too.

'You have a powerful resonance,' Pascal told her. Then he

charged her fifty bucks. He referred her to a kinesiology clinic, where she learned all about which foods were bad and good for her. Donuts were one of the worst. But, with a kind of spurious defiance, she ate them religiously all the same.

Gloria called her with an invitation to go on the *Miami Vice* set. Cookie said she had a cold. The haunted-house sandwiches mounted like laundry. She started being afraid to go out, which she knew wasn't a good sign.

She was also getting a lot of phone calls where the caller hung up as soon as she picked up the receiver, leaving her with that weird singing dial tone. These freaked her out. She felt stalked, and she started screening all her calls.

Then Agnes called and invited her over. Nervously, Cookie went. She was starting to imagine she saw golems on the sidewalk when she drove down the street.

'I don't know what to do. I'm gaining weight again. My jobs are killing me. I feel all dead inside. I can't keep this up. But I don't know what else to do. Things keep . . . appearing. Look at this!'

Cookie drew out a glossy Playbill for a Broadway show called *Grid Attack*. Agnes scanned it, brows furrowed.

'This is a Playbill for *Cats*,' she said. 'I don't get it.'

Cookie snatched it back. 'Never mind.'

Agnes nodded, patted Cookie's hand, oozed sympathy and *Cinnabar*.

'You have an undeveloped talent, Cookie. You have to confront it. This is a spiritual test for you.'

Cookie shook her head. 'I don't mean to be nasty to you, but the truth is that I don't believe in any of my mom's stuff. I just don't believe in it. I've been to fourteen different people. None of it is working for me, Agnes.'

'That could be part of the test, too.'

Cookie sighed. 'I think I might need a shrink. But I can't stand the drugs, I really can't. I wish I could find a really good shrink, somebody I could trust.'

'Actually . . . I may know of somebody. There's this amazing healer who has just come back from Hawaii. He's totally awesome, Cookie. I've heard nothing but good things about him. I'll write down his number.'

'Is he an actual psychiatrist or what?'

Agnes waved her hand. 'Psychiatrist, psychologist, something like that. But he's studied all these Native American things, and he's been to Nepal, and he's the best. He's only been in Woodstock three weeks but the word is going around, so if you want to work with him you'd better call him right away.'

'And . . . he's totally legit? You promise?'

'Totally legit. Too legit. I mean, Victor is, like, beyond all that. He left it behind years ago. He's so evolved. He's awesome. *I promise.*'

Bearsville, New York. Against her better judgment, Cookie finished her donut and got out of the car. It smelled good up here. Pine trees, sunshine.

A tepee was balanced on a scrap of lawn in the middle of a steep, heavily wooded hillside. The house that overlooked it must have been worth nearly a million: all redwood deck surrounding the kind of place that would have huge open-plan rooms, high ceilings, and funky artwork. Great expanses of glass overlooked a rushing stream.

Victor walked down the lawn toward her. He wore baggy cotton clothes and black tai-chi slippers, and he looked young but had a streak of gray in his long curly hair. Cookie's first impression was that he was soft-spoken, small, unprepossessing. He had something of a pot belly. He gestured towards the tepee.

'I just got back from Hawaii,' Victor said. 'We're living in this until we get a place.'

'We' turned out to be Victor and his beautiful young wife

and their baby daughter. The daughter had a wide face and china-blue eyes that laughed at Cookie over her mother's shoulder as they made tracks up to the big house.

Inside the tepee Victor sat down on a mat opposite Cookie. He lit some Tibetan incense. Then he looked at Cookie with doe-brown eyes. He seemed to be waiting for something.

Cookie looked back at him. Contrary to Gloria's assurances, Victor showed no sign of being an authority on anything. He just sat there, with his small and rather soft body and his long curling hair and his deeply lined fleshy Jewish face. His eyes and his curving lips questioned her.

Here we go again, she thought. *What am I doing here? I'll tell him about my little problem, I'll listen politely to his description of his therapy. I'll want it to help so badly that I'll fall for it. Then I'll give over my money and feel wonderful . . . for a while. Until I watch an episode of LA Law. Arsenio Hall. Maybe Regis and Kathie Lee. And then the Synchronicity will creep back in again and I'll have to hide the TV at the back of my closet.*

'What is that?' Victor said, as if Cookie'd said something even though she hadn't.

'I don't know.'

'Yes, you do know.'

'It's . . . look, I don't think you can help me.'

Cookie waited Victor him to defend himself, or attack her, or try to sell her his system of self-development. They always did. They always needed her more than she needed them. She could hear it in their voices on the phone from the very beginning. But for some stupid reason she kept trying, hoping that somewhere in the mix of astrology/crystal healing/past-life regression/yoga/color therapy/acupuncture/numerology/chiropractic/Bach Flower Remedies/homeopathy/rebirthing/polarity therapy/Alexander technique/tarot/aura reading/Silva Mind Control/palmistry/iridology/macrobiotics she would find something she could use.

She had to.

It was either that or thorazine.

But the tepee was too much. It was just too much.

Not that it wasn't a nice tepee. It smelled nice, and there was a scrap of blue sky visible where the poles came together at the top. But really . . . this guy sounded like he came from Brooklyn. So what was with the tepee?

Victor had tilted his head a little and was watching her. Cookie was aware of him being present. It was as if he occupied an extra dimension: he was present in the places where other people were absent. And all this was amusing him, for some reason.

'No,' he acknowledged at last. 'I can't help you. So why are you here?'

'I shouldn't be,' said Cookie, standing up. In an instant, she was cured of all desire to consult psychic experts of whatever stripe. Looking for answers from teachers wasn't going to help her. She should have learned that from the experience with Shihan Norman.

And yet . . . it could be argued that even in letting her see this, Victor had done her a favor. And she felt guilty for wasting his time. And she didn't want to insult him.

So she said, 'Thank you for helping me see that. I'm going to go now.'

She pushed the tepee flap aside and bent to leave.

'The guy you're worried about, he's looking for you, too. Are you aware of that?'

Cookie's nostrils flared. She froze, half in and half out of the tepee.

'Who?'

Victor shrugged. 'You know more about him than I do. He's one of the invisible ones. But not in a good way.'

Cookie turned around and stood over Victor. She gazed down at him like a mother confronting a child.

'Did Agnes talk to you about me?'

Victor rocked from side to side on his seat bones, smiling a canary-cat smile.

'Agnes?'

'Agnes Peretti.'

He shook his head slowly, the smile broadening. 'Don't know her.'

'So how do you know about me?'

'I've been expecting you for a long time.'

Cookie frowned and popped her knuckles.

'Victor, I've messed people up in my life.'

He gave one of those 'Whaddaya want me to do?' Jewish shrugs, lips pursed. 'That physical-violence stuff, it's a lot less insidious than what most people do to each other. I can see into the thought realm, Cookie. I can see the knives. I can see the guns. People do violence to their children every day. They tear each other's throats out. They're cannibals. I can see this. I can see where you're hurting.'

'Yeah? And you're going to regress me to my past lives, right? Gonna unearth some sexual abuse, maybe? Isn't that how all you guys get your kicks?'

Victor didn't flinch. 'It doesn't matter what *I* can see, Cookie. It's what *you* see that counts.'

'Don't play with me!'

'I'm not playing,' he said mildly. 'Are you taking something out on me here? Is there something I've done to make you angry?'

Cookie sat down, frustrated and hurt. She felt as if she'd been hit by her own boomerang. Her chest was tight.

'It's good if you need to cry,' he said. The next thing she knew, the sobs were bursting out of her.

'That's good,' said Victor. He reached over and touched her shoulder. 'Go into that place.'

Cookie closed her eyes.

'I'm sorry if I was confrontational,' she said suddenly. 'I just don't like being laughed at.'

'I'm not laughing at you. But I can see that it's easier for you to dismiss me than it is for you to look at reality square-on.'

'I'm trying to do that,' Cookie said.

'Don't try to do it. Do it.'

They locked stares. He gave a big smile. Cookie felt foolish.

Victor said, 'I can't help you. All I can do is hold the space for you.'

'What does that mean?'

'You know what it means. You want to pin it down with words. And you know that by nature it can't be pinned down. So you're caught in your own trap.'

Cookie said nothing.

'Why are you here, Cookie?'

'Agnes thought that I should look you up.'

Victor reached over and touched her over her left eye. His tongue protruded slightly in concentration as he did this. She wondered if this was all bullshit or if he believed in it. He radiated a weird jocularity.

'Do you do everything Agnes says?' he said.

'I don't buy into this New Age voodoo shit,' Cookie replied.

'Shit?' said Victor, as if shocked. She knew why he was surprised, too. He was surprised to hear her swear. *He knew*. He already knew.

Cookie felt her face go hot. 'I'm practicing saying expletives. It's part of getting back my power.'

'I see.'

'Do you? Because I'm sick of being conned. I don't want to spend my whole life being the victim of other people's head trips.'

'What other people?'

'Because I have this problem with reality, and the only people who seem to be able to take it seriously are the New Age crowd, but none of them I've met so far had the faintest idea how to help me. In fact, most of them were quacks or loonies. My mother was into this stuff and it didn't help her one bit in her life.'

'How do you know that?'

'Because . . . it was obvious. It never got her anywhere.'

'How do you know that?'

'Well . . . I guess she could have been worse off without it, but I doubt it.'

'And yet here you are.'

'So here I am. In your tepee.'

'Calling me out.'

Cookie considered this.

'Yeah, I guess you could say that. I want to know what you meant before, about the invisible guy.'

Victor inclined his head.

'OK. I can show you something. But first you have to give *me* something.'

'What do you want?'

'What do you want to give me in exchange for this information?'

'I don't know . . . twenty bucks?'

'Not money. Something else.'

'I don't have anything else on me.'

He nodded at her hand. 'What's that on your wrist?'

Cookie snorted. 'It's a friendship bracelet. I got it in prison.'

Victor nodded.

'You want that?' Incredulous.

He nodded again.

'This is important to me.'

'I know.' That happy-Buddha smile.

'I can't take it off. I'd have to cut it.'

'It's up to you.' He produced a Swiss Army knife.

Cookie sighed and cut the bracelet off. She gave it to him.

Victor said, 'What you do about this guy is up to you. He's shadowy. He's like a spider. You can't confront him; he'll retreat and change shape. He's a manipulator. He doesn't have your kind of courage.'

'Is he creating the problems I'm having? Is he making me see things? Because it's not just in the TV anymore. It's breaking through, and I can't tell what's really real anymore. At all.'

'You can find the answer to that if you really want to. Lie down over here.'

Cookie lay on her back on a Mexican horse blanket.

'Scared?'

'Yeah.'

'It's good to be scared. But you can go past that.' Victor put one hand on her shoulder, one on her abdomen. He said, 'You know the difference already. You know what to trust. It's not in your head. It's in the middle of your body. Go to that place.'

Cookie burped. Then giggled.

'Excuse me.'

'If you want to avoid your stuff you don't need me. You got Dunkin' Donuts for that.'

'Sorry.'

'Never apologize.'

She closed her eyes. In the middle of her body was a cave. She could feel thoughts and emotions criss-crossing that space like bats. Words and pictures tangled in there.

'Good. You know who the guy is. You already know everything you need to know about him. But you've chosen to forget it, because he's good at what he does, and he's made it easier for you to not see him. You'll see him when you want to see him.'

Cookie opened her eyes.

'I cut off my friendship bracelet for this? I'll see him when I want to see him? You're just the same as all the rest.'

'That's OK,' Victor said softly. 'I can take it. If you feel you need to attack me. But how is it serving you to lash out at me?'

'This isn't about me!' Cookie snapped.

'Yes, it is. I'm not a psychic. You are. I'm a guy who holds the space for you.'

'How do you know I'm a psychic?'

'Because it's written across your hiney in big letters.'

Her eyes flew open. He was holding back laughter, eyes sparkling.

Cookie didn't say anything.

'What was that?' prompted Victor.

'Nothing.'

'Come on, mama, what you want to say to me?'

She felt like she'd been slapped. '*Mama?* Are you trying to piss me off?'

'Is that what you think?'

'See, why do you keep throwing it back on me? You're the one who's acting weird.'

'I'm not the one with the head problem, girlfriend.'

'You are definitely starting to piss me off.'

'Am I? Good. Maybe that's how you do it. Maybe that's where your truth lies.'

'My truth? Baloney.'

'Baloney is something you've been eating too much of, big mama.'

'I don't believe I'm hearing this,' said Cookie. 'Are you for real?'

'Oh, and speaking of baloney, I just thought of something. You remember the Oscar Mayer jingle? "*My baloney has a first name, it's O-S-C-A-R*",' he sang. 'You could try singing it. Sing your baloney. Sing out his name!'

'Victor, dude, it's not a good idea to get me upset. Bad things happen to people who do that.'

'Let me guess. You turn green and burst out of your clothes. "*My baloney has a second name*" . . .'

Cookie sat up.

'I'm not gonna lie here flat on my back and take this crapola, motherfucker.'

'Oh!' cried Victor. 'Two curse words in a row! The water buffalo's on the loose!'

'I'm going. Give me back my friendship bracelet.'

'Tell me his name and I'll give it back.'

'I don't know his real name, dipshit,' she said, standing up. 'That's the whole point. Now give me the bracelet.'

He held it behind his back. Playground stuff.

'You do know his name, it's on the tip of your tongue.'

Cookie snorted, feeling frothy. She balled her fists.

'You,' she said, 'are such an asshole.'

'Tell me his name and then we can have some fried chicken and shrimp.'

Cookie, seeing purple, shouted, 'His name is Gunther Stengel, jerk-off!'

'Not his name *then*. His name now. His invisible name.'

'Borland, fuckface. Michael Borland. Now give me my friendship bracelet!'

Victor smiled.

'Good work,' he said. 'Although we might need to teach you some new curse words.'

Cookie quivered, swayed on her feet, and then abruptly sat down.

'Michael Borland. Where did that come from?' she whispered.

'Keep following it,' Victor said. 'Anger opens a pathway for you. Use it.'

'His name is Michael Borland and – I don't believe this. I just talked to him on the phone. I didn't know it was him. But it was.'

'He's good,' said Victor. 'What did he say to you?'

'I can't remember. I thought I was only on the phone for five minutes, but when I looked at the clock it was twenty. We were talking about the things we see when we watch TV.'

'He doesn't see them. He was faking you out. He was planting suggestions in your mind while you were on the phone.'

Cookie looked closely at Victor.

'I've been getting a lot of phone calls where the person just hangs up.'

'But he doesn't just hang up. He talks to you. Afterward, you don't remember.'

'How do you know that?'

'It's what you know that counts.'

'But he doesn't know my phone number.'

'How hard could it be to get your phone number?'

Cookie thought. Miles had tracked her down. Gunther could probably do the same thing. Or . . .

'Gloria!'

'In excelsis deo?'

'No, my friend Gloria. She told me she gave my phone number to this guy from *Miami Vice*. She told me he wanted to meet me. But she couldn't even *remember* Gunther, or she said she couldn't.'

Victor said nothing. He nodded and smiled.

'I'm going to check this all out when I get home,' Cookie warned. 'This better be the real shit.'

'It's your shit, so of course it's real.' He smiled. 'Tell me more about him.'

'It's coming back to me now. When I knew him, he was Gunther Stengel and he worked for Dataplex. He hypnotized me. He told me I would be witnessing a war in another part of the galaxy, and that my input was essential for our agents to survive. He told me I was paving the way for human progress. He swore me to secrecy. Then he showed me Froot Loops commercials and stuff like that. I thought it was a real war.

'But it was all made up. He was working on a project for Dataplex, but there was no Department of Extraplanetary Hauntings. There were just me and the other deluded idiots. He was using us for some kind of computer project. All along, he was trying to convince Dataplex of this software he was writing. He was into the whole computer thing, just like Miles. People are supposed to be like computers. We have hardware and software. He told me he was giving me new, better software. He told me I was the next wave. I could integrate with machines and with people. I could read the Grid.

'Shit, it's all coming back to me now. I'd go in there to debrief, and he'd hypnotize me. He'd tell me stuff, and I'd believe it. He wanted these logic bullets, he wanted to know how the Grid worked so that he could design the software to control it. He wanted to control the marketplace through the Grid. But I didn't want to give it to him. The Grid is wild. It has its own patterns, its own intelligence, its own purposes. But Gunther told me that if I didn't give up the logic bullets, then Machine Front would have to destroy the Grid and everything in it.'

'Did Gunther have that power? What's the Grid?'

'I guess . . . I guess the Grid is an underlying order. I think it's a mathematical order, but it's very strange. Maybe it's like the collective unconscious. It doesn't exist on a physical level but it influences us anyway. No, he couldn't have destroyed it. I know now he didn't have that power. But at the time I believed that he did. You see, he thought the Grid was just a figment of my imagination. But it isn't. I mean, it might not look like what I think it looks like, but it's real, and it's there.'

Victor nodded.

'And this is still going on. What does he want? Why is he pursuing you?'

'I don't know!'

'Yes, you do, big—'

'Oh, don't start that again. I think . . . I think . . . see, I brought something *through*. I brought someone through. I tried to save her. She was . . . someone damaged. Someone special. Almost like a goddess, or part of a goddess. And when I did that, I brought Gunther's machine monster through, too. I brought them both here. And ever since I did that, the world has cracks. There are places where I can see through. Stuff passes through from other places. I don't even think they're real places. They could be fictional places. Do you believe that?'

'It doesn't matter what I believe. Tell me, how did he hypnotize you?'

'Music,' Cookie heard herself saying. 'He always had a tape deck in his office. He used music.'

Then she told Victor everything. About Karina and the TV. About the haunted-house sandwiches. Her mother's death and how she hadn't been able to eat. The bodies floating under their balloons in the Grid. Everything.

Then Victor started to talk to Cookie, and she didn't quite get where he was coming from at first. But he seemed to think it was very important.

'The Indians have this idea about invisible people. The more powerful a person is, the quieter they keep it. Like, with the Indians, if a warrior wanted to count coup on you, his objective wasn't to kill you, it was to humiliate you. It was to show you he could have killed you so easily, but didn't. Invisibility is more powerful than strength.

'And a medicine person doesn't talk about what they know. If you have some medicine, you don't go around bragging about it. And the other thing is, if you know something and somebody asks you for help, you have to give it to them. That's part of your place in the world. Now I think your friend here has some of this knowledge. But he isn't any more Indian than you or me. He has no respect for the Great Wheel. In fact, he's amoral. He's twisted. He exploits. That's all he knows how to do. He wants to use you. And he'll keep pursuing you.'

'But why me? Why can't he use somebody else?'

Victor let the air out through his nose. Cookie sensed his weight settling deeper into his seat bones. It was like watching a bird get serious about sitting on some eggs.

'There's something about you,' Victor said. 'Isn't there?'

'I don't know.'

He smiled from his eyes.

'It's your superpower,' Victor said.

'Why do you have to be such a wiseguy?'

'Oh, come on. A lot of people have superpowers. And you have one, too, but it's not the power you think it is.'

'Oh, really? And what do you think I think it is?'

'You tell me. It's *your* superpower.'

'All right, then – I see things. I see things I should have no way of seeing, and I usually see them before they happen. Sometimes the information just comes to me in a flash. Sometimes I see it on TV. I can't control it. It doesn't seem to have any purpose. It just happens. Like sneezing.'

Victor was shaking his head *no*.

'What? Are you saying I don't know my own superpower?'

'You're missing the big thing about it, Cookie.' He leaned forward. 'It's not the fact that you see things before they happen, it's more than that. By seeing things happen you *make things happen*.'

'I refuse,' said Cookie, 'to be psycho-girl from a Stephen King movie.'

Victor sat back. He looked disappointed.

'Think about it. When was the first time this happened to you?'

'The first time? Probably the anaconda in the bathtub when I was a kid. I said something about it, our neighbor denied it, and when he went downstairs there was an anaconda in his bathtub. It had nothing to do with me. I just saw it in my head, and I told my mother.'

'You made it happen,' said Victor.

'How the hell do you know?'

'I know because *my* superpower is knowing what other people's superpowers are. That's my job.'

'Well, you're wrong about me. Because if I made those things happen, that means I made a guy get killed, and I don't buy that. I'm not a murderer!'

'I know it's upsetting. But I'm not wrong about you. You make things happen. You see them, and then they happen, and it isn't something you can control and it doesn't make any sense to you. That's why you've got to learn to use it. This whole situation you're in right now, it comes down to that.'

'Victor – this is all way too philosophical. I need practical help here. Like with Gunther and stuff.'

'He's stalking you. He's trying to draw you to him. And you've been passive. You let Karina's TV grab your attention, but you try not to watch TV because you're still afraid of it. This is something you have to turn around. Now that you know the name he's using, you have the advantage. But you can't confront him. Not yet. You have to find your weapons. Learn how to use them. Then you can deal with him face to face. And you will have to do that.'

When Victor said *weapons* Cookie flashed an image of the knight in armor in the Haunted House. There had been crossed pikes on the wall.

'Weapons? I'm not even sure what we're talking about here,' Cookie said nervously. She could sense Grid shimmering and humming under everything.

Victor eyeballed her. She felt herself flinch away from his gaze.

'That,' he said. 'Look at me. That. Right there. What you're thinking about right now, that's what you have to do.'

'But . . . it's crazy.'

'So are you. That makes it right. Cookie, you can't run away from this. Next time you aren't going to get sucked into a TV. You're going to jump in.'

'I can't do that.'

'I told you I can't help you. And I can't. But that's my advice. When I see somebody drowning, I throw them a cement life jacket. This is yours. You don't have to grab it.'

Cookie just stared at him.

'Come back when you've mastered your weapons and we'll talk again.'

Victor put the friendship bracelet in his pocket.

The Map is Not the Territory

There was a message from Gloria when she got back. Cookie called her.

'Cookie, you're not going to believe this, but he wants to meet you.'

'Huh?'

'Philip. The guy from *Miami Vice*. And, you want to know what? He's really into all that psychic stuff, too. Now, he *has* a girlfriend but I still think, you know . . .'

Cookie sighed.

'Gloria, I really don't have time for this. Look, Philip Michael Thomas is a big star. He's not going to be interested in somebody like me.'

'But he really wants to meet you. He's such a sweet guy, Cookie, why can't you just go and meet him?'

'Because I'm not the kind of woman guys like that go for. Because he's only doing this because he likes *you*, Gloria, don't you get that? He'll give me an autographed photo. And I've never even watched the show . . .'

'Well, it's not as good as it used to be, but that's not *his* fault. Oh, just come and meet us. We'll be at TGIF on Wednesday around eight. Just come. It'll be fun.'

'Yeah, OK.'

'Do you *promise*?'

'OK, OK, I promise, I'll be there. But I'm not staying. I have things to do.'

Cookie hung up, made herself a cup of coffee, and set the milk down on the counter with a splash. Instead of a missing child on the carton, there was a dead soldier floating in the Well.

Wednesday night at TGIF was supposed to be quiet, but the place set Cookie's nerves on edge. It was dim inside, with big TVs by the bar that so that she had to find her way to Gloria without getting caught up in the Synchronicity. It was like trying to swim a rip tide.

Gloria was with a bunch of people near a window overlooking Route 4. There were cocktails and buffalo wings and much laughter. When Cookie appeared, Gloria leaped up. She pointed to the bar.

'He's there!' she said. 'He's over there, in the leather jacket – see him? Look, he's waving to you.'

Cookie looked.

She couldn't see anybody remotely like the *Miami Vice* actor. But there was a skinny, balding white guy in a neon-green T-shirt waving frantically.

She blinked.

It was Gunther.

Cookie turned back to Gloria. She was shaking with rage. This was just like a joke some girls had played on Cookie when she'd been a junior in high school, telling her they'd set her up with a reasonably OK-looking chess player in the senior class. Cookie had been wary, but too polite to do anything but walk into the trap. She had even been stupid enough to buy a dress.

Now she heard herself say, 'Meet your prom date,

Cookie – hope you'll enjoy dancing with this sexy St Bernard.'

Then she burst into tears. She was peripherally aware that Gunther had started to come over.

Gloria's brow furrowed. 'What?' she said, all innocence.

Cookie hauled off and belted Gloria right across the face. It wasn't a slap, it was a punch. Gloria's head whipped around and she spun, crumpling against the nearest table. People leaped to their feet.

'I thought you had a black belt,' Cookie said. Then she turned and fled. Gunther was trying to get to her, but the place was too crowded, and by the time he'd reached the entrance she was already unlocking her car.

He ran after her and she fought the impulse to back up and run him over.

They couldn't send her to prison if she vanished into the Synchronicity, could they?

There were no messages when she got home. She might as well split; the police would be coming here soon.

Weapons. Victor had said weapons.

So on Thursday morning Cookie walked into the haunted house carrying a knapsack. She tried to take the crossed pikes but they were huge and heavy; she couldn't even wrestle one of them off the wall. She put a pair of silver candlesticks in the knapsack instead. She took the gauntlets off the suit of armor and put those in, too. She tried to get to the stairway but when she got closer to it she discovered that it had only been painted on the back wall of the room.

Cookie closed the knapsack and left. She put it in the back of the Rabbit. It was heavy and made clanking noises. She drove all the way to Paterson, to a pawn shop.

'How much can you give me for these?' she asked, and put the candlesticks on the counter. She'd never been inside a pawn shop before, and her hands were sweating. The owner looked at the candlesticks impassively. He picked them up and studied their bases. He held up a magnifying glass.

'I can do fifty bucks each.'

'They've got to be worth more than that,' said Cookie.

He shrugged. 'They might be. As a favor I can tell you that they're solid silver, not plate. But I don't do much business in stuff like this. You got a watch? Jewelry?'

Cookie shook her head. 'How much are they worth, then? To sell?'

The shop's owner blew air through his nose, scratched the back of his neck. 'You wanna sell them for permanent? Go to an antiques dealer. Like I said, I don't got the market for it down here.'

She chucked the gauntlets on the counter.

The guy laughed. 'I can't deal with this. Tell you what. I'll give you a hundred and twenty for all this, we call it a day.'

Cookie hesitated. 'You just said you don't deal in this stuff.'

'Maybe I know somebody who does.'

'That's OK,' said Cookie. 'I'll take them to an antiques dealer, like you said.'

'OK, two hundred.'

'Um . . . thanks, but, I'd rather get them appraised just to be sure.'

He shrugged. 'It's your life. Hey, five hundred bucks cash now, my final offer.'

Cookie smiled, gathered up her stuff, and walked out. An hour later she was leaving A Touch of Class in Wayne with just under three thousand dollars in her wallet. Cash. For stuff she'd taken from a house that no one else could see.

Cookie was dizzy with power. She went to Dress Barn and got herself some real clothes. She chose strong, Caribbean colors. She dragged her hair back and put a scarf around her head. She dug out the Japanese lipstick that she'd found in a

haunted-house sandwich incident and, with a sense of defiance, painted her lips. She started holding her head high.

On Friday morning she played hooky from work. She dragged
the TV out of her closet.

It was going to be different this time. This wasn't going to be
Gunther's trip, not anymore. This was going to be Cookie's
trip.

She turned the set on.

Now here's the thing. Here's the really big difference which is
all the difference in the world and none at all, depending on
where you stand when you look at it: a location-specific para-
dox. Cookie took her body with her. This was truly a strain on
her conceptual rigging and possibly the cause of all her
unpremeditated zaniness in future chapters, because of course
the thing about edges is that once you go off them, you don't
get to go back on. That's what makes the thing an edge.

So: Cookie went into the Synchronicity and left nothing
behind.

She walked through the place, looking for something familiar.
Baskin Robbins, maybe, or a Toyota dealership, or even the set
of *Anything Goes!* from the 1970s. Something hat-hangable.
Nosuchthing, however. No Bambi, no Thumper. A lot of different types of carpet on the streets, if you could call the passages
of the Synchronicity streets. The carpet was useful, a kind of
popcorn-trail phenomenon that kept reminding Cookie with
every step she took that she was inside the Synchronicity as
opposed to the real world. Otherwise she might have gotten
confused.

She bought a newspaper with Monopoly money and read
some of it. It all made perfect sense, but she couldn't have said
what it was about, only that she noticed several small gram-
matical mistakes. Particularly sentence fragments. Which

seemed to be common, run-ons and punctuation mistakes were frequent: too.

Cookie carried the newspaper anyway, because it gave her something to do and because it gave her some sense of anchorage every time there was a dislocation and she found herself jumping to another avenue of the Synchronicity.

All this was uneventful until she stepped through an innocent doorway and found herself in a glass elevator, going up fast. She lurched and swallowed her own gorge as she took in the panorama around her: the wild city with its tiny perfect gardens growing up the sides of buildings and its traffic moving upside down, glittering in the sky. The Synchronicity had grown. It was still growing.

The elevator stopped. The doors opened. Light dazzled her. She was looking across a construction site high above the Synchronicity. The concrete floor was newly laid, and bare girders marched away in unlikely curving patterns. Wind lifted bits of plastic packaging and dragged them across the open expanse.

Cookie stepped out of the elevator and took a few hesitant steps.

She heard voices. They were angry. She began to walk toward the sound of the confrontation. Soon she came to a large diamond of *Wizard of Oz*-green corporate carpet. On the carpet was a fully furnished room, but without walls or ceiling. There were, however, a series of windows floating in midair.

The players were familiar, but she couldn't have said where she'd met them before.

Lipstick One and Lipstick Two were having a heated discussion across a shiny black conference table. The whole place smelled like new carpet and Lipstick Two was wearing his best hat.

Lipstick One said, 'There's just no way I'm going to be some vehicle for you to exercise your deep-seated need for your black nanny and her cooking and disguise it as some kind of hip New Age professionalism. As if – duh – I'm going to be that superficial.'

'Rhubarb pie is not superficial,' argued Lipstick Two, banging a meaty fist on the table. 'And it's not racist, either.'

'I never said it was racist, I said it was *stupid*.'

Cookie interrupted, 'Just what is going on here with you two?'

Lipstick Two raised his eyes to her imploringly.

'I have tickets to Barbados this weekend. Can you tell Mr Surf's Up here that the next wave is not Brainwave and it's not Shark Blood, for God's sake.'

'I never said Shark Blood—'

'I mean, why don't you just call yourself Used Tampon?'

'Look,' said Cookie. 'I don't know what all the fuss is about, but—'

'I'm punching through!' yelled Lipstick Two. 'And I'm not going to let Bimbo Red Corvette stop me, OK? Rhubarb Pie is coming through and that's final. I'll see you both in Bloomingdales.'

That was about when things started getting ugly. Lipstick One flew across the table at Lipstick Two. There was a clumsy, inefficient scuffle.

'Break it up!' yelled Cookie, grabbing the nearest pitcher of ice water and dousing them both.

Lipstick Two burst into tears, evidently distressed at the damage to his hat.

'Oh, it doesn't matter,' he sobbed. 'You can do it, Cookie. Bring me through and you won't regret it. Look, I can trace my associations back to the seventeenth century . . .' and Lipstick Two grabbed a handful of what Cookie had taken for his hair but turned out to be a lot of fiber-optic-type cable of the sort she had previously seen only in the Grid. Some of it, thin as fishing wire, was longer than the rest, and it went out the floating window and vanished into some other dimension of the Synchronicity.

Lipstick One, who was bald, sneered.

'Genius doesn't need to advertise its pedigree,' he announced.

'I need,' said Cookie through clenched teeth, 'to talk to somebody who has a clue. I need some explanations. Now are you guys going to help me out, or am I gonna take these scissors –' she snatched up a handy pair of pinking shears that she had just noticed on the sideboard '– and chop all of your MaxFact associations *right frigging now*?'

'No need to do that!' exclaimed Lipstick Two. 'Down that hatch, you'll get all the explanations you can handle.'

He indicated a manhole cover that was embedded in the carpet. Lipstick One went so far as to grab a presentation pointer and prise up the lid. A shaft of orangey light blasted forth. Lipstick One bowed elaborately.

'OK,' said Cookie, shaking all over because she hated getting aggressive. She tried awkwardly to go back to being nice. 'Thank you. Appreciate it.'

And she lowered herself through the hole.

She was dangling above a slumping brown sofa. The orange light faded. Cookie let herself down to her elbows and hung there, but she couldn't see much of what was below and her triceps were about to give out, so she let go. She thumped into the sofa and, breathless, collected herself as quickly as she could.

It was an office with plexiglass all along one side overlooking a factory floor. At a drafting table covered with paint chips sat a small dark man. He might have been Indian or Indonesian. He was dressed in a pale blue short-sleeved shirt with a dark tie, and his hair was slicked back 1950s style. He had left a cigarette burning in a plastic Budweiser ashtray, and with ferocious concentration he was writing out lists on a yellow legal pad. On the drafting table was a small transistor radio playing 'Heroes' by David Bowie. The small man hummed along in between mumbled comments, apparently to himself, in a California accent.

'Burnished Mangrove. What does that say? Ripe Manticore. Hmm. Lime Quickness. Too arch. Maybe Florentine . . . Florentine . . . Florence . . .?'

He shuffled his paint tiles in evident displeasure. Then, in the same tone, he added,

'You fucked up big time. You let the thing in and now look.'

Cookie didn't say, 'Excuse me? What are you talking about?' There was something in the guy's manner that wouldn't have brooked that. He was an autocratic little fellow, and he'd caught her off guard. So she tried to rally.

'What choice did I have? If I let the MF take the last iteration, then MF really would own Grid logic. The Grid would all be broken down. I couldn't let that happen.'

The man snorted. 'Gimme a break. You let the Grid tweak your nose. All those cute little kids, helpless little girls getting gobbled up by the bigbad monster machines. You fell for it. And now she's here, and so is IT. Not that it matters. Would have happened sooner or later. The Ascension of the Abstract has been on the cards for a long time.'

Cookie said, 'Do you mind telling me who the hell you are?'

'Yes. I do mind. Which is the difference between you and me. I mind; you don't.'

She just gaped at him.

'There's no need to be insulting.'

The small fellow laughed. 'You're a real piece of work. You think you can come here, fuck things up for everybody, ask questions, and everybody's got to jump on your tuna frigate. But you aren't even invisible. You don't even know the score. What's a couple of candlesticks, what is that? Big magic. Come on.'

'What do you mean, I'm not invisible? Are *you*?'

'I'm here, aren't I? What do you think of Sheer Plasma? Too funky?'

'It sounds like a pantyhose.'

He sighed. 'Yeah. OK, how about this?' He held up a chip. 'Bedouin Spice.'

'Looks like puce to me.'

'But who wants a paint called puce? It sounds like puke.'

'So what should I do? Can't you give me some kind of advice, since you know so much?'

The man sniffed. Regarded her with lips twisting in consideration of her question.

'Take control. Yeah. What else can you do? If you don't put it together for yourself, no one will.'

'And how do I get to be invisible?'

'It's just about doing your shit without advertising it. You have to live in the world. I ride my bike to work. That helps.'

He put out the cigarette. 'And don't smoke. It turns your teeth yellow.'

He waved his hand at her with a magician's dismissal.

'But – I need help.'

The small guy sighed. Put his face in his hands.

'I need help,' Cookie repeated. 'And Victor said if you're invisible and somebody asks you for knowledge, you have to help them. Help me!'

'Help you do what?' he moaned, still not looking up.

'Help me figure this place out.'

Long sigh. 'It's associational. It's like following thought. Don't think of it like a physical place. It's not ordered like that. If you want to go somewhere, you have to find your way in your head. You have to trace the associations. That's why things like brand names are so powerful. They encode all kinds of other information.'

'What about going in and out of TVs?'

He looked at her then. 'Hey, that's your special fetish, I don't do TV myself. I stick to the material world.'

'So you're saying . . . I'm really jumping around from one

location to another? Does that mean the Grid was real? I was really on another planet?'

'What you call the Grid is real, but it only looks like that to you. Your senses are interpretive, you know.'

'Whoa,' said Cookie. 'I think I get it.'

'I think I've helped you enough now. Think about something else so you can get the hell out of here.'

She was thinking about Miles.

There were streets and alleys of nothing much. Then Cookie spotted a white man in a blue suit standing on a plinth outside a carwash. He was holding a briefcase. He appeared anonymous. He was waiting for his car, which was an Oldsmobile. *Brand name.*

'Miles!' screamed Cookie, and started to run.

But it wasn't Miles. It was some other poor fool in a blue suit, and he scrambled into his car and swerved to avoid her. Then he drove off in a big hurry. But he left deep tire tracks in the beige carpet, and Cookie followed them. They led her all the way to the IBM parking lot, where it was raining.

There was no longer any carpet. Somewhere the carpet had changed to asphalt; Cookie couldn't remember where. She looked around herself with a sense of slightly dazed forgetfulness. It was the feeling you get when you open the fridge and then stand there, blinking in the light, forgetting what you came for. IBM's plant confronted her with a certain smug certainty about its own reality, and she couldn't measure up.

Cookie put the newspaper over her head and walked up and down the rows of parked cars looking for Miles's. This took half an hour, and in the end she wasn't successful. A security guard came out and asked her what she was doing.

'There's no more carpet,' Cookie said.

'You seem a little confused. Did you lose your car?'

'You're very nice,' Cookie said. 'But it won't do any good.

I've come a very long way to get here and if you knew how that worked, you'd go straight home and get back in your bed.'

The guard cleared his throat. He rubbed his fingers over his upper lip a couple of times, thinking.

'OK, I'm going to walk you to the edge of the premises and then I'm going to say goodbye to you, all right?'

'I want to see Miles Siebel,' Cookie said. 'He works here. Can you tell him Karen Orbach is here?'

His expression was suspicious. Like he thought she was playing a joke on him.

'Miles Siebel.'

'That's right.'

He took out his walkie-talkie and said, 'Christie? It's Les. Do we have a *Miles Siebel*?'

'*Yep. Extension 2109.*'

The guard's eyebrows lifted fractionally. 'OK . . . can you call him and ask him if he's expecting a—?'

'Karen Orbach,' Cookie supplied.

'—*Karen Orbach*?'

'Will do.'

They waited.

'Les,' Cookie said. 'Do you watch a lot of TV?'

He shrugged. 'Mostly sports.'

'Well, if I were you—'

'*Les? Miles is on his way down to pick her up.*'

'I'll walk you to reception,' said Les, smiling.

Miles had had a significant haircut. He had also grown a full beard. He looked scientificky-establishment to the max. He worked in a large office shared with several other male geek-types. When he walked in with Cookie, Miles's colleagues didn't react; they were all bent over their keyboards working assiduously, except for one Middle Eastern-type guy who had his feet up on his desk and was throwing a superball repeatedly against the wall of the office and lunging this way and that to catch it.

'I'm not really here,' Cookie said in a rush. Miles nodded as though this were a perfectly ordinary thing to say.

'OK . . . but you'll be on security camera, you know that, right?'

'Will I?' said Cookie, raising one eyebrow. Miles laughed.

'Not to be an asshole, Cookie, but I'm like *really busy*. Can I meet you after work? Say about seven? We could grab something to eat—'

'No, no, it has to be now. This won't take long, I promise.'

Miles picked up the phone. He told someone that he would be tied up for half an hour. Then he addressed his attention to Cookie.

'Shoot.'

Cookie took a deep breath.

'Do you mind if I skip the bullshit and come right to it?'

'You said bullshit!'

'Do you mind?'

'Of course not.'

'Miles, here's the thing I haven't explained. In the Grid, the logic bullets weren't resources being mined by MF at all. They were bait. The Grid was offering them up on purpose.'

The beautiful thing about Miles, Cookie thought, was that you could be absolutely straight with him and he'd never take advantage of it. He always matched you point by point. He never pretended not to get it. Like now:

'Why?' said Miles. 'Why would the Grid do that?'

Cookie said, 'Maybe it wants us.'

'What do you mean?'

'Maybe the colonization effort isn't what it looks like. Maybe it's the other way around. Maybe the Grid wants to come here.'

'Pfffff!' said Miles, giving Cookie a pseudo-gay, *go-away* hand-wave. 'Now that really is paranoid.'

Cookie shrugged. 'I'd call it perspective.'

Miles drummed his fingers on a stack of file folders. His desk was L-shaped and dominated by an enormous computer monitor, an extended keyboard, and a lot of empty coffee cups. A Bill the Cat calendar hung next to Cookie. It had suction-cup darts stuck on it. The office had no window and Cookie found it claustrophobic. Miles pulled at his lower lip.

'Come here in what sense?' he said finally.

'What if it could re-order us? Our world. According to its logic.'

Miles scrunched his eyebrows and said, 'What do you know about digital music?'

'You mean CDs? Not much. They're expensive? They sound colder?'

'See, here's what I'm thinking. I'm thinking about how you can digitize something, chop it up, and reassemble it. They do it with Madonna's voice, to make her sound better. And I'm thinking about strobe lights. In between moments. Flash snapshots. Other rhythms. Strobe. Subliminals. Hmm.'

'Hmm? Hmm what?'

'Digital music breaks everything down into quanta.'

'What's a quanta?'

'Not *a* quanta. Quanta, plural. More than one quantum of information. A quantum is just a very small unit. And in music, you can break sound down into many quanta and then build it up again by adding them together. But we don't experience music as discontinuous flashes. We perceive it as continuous. We perceive life as continuous. When, in truth, our whole mental function occurs in flashes. So, the question I'm asking is in what way is it meaningful to know this?'

'What do you mean, "our whole mental function occurs in flashes"?'

'I mean just that. It does. Don't you read *Scientific American*?'

'Sometimes I read *Discover*, in, like, the dentist's office. I prefer it to *Omni*.'

Miles rolled his eyes. 'Well, take my word for it. Our consciousness functions in cycles. But is that important? I mean, if something is outside our perception, why worry about it? If something is going on in the cracks between our awareness of time, so what?'

'Grid,' said Cookie. 'You think the Grid is on a different timescale?'

'Not exactly. Say your consciousness is like a searchlight. Say it's like the beam on a lighthouse and it spins on a regular cycle, around and around. Your heart beats, you breathe, chemical interactions occur on their own minute timescales. Your brain takes a picture every one-fortieth of a second. Now imagine a band of fugitives ducking down every time the searchlight passes, then running when darkness comes. What I'm saying is, there could be all kinds of events happening in our perceptual blind spot.'

Cookie noticed that Miles had broken out in a light sweat as he was telling her this.

'Are you OK, Miles?'

'What?' He gave himself a little shake. 'I don't know. I mean, we're only talking theoretically here, right? And anyway, I'm not sure that that idea flies for me. If the Grid was operating in between our cycles, then we'd never perceive it at all, would we?'

'Maybe it's in the process of changing frequencies,' Cookie said.

Miles made a face.

'It's not *frequencies*. You New Age people, you have no concept of actual physics.'

'Sorry,' said Cookie. 'Actually, I'm amazed you're even willing to talk about it at all. What did you say last time? Winnie the Pooh?'

'You're calling it the ascension of the abstract,' Miles said, ignoring her sour comment. 'What could that mean? The assertion of invisible patterns upon the energy of a system. It's a neat idea.' He leaned back in his chair and hooked his hands behind his head. 'Of course, I can't find any basis whatsoever for it in reality, but it's still a neat idea.'

'There *is* a basis for it,' Cookie said. 'I've seen it. I've heard it. *Something's going on, Miles.*'

'Keep your voice down!' Miles whispered. 'You already don't exactly fit in with the decor here – I mean, what is that you're wearing?'

Cookie glanced down at herself. She had on a pair of her mother's old slacks, tight green and white polyester ones from the late 1970s with patterns of different medicinal herbs traced on them, complete with Latin names in pseudo-handwriting. And an oversized Salt 'n' Peppa T-shirt that Karina had given her. And riding boots. She wasn't quite sure where the riding boots had come from.

'I guess the boots don't really match,' she mused, inspecting the soles for traces of manure; they were clean. 'Strange . . .'

'Cookie,' Miles said. 'I think you'd better go now. I have a lot of respect for you and your point of view, but this isn't the time or the place.'

Cookie stood up. She narrowed her eyes. 'Since when do you have all this respect? Has something happened to you? Is this about Gunther?'

He shook his head rapidly. 'No. It's not about Gunther. But I . . . look, I can't talk about this here.'

As Miles spoke he took Cookie by the elbow and walked her out of the work area. No one paid attention to them. He walked her to the elevator.

'Something happened to you,' Cookie said in her anaconda-in-the-bathtub voice. 'You've discovered that I'm right. Haven't you?'

'No!' he hissed. 'No, I haven't. I just . . . look, after I visited you that time, and you told me about the Daffy Duck thing, that same evening I was down in Hackensack and I . . . I . . . maybe I saw something. I must have imagined it. I'm *sure* I imagined it. It wasn't so much what I saw as what I thought I heard. The sound was . . . very strange. Ever since then I've been looking into computer music and stuff like that to try and find that sound.'

'Sound? What sound?'

'Well, I can't describe it, and I can't very well yodel it!'

The elevator came. He ushered her into it.

'Call me,' said Miles. 'Please don't come here again. Nothing personal. Call me, or I'll call you.'

'But . . .' said Cookie desperately, sticking her foot in the elevator door. 'I don't have my car with me.'

'How the hell did you get here, then?'

'I . . . walked. I don't remember the boots . . . must have found them on the way. It's not always clear . . .'

Exasperated, Miles stepped into the elevator with her and shut the doors.

'Do you have any money?'

'No. That is, I'm not really here. Like I said before . . .'

'I'll give you bus fare.' He dragged out his wallet.

'I don't want bus fare. I want your help finding a guy called Michael Borland.'

'Who is Michael Borland?'

'He's the . . . er . . . alter ego of Gunther Stengel.'

Ding! The elevator arrived in the lobby. More people in suits. Aftershave. Breath mints.

Miles had been staring at her with the kind of fierce concentration that he usually reserved for designing new pit traps. Confronted by the wall of suits, he led her across the lobby to a quiet spot beside a potted palm tree. He gave her his car keys.

'This is a big act of faith,' he said. He took a business card out of his wallet, wrote an address on the back and scrawled a tiny map. 'This is my house in Rhinebeck. Come back and pick me up at six. Don't get out of the car. You'll find change for the bridge toll in the ashtray. Help yourself to anything you want at the house. If Nina is there, try not to freak her out. She knows about you, but still. Try. OK?'

Cookie's eyes welled with tears. 'Miles, truly, you are such a mensch . . .'

Miles looked at the carpet and made frantic negating gestures.

'Shh! Emotion is the bane of reason. Et cetera. Now off with you!'

Miles's new house had seen a woman's touch. Cookie recognized most of the furniture, but now there were knickknacks on the bookshelves. Many of the books were printed in Cyrillic. There was artwork on the walls, brilliantly colored computer images involving fractals and suggested faces. The effect would have been sophisticated, but the stack of *Mad* magazines next to the sofa kind of negated that.

Nina was not there, but she arrived after Cookie had been sitting in the kitchen for about half an hour. She was sallow, heavy-set, with sharp spiky hair and too much jewelry.

'Miles called me and told me you were here,' she said in a Russian accent. 'Do you want something to eat? Some coffee?'

'Tea?' said Cookie. Nina got busy.

'I'm glad you finally decided to come up,' Nina said. 'Miles has been missing you. He always talks about Monty.'

'Monty?'

'Your paladin? It was Monty, right?'

'Oh, yeah.'

'You know,' Nina said, 'it has always been my opinion that D&D has ruined fantasy. How can you make magic statistical? And what about this idea of alignment? Good and evil, lawful and chaotic? It's too simplistic. What do you think?'

'I guess so . . .'

'You know what I think, Cookie? I think it's the nerd's way of ordering the world so he can deal with it. All those tables and charts . . .' She gave a faint shudder.

'What are you into, Nina?'

'Me? For a living? I do computers. The money is too good to do anything else. I do art, too, but that's just a hobby.'

'Are those your pictures?' Cookie said, gesturing at the walls.

Nina nodded. 'You don't get them, right? That's OK. Nobody does. I'm used to it. You know what I mean, right?'

'Well . . . I know what it feels like when people don't get you.'

'Did Miles tell you about his dragon?'

'No – has he created a new species?'

Nina laughed. 'Not D&D. The one he saw in Hackensack last year. With the weird music. In the sky. He didn't tell you? When we met he went on and on about it. At first I thought he was—' She made a characteristic whirlybird gesture alongside her head, the sign for *crazy*.

Cookie tried to laugh, but inside she was flipping out. No wonder Miles had 'respect'. He had seen the MFeel.

So IT was definitely here – no way to deny it now. Cookie had brought IT through, just as she'd feared.

She'd been hoping that maybe IT hadn't survived or something.

Nina took Cookie along when it was time to pick Miles up. Cookie learned that Nina and Miles had met at an electronic-music symposium in California, where Miles had been searching for inspiration for composing his latest rock opera and Nina had been hanging out with friends. Nina had moved in with him only a few months later.

'He's so cuddly, and not at all arrogant like most of the men in my field,' Nina said. 'He's very well-rounded. He knows who Schoenberg is, which is unusual for a nerd.'

As Cookie herself did not know who Schoenberg was she

didn't comment. All she said was, 'You don't think he talks too much?'

Nina laughed.

And, true to form, Miles was talking even as he got in the car. 'Did you tell Cookie about NLP?' he asked Nina.

'We didn't have time,' Nina said. She caught Cookie's eye in the rearview mirror and said, 'Cookie, Miles wanted me to tell you that NLP, neuro-linguistic programming, is this New Age fad among psychotherapists and business . . . how shall I say? Business gurus? It's all about using language to control people's thoughts and behavior. And Miles found out that Gunther had studied it and was probably using it in his work with people. Was that what I was supposed to tell her?'

'Yeah. So anyway, there's this basic tenet of NLP, and it says "the map is not the territory".' Miles said, 'I put it to you, Cookie, that in your case maybe the map *is* the territory. Maybe, for you, the map is the Grid. I mean, come on . . . the *grid*?'

'What? What are you saying?'

'Don't you get it, Cookie? D&D? Graph paper? The Grid! It seems obvious to me.'

'So you're saying . . . the Grid is a map of my inner reality. On graph paper.' Cookie thought the sarcasm in her voice was pretty obvious, but Miles didn't react to it at all.

'Except it's not so inner anymore. It's like my sister's belly button when she got pregnant. She had an innie but her stomach got so big it flipped around and became an outie. In fact, topologically speaking, you could say—'

'What about the logic bullets?'

'The logic bullets are the insights that you've been offering up to Machine Front. Machine Front are Dataplex. They're trying to quantify your inner world and your inner world doesn't like it. So it fights back.'

'Yeah. OK. *Maybe* I could follow you there. But where do

Serge and the abortion and the nine versions of her daughter come in?'

Miles scrunched his eyebrows in annoyance. 'I don't know. Cookie, it's *your* inner reality. I'm just offering a possible interpretation of events. Those things probably have something to do with the products that you were supposed to be assessing.'

'Nine Lives cat food,' said Cookie. 'That's probably why the golems are nine. But the other stuff I really don't get.'

'I think the part we really have to look at closely is the synchronicity. You rendered that missile into a city made of human abstractions—'

'I didn't render. Serge's daughters did that. I was only watching.'

'Cookie, Cookie. It's all you.'

'No, Miles, I beg to differ. It *isn't* all me. It's all the world. Don't you get it? The Grid is not just some head trip belonging to me. All these things are connected. Something is really going on in the Grid. The Grid is the invisible place. It's a world we can't see or hear or touch directly, but it's reflected in all the products of our culture. Our art, the things we buy, the objects we make, the words we use. The war I was watching wasn't happening inside me. It was happening in the Grid. The only one single thing I personally actually did was use Gossamer's eyes to pull Serge's daughter out of the synchronicity and through the well and into this world. That's all I did. The rest is nothing to do with me. I'm just an observer.'

'Ah,' said Miles, with a smug grin. 'But there's no such thing as just being an observer anymore, Cookie. It's a dead-cat idea.'

'A what? Oh Miles, don't confuse the issue. This isn't about quantum physics. Listen. I have reason to believe that in some way this guy Michael Borland is using music or sound to get information out of people like me.'

'There's no doubt that music can have hypnagogic effects,'

said Miles. 'But we're stretching it here. It's too much hocus-pocus for my liking.'

'Ah, but is it?' said Nina, and pulled the car into Miles's garage. She winked at Cookie, and Miles sighed as if this were some old bone of contention between him and Nina. They went inside.

'Listen to this guitar,' Nina said, and slid a CD into the stereo. A weird misty shivering came into the room.

'That's not a guitar,' Cookie said.

'Oh, but I beg to differ. It is very much a guitar, but I've broken down the sound and changed the wavelengths. I've doctored it. It's still a guitar, but it's been processed by a computer. Or, if I wanted to, I could build a guitar sound from scratch. Just add up the wavelengths. *Ceci n'est pas une guitare*, so to speak.'

'Weird.' Cookie looked at Miles. 'I can't quite connect . . .'

'I think what Nina means to say is that it's all context. Computers let us decontextualize the world. We can move things around, manipulate them. We can create models and watch them run. It's playing with reality. It's playing with ideas, and nobody gets hurt.'

Nina altered the EQ. The 'guitar' was shivering and thrashing like a living thing.

'It gives me the heebie-jeebies,' Cookie said. 'You can't call that music.'

Miles kicked back into the leather sofa and said, 'That's because underneath it all you're a conservative, Cookie. You don't want to get out there on the edge.'

Annoyed, Cookie stood up.

'What the hell do you know?'

'I didn't mean it as an insult. It's just who you are.'

'Just because I don't advocate treating the natural order of things with total disrespect . . .'

'See? What do you mean, disrespect? Nature's just a set of

rules. All the universe is a game. Why shouldn't we play too?'

'Maybe,' Cookie said, 'one day you'll get taken down to your bones and then you'll see that not everything in this world will submit to your rationality.'

She glanced at Nina, who had turned off the music and was watching them, arms folded, with a distant, amused air.

'Maybe,' Cookie said, 'something will come out of the abstract and bite you on the ass.'

'That would be really cool,' said Miles. 'But all the evidence points to us humans being the only intelligent life out there. So I'm not going to lose any sleep.'

'You're assuming that the alien is an alien species,' Cookie said. 'But aliens could be more alien than that.'

Miles made a *my-God-you're-stupid* frogface.

'Right, Cookie,' he said. 'And what would that be? One day my fried eggs will leap off the plate and blast death rays into my retinas?'

'You never know,' Cookie said darkly.

Miles roared with laughter. 'I'll be sure to be on my guard, then.'

'Speaking of eggs,' said Nina, 'it's time to eat dinner.' She ushered them into the kitchen and made them help set the table. She tried to get Miles to open a bottle of wine. Miles and Cookie glowered at one another throughout.

'The KGB has studied all these mind-control things,' Nina said. 'In Russia we didn't scoff so much at the paranormal, you know, Miles.'

'I'm not scoffing. I was the first to suggest mind control to Cookie, but no. Unlike your garden-variety paranoid schizophrenic, she's not worried about the CIA or UFO abduction. She's worried about the entities in her breakfast cereal now. But no matter how you shake it, Cookie, I can find no concrete mechanism by which Gunther accomplishes what he does.'

'Shouldn't that tell you something?' Nina pitched in. 'Maybe Cookie has a point.'

But Cookie had seized on Miles's choice of words.

'Mechanism? What is the mechanism of consciousness? Is it a tipping point? Is it just a difference in how much brainpower we have compared with animals? Or is it some special pattern? And why does it have to be a mechanism? I mean, take love. Take bonding. Those things are at the very root of what we are, but do we understand them? ArtIQs can't do these things, not in a way we can recognize. Everyone knows what love is, but nobody has ever broken it down mechanically, have they?'

'OK, maybe that was the wrong way to put it,' said Miles.

'In the synchronicity,' Cookie replied, 'choice of words is everything. The synchronicity is the map. This is the place where words cross over into things.'

Nina took the bottle away from Miles and opened it. She gestured for Cookie to sit down.

'I think,' Cookie said, 'the Synchronicity is one place within the Grid where we can actually stand, secure within our own mental structure, without falling into the well. And it's growing. The Mfeels have seen to that.'

Nina passed Cookie the potatoes, for all the world as if discussion of Mfeels was perfectly ordinary dinner conversation in their house.

'And . . . isn't that a good thing? Doesn't that mean we're colonizing it? Right, Cookie?' Miles handed Cookie a glass of wine.

'I know you think this whole thing is just my bullshit,' said Cookie, looking into the dark liquid. '"*By what mechanism can you come here?*" That kind of thinking just doesn't apply.'

'By what *means*, then,' said Miles, sounding petulant.

'Means. By the means of meaning. This is what it *means*, Miles. This is the means. This is meaning—'

'Look, just shut up for a second, Cookie. You're going off the deep end again.'

'No, I'm not. Because the Grid is real and it wants to come here. It's an aspect of the world that is starting to poke through. And the way it comes through is by words and images.'

Miles and Nina exchanged significant looks over the beef stew. They must have discussed Cookie extensively.

'Don't you see?' said Nina gently. 'Gunther Stengel brainwashed you. All those long hours they made you work. It's classic. The secrecy. The isolation. You were vulnerable. He knew that. He used that.'

Miles added, 'Gunther's trip at Dataplex was just like a god-damned cult, Cookie.'

'But, Miles,' Cookie said, 'there's one thing you're conveniently forgetting. They paid me. They paid me good money. In a cult, it works the other way.'

'I know. I'm not forgetting. And this is the part I can't wrap my head around. You *are* good at it. You actually *can* predict the stuff he says you can. Not for the good of humanity, just for the good of Gunther. You made him money and you made Dataplex money. But he's history now.'

Cookie snorted.

'I wish he were. There's one other thing you're forgetting, Miles. Or maybe you don't believe it in the first place. The Grid is real. All that stuff about seeing into the world of the abstract? It's true. Gunther thinks he can mine the Grid. Gunther thinks he can use this source of structure and it won't bite back. This is the big problem, Miles. The Grid isn't just a great big chocolate pudding. It has teeth.'

'Whoa, hold the pickles and the metaphors and the image patterns. All I really know for sure, Cookie, is that one night in Hackensack I actually hallucinated something. I don't know what and I don't know why.'

Cookie said, 'It was the MFeel that got Serge's daughters. It followed Cassidy across. That's what you saw. I'm sure of it.'

'But you just said all that is only an abstraction . . .'

'Wait,' Nina interrupted. 'If we're talking about events in an abstract realm, then it really doesn't matter whether the phenomenon is legitimate or not. The brain can't distinguish truth from fiction. If you are suggestible and somebody feeds you a line of nonsense, your mind will take it up as real and make it real. It's like carbon monoxide. Your body can't tell the difference between CO and oxygen, and that's how people get poisoned.'

'But that's a fallacy,' Miles said. 'Because if we applied that analogy to Cookie, then she'd be able to breathe carbon monoxide and it would work for her. It wouldn't poison her.'

'Yes, exactly,' said Nina. 'Because from what Cookie has told us, I believe that this is what happens in the Grid.'

Cookie said, 'I don't get it.'

And Miles said, 'That's OK. Nina's just being fanciful. Have some more wine.'

'No, tell me, Nina. What do you mean?'

Nina, flustered, drank more wine and waved her hands as if to distract attention from what she'd said.

'I just think it could be a kind of magic, you know? Not science at all.'

Miles stared at her.

'Yeah, but you don't believe in magic!'

Nina stood up. 'I'm going to bed,' she said. 'Miles, can you load the dishwasher?'

'What? Oh, yeah. Thanks for the meal. Nina, are you OK?'

'Of course!' said Nina. 'Cookie, you have everything you need?'

'Yes, thank you. The food was delicious,' Cookie said. But she couldn't remember eating any of it.

'We are your friends, Cookie,' Nina said. 'I know you and Miles argue, but you can believe that we want to help you.'

Miles looked at the carpet and swung his foot to and fro like a schoolboy.

'She knows all that, Nina.'

'Thank you. Both.' Cookie looked at her watch. 'I'd better be going.'

Miles snorted.

'Don't be stupid. Of course you're staying. There's blankets and pillows in the hall closet. Tomorrow's Saturday; we'll drive you home. We can talk more then.'

Cookie waited until they had gone upstairs and the house was quiet. She found a plexiglass note-cube on a book shelf; it had a thick stack of white paper inside it, and the margins were musical staves. She found a Bic pen and left a polite thank-you note.

Then she turned on Miles and Nina's gigantic Sony TV to Channel One and walked through its cool curving boundaries into a swamp in the rain. In the swamp were a series of lamp-posts curving off, yellow and smudgy, into the night mist. Cookie trudged from one to the next until the swamp gave way to the echoing aisles of a vast open-air warehouse and then to recognizable urbanity. She walked past street signs reading 'Dancing in the Dark' and 'Runaway', until ahead of her out of the mist appeared the neon sign of Tony's pizza and then, a rhombus of dim fluorescence, her own bathroom window, and she knew she'd made her way home.

Now here was the fun part:

When Cookie opened the door of the apartment, she didn't find herself sitting on her own sofa watching Channel One. She found her home empty except for the cats, who were complaining that she hadn't left them enough food to last the whole day. And a string of messages from both of her blown-off employers and then one from her parole officer, who said,

'I hope you have a good explanation for this, Cookie.'

The B-52s, Sunbathing

At six a.m. Miles phoned and left a message demanding to know how Cookie had left without unlocking any doors. He kept calling her until finally she picked up the phone.

'Yeah, I got back OK,' she said. She ignored his questions about why she'd left in the middle of the night or how she'd gotten home with no car and no money.

'Nina is worried about you. She thinks you have anger issues.'

'Who doesn't?' said Cookie. 'I guess you told her about my stint in prison.'

'Nina thinks that living outside a family or community is too stressful for someone like you. She thinks you should go back to college.'

'Join the front,' said Cookie. 'Get in step with the masses. Stop thinking for myself.'

'Oh, give it a rest. Listen, promise me you'll steer clear of this Michael Borland character.'

'Don't worry about me, Miles.'

'Cookie, I mean it. The guy is a whack-job. I checked him out under that name, and he's put himself out as a self-help guru. I found him through the NLP lecture circuit. He does motivational speaking for creatives and business people. He does hypnosis tapes. He must have been cooking it all up while he was at Dataplex, because in the last year he's hit the self-help scene like a tornado.'

'So he wasn't so easy to get rid of, eh, Miles?'

'I'm really sorry, Cookie. I thought I was helping you out.'

'It doesn't matter. Like I said, I already knew he changed his name, and I knew he'd done something to Gloria. Messed with her head. So he might have been planning this, anyway.'

'I still feel like a jerk. Anyway, now he's got some kind of New Age cult going. He runs it out of his new house.'

'In Pearl River? That's close.'

'How did you know it was Pearl River?'

'Ah, so it *is* Pearl River. You know his address.'

'Stay clear of the guy, Cookie. He's a snake charmer.'

'Just give it to me, Miles. You'll save me a lot of time wandering around in my TV.'

'I think you're making a mistake,' Miles said.

'You don't even know what I'm going to do.'

'If you firebomb his house you'll end up in prison for a lot longer.'

In her apartment with Rocky and Nebbie, Cookie made lists on a vinyl-covered clipboard with one of those fat four-color ballpoints where you can click from one color to the other.

She wrote *Missions:*

And then thought for a long time.

1. *Explore synchronicity. Map if possible.*
2. *Get Gunther out of the way.*
3. *Find Cassidy before he does.*

Then she sat back, sipping Diet Coke. Nebbie climbed into her lap and began to knead her thighs with claws out.

'Ow!'

She wrote *Means:*

1) *Sell valuables.*

2) Find shortcuts from point to point.
3) Invisibility?

Cookie didn't feel so sure of this last one. Sounded too mystical. But raiding the synchronicity for cash was fun. It was D&D without the monsters.

She wrote *Equipment:*

1. Flashlight
2. Rope
3. Knapsack
4. Food/water supplies
5. Map, compass
6. Weapon?

She settled on a Swiss Army knife. But Cookie doubted she could get the knife part open in time to protect herself with it in an emergency. Knowing herself, she'd probably stab somebody with a corkscrew. But not to have it would have meant giving up in advance.

When she had all her stuff, she made sure the cats were well supplied. Then Cookie set off into her television as if it was the Borneo jungle.

High in the girders the whisper of many voices wrote pale shapes on the sky. Metal seemed to accrue out of blue sky and pure tones. It warped and molded to itself in accordance with the mouth-sounds of unknown entities. Cookie watched it happen as if she were watching wasps build a nest out of paper and butt-spit. The synthesis of the Synchronicity seemed no less likely than any other natural phenomenon, now that her eyes were open to every theoretical possibility.

Cookie was thinking about the Grid. She was thinking about the musical abominable multichildren traveling around singing and changing the world like the Partridge Family à la David Lynch. It seemed to her now that the Synchronicity itself must be wrought of sound.

She couldn't see Cassidy. She didn't know if this sound was Cassidy's song, or the song of the MFeel that had eaten the eight other Cassidy-sisters. But she knew one thing for sure: the ground beneath her feet could be taken away as a matter of utterance. For that matter, a cage might spring up around her at any time, trapping her in between idioms forever.

After that, she started packing a blowtorch, just in case.

In time, she learned that the Synchronicity had its own organizational principles, and they weren't obvious at first. What *was* obvious was that the place was incomplete, a partial rendition of some inexplicit structure. There were windows hanging in the air, without walls. There were transparent floors beneath which moved giant images of microorganisms as if under a microscope slide. There were people walking around with gaping holes in them, or no heads, or moving apparently backwards.

Once Cookie opened a door onto a purple swamp that stretched as far as the eye could see, stinking and insect-ridden.

Once she rode an escalator to what looked like a stereo outlet store until she got up close and realized that it was a garbage dump of epic proportions.

She found a tiny functioning airport floating on a paper plate in a fountain outside a boarded-up FAO Schwartz.

Her efforts to map were sporadic and, indeed, pathetic. But she kept trying. Every dungeon she had ever played in had felt like this at first. So many dark turns; so many unknown doors. But, eventually, familiarity would come.

It was a funny thing, this fearlessness of Cookie's. She had been afraid to go on a date with Emilio the janitor. She had been afraid to wear unmatched socks to Jack La Lane lest someone ridicule her. She had been afraid to go back to college. But now she scaled the face of reason with only the contents of an LL Bean knapsack to support her, and this didn't seem unnatural.

It was as if the world, hitherto an insoluble riddle, now presented itself as a Sunday crossword.

It was doable.

It just needed a little persistence.

Cookie could stroll alone through the entire stock of Cartier, in the Abstract Palace of Cartier. And she did. There were no security cameras: it was not Fifth Avenue. And yet, the pizza delivery boys on bikes and the falafel stands of the 'real' New York were only a shrug away across a membrane of the Synchronicity. Cornfields waited on the other side, combine harvesters churning against a sweet blue sky. In the Synchronicity, the world had folded itself into some new origami creature.

But about Cartier: At first Cookie concentrated on treasure, because that was the obvious D&D thing to do. And because it was easy. The objects of the world had been abstracted and stored in their own separate reality. Out of the Synchronicity she plundered Persian lamps and Franklin personal organizers. Silk scarves; rare first editions of Victorian novels; a whole payload of obscure and valuable stuff that would not exist in the real world until Cookie brought it out.

Unfortunately, the Synchronicity hadn't been organized in a user-friendly way. Mapping it was an exercise in mental gymnastics that made those nasty object-rotation exercises in IQ tests look like child's play. Cookie was lost for what felt like a week in a reality she dubbed Litterbug, because it consisted entirely of candy-bar wrappers, dead leaves, cigarette butts and bird shit. Litterbug was inhabited by a sonic presence that could turn Cookie back and forth like a wind. She became disoriented and even forgot who she was. The sound posed her and made her walk and run and lie down. The sound manipulated her like a puppet. She managed to escape when she recognized some writing in the sky. It belonged to the ingredients list on a box of Ritz crackers. Cookie knew this on account of being a compulsive reader. Amazing how one's minor talents could come in handy in a pinch.

So it was that she found her way to the realm of cereal-box literature, and thence to Hoboken where she caught the Path to Penn Station. She sold a load of her plunder in Alphabet City and got a taxi all the way home to Wayne.

But there were only so many pawnshops she could go to before she'd be recognized at all of them. Sooner or later she'd arouse suspicion. Then she'd have to find a fence just like thieves did, and she didn't want to do that. The people involved were too scary. Besides, she had to come up with something bigger. So she set out to find Wall Street's location in the Synchronicity. This was easier said than done: she kept getting diverted sideways into Eastern European state cinema and, sometimes, Chinese government statistics depots. When she finally tweaked how to get there, she found Wall Street heavily guarded. Almost before she knew what was happening she found herself confronted by a squad of cartoon cowboys in black-painted ex-German-Army-issue panzer tanks.

'This here's a no-go zone, ma'am,' said one, pausing to spit politely before swiveling his gun turret in her direction. And behind him she could see and hear a shivering in the air; it reminded her of Nina's computer-guitar sound. Something was poised to break through from some other area of the S'city, and it wasn't something friendly. Lights flickered through the wavering sound, and Cookie had the impression of phosphorescent tentacles and many, many eyes . . .

'I don't need a lot of bread,' Cookie said hastily, showing her palms like Jesus. 'I won't be any trouble.'

'You're green as Bacardi puke,' said the cowboy. 'Go back to playing Lotto.'

Cookie made a face.

'Give me a break, will you? You can block me here, but I'll find another way in. You know as well as I do this place is full of holes.'

The cowboy laughed.

'Well, now, that's a pretty spunky thing to say. Who you working for?'

'Nobody. I'm not a threat,' Cookie said. 'You won't even know I've been . . .'

'Nope, nope, can't break the regulations. On the other hand, if you were looking for advice . . .'

'Yes?'

'Let's just say garbage-picking can be real lucrative around these parts.' The cowboy pointed over Cookie's shoulder.

As he spoke, Cookie became aware of a stench. She went in the direction he indicated and the smell grew stronger. She came around a corner and confronted a garbage mountain, complete with seagulls and rats. Cookie retched as she began to climb, kicking half-heartedly at the trash and feeling hard-done-by.

'What am I doing here?' she muttered, but she couldn't help looking.

She only lasted ten minutes. Then her gaze fixed on a bag with a big brown envelope taped to the side. She waded toward it. In red Magic Marker on the outside of the envelope were scrawled the words: *Unclaimed NYC teachers' pensions.*

The envelope was empty. But the black garbage bag was full of cash.

Cookie picked it up and stepped sideways, into a Korean grocery in Park Slope.

She looked inside the bag. A hefty weight – and it was all hundred-dollar bills. She got a meal at the salad bar of the grocery, then headed back to Manhattan where she caught the Hoboken ferry.

People stood back from her. She did not smell good. Suspiciously, they eyed the bag she was dragging behind her.

'I work for the Department of Sanitation, OK?' said Cookie to a woman in a suit who was carrying an Abercrombie & Fitch briefcase. 'I'm just bringing work home with me. Don't you ever bring work home?'

The woman seemed to wilt, and edged away. Cookie laughed.

But every so often, when no one seemed to be looking, she peeked inside, just to make sure it hadn't turned into Monopoly money.

'I think I've got my weapons, now, Victor. I'm ready to fight him, but I'm scared. I still don't understand what he's really up to.'

Cookie rehearsed what she would say to Victor as she drove up the Thruway. This time, Victor would not toss her around with that mind-reading stuff. This time Cookie would show that she had her shit together. Yes, *shit.*

Except, Victor wasn't there. The house was there. The river was there. But when Cookie got out of the car and walked around, there was no tepee.

Maybe they'd found a permanent place to live. Cookie was about to go up to the house and ring the bell when a skinny blonde woman dressed in a tie-dye peasant blouse over bleached jeans came sauntering across the lawn to her

'Can I do something for you?' The woman was small and sprightly, but not young.

'I'm looking for Victor. The guy who lived in the tepee.'

'Oh, that's interesting,' said the woman. 'I don't know him. Did you meet him somewhere around here?'

'It was right here,' Cookie said, annoyed. She pointed at the ground beneath their feet. 'The tepee. He lived here with his wife and their little girl.'

'That's really weird,' said the woman. 'I don't know anybody named Victor. And as you can see, we don't have a tepee.' It was true that the grass was long and thick, unmown and also untrampled.

'But . . . his tepee was right here,' Cookie said.

The hippie lady's eyes crinkled up. She had to be pushing fifty.

'Are you . . . tripping? Or something?'

'No, I am *not* tripping,' said Cookie through clenched teeth.

'I don't mean to be uncool,' said the hippie. 'But sometimes people try to use my property to get pictures of the B-52s sunbathing, and I'm sure you can understand that I'm protective.'

'Of course,' Cookie said. 'The B-52s. I wouldn't do that.'

The woman smiled. 'Of course you wouldn't. You just got a little confused, that's all. Is that your car?'

'Yeah. And my donuts. I guess I better be going.' There was only one thing to do, and Cookie had been counting on Victor to help her get ready to do it. Now she was on her own.

The hippie said, 'There's a good bookstore in Woodstock. It's called Mandala. Maybe they know your friend.'

'He's not a delusion,' said Cookie, too intensely. She ducked her head so the woman wouldn't see her tears. 'I would know it if he was a delusion.'

But she wasn't so sure. And the woman's pity drifted to Cookie across the sunlit air together with her perfume. Both cloying.

'Oh, hey. It's, like, no problem. I know how life can be.'

'Not my life, you don't,' Cookie said.

The Wellspring Process

Cookie did not like dogs. She did not like big dogs. And she especially did not like the kind of big dogs who hurled themselves at the door when you rang the bell. She could hear their claws on the inside of Gunther's front door. They were in a frenzy.

'Freya! Thor!' Gunther yelled as he fought his way around the edge of the front door. He tried to step out and shut it behind him but the dogs took his legs out from under him from behind and he ended up sprawling on the welcome mat. Two Dobermans raced out and circled around Cookie, sniffing. One of them stood up on its hind legs and planted its front paws on Cookie's chest.

'Down, Thor!'

Cookie forced a smile. 'Hi there, Thor,' she said, trying to close her nostrils against the influence of Thor's breath, which smelled like herring. 'How's it going?'

Gunther hauled Thor away by the dog's studded collar. He was looking richer and healthier. He was tanned, his bare arms looked almost muscular, and he even seemed to have more hair. Cookie was shaking.

'I'm *so* sorry, Cookie,' Gunther said. 'Please, come in. I'll lock them in the kitchen.'

By the sound of it, some other dogs were already locked in the kitchen. Gunther had always been a big one for adopting strays, but he had no actual way with animals. At least, his dogs never listened to him. Maybe that was because he talked to them in lovers' baby-talk.

'You stay in there, pookie,' Gunther said to Freya as he shut the door in her face. Then he led Cookie into a paneled study lined with books. He gestured to a leather couch, but Cookie perched on its arm. Gunther sat down on the corner of the desk. She could hear his clothes rustling as he settled himself. He was perfectly clean and perfectly shaven. His gestures were relaxed and warm: no hint of any bad blood between them, ever.

'It is so good to see you. Hey, sorry if I freaked you the other night.'

Dominating the wall in front of her was a framed poster of *Here the Music* by Michael Borland. Cookie cleared her throat.

'Is Gloria OK?'

Gunther laughed. 'She has a black eye like you wouldn't believe, but she's OK. Don't worry, she doesn't blame you. I've got her thinking she fought off two muggers outside Egghead Software.' He beamed with self-satisfaction, then quickly checked himself when he saw that Cookie wasn't smiling back.

'So what can I get you? Iced tea? Coke?'

'Just water, thanks.'

Cookie watched him bend over to a minibar that was tucked among the bookshelves. He opened a dark blue bottle of sparkling water and carefully added a slice of lemon. The weirdness of this filled Cookie's mind like a clawed monster. She held the glass without drinking. On Gunther's desk, partially obscured by a remote-control unit, there was a press release.

Do You Here Music? it began. *Michael Borland, author of* Reality Manifest, *is giving a series of seminars on the power of sound and the unconscious mind. Beginning on November 18th at Montclair State College—*

'Excuse me,' said Gunther, and Cookie realized that he'd seen her peeking. 'Can you hand me that remote?'

She gave it to him. He pressed something and there was a faint, almost subliminal chiming, and then silence.

'So, um, your life seems to have changed,' Cookie said.

'You know, I'm glad you said that.' He flashed a smile. 'Because it's a little awkward, sitting here like this with you, with so much water under the bridge.'

'Yeah,' said Cookie. Face to face with Gunther, it was very hard to see him as a badguy. There was something friendly in his air. The way he used to tell jokes around the water cooler. The children he sponsored in Ethiopia. The impromptu Nerf basketball games . . .

He said, 'You know, you screwed everything up for me.'

'Oh?'

Gunther nodded in a way that made her almost begin to nod along with him. He was good. Soft sound began to creep into the room, pulsing. She couldn't see any speakers. The sound crawled on the air like a swarm of tiny insects. Cookie blinked, but now Gunther was talking to her and she couldn't seem to listen to the music and him at the same time without feeling sleepy.

'Dataplex wanted to know why none of my simulations could compare to you. They figured out that it wasn't the pro-gramming I was writing that was picking the hit material, it was you.'

Cookie looked at the bookshelves. Mostly academic texts. Psychology. Business management. Every so often there was a discreet ornament on a shelf. The ones nearest to her were old-fashioned ships in bottles labeled with stamped copper plates.

The Mary Jane. *From Singapore to San Francisco, carrying a cargo of silk, spices and gold.*

Gunther touched her knee and she had to look at him.

'That's all water under the bridge. I know you tricked me. Pretending you couldn't fly. Picking the wrong names. All of that. It was good. I'm impressed! No, don't look so uneasy. Ah, Freya, goddamnit!'

Cookie jumped up on top of the desk as the dog arrived in a scrabble of claws. The other dogs were hard on Freya's heels. They came into the room in a black sea of movement. Cookie felt confused. She didn't remember hearing the kitchen door open, nor the sound of their approach. They seemed to have just *arrived* as if they'd been teleported.

Gunther dragged them all back in and shut the kitchen door again. This time he put a chair in front of it.

'She's young. So rambunctious. Now, where were we?'

Cookie glanced at her water glass and saw that all the ice had melted already. Surreptitiously she checked her watch. Half an hour had gone by.

But she'd only just sat down . . .

Wait a second. This was just like her phone call with Michael Borland of Cedar Rapids.

He was hypnotizing her.

No!

Gunther sat down and studied her face. 'Ah,' he said. 'You're closing up on me. OK, I can respect that. Here's my question. What would it take, Cookie, to get you back on my team?'

Cookie felt a strong urge to remix Gunther. Stick him in the well and make him into something else. Purge him of all brand names and other symbolic associations, degrease his bullshit, and take away all the power of his words. What was really underneath all his mannerisms? He was all body language, lines, and emptiness.

And he was taking her for a ride. Always.

'I think,' Cookie said carefully, 'that you're all about words. And there's nothing behind your words. Or rather: you don't believe there's anything behind them. But there is. Words have power.'

'Eminently true. Words do have power. That's my business.'

'But you believe all that "the map is not the territory stuff. Don't you?"'

'Ah, reading our NLP, are we? That's right. The map is *not* the territory,' said Gunther. 'The map is just our beliefs about the world. Change the map, you change the world.'

'But you told me there was a gravity-torsion generator in Vermont.'

'Maybe there is.'

'Maybe there isn't.'

'Maybe there is, and maybe when you entertain that possibility your map becomes a little bit more rich. Or a lot more rich.'

'I'll tell you what's rich,' Cookie said. 'According to *my* map, the Grid is coming here. Now.'

'Now that,' said Gunther, 'is the first interesting thing you've said today. I wonder—'

There was a knock at the door and Gunther rolled his eyes. 'Yes?'

A female voice said, 'Excuse me, Michael, Buzz is on the phone from Nepal.'

'I'll be right there, Chi An.'

Gunther stood up.

'Who's Buzz?' said Cookie. 'A clairvoyant yak?'

Gunther opened the door and there was Chi An, wearing a bikini and a fur jacket. She handed Gunther a portable phone and smiled at Cookie.

'Buzz?' said Gunther, leading Cookie through the kitchen – the dogs were no longer in evidence – and into a fenced pool area out back where steam rose from a kidney-shaped swimming pool. 'Hey, did you drink your own pee yet, dude?'

Gunther's house turned out to be full of people. Some were staying there (Chi An informed Cookie that Gunther had seven bedrooms and a pool house) while others drifted in and out, parking their cars in the big circular driveway with its perfect black macadam. Small birds blustered in the shrubbery. Chi An escorted Cookie to the pool area while Gunther trailed behind, laughing at whatever Buzz was saying.

In a low, amused voice Chi An said, 'Oh, before I forget – it's a clothing-optional pool, just so you know.'

Almost before Cookie could take in those words, a naked blond guy with a beard and no tan lines came striding over and shook Gunther's hand. He was soaking wet. Gunther handed the phone back to Chi An.

'Hey man,' said the naked guy. 'Great visualization this morning – that's really working for me, dude.'

'Hey, Jimbo,' Gunther replied in a guy-meets-guy roar . 'Jim, this is my buddy Cookie. Cookie, Jim here's chilling out after some heavy action on Madison Avenue. '

'Oh, total rehab from the straitjacket of the office deathfume,' said Jim. His penis bounced as he laughed. He took a big towel from Susan and began to rub himself down vigorously. 'And the IRS can't find me here! Michael's got me tripping on life, woooo!' He threw back his head and gave a wolf-howl.

'Eat your cake and have it too,' Gunther said genially.

'Hey, Cookie, can I get you anything?' said Jim. 'Hibiscus cooler? Root beer?'

Cookie shook her head. She was becoming progressively more confused. Her manners warred with her anger that Gunther was subjecting her to this circus.

'Cookie is a consultant,' Gunther said. 'I'm trying to svengali her into our project, so if you could—'

'—get my ass out of your way you'd appreciate it, yeah, yeah,' Jim said. 'OK Mike. See ya later, Cookie. I'm gonna go get an apron and start the barbecue. Apron, get it? Hah, hah.'

He was shivering. Everyone else seemed to be in the water: a couple of older guys and a smattering of too-pretty college-age girls. An enormously fat woman in a cherry-red ski jacket and a bathing-suit bottom sat dangling her feet in the deep end, reading a Danielle Steele paperback.

Cookie narrowed her eyes and shook her head at Gunther. Through clenched teeth she said, 'I need to know how you did it. How did you make me see the Grid?'

'Trade secret. Does it matter? The Grid is inside you. It's yours. You don't even need me. But I need you. Doesn't that make you feel powerful?'

'Shut up. Shut up. I have to think.'

She pressed her index fingers furiously against her temples. She could feel her brain all stoppered up, clogged with half-formed and possibly stupid ideas.

'Gunther. The Grid is not just inside me. I keep telling you. It's real it's real it's real. And it wants to become realer. It wants to come here.'

'O-*kay* . . .'

'You have some way of doing it. That music you were playing before. What is it? Where did you get it?'

'Why?'

'What?'

'Why? What do you want to know for?'

'Because I have to stop the Grid taking over.'

'Ah! A quest! OK, forget the market research. We'll do a quest. Sounds like fun. I'd love to work with you again, Cookie. I need to know what makes people like you tick.'

'No.'

'What do you mean, "no"? What is this, "just say no to drugs"?' He laughed. 'You know, I'll do it with or without you. We're all archetype-driven anyway. You think brand names and video games have nothing to do with the African savannah. With our point of origin. With our true selves, right? That stuff is all about where civilization went wrong, isn't it? But that's not true. Brands have everything to do with our true selves.'

Cookie arched one eyebrow. 'Speak for yourself.'

'I can speak for all of us on this one. Brand names play into our instinctive archetypes, and all I'm doing in my market work is making those archetypes work for me. When you were flying, you were helping me find the paths back to what the brand names really mean. You were helping to figure out what really makes us tick. When something resonated for *you*, I knew that meant it would work in the market.'

'That made me a well-paid guinea pig,' said Cookie. 'How flattering.'

'No. Because I could have hypnotized anyone, I could have used focus groups, I could have done a bunch of other things. The reason you worked so well is that you tap into something bigger. You call it the Grid.'

'I thought I was doing something noble. But it was the opposite.'

'See, that's where you have it all wrong. Like I said, there's nothing wrong with making use of archetypes, or inherent behaviour patterns, or suggestion, to sell people stuff. Those buttons are there to be pushed. I didn't make them. I mean, hey, you could argue that even *God* is just a brand name. So what's wrong with what I'm doing? I'm exploiting the fact that these touchpoints are embedded inside us, just like a chef exploits the taste receptors in your mouth.'

'But you're not a chef,' Cookie said. 'You're McDonald's. Chefs are artists. You're just somebody who packages things to make them look like something that they aren't.'

'Everybody can afford McDonald's,' said Gunther. 'Chefs are for the elite.'

'Yeah, but you don't have to be rich to cook your own food, and I'd take my mom's cooking over anything at McD's.'

Gunther laughed. 'It's always about food with you, right,

Cookie? OK, OK, let's go back inside. We need to keep this private.'

Everyone watched them as they went back into the house. Cookie couldn't help sneering.

'The Hugh Hefner act would work out a lot better if you moved to a warmer climate,' she said.

'Hugh Hefner? I was thinking more like, I don't know, Salvador Dali.'

Cookie didn't know who that was. She wondered if he was a South American dictator.

Back in the study, as they came in the room Cookie detected a faint music. But after a few seconds she found that she couldn't hear it anymore.

'What's that sound?' she said.

Gunther gestured for her to sit.

'So you want to know what The Process is. I've been working on it for years. What I have here is nothing more and nothing less than the gate to . . . the well, as you would call it. I prefer to call it the Wellspring – it sounds more optimistic, don't you think?'

'It sounds like a soap,' said Cookie.

'Hey, that's good. That's very good. Irish Spring, luck of the Irish, springboard to success, Wellspring . . . you can picture the focus group, can't you?'

'I'd rather not.'

Gunther's brow furrowed in a frown. 'I'm sorry you feel that way, Cookie. I expected you to take an interest in this. The Wellspring Process is something I've plumbed, hah-hah, thanks to all the insights you gave me back at Dataplex.'

'They fired you,' said Cookie. 'See, I thought Machine Front were taking over. I thought you weren't going to need me anymore because you'd have the logic bullets and the Grid would be decoded and you'd be able to make it dance like a puppet on strings. That's what I thought the war was all about. Taming the Grid.'

Gunther cleared his throat.

'It didn't quite work out that way. After you left, my bosses were kind of disappointed when I couldn't generate the code to support my Nielsen's predictions. Their expectations on product-placement algorithms were totally unrealistic, so it was time for me to move on. I had all the data from our experiments, Cookie. From our war.'

And he looked at her intently. Gunther was charming: Cookie had to give him that. You could see it in the body language of everyone as they moved around him. You could feel it in his air: Gunther's satisfaction with himself slid away from his skin like cooties and jumped to everyone around him.

'About the war,' he repeated, and his voice went soft and intense. 'You know why I had to be a double agent. To get the revenue in. To get the support we needed. But now we aren't dependent on anyone. We've achieved escape velocity. We're ballistic. We've launched. *And the only thing missing all this time has been you.*'

Cookie found herself totally unprepared for this. She had expected to find Gunther evasive, maybe defensive, but this self-congratulation was all coming out of left field.

'Cookie, the message is simple. I want to know what it would take to get you back. There's no one like you!'

'That's a Scorpions song,' Cookie said. 'Don't tell me I worked on that, too? The video where they escape from Alcatraz?'

'An unfortunate reference,' said Gunther. 'I'm being as serious as I know how to be. I'm sorry if you felt deceived in the past. The truth is, since you left nothing's been going to plan.'

'And it never will,' Cookie said. 'Gunther, try and picture this. You're selling something that doesn't exist. You're basing your life on a lie. You're so busy convincing people of what you're selling that you almost begin to believe your own bullshit. And then, one day, you find out that in some sense your bullshit really is true. It has a basis in fact. What do you do then?'

Gunther offered Another Winning Smile. 'Which specific thing is actually true, Cookie? What are you saying here? Because, I mean, I believe passionately in everything I teach people. And I believe in our Grid project. You know that. I don't blame you for being angry. I shouldn't have kept some things from you. But it was for your own protection. You were a danger to yourself—'

'Is that really the best you can do, Gunther?' Cookie said. But even as she said it, she knew that he was getting to her. Cookie had never been one of those people who could shrug off what people said about her. It wasn't that she was thin-skinned; it was that she was skinless, and mostly boneless, too – speaking of chicken. She was totally permeable to suggestion.

'If you've had a new insight and you'd like to share it with me, I'd be very happy to hear it. You can always talk to me, Cookie.'

Gunther's voice was pitched low and he was speaking slowly and with perfect enunciation. He was trying to disguise his excitement. But his pulse had quickened; she could see it in his temple. She could see his toes moving inside his tasseled Italian leather shoes, betraying the restless energy of a spectator at a sporting event.

Don't tell him, Cookie, she commanded herself. *Don't tell him about the Synchronicity.*

At the same time, the urge to tell him was becoming stronger and stronger. She could track it in her mind like a physical sensation.

'You hypnotized me,' she accused.

'I'm hypnotizing you right now, Cookie. You're a good subject. You like it.'

'Maybe I should read your script back to you.'

'My script?'

'Yeah. I've got a copy of it right here.'

Cookie smoothed the xerox paper out on her thigh.

'Scientists have recently discovered that there are many dimensions. The universe is composed of tiny vibrating strings, and nested
inside the four dimensions we know are seven more dimensions
folded up in incredibly tiny packages. You are aware of all this. There
are now no limitations to what you can perceive. All time and space
is open to you. And now what I'm about to suggest to you is so powerful I don't know if you can really imagine the changes that you are
capable of. Because your mind can even travel into the limitless
realm of the abstract. You can transcend the physical world and
directly access the secret order of the universe. And you can know
anything you need to know about the past, the present and the
future. You can know next year's hit songs. You can know next
year's top movie. You can know what product will revolutionize
people's lives.

'Your mind is a supercomputer of unlimited power. The universe is
just a state of mind, and your mind is a reflection of the universe. Your
mind can transcend the eleven dimensions and see them all at the
same time. Your mind can penetrate the hidden patterns of reality. You
will build image patterns to hold all the new information that your
subconscious is collecting and ordering, every day, all day, as you go
about your ordinary business. These image patterns will be available
to you whenever you are working, and they will evolve as you evolve,
into the next wave of human enlightenment. You will become unconsciously conscious, and consciously unconscious. You will channel the
collective unconscious through your visions and dreams.

'What I am telling you now will become invisible in your memory
after you awaken from this state. You know that you are working for
the greater good of mankind. Your mind will act as a template, so that
all your powers can be computerized and offered to all humanity, and
everyone will become like you. You are the first pioneer. You are the
new wave of human being. You will understand this information on
a subconscious level, without knowing how you know what you
know. Everything we have done here today will lie dormant in your

subconscious mind until it is needed, and then it will be produced on
an instinctive level to aid you in your quest.

   '*I am now about to offer you a suggestion which is for your bene-*
fit. You will follow my suggestions, which are designed personally to
assist you in everything you do and will harmonize with all human-
ity. You will keep quiet about the Project. The success of all our efforts
depends on secrecy. We truly will be able to decode the hidden logic of
human beings provided we are allowed to operate undetected, like a
naturalist studying animals in the wild. We will contain our true
purposes and protect our interests from outsiders. We will even speak
with one another in a way that is guarded and safe. In doing so we
protect the integrity of the Project and guarantee its ultimate success
as well as our own enlightenment and continued well-being.'

   Cookie paused. 'There's more,' she said. 'Shall I go on, or do
we have the gist of it?'

   Gunther rubbed the back of his neck, blushing. 'Did I really
write that? It's not bad, is it? I wonder—'

   'Gunther! We've got big problems here. All that stuff about
accessing the limitless realms of the abstract? And all that
wartime lingo about targets and strategic objectives and bullets
and moving units and all of it? And the map is not the territory?
Well, what if the map *is* the territory, Gunther? What if someone
we know took the map and *actualized* it into the territory? What
if someone we know *mobilized* her *resources* and took the *initia-*
tive and *made her dreams real*? Gunther? What *if*? Goddamnit?'

   Gunther's laugh sounded muffled and sheeplike.

   Cookie said, 'See, here's my theory. Somewhere, even within
all the commercial BS that we take in every day, there are unin-
tended truths. Subtexts that are unconscious, maybe even alien
to us, but using us to come into being. Stealth thought-worms.
And the commercial success of a show isn't formula, it isn't the
intended message or conscious choices of its creator. The success factor is something else, something that makes the subtexts
replicable. Something that makes everybody want them. And

that something is something Other. Something Grid. And it wants to come through.

'It wants you to find it, Gunther, not so you can capture it but so it can capture you.

'It's lying in wait.

'Don't you understand that?

'Sometimes when I watch TV I can see the other world.

'It's bound to our world but it's different. Totally different. The logic's a force-fit. When you try to marry the two you get a nonsense. Except in her.

'Except in her, in Cassidy, and where is she? Where can I find her? And what will I find *in* her?'

'Aha,' said Gunther. 'Who is Cassidy, may I ask?'

And he let rip a very big smile.

A Hill of Beans About Samsara

The music seemed to be ever so slightly more noticeable. It was elusive, like the imaginary tunes you could hear within white noise between stations: you'd swear it was Mick Jagger singing 'Satisfaction' and then in a heartbeat you'd realize that it was actually Donna Summer's 'She Works Hard for the Money', but in truth it was nothing but noise. Cookie knew she should stop up her ears somehow, but she was trying to play it cool. Trying to pretend she was in control. That simple fact was probably the source of her whole problem in life, she thought glumly. That, and not being able to stop eating the whole carton of Häagen-Dazs in one go.

'Never mind about Cassidy,' Cookie snapped. 'You want me to work with you? First I have to satisfy myself that you can and will answer my questions.'

'I can see that being in prison has made you more assertive – oh, I'm sorry. Did that sound patronizing? Honestly, I didn't mean it that way. I just have to get used to the new you. Go ahead, ask me anything.'

'What *is* this *Process*, anyway? How did you arrive at this Wellspring thingy?'

Gunther smirked. 'You wouldn't believe me if I told you.'

'Try me.'

'You probably think I know somebody at Caltech who does research on sound and the brain, or that I've encoded some kind of formula in a melody, or that it's all about frequencies that vibrate in synchrony with certain cells in the brain. Right?'

'Is it?'

'No! I went to a guy in Chicago who does soundtracks for video games and corporate presentations. I hired him to write something that would sound really high-tech and cool for the induction part of my work. I think he did a really good job, don't you?'

'But . . . ?'

'I know it's hard to take,' said Gunther in a consoling tone, nodding like a wise grandfather in a lemonade commercial. 'See, it's the meaning of no meaning. It's all suggestions. Very Zen. Zen and the art of selling stuff. Maybe I'll write another book.'

He laughed again. He said, 'Don't you have to just surrender to that? I mean, it's cool, isn't it? The emptiness of it all. You just have to give in.'

'So you're saying this induction music, it's pure fluff.'

'Cookie, I'm starting to believe that pure fluff rules the world. Now, all I do is pipe the Wellspring soundtrack into one ear and the video soundtrack into the other, show you the visual, and *voilà*! You're off. You're off into the infinite dimensions within your own navel.'

'If we're talking about events in an abstract realm, then it really doesn't matter whether the phenomenon is legitimate or not. The brain can't distinguish truth from fiction. If you are suggestible and somebody feeds you a line of nonsense, your mind will take it up as real and make it real. It's like carbon monoxide. Your body can't tell the difference between CO and oxygen, and that's how people get poisoned.'

So the Wellspring Process, even if it was pure bullshit, was legitimate as far as its effect on Cookie was concerned. That was what Nina had meant.

Cookie said, 'The one thing that makes you really dangerous, Gunther, is your pig ignorance. You really think you're going to get away with all this, and it won't really matter, and you'll drive off in your Audi and everything will be fine. Well, you won't. I won't let you.'

'But it isn't anything, Cookie – don't you get it? The Wellspring Process is a placebo. It's not real. The whole effect is in your mind.'

'In the Synchronicity, in the Grid, there's no damned difference. You've set something in motion and it's out of your control now. Your placebo? I think it's actualized itself. It may have started out as a placebo but now it's an archetype. I've made it real, goddamn me, I've made it real by believing in it and now it's here and we've got to get it back where it belongs.'

'No, you're just being fanciful, Cookie. I'm really close to something here. I can feel it.'

'Yeah, you're close, all right,' Cookie muttered.

'If I can get to the bottom of this thing you call the Grid, I can use it. What a breakthrough! And you can help me.'

'You don't get it, Gunther. You want a breakthrough? How's this? The Grid is coming here. It's already *breaking through*. I've seen things, done things, and I can't undo them. The only chance I've got is to find this MFeel I brought through and try to bring it back where it came from.'

'OK,' he said equably, folding his hands. 'We can work on it together.'

'*No, we can't*. I need that tape, Gunther. I don't care if it's fake or a placebo or whatever, I need it.'

'So that's good, see, we've got some basis for negotiation here and I'm sure we can work something out.'

'Gunther! When are you going to wake up? Do I have to take you there? Do I have to show you?'

His eyebrows went up, whether in real or mock surprise Cookie honestly couldn't tell.

'Really? You could do that?'

'If you have the guts to use this Process of yours.'

Gunther shrugged. She could see him thinking: *It's all garbage, it can't hurt me, it's all in Cookie's head.*

'All right. I'll try it. You show me what you need to show me.'

He was very careful not to sound too condescending. He was good that way. He'd fooled her for a long time.

Cookie said, 'By the way, Gunther, did you notice my car pull up outside?'

'No, but—'

'That's because I actually walked here through my TV.'

'Hey, who needs Greyhound?' Gunther quipped.

'I have access to the Grid anytime I want. It's not the same Grid it used to be, not since you and your computers started messing with it. Not since . . .' She almost said, *Not since Cassidy and her other iterations started investing it with consciousness*, but checked herself. '. . . I started taking control.'

Gunther's eyes sparkled.

'You know, seeing you so *in control* is really awesome, Cookie—'

'Can it,' Cookie snapped. 'I can go there anytime I want, and today I'm going to take you with me. I want you to see it with your own eyes. Hear it with your own ears . . . or should I say, h-e-r-e it, Michael Borland?'

A genial shrug. 'OK. How's this going to work?'

'*You* put on the headphones. *You* watch the video.'

'What video?'

'Any one you like. But not here. I don't like this room.' Cookie just knew that whatever that subliminal music was, it wasn't doing her no good.

'OK. There's a TV in the kitchen, above the microwave . . . but it isn't very private,' Gunther said.

'Doesn't matter.' There was actually *swagger* in Cookie's voice. She followed him to the kitchen. Through the open window she could hear 'You Can Call Me Al' playing poolside. A chill wind blew in, but steam was coming off the water.

'OK, I'm going to put in the most recent footage we're working with. We'll wear these headphones. I've got an extra pair somewhere . . . here you go. We'll be totally in sync with each other.'

'I don't need them,' said Cookie.

'Are you afraid I'll take over?'

She took the headphones and put them on. She still cared what Gunther thought of her.

The Wellspring Process music came creeping in.

It was pretty neat watching the Synchronicity grab ahold of somebody else. The screen of Gunther's TV opened like a flower and Cookie watched him step through it into leafy darkness.

'Oh my God . . .' Gunther stopped in his tracks, looking around in what Cookie felt was exaggerated surprise. She *had* warned him. She followed, slipping off her own headphones as a precaution against monkey business.

'Tell me where we are,' Cookie said. 'What is this place?'

She could see it as well as he could, but she relished the feeling of being in control.

'The woods. Night. It's chilly – aren't you cold? I can hear music . . . I think it's music . . . coming from over . . . there!'

Gunther pointed. It was hard to tell the expression on his face because there was very little light; some of what there was came from a series of orange lampposts that lined the dirt road they were standing on. Some came from the lit windows of the big wooden building behind them. Ahead, through the trees, where the sound originated, there was a small, squat house. The sound that emanated from its walls seemed to shimmer and shake the air. Yet it was very faint.

'That sign says "Woods Studio",' said Gunther. '"Photo-graphy and Sculpture." What is this place?'

'What's with that music?' Cookie asked. 'Go and check it out.'

Gunther started walking through the dry leaves, but after a minute he stumbled and, cursing, came to a halt.

'What the hell is this?'

He sounded freaked out.

'It's a miniature city. It looks like a diorama. I . . . wait, I think I've got gum on my shoe . . .'

A feeling of warning came over Cookie. The sound coming from the house in the woods was clearer now. It was a groping, uncertain sound. It wasn't random, but it wasn't exactly con-trolled, either. There was a lot of twanging, purposeless bass – that was the part that carried across the night air, anyway. In the windows of the little house she could see the silhouettes of people, moving.

Gunther examined the bottom of his shoe. Cookie looked at the dark mass around his feet and saw tendrils of Grid begin-ning to creep out of the shadows, pretty and menacing, like animate tinsel . . . she began to back up. From the photography studio behind Cookie came the sound of a phone ringing. It seemed to get progressively louder.

'Don't worry about that,' said Gunther quickly. She couldn't see his face clearly in the darkness, but there was tension in his posture; he was half-crouched in what she first thought was fear. Then he said,

'Just tell me where you think she is. That music over there – is that her?'

Cookie went cold. He had slipped. There was eagerness in his voice.

He'd tricked her again.

She was not in control.

She was here because he wanted her to be here, and he was looking for Cassidy.

'No!' she cried, and looked around for a way through the Synchronicity, a way out of this . . .

'I think that's enough for today,' said Gunther in a different voice. He shuffled some papers and stapled them. Cookie felt the staple crunch into the paper as if it had bitten her, personally. Her eyes snapped open.

'Don't you dare.'

'What's the matter? I counted you down out of it. You should be *wide awake, refreshed and alert.* Cookie?'

'You're *there*,' said Cookie. 'You're *there*, don't you get it?'

They were still in Gunther's kitchen. He was sitting on the counter, watching her. Barbecue smoke, stale beer and chlorine salted the air. The screen was blue. The phone had stopped ringing and Chi An's voice could be heard greeting the caller on the answering machine.

Gunther had gotten the better of her again.

Cookie grabbed the remote.

'We're both there,' she snarled. 'We're *here.*'

She switched from AV to TV. It was Saturday afternoon, *Wide World of Sports*, Formula One racing.

That was when it happened.

The fourth-position Ferrari came through the side of Gunther's pool shed, went airborne over two deck chairs and snapped a third on landing before plowing through the roses and taking out the pool fence. Gunther fell off the kitchen counter. Outside, women screamed. Cookie was so scared that she clicked to *This Old House* defensively. The car snapped into nonexistence, but the pool fence continued to sag slowly into the ruined hedge. The smell of burning rubber drifted through the screen window.

Gunther came up quivering. 'How did you do that?'

Cookie was fuming. 'You think the Grid is just some way you can get yours without being accountable to anybody. But it isn't.

It's bigger than that. And as far as I can tell, it's real. So how about you stop playing me and hand over that audio track you're using to mess with my head.'

'Wait a minute, wait a minute,' Gunther said, blotting his face. 'This is not the way it works.'

Chi An burst in through the back door, waving her hands and jiggling all over with excitement.

'What's going on?' she cried. 'Josh almost got run over!'

Gunther made placating gestures and went to her. 'We're doing some manifestations,' he said. 'Was it real for you? Was it really real?'

'Shit, yeah,' she answered, her black eyes sparkling with fear. She had gone all stiff, but Gunther just took her arm and steered her back outside.

'Everything's cool. I apologize for alarming you guys. Hey, you know what? If you go in my car in the glove compartment there's some X. Free to anybody who needs it.'

A moment later he came back in.

'Give me that remote.'

Cookie snorted. 'I can live with the idea that I have delusions,' she said. 'But I refuse to be hypnotized by one. So just cut it out with the funny business.'

'Don't be ridiculous, Cookie.' Gunther's voice was shaking. He looked really alarmed. 'Of course I'm not a delusion.'

'It's OK,' Cookie said. 'I don't mind a few delusions. I say, have as many as you can get away with. Life's more fun. But when it comes to you *specifically*? I'm here today to tell you I've had enough of you.'

Gunther coughed. He surreptitiously slid a Maxell XLIIS tape out of the stereo deck and slipped it into a Staples bag. Then he wrung the bag between nervous hands.

'What were you stapling just then? Let me see those notes!'

'It's nothing, it's just some stuff about—'

'About Cassidy? How do you know about her? You couldn't

know about her. I never told you. And this proves that you *aren't real.*'

'Cookie, I'm *not* a delusion. Can you please give me that remote?'

'Victor was a delusion. And he's maybe the most real person I've ever met. But as for you, Gunther, Michael, whatever your name is – think about it: what proof have I got? Dataplex claim not to know who you are. Gloria thinks you're Philip Michael Thomas. So: are you a secret agent, or are you a bullshit artist? Or are you a fig newton of my imagination?'

'Figment,' said Gunther forcefully. 'Figment. Look, the Buddhists think this whole life is just an illusion, they call it samsara—'

'I don't care a hill of beans about samsara. The best thing for my life would be for you to disappear. See, I can deal with the Synchronicity. I got the cash to prove it. Now, maybe the police are going to come along someday and arrest me for holding up liquor stores, but I don't think so. I think the shit is real.'

Cookie liked saying 'shit', probably because she felt like someone else when she said it.

'I don't know what you're talking about. Why would you hold up a liquor store?'

'Gunther. I'm warning you. Get out of my way. Or I'll have no choice but to deal with you. Now, give me that tape or else.'

Gunther slid across the counter and pressed some sort of intercom button. 'Security to the kitchen!' he croaked. 'Now, Cookie, let's keep it reasonable. We're all friends here.'

Cookie could hear herself breathing.

'I don't know why people take me for such a mug,' Cookie snapped. 'Why do they smile at me while they're trying to kill me? And why do they look surprised when I don't smile back?'

And, stupidly in hindsight, Cookie lunged across the kitchen and made a grab for the Staples bag containing the tape that Gunther had removed from the machine. There was a scrabble of hands and arms as Gunther in turn tried to get the remote off her. But he hadn't reckoned on Cookie's anger.

At first was just like with Shihan Norman, only Gunther fought back harder. Cookie couldn't get the tape, but she managed to head-butt him and then throw him onto the lino, where she jumped on top of him and gained a momentary advantage.

Then things didn't go so good. Gunther did some kind of wrestling reversal, and within thirty seconds Cookie found herself kneeling on the floor with him on her back beating her about the head and shoulders with a pot of hot coffee. It broke, scalding her, and he continued slashing at her with what was left of it. She managed to scramble away from him and flip over at the same time, keeping him away with her feet. Cookie was beyond pissed off.

'Now, Cookie,' Gunther said. 'Let's just cool down and think this one over.'

'Give me the tape and we're finished,' she said. 'Give it to me *now*.'

'You know I can't do that.'

The burns were blindingly painful and he was *still smiling*. Big mistake.

Cookie was sitting on the remote. She got hold of it and zapped through Billy Graham to MTV, where the Mad Hatters bass player was thrashing around to the sound of heavily flanged guitar and gunfire. The video was set in some Asian war – Vietnam? Korea? – and an enemy soldier came after the bass player in slow motion. The soldier reached out of the TV and grabbed Gunther by the scruff of the neck. In a flash Cookie saw Gunther, beautifully pixilated in the TV's frame, dressed up as a soldier, his face vacant with disbelief. She zapped again to Channel One and saw Gunther stumble into the dark musical wood they had just left behind, clutching a bayonet that had been stuck in his gut and making gagging noises.

Just then, two guys burst into the kitchen from opposite

directions. One was Jim, wearing only an apron that said *Kiss the Cook, She's German!*, and the other was a fully dressed security guard with a tonfa in his belt. The Dobermans shot past him and sprang at Cookie.

In a panic, Cookie accidentally changed the channel.

'*—my preferred technique with the plastic wood is to use an X-acto knife first just to make sure all the edges are trimmed—*'

She was back to *This Old House* again, and Gunther was gone.

'OK, lady,' said the security guard. 'What's going on here? Where's Michael?'

Cookie switched to MTV and leaped.

Big Mistake

The Mad Hatters video was over and Cookie found herself in the middle of a commercial for some deodorant body spray. She ducked behind a park bench as some skinny fifteen-year-old in a miniskirt came scampering past, scattering flowers and laughing. A blood trail crossed her path, leading across the grass and into the hydrangea bushes. Once the commercial girl had passed and Cookie was sure that she was not in shot, she followed the blood to where it spattered the flowers. When she parted the foliage to look among the bushes, the body-spray reality began to break down to Grid.

The music of the commercial faded to be replaced by a rhythmic cold snapping sound, highly syncopated and dizzying to listen to, its patterns so subtle that they were balanced just this side of random mechanical noise. Cookie couldn't imagine who or what was producing it. Maybe some giant machine. The sound seemed to be coming from all around her at once, even from above and below.

The hydrangeas had dissolved into nothingness. She was holding in her hand a sheaf of papers stained with blood. When she tried to see where she was, filaments of Grid crept around her like a net.

Cookie tried to read the text. Seemed to be some hybrid of a shooting script for a Mad Hatters video and Gunther's notes titled 'Cookie Orbach Wellspring Trance October 14, 1987 2:30 p.m.'. And in her mind's eye she again saw him stapling the notes together as she came out of the Synchronicity. She heard the crunch of the staple and recognized it as no different to the sound that now surrounded her: she was listening to a symphony of manic staplers.

Where was the Wellspring tape? It had to be here somewhere. *Where?*

If she had been in the Synchronicity, the question would have taken her somewhere: the city would have thrown up some physical response. But she was still in an unfixed location, inside the sound itself. And now, above the mechanical noise, there began a high, tuneless wailing. Sounded like a sick bird or a badly played violin.

Cookie shut her eyes.

Darkness. Still the noise of staplers like terrible teeth chattering. Gunther had stapled the papers, and then he had shoved the tape in a Staples bag. So what was with the staple thing?

The Synchronicity is associational . . .

Something was punching through. Quite literally, the world and the Synchronicity were interpenetrating one another. Gunther wasn't here. He and his Staples bag had punched into the solid world at some new point, and now all that was left was sound.

She had to get out of here. This wasn't a place. Unlike the Synchronicity, it didn't even pretend to be a place.

Cookie remembered where she had been just before zapping Gunther. Dark woods. Fallen leaves. Cold.

Try to get back there.

It should be easy. She knew the Synchronicity's ways now. She should be able to step to that place with a thought. She clapped her hands over her ears and shut her eyes and thought herself in the direction of the woods where she'd gone with Gunther.

A white gulf of sound. The beating of wings. The searing backtrail of passage.

She couldn't get there. The sound wouldn't let her in.

The dragon had already been here.

The dragon was coming.

Do you here music?

The dragon, here. NOW.

And Cookie knew that the dragon would always be waiting for her inside this sound. No matter what else it had been doing, always it would turn on its tail and come toward her with open mouth and compound geometric eyes and teeth made of cutting numbers. Just like it was doing now, its sinuous MFeel body pumping in the air with circuits displayed like jewelry and the voices of the swallowed children running up and down its length like flute music—

And as the image of the dragon MFeel came clear, Cookie found her orientation. She was in a blind alley of the Synchronicity and the thing was behind her, unwinding from out of subway steam and bricks. Cookie lurched forward. Stumbled over cardboard boxes and around a dumpster, until she reached the back end of the alley.

Nothingness. The walls ended on either side and after that there was nothing. Before she could check her forward momentum she'd fallen forward into white empty space, a blank paper of sky.

Down, down, into the cold white, with the sound of Serge's daughters all screaming following her until her senses were blasted away and she knew nothing.

There was no landing. Cookie was simply motionless in the cold and the white, and the dragon and the screaming were gone. As her surroundings materialized, she realized that she was up to her knees in the snow piled at the bottom of the support stanchion of a ski lift. She was not dressed for the occasion, and the cold took her breath away. The burns on her back were singing to the beat of her pulse.

'Damn it!' she said. 'Damn it, damn it, damn it! I didn't get the friggin' tape.'

Cookie started to walk down the hill. It wasn't very steep, but she wasn't dressed for this, and she was upset, and little kids kept zipping past her, shrieking, and making her feel like a fool. Little kids, like four years old, zooming bandits that streaked downhill while Cookie did all she could not to slide down on her ass.

Halfway down, a ski instructor asked her what she was doing and she said, 'I wiped out, buddy,' in a tone that got rid of him.

'But where are your boots?' he called after her, and she flipped him the bird.

The place turned out to be Sterling Forest ski center. *Sterling Forest*, she thought. Why here? Why did the Synchronicity seem to focus on upstate New York when it dumped her places? Why wasn't she in Finland, or Guam?

Eventually she made her way to the ladies' room, where she soaked paper towels in cold water and patted the burns and carefully picked the glass out of the back of her neck. The cuts opened up again and her clothes were a disaster, what with all the blood and rips.

A toilet flushed and a blonde girl emerged from a stall, perfectly dressed in expensive ski clothes. She glanced at Cookie and then began to wash her hands. Cookie assessed what the other girl was wearing.

'Not my size,' Cookie muttered. 'Too small.'

The girl assiduously didn't look at her.

'It's not even the right time of year,' she said to the mirror.

'It's supposed to be October.' She tried to catch the girl's eye in the mirror. 'Excuse me, can you tell me today's date?'

The girl glanced at Cookie and her heap of bloodstained paper towels. Instantly she withdrew from the sink and backed away without drying her hands. 'Saturday,' she said. 'It's Saturday.'

'Date,' said Cookie. 'Not day of the week. Date.'

The girl shook her head. 'I don't know!' she said, and hastily scurried out of the bathroom.

'Good riddance,' said Cookie.

The snow thing made her uneasy. It was like, you know, old stories where people wandered into Faerie and spent what they thought was a few days, but a hundred years had gone by. It was like in modern stories where one way you knew for sure you'd been in a fantasy world was that, when you got back after many adventures, no time had passed at all.

And it was a little like her old Flying sessions in the Grid. Time playing accordion.

Still, no point in freaking out about it.

Cookie went outside to look for a way back home. First she went to the ski shop and picked out a nice jacket in lavender and cream. Then she remembered she had no money on her. She had no money on her because she had gotten Gunther stabbed and then had fled through the Synchronicity and now here she was.

'I had to do it,' she whispered. She said it to herself over and over. But she couldn't make herself believe it.

She hadn't *had* to do it. But it was done, and she couldn't say she regretted it.

Even though she knew it had been wrong.

In truth, she felt pretty good about it. Actually.

'Can I help you with something?' The sales attendant was very very white. Cookie felt her mouth working. So she was a shoplifter now? Black – probably the only black person here who wasn't an employee – bleeding, hardly built like a skier . . . and no money on her person.

'I need this jacket,' Cookie said. 'I'd offer to pay for it later, but I doubt I can find my way back here. So you'd better call the police.'

Then she bolted. Well, she tried to bolt. Her legs weren't doing her any favors. Luckily the salesgirl didn't come after her. Cookie made it to the parking lot and then realized she had no car and no idea of how to steal one by hot-wiring. So she intercepted a Volvo that was just pulling in to the lot.

'How ya doin', folks? We're really full up today,' Cookie said, leaning down to the driver's window. 'Free valet parking, just get out here and I'll take care of it.'

She helped a family unload their equipment, handed over the price tag that was still on her jacket as if it were a claim ticket, then accepted a dollar tip and drove off in their car.

There was something to be said for hypnotism after all.

In her rearview mirror Cookie saw the guy turn the price tag over. He stopped in his tracks, looking at it. He turned to see where she'd gone with his car, but by then she was already turning onto the main road and peeling off in third gear.

There was plenty of gas. Cookie was scared to go home. She had to talk to Miles. He would know what to do. She found her way out to 17 and then picked up the Thruway north.

Cookie knew where Miles lived, roughly, because she had driven to his house from IBM. She had crossed the Kingston-Rhinebeck bridge and taken 199 into Red Hook, then north on Route 9 to the house he shared with Nina. But when she drove up the Thruway there were no eastbound exits between New Paltz and Albany. No signs for the bridge.

She pulled over on the shoulder and rummaged in the glove compartment. Map.

There was no Red Hook. The Hudson River was still there, and the towns on the west side of the river, like Kingston, were still there. But nothing to the east north of Poughkeepsie, until you were halfway to Albany.

This was not the world that Cookie knew. Whole chunks of the Dutchess County map were missing. Miles's house – the whole town that Miles's house had been in – just wasn't here. And from the look of the landscape, it couldn't be October. The trees were gray and naked. Dirty snow lay everywhere, plowed snowbanks with their truck-exhaust mustaches.

Cookie turned off at Kingston and asked directions to IBM. She had no trouble finding the compound, but there was a different guy on security duty. He wouldn't let her in and he said Miles Siebel wasn't on the phone list of employees.

'Where's Les today?' asked Cookie, smiling, hoping to get the guy to lower his guard a little.

'Who's Les?' he said irritably, and she knew something bad was happening.

'This is totally uncool,' Cookie said to the rearview mirror as she backed out of IBM. Her back was itching like crazy. She kept reaching over her shoulder to try to scratch at the peeling skin, but it was hard to get her arm right to the middle of her back.

What had happened to November, anyway? And what had happened to Miles?

It was as if the Synchronicity was invading the world, and at the same time pieces of the world were disappearing – did that mean they were going into the Synchronicity?

Only one way to find out.

If she'd had any money, she'd have gone to a motel. But she didn't even have enough gas to get home on in the tank, and she didn't want to risk getting caught with a stolen car. So she parked the Volvo on a suburban street outside a house that looked as likely as any. There was no garage, no car in the driveway, and no lights were on. She went around the back and knocked on the storm door. No dogs, either. She'd had enough of dogs for one day.

She put a rock through a window. When she got in she checked the whole house out to make sure that nobody was there.

Cookie wrote a note:

To the occupant: I'm really sorry about breaking your window. I didn't steal anything. I've left a car outside. You can keep it, or turn it in to the police. It's stolen. Thank you.

Cookie.

She left this on the kitchen table, and then sat down in front of the TV.

The Synchronicity is associational, she reminded herself. If she was going to find the Process tape, she was going to have to do it by some lateral association – not by a straightforward map.

Gunther had disappeared with the tape into a music video.

So that was where she would start looking.

Cookie picked up the remote, took a deep breath, said:

'I want my MTV.'

part three
rendition

January 1988

Red Hook

Foul Play

Jeremy answered my knock on the door of the House. He'd grown a full beard and it made him look like a Talmudic scholar. In keeping with this part, he took a long look at me without saying anything. At length he stood aside so I could come in.

The House was freezing – no wonder he needed the beard – and smelled strongly of stale pot. We went into the kitchen, where Anitra hugged me. They had rigged a camp stove. Anitra was making an omelette.

'Look,' she said, pointing with her spatula. 'We got chickens.'

There was a henhouse in the back, chicken wire, a dog lying wearily in a house made of cut-up old tires.

Jeremy was still watching me.

'You've been across, haven't you?' he said.

I nodded. I told them the gist of it, adding, 'I think the whole thing started at Bard. They are the most fucked-up there, and the place seems to be in a state of flux. People disappear and don't come back. I don't know where they go, because when I tried to take someone out he popped back in through at the other side.'

'Never mind that,' said Jeremy. 'What about the real world?'

'Red Hook doesn't exist,' I said. 'We never did. The maps have closed up around us like a wound. The edges have knit together. If I tried to tell people, they'd think I was crazy.'

Jeremy shook his head. 'But that can't be possible. We're still on a planet. We're still orbiting the sun. There has to be a way to show physical proof that we exist. What? Why are you looking at me like that? You don't even look like you want to try.'

I said, 'Tell me what's been happening here.'

Jeremy drew a long breath. As always, he was happiest when lecturing. He gave me all the news, liberally sprinkled with his own interpretations. He talked about all the things that were now worthless: books, tapes, records, electronic equipment, domestic animals. Instead, everybody wanted axe blades. Greenhouse glass. Seeds. Rifle ammo. Soap products.

'Next door they're having pray-a-thons. Every so often one of them comes over here and tries to convert us. We talk Bible. They brought a nice fruitcake last time, didn't they, An?'

Anitra nodded. 'Yeah, it was a good tactic. We let them in because of the fruitcake. I've started doing it with the Antiques guys. Bring them some food, try to win their trust.'

'You're wasting your time,' Jeremy said, and it was obvious this was an old argument. 'Tom just likes being important in this crisis, or he'd see that Alvin's at a dead end. I'm the only one who's really thinking about long-term solutions.'

I glanced at Anitra to see whether she agreed, but she didn't say anything.

'What are you guys doing for supplies?' I said.

'Dealing,' said Jeremy. 'Big demand for product. I'm using the whole upstairs. Put in a skylight and a little woodstove to keep the seedlings happy. We'll be OK.'

I must not have looked convinced, because he got all defensive.

'If you can walk in and out,' Jeremy challenged, 'why'd you come back? Why are you here, anyway? If you're so smart?'

I didn't answer. But he persisted.

'Cassidy, answer my question!'

'I don't have to answer shit,' I said. Then I went into the back yard to meet the dog.

When neither of them was paying attention, I found my stuff. It was mostly untouched. I got the Wellspring Process tape out of my boot, together with my other session tapes and the Walkman itself. While we were putting 'dinner' together I tried to find out where I'd have the best chance of getting portable supplies to bring back to Bard, but I didn't want to ask questions outright because nobody believed in Bard and I didn't want them to know I was planning to go back there. Anyway, the supply situation didn't sound good. Nothing worth having had been left lying around. Everything was rationed by Sweeney or one of his associates. I wondered if I should risk going back to Lake Katrine via the bridge to get stuff instead. But every time I crossed the barrier, I had to worry about IT.

'And what about . . . the explosions, and stuff? Any more developments there?'

Anitra looked at Jeremy. Jeremy looked at the ceiling.

'I find it hard to say this with a straight face,' he said. 'But you know that kid you used to work with up at the horse place? He was down here the other night looking for you again. No one knew where you were.'

'I did what you wanted, remember?' I said. 'You wanted me to cross, and I did. So maybe you could lay off the guilt trip.'

Anitra started humming 'Bishop in a Tutu' while she mixed dog food and water in a plastic bowl.

'I'm only saying. The kid shows up and he says there are monsters in the hay barn and he thinks you have something to do with it.'

I didn't say anything. Still humming, Anitra went outside with the dog food. Jeremy watched me. I stared right back at him.

'Do you want to know *why* he thinks you have something to do with these monsters?'

'No,' I said. 'I'm not interested.'

That wasn't going to stop Jeremy from telling me.

'He says – get this – he says when they open their mouths, he can hear your voice singing.'

I said, 'Ray is fifteen. Ray is weird. Forget Ray.'

We locked stares again and this time after a second Jeremy shrugged and laughed.

'Well, that's what I thought. I gave him some free weed and told him that whatever he's using, it's too strong for him. He started kicking things and cursing me out, and then he left.'

Anitra came in, rubbing her arms for warmth and stamping her feet up and down.

'OK, the dog's fed,' she said. 'Let me just break out the caviar and then we'll move on to the chateaubriand.'

I stayed at the House that night. It felt empty without Tom. The residents seemed to be into 'sampling the product' which meant that the scene was laid-back, there was a lot of talk about nothing, and when the munchies struck there was nothing to raid but popcorn dusted with cumin. I did manage to find out that Jeremy had a scooter with some fuel in it hidden out back under a tarp, and in the morning I told him I'd take it to Poughkeepsie to get supplies from 'outside'. He was suspicious, but he didn't have much choice – it had been his idea to use me as a runner between worlds. He let me take the scooter.

I only headed south a short ways. Then I cut back through side streets until I was going north again, toward Moonshadow Farm in Livingston.

*

'Your friend, that black guy? He was looking for you.' Ray's filthy hair was jammed under a ski hat, and the shavings fork he was leaning on had several broken tines.

'Which one?' I hoped he didn't mean Chester.

'He talked real strange. Not like a regular black guy. Like somebody from Channel 13.'

'Oh, Tom. What did he say?'

Ray shrugged. 'Just looking for you, that's all. I said I didn't know where you was. That was like weeks ago.'

There was a bleak look on his face.

'You were afraid this would last a long time,' he added. 'I didn't believe you. Where you been?'

'Around. Hey, so what's this I hear about monsters?' I tried to keep a laugh in my voice.

'Oh, them. In the hay barn. I ain't been up there in a week. First there was these floating bubble things, and then they hatched, and now there's baby monsters. I'm like, if their mom comes looking for 'em we're totally fucked. Luckily, so far they didn't go for any of the horses, but they blew up one of the tractors.'

He was not kidding.

'Oh,' I said after a while.

'And I could hear your voice, Cassidy. I could swear it was your voice. First time I went in there, when it was still just eggs, I thought I heard you calling. But it wasn't you. It was them.'

I'd long since gotten used to the idea that I was the only one who could see and hear various things associated with IT. So to hear Ray of all people talking so matter-of-factly about monsters that had my voice – well, it was totally bizarre.

'Has anyone else seen them?'

Ray shook his head. 'Only my mom. And she told me to stay away from them. I was going to try and get Sweeney out here, but I was afraid that if he saw it was just me and Hannah he'd try to take over.'

'So you're just ignoring them?'

'For now.' He was edgy. There was stuff he wasn't telling me; that was pretty obvious.

'What about Hannah? She paying you?'

'Paying me? With what? Nah, she's still locked in the house. Still waiting for Dominic to come.' Ray snorted. 'Last time I seen her, she was down to dried spaghetti and Cheetos, and she tried to trade me cigarettes for toilet paper but I don't smoke, so I said no. Maybe it was mean of me, but she's Dominic's wife and she should care enough about the horses to come out and give me a hand once in a while, or ask how Whooser's foal is doing.'

'Whooser had her foal?'

He nodded. 'Windswept, but these don't got to be track horses no more, do they? We'll be able to use him for something.'

'We?'

Ray looked at the ground. 'You came back, didn't you? You could have Sally's trailer. I sleep in the barn, on watch.'

I gaped at him. What fifteen-year-old kid puts himself out for animals he doesn't even own, especially at a time like this?

There was no way I was staying here. But Ray shouldn't be taking this shit, either. I went up to Dominic's house and knocked on the screen door.

'Hannah,' I yelled. 'I got toilet paper. Answer the door.'

Hannah's long face appeared in the window, yellow-streaked by the nicotine-stained glass.

'You're lying,' she said. 'Go away.'

I was getting a little pissed off with her attitude and I probably wanted to show off for Ray, so I kicked the door open. It hadn't even been deadbolted, but there was a pile of furniture blocking it so my movie-style push-kick didn't have much effect. I had to give a bunch of big, grunting, leaning shoves to get a wide enough wedge of open door to go in.

Hannah came at me with a cordless curling iron. Her eyes

were bloodshot and her teeth yellow, and she looked even skinnier than usual. I picked up a chair and threw it at her.

'Get upstairs and stay out of the way,' I said. 'We need to use the house.'

'How dare you?' she said, quivering. 'Get out of my house.'

I picked up a riding crop and pointed it at her.

'Either you help us do the work, or you can fuck off and go somewhere else,' I said. She scurried up the stairs and I heard a door slam.

Only after she left did I notice that the TV was on. For a second a shaft of hope stabbed upward in my throat – had she gotten reception somehow? Then I realized *Foul Play* with Goldie Hawn was playing off a video.

I looked at Goldie and felt a pang. It's like with my piece, 'Nuclear Day Dream'. What happens after? The world's blown up and everybody's dead, but there's Goldie Hawn and Dudley Moore and an inflatable sex doll.

I switched off the TV. 'Where's the generator? Basement?'

Ray was standing in the doorway, watching me take a visual inventory of the room.

'Not . . . exactly.'

I tilted my head, questioning.

'OK, but you can't say anything, Cass. Since them dragons came, we got power. Not much. But some. You can hear 'em singing away at night. Well . . .' He looked away. 'Actually, it sounds like *you* singing.'

I whispered, 'Holy fuck,' and then wished I hadn't. Tried to pull myself together while he watched me in that stupid-not-stupid way that Ray has. Then I said:

'You better take me out to the hay barn.'

The door of the barn shrieked when I dragged it back on its hinges, and a cloud of hay dust rose up when I first set foot inside. The nest was up in the loft, just visible from below. I counted eight baby monsters in it. They were each about five feet long, reptilian with bat wings and doggy, intelligent eyes. They stirred awake, emitting blasts of ragged IT-sound so that I had to clap my hands over my ears. The sound made the air crack and part, revealing glimpses of a futuristic city rendered in translucent aquarelle softness beneath.

Ray's eyes were bugged-out.

'Don't go in there, stupid!' he yelled. He grabbed my arm and tried to drag me outside, but I shrugged him off, my hands still covering my ears. Visually, the hay loft was breaking up: I could see glimpses of other worlds like shoebox dioramas from grade school, all slipping and sliding and wavering in the body heat of the little fuckers as they slithered around in their nest, singing.

In the nest there were shards of eggshell, and these acted like curving TV screens. I could see scraps of old TV shows playing away in there, just like Goldie and Chevy on Hannah's TV.

Ray stood in the doorway, waving his arms and yelling at me.

'Are you psycho? Come on!'

I just stood there.

The monsters started coming toward me. They couldn't fly yet. They slithered out of the nest, and one began to creep down a beam that was supporting the loft. They were ugly, their movements halting and quasi-mechanistic.

They stopped singing. The nearest one had almost reached the floor.

It opened its mouth and sang wordlessly in my voice. The rest joined in.

I fled.

Back in Sally's trailer I found a bottle of Hennessey under the sink. After a shot and a half, I stopped shaking.

'OK, Ray, here's the deal. We run the place together. We don't tell anybody what we're doing. We don't show off. We keep the horses away from the road, out of sight. Anybody comes up asking questions, as far as you know all the horses ran off or starved. You're just crashing here for a while. Got it?'

'Where you gonna sleep?'

'Here. You take the house. Don't worry about Hannah; I'll deal with her. Either she can work, or she can get out.'

Ray's eyebrows shot up. The idea of kicking Hannah off her own property had evidently never occurred to him. He was a nice kid. I wondered if I ever had been.

'What is this supposed to be? You taking over or something?'

I shrugged. 'I'm willing to do it. Or do you have a plan you're not telling me about?'

'But you can't keep the horses a secret. How will we get stuff? We got to deal for feed and meds. Maybe not right away, but we'll need more Bute for sure.'

'Leave that to me,' I said.

We decided to take turns on night duty. Northern Darling was due to foal any day now, and someone had to sleep in the next stall in case she got into trouble. On my first night bunking down in the hay, I was a wreck. I didn't know what to do – how would I know if something was going wrong? There was no vet to call, and even if I went and woke Ray up he'd probably be out of his depth. He told me not to worry, that everything was usually fine. He also told me he knew where to shoot humanely, if the worst should happen. Then he made an awkward pass at me.

'Are you nuts?' I said.

'Quit acting all surprised. We're the only ones here. We could die any time. You know? Come on, what's the big deal?'

'The big deal is you gotta be off your rocker. You're fifteen. There's just no way.'

'Oh, thanks a lot,' Ray said. 'You're not exactly Miss America that you can go acting all picky, you know. You don't gotta act like the ice princess and stuff.'

'*Ice princess*? Look, Ray. We're in this together, OK, fair enough. But I'm not into you, not like that. I'm not into anybody right now. Let's just forget it.'

After he left I was annoyed. I was dirty and tired and stiff from working all day, but I couldn't sleep for wondering if Ray was going to be a problem. I listened to Northern rustling around in the next box and fought the strong urge to leave, just go, get up and not come back.

Then I heard a noise out in the aisle. The main door slid open with a squeak. A rake fell over and there was a whispered '*Shit!*'

I got up. I was starting to get sick of Ray.

But it wasn't Ray. It was a pot-bellied guy in work boots and a bomber jacket. I eased out into the shadows of the barn and watched him go to the first stall, opposite the feed room. He took the halter and lead rope off the door and started clucking to the occupant, a gravid chestnut called Tequila Mockingbird.

I slid back into the stall, where the foaling supplies were piled near my 'bed'. Picked up the gun that Ray had shown me and fiddled with the safety. Then I crept out again and made it to the light switch opposite the break room. I flicked the switch.

'Holy shit!' the guy said, jumping about a mile. Tequila kicked the back wall of her stall, startled.

'What the hell do you think you're doing?' I snapped.

'You scared the hell out of me, girl. Don't worry. I'm not here to hurt nobody. I got a trailer just outside. I'm supposed to bring this horse down to Rhinebeck, to her new owner. Dominic tried to contact you to tell you he sold her.'

'Not that one,' I said. 'She's due to drop her foal in February.'

'Aw, that's OK—' he started to say. Then he saw the gun.

'Step outside real easy,' I said, walking toward him. 'My aim isn't too good and I might shoot you in the head by mistake if this thing goes off.'

He put his hands up. 'Hey, whoa,' he laughed. 'Now I'm a friend of Dominic's, and he asked me to help out here, and that's what I'm doing.'

'How nice of you,' I said. 'You selling pregnant mares so people can ride them? That's kind of short-sighted, isn't it? I mean, if you're going to set yourself up in the horse business you should be thinking ahead to the next generation.'

'Well, then, you could be right about that, honey. But she'll be getting the best of care where she's going, I assure you of that.'

I kept the gun raised and I kept walking. I was close enough that I probably would hit him if I fired.

'Honey, you don't want to use that thing. Come on, now.'

I said nothing. *Honey, my ass.*

'I'm not alone here,' he said loudly, and I knew then that he was alone. And stupid.

'You haven't seen Dominic. You probably don't even know him. You're outta here,' I said. '*Now.*'

He lunged at me, grabbed at the gun. I fired. The shot went up into the rafters. The horses screamed and kicked. I kicked at the intruder, aiming for his balls but missing. Behind me, Patriot was rearing up in his stall and trumpeting with that high-pitched ululation only a stallion can make, which should sound ridiculous but in the hindbrain goes down pretty scary if you ask me.

The guy's weight hit me. I smelled alcohol on his breath as he wrested the gun away. The catch of Patriot's stall dug into my back. I reached behind me, fumbled – *ow* – jerked it open and jumped sideways out of the way.

Patriot shot out of the stall, blowing plumes of steam from his nostrils. I saw his brown flanks flash past me as he careered into the aisle. The barn door was closed; nowhere for him to run. The guy had dropped the gun in the dust and now he stood there, knees bent, saying, 'Easy, boy' not very convincingly. He was looking toward the feed room, where I could just make out the lines of a shotgun propped against a barrel of sugar beet.

I threw a bucket at Patriot's butt to spook him a little bit more, and then dove into his empty stall.

'Try riding *him*, asshole,' I yelled.

While Patriot was rocketing up and down the barn I climbed from stall to stall over the tops of the iron dividers until I'd reached the feed room. Patriot was now actively chasing the intruder, and twin plumes of steam came out of his nostrils. His neck arched and his muscles bunched. I dropped down. There was so much dust in the air that I could hardly see. I got hold of the shotgun and aimed it at the guy's legs. The gun kicked back hard against my stomach and I fell over on my ass. The shot hit the dirt in front of the guy; Patriot bolted again and the mares continued to scream. The guy called me a crazy bitch and shoved the barn door open. He ran out into the night. Patriot followed him, still screaming.

I walked up and down the aisles, checking on the mares.

'Sorry about that, ladies,' I said. 'Nothing to get excited about.'

After a while Patriot came wandering back and performed his own inspections. I lured him into his stall with grain before I more or less collapsed in the dirt of the aisle.

I had a little pity-party there, all by myself. I needed someone to talk to. This was all way too personal. Why couldn't I hand it off to somebody else? And why didn't any of it make any sense? The last several months had been like trying to figure out a math problem that was way over my head. Like asking a six-year-old to do algebra.

Not fair.

Not what I had been led to believe the world was.

Boo-hoo.

I reached in my pocket for a tissue to blow my nose and my hand closed on the Bergenfield snow globe.

'Then again, Cassidy,' I said aloud. 'At least we're not in Bergenfield.'

Jesus H. Frick

Before I had time to decide what to do about the dragons, Sweeney showed up in person. He'd heard what I did to the other guy and thought I 'had spunk'. He wanted to 'work with me'.

That meant he wanted horses. Specifically, he wanted a couple of brood mares and a stallion, and he was prepared to haggle.

I wasn't sure how hard to drive him. I knew that if I pushed it too far he would just call in his private militia and take over. He brought a shovel to every meeting and sat there holding it as if to say, *This is the Irish man's weapon of choice, so turn your back on me at your own risk.*

Never mind the fact that he wasn't Irish. He was second-generation American with a Long Island accent. I thought about getting my own shovel but I figured the gun was probably better.

Sweeney's main offer on the table was labor. He could see that Ray and I were going to need help, long-term, to repair fencing and spread muck and make hay and all that shit. But I wasn't planning on staying here that long. And I was uneasy with the idea of having too many people around. Especially

Sweeney's people. What if this 'deal' was just an underhanded way of taking over my operation?

So I decided to let him take Badger for a test drive.

I warned him extensively that Badger liked to run under tree branches.

'There are no tree branches for a mile,' said Sweeney, with a big yellow smile.

'Just so's you know about it,' I said in my best country accent.

Sweeney didn't seem to understand that Badger could cover a mile in a couple of minutes. He didn't seem to know that stallions, apart from being jumpy as shit, can be sadistic bastards who love the idea of hurting their riders.

'Ah, the noble horse,' he said when he saw Badger, who really was a pretty thing.

I suppressed a smile. I'd never yet met a horse who was noble. But that was for me to know and Sweeeney to find out.

The next day, Sweeney's guys came to see me and told me they'd fix the barn roof and bring a load of hay down for me if I could please just keep my mouth shut about what happened.

'He's lucky he wasn't decapitated,' I said.

Badger hadn't bothered to run as far as the nearest tree branch. He'd run under the arm of the telephone company hoist that was parked in the driveway, out of gas and flat-tired. Sweeney's head had hit the thing with an unholy clang.

It had taken me an hour to catch Badger, and he got all randy on the way in. His dangling dick wiggled and danced all the way into the barn, all long and skinny; I thought it was going to hit the ground.

I missed Bard, I missed Bard, I missed Bard.

But I showed Sweeney's guys what to do on the roof and they did it. I watched. My fingers were yellow and felt like little icicles when I pressed them on my face.

'How much hay you need brought down?'

'That's OK, I can do that myself. But can you get me a bottle of Smirnoff's or something?' I said.

Sweeney's guys nodded, and for a moment there we were all brothers.

My body was changing. There were ropy veins in my forearms. I had calluses across my palms at the bases of my fingers. The bottoms of my feet were hard. There was no more padding on my hips or butt. I could see my pelvic bones. Muscles had sprung out in my legs. I felt primitive and strong. There was a sense and order in my own body that I was coming to trust. I was moving from the inside. I was learning to line up my bones and joints when I moved, so that I became stronger even though there was less of me. I was learning to use gravity.

And I'd started seeing out of a place that was deeper behind my eyes, some hindbrainy knowledge always switched on now. I had experienced so many adrenal firings that I came to appreciate the vast gap of one or two seconds between the precipitating event and the release of cortisol that made my blood run hot. That rush usually came late, but better that than never. I learned to think in compressed time.

In practice this meant that in moments of crisis events seemed to slow down. When Patriot startled at a noise and reared, I could see the slow pawing of each of his hooves in the air as a discrete event. I could anticipate where his weight would fall. I was moving before thinking.

And my mind was getting used to being left behind.

My body knew what to do. My mind trotted along afterward, like a reporter with a notepad chasing a moving police car and asking dumb questions, offering cute headlines:

CASSIDY DODGES BULLETS, WATER TROUGH SAVES COLLEGE GIRL'S LIFE

Some idiot hunters had been shooting in the patch of forest adjacent to Moonshadow just as I was out checking the perimeter fence. The water trough did save me, but I still had to bleach the shit out of my pants afterward. I thought I got it all out, but the next morning Barney the yard dog kept sniffing my butt.

DOGGY INTIMACY RUMBLES DIRTY PERSON

I wanted to sit down in a snowdrift and cry, but I could see Hannah watching me from out of her upstairs window, so I went to muck out instead.

And so winter went grinding along. It was all work, which was bad enough. Hannah was getting on Ray's nerves and he kept hinting about us changing places – me in the house, him in the trailer – or, worse, both of us in the trailer. I fantasized about escape. Short of taking a horse and riding, there was no way I could get back to Red Hook to talk to anyone – the snow had blocked the roads and the only vehicle we had was Ray's mother's Geo, which had gotten stuck in the snow up here weeks ago. Ray's mother had come once on a snowmobile, bringing food and kerosene, but she had been our only visitor.

If I rode to Red Hook, it would take me all day. And if I got bucked off in the middle of nowhere . . . well, it wasn't worth the risk.

So I waited it out. I felt like I was holding my breath. Every night the baby dragons sang. I didn't go back to the hay barn. I don't know what I was waiting for. But I couldn't face them.

Ray stopped making passes at me. I noticed he'd assembled a small collection of porn movies that he watched in Hannah's house while the dragons were singing. I didn't ask him where he got them, but I started keeping tabs on him. Some nights he'd take a flashlight and saunter down the road in the direction of Red Hook, and he'd come back carrying stuff. A cardboard box; a black plastic garbage bag; a knapsack.

One night I followed him. This was nerve-racking, because it's impossible to walk silently in the snow and the night was silent and still. No wind, no animals stirring, nothing. I could just about keep his flashlight in sight as I tiptoed along in his footprints.

About a quarter-mile down the road Ray turned off into the deeper snow. There was a patch of woodland to the right of the road, and it was here that hunters had been shooting a little while back, firing the shots that had nearly hit me when I was out checking water troughs in the five-acre field.

A big grey Isuzu Trooper was sitting in the road, up to its wheel arches in snow. The headlights were off but there were lights in the cab and I could see two guys inside. Ray trudged over and they talked. Ray was putting stuff in his empty knapsack. I saw liquor bottles and videotapes and some smaller boxes, might have been food. Ray pointed off into the woods, they talked a little more, and then he started coming back toward me. I had to run to get out of his line of sight.

I was out of breath when I got back to the trailer.

What was Ray up to? I hadn't seen him give the guys in the truck anything in exchange for what they gave him. So what was he dealing in?

The next day I told Ray I was too sick to work, and when he went up to the track to get some of the hay supply stored in the second barn I jogged out to the spot where I'd seen the truck. I followed its tracks offroad and then behind a stand of trees, and there was the truck, wedged against a snowdrift like a ship run aground. Crows were flying in tired circles around it. Some of them sat on the hood with their feathers fluffed up. There was nobody inside. Footprints led away from it across the snowdrift and down into the next field.

Faintly, I could hear IT.

The black of plastic-wrapped circular hay bales stood out against the snow: the baler that had been packaging the hay had been abandoned on the far side of the field and the bales had never been collected. Nearby, I could see stock fence topped with barbed wire. Within the squares of stock fence were embedded many TV screens.

Trickling from the tiny speakers on the TVs, I could hear IT like a Metallica guitar solo coming out of a baby's throat.

I walked closer. I had to stick my fingers in my ears to blot out the sound of IT. Then I saw the two men. They were sitting with their backs to me on a hay bale that they'd swept clear of snow, drinking from a flask and watching the TVs like kids. They were joking with each other, drunken to idiocy. I stayed still, watching.

As far as I could tell, I was looking at a lot of old commercials. Mesmerized, I watched for maybe twenty minutes before I realized that the same commercials were cycling over and over again. I remembered most of them – they weren't recent. I had watched a lot of TV after the *Golden Dragon* incident in 1984 and I recognized these as having been shown at that time. Seeing the old commercials again now, in this context, felt creepy.

'Ah, man, fucking awesome!' roared one man and the other threw his hands up in the air. I couldn't see what had been so great: they were watching a commercial for control-top pantyhose.

They punched at each other and passed the flask. As they did so, one of them turned his head, spotted me, and startled violently.

'Jesus H. Frick!' he yelled. 'Where'd you come from?'

'Sorry,' I said, trying to sound nonchalant. 'I found your truck. Are you guys OK?'

They looked at me like I was nuts. I guess they had a point. Like, what was I going to do if they weren't? Offer to bake cookies?

'Yeah, we're OK. How 'bout you?'

Snickers.

'Is there a reason why you guys are sitting around out here drunk off your asses?' I asked.

'You got eyes,' said Frick. 'TV! Movies! Anything you want to watch, it's here. It's fantastic. Hey, you pay to get in or are you crashing?'

'I paid,' I said hastily.

'I don't know, Jerr,' said Frick. 'You think she's telling the truth?'

I looked at Jerr. I had had to take my fingers out of my ears, and the sound of IT was becoming more and more uncomfortable. I shifted from foot to foot. I probably didn't look especially credible.

Jerr said, 'Ray told us about these here TVs. And about the hunting. How the animals, they kinda just show up.'

'Yeah, they jump in your lap,' said Frick. He pointed at the ground with his bottle. 'Right here. They just show up, and they're confused, and they don't know where to run. Easy to shoot 'em, that way.'

'Oh,' I said. I was trying to take it in. I was trying to figure it out. 'So, um . . . whatcha watching?'

'New Mel Gibson movie,' Jerr said, jerking his head toward the screen. 'Want a beer?'

'Uh . . .'

I was finding it impossible to think. ITsound was winding ITs way around my spinal cord and creeping into my brain. IT was gobbling my eyes. The commercials bleached to white.

I was aware that I could no longer see the commercials on the screens. I knew the two guys were staring at me but I couldn't seem to bring myself to respond. It was like being on the verge of passing out. I tried to look away, but I was stuck watching. And listening. As IT came closer. Then, inside all the TVs, I could see different shots of some mad-ass unreal city.

'I think maybe I should go,' I said.

Something was moving among the buildings. Something sinuous. Something flashy. Something like mamadragon, to use Ray's phrasing.

I started trembling all over.

Confusingly, this was nothing like a movie.

The sky was a flat gray, that dead winter color: visual asphyxiation in toneless white. Telephone lines scored the sky. The wind was dull. It was just a slice of a February day, and here I was with two drunken hunters, nose running, shivering, feeling like a rabbit.

Because I could hear IT, and IT was coming out of the TVs.

IT was the agent. IT was compressing the sound; IT was slicing the sound; IT was riding on the sound. And IT was all *the sound*.

Because the one thing that's clear about sound is, that you can't divide it. Sound isn't like image. It hasn't got that kind of integrity to be broken. Sure, in a recording studio you can separate a sound into tracks. And you can chop it digitally and move chunks of it around. But when you do that, the sound becomes something else. All sound happens in the context of time, forward, backward, retroactively self-inflecting: sound is a verb that is always becoming another verb. The life of a sounding is holistic, incident-specific, and subjective. So IT was the sky, the dragon, the city, and the movement of all these things against each other.

'Look out!' I was screaming at the top of my voice, but I couldn't actually hear myself. 'IT's coming! Get down! Get out of ITs way!'

But the two guys just gave me slack are-you-kidding faces, and the last I saw of them they were turning back toward the TVs. Then I was flat on my face in the usual pose, snow in my nostrils and shit in my pants.

Nested Patterns

When the sound died down I stayed right where I was until I was so cold I knew I had to move. I opened my eyes. A bunch of the TVs had shattered, leaving things really messy. The screens were blessedly dark and silent. The hunters lay among a lot of glass shards and blood. Maybe the snow made the blood seem more than it was, but I don't think so. I didn't bother to try checking for a pulse or anything. It was pretty obvious they'd been killed instantly.

I took off my jeans and underpants and wiped my ass in the snow, then put my jeans back on and buried my underpants. I started trying to bury the remains of the hunters, but I had to stop to be sick, and then I started crying, and then I gave up on it. I knelt in the snow crying for a while because I didn't know what else to do. I felt pretty bad. I could hear the melting ice dripping; it drummed against a big hollow log, and when the wind blew there was a tinkling sound as little bits of icicle fell off and hit the ice-covered rocks. I paused in my work, listening, holding still like a child waiting to be tickled. Old habit even made me reach for the Pro Walkman I used to wear on my belt; then I remembered I wasn't composing anymore.

If I ever had been. Surely I'd only ever been doing music to survive. Just like the Open Space group playing to stay in the reality game: it had been that kind of addiction. Addiction to air. Addiction to water. That level of motivation.

Not what you could call art – right?

I remembered Dr P's advice to me, back when we used to trawl unsuccessfully for my drowned memories. He said that I lived too much in my head. He said I spent too much time with my guitar: music was too abstract to get me anywhere.

'Music isn't abstract,' I said.

'Music is the fault line,' he said. 'It's partly abstract and it's partly physical.'

While we were talking Dr P's white Persian cat had a habit of standing on the desk and batting at pencils with a curled paw. This tended to take the intellectual bite out of Dr P's words.

'You should consider taking up something more practical,' he said. I ignored him. I thought he was being a clod. I was still at that stage of my life when I was going out into the woods on moonlit nights looking for fairies, because I'd read in this book called *The Magic of Findhorn* that they really do exist and they're very subtle but they can be perceived if you're tuned in.

Well, I thought. *Here I am in the middle of fuck-all nowhere, two dead hunters, a stalled pickup and not a fairy in sight.*

'That's two points to Dr P,' I said to the frozen trees. Then I went back to the truck. It was in good shape. It had a shitload of gas in back. I could use it. Or bring it back to Alvin for masses of brownie points. I got a can of carburetor spray out of the back and opened the hood. I was going to have to get this fucking engine started, or else.

It was a good truck, and it roared to life after a couple shots of spray. The guys had left a thermos with coffee that was still warm. They had maps, they had emergency rations. They had blankets and a first-aid kit. Everything was neat and efficient. They had a dead deer in the back too. The dead deer comes as standard in a pickup this time of year. Hunters.

Guys like this could come in handy in a tight spot. But the truck was better.

It was nearly dark by the time I stormed into the main barn, where Ray was shaking out fresh straw into the foaling box.

'I thought you were sick.'

'What the fuck are you up to?' I shouted. 'You knew about those TVs. Just like you knew about the power. What were you doing, selling tickets?'

He didn't actually hang his head, but he got all shifty.

'Why not? How else are we gonna get by?'

'Who else knows about it?'

'Nobody! Well, hardly anybody. I can't help it if people talk.'

'Oh, fucking shit . . .'

I kicked the bottom of the stall and spooked Tequila.

'Sorry,' I said to her rolling white eyes. 'Ray, just tell me what you know. How did you find the TVs? How long have they been there? Have you seen the city?'

'City?'

'Just tell me what you know.'

'I found them when the monsters started hatching. There was something down there, some kind of really loud noise, and when I went to check it out I found the TVs. No big deal. All's they show is movies. People bring me their videotapes and I play them on Hannah's TV when the monsters is making the juice.'

'Why don't you just go out there and watch the TVs yourself? Why do you have to involve other people?'

'Because I can get more stuff if I trade. I can only watch so much TV. But people bring me useful stuff. You didn't complain the other day when I gave you those gloves, did you? Well, there you go.'

'And what about the animals?'

'Dunno where they come from, but they do. Maybe it's some

kind of boundary. So I told some friends. So what? They don't know about the electricity.' Ray grinned. 'If they did, they'd all move in. But I don't see as I done nothing wrong. We got to help each other survive. And you can't blame people for wanting to eat.'

'Or be eaten?'

'Huh?'

'The dragons' mama came back,' I said. and I told him how the hunters had died. 'How you feel about that?'

He just stared, slack-jawed. I stomped out of the barn.

'Where you going?'

'For a walk. You do the feeds.'

Ray didn't say anything. I went out into the cold and the dark. It was a chilled-glass night, the moon like the sail of a Phoenician ship billowing in the wind. Blurred, smoky galaxy and pinpoints of dazzling individual stars. I breathed deep and kicked at the snow.

I'd never meant to stay here. The whole thing was a mess. At Bard, were they looking up at this same sky, playing to it – singing for supper or heat or just the integrity of what little reality they could contrive to make while clinging to their shaky raft of a world? And in the outside world, could they even see the sky I could see, or was it blotted by groundlight and pollution?

Did it matter?

Not as far as what I had to do was concerned, it didn't.

I had a handgun but I didn't know how to shoot. I went out behind the track and set up some targets out of sight of the road. I'd taught myself to type and I figured this couldn't be too much different.

It was different. It hurt my ears and my arms and hands. But it was kind of fun, in a nasty nihilistic kind of way. I practiced for about a week.

Then I did it for real.

I got drunk first, thanks to Sweeney's Smirnoff. I waited until I knew Ray was 'busy' watching TV at Hannah's house. Then I went up to the hay barn. What happened was that at first my aim sucked, and I hit a couple of them in the wings and feet, which made them scream like babies and their music got much more complicated and beautiful. I panicked and winced and looked away and looked back. They weren't attacking me. They were writhing around each other, though, in a way that was kind of gross and threatening. Their wings flapped with reflex precision. It was disgusting and at the same time, the way they looked at me as they bled clear fluid over the straw, I felt awful doing it to them. They kept trying to get to me. I had the awful sense that they wanted to communicate with me, but whatever message they were bringing I didn't want to deal with it. In no way were they going to be anything other than monsters to me.

I had to destroy them. I had to. They wanted me but it wasn't mutual.

Halfway through, I wanted to drop the gun and run away.

But I didn't – and that's the bottom line. I saw it through. I whispered, 'Sorry, sorry, sorry' and I shot them in their heads. I stopped to reload. The first one was the hardest. By the time I was killing the last one, I hated it passionately and wanted to get it over with as quickly as I could, because I knew it had witnessed me killing the others and it had soaked up my guilt. I blew multiple holes in its head, shuddering.

They lay there, smoking, their music lingering in the air. They lay in a familial heap. It took a long time for the sound of them to die.

I had never felt so bad. I wanted to tell someone and cry and drink and hide and I wanted my mother.

None of these things were an option.

I wanted to beg someone for forgiveness but who would that be?

I wanted to run away, get so far from that place and never go back. But I made myself look at the bodies. They were real. They didn't vanish, sizzling. They didn't melt into the floor. They were real. They didn't have blood, as such, but they had flesh. They had bones. Their wings were furry on one side. Bugs crawled away from the corpses: parasites abandoning ship.

The desire for consolation was beyond any hunger, any thirst, any pain. I didn't want the world to be about this, but it was. And I was part of it.

When he found out, Ray was pissed off. No more electricity. No more black market in television and movies. I knew that soon he would take the truck I'd recovered and leave. He'd probably go to Sweeney and we'd be taken over, maybe even by the idiot that Patriot and I had chased away. I was sick of playing tough girl. I'd taken the action-hero solution: I'd exterminated the offspring. And so what?

Coming here had been a waste.

When I went back to the trailer I packed some food in my backpack together with the tapes. It would be a long ride across country back to Bard, and I couldn't make up my mind which horse to take. Little Nooky was the most likely choice because she had no foal this year; but I didn't like her much and the feeling was mutual. I wondered if I dared ride Patriot.

Had a bad feeling I was going to end up with a broken collarbone in a snowbank somewhere. But it was either that or move in with Hannah.

The next day Ray was acting somewhat normal, and I wondered whether I'd been right about him selling out to Sweeney. It was what I would have done if I'd been him; but he wasn't acting shifty or defensive, only grumpy. I started feeling guilty about my plans to ride back to Bard and abandon him.

We knocked off early in the afternoon. We were both

whacked with too much work and too much emotion. Ray dragged the stag out of the back of the truck.

'We gotta hang it up,' he said. 'Then we'll get my ma to help us cook it.'

Yep, I was feeling guilty for real now. I walked away while Ray struggled to get the deer out. He managed to hoist it on his back and I watched him stagger across the wet gravel of the yard toward the house. He reminded me of a three-year-old trying on his mother's full-length fur coat. The horns flopped around and stabbed him in the legs. He yelled. I reached down to pet Sneakers.

Ray dumped the stag on the porch and then went out to the barn.

'I'm going to get some rope. We'll do feeds at five,' he called, and disappeared into the gloom.

I started to go back to the trailer to finish packing, but I heard an engine on the road. The sound seemed to come out of nowhere. I turned around and a shining new Hyundai turned along the drive, spinning its wheels in the snow. A big black woman got out and trudged toward me. She was dressed in a fuschia polyester pants suit topped by a puffy metallic purple ski jacket. Instead of saying 'Hi' she pointed at the dead hunters' truck.

'Whose truck is that?'

'Who wants to know?' I thought I sounded impressively local. There was no need for this woman to know I'd come from Bard.

'My name's Karen Orbach. I drove up from Jersey this morning.' She seemed to be groping for words. She looked down at her feet and I noticed she was wearing riding boots. 'I'm . . . uh . . . looking for a horse.'

I squinted and cocked my head. I'd picked up the posture from watching Sally, and it made me feel Country.

'You got a car. What you need a horse for?'

'That's my business.'

'See,' I said, 'these here horses are valuable. With the gas running out, they're the only way people are going to be able to get around. Tell you what. I'll sell you the truck, you want it.'

'I don't want the truck. But I've seen it before.'

I shrugged. 'Yeah?'

'On TV,' she said. 'I saw those two guys get killed, too.'

I staggered back a step. Karen Orbach advanced on me. She was staring at my hands. People do that, but they aren't usually so brazen about it. I shoved them in my pockets and stared right back. She looked inordinately clean. I could smell her shampoo from where I stood. I think it was Breck.

'What's your name?'

'Sally,' I said. I couldn't explain why, but I didn't want to tell her my real name. And I didn't want to act like the real me. 'Sally Travis.'

'Hmm,' she said. She was looking at me in a placid, dull way. I thought that probably she wasn't too bright.

'Well,' I said. 'Sorry we couldn't help you.'

'Aren't you interested in how I got here from Jersey?' Karen Orbach said.

I shrugged again. 'Not really.'

Again the flat turtle-like gaze.

'You have got to be kidding me,' she said in a scathing black-woman tone. 'I drive up in a clean, brand new car in the snow with a tank full of gas – you know what? That car's a Sonata. It's not even available for sale in this country yet. Name mean anything to you? *Sonata?*'

'Nope,' I said. 'But I guess you got chains on your tires. Must be some fancy car to go that good in the snow.'

'Oh, come on. Look down the road. You won't see tire tracks.'

I met her insistent gaze. My John Wayne act wasn't working. I tried harder. Tried to stare her down.

'I'm not interested,' I said. Actually, I was terrified. 'What's your car got to do with me?'

She held my stare a little longer. She shook her head slowly from side to side.

'OK,' she said. 'If that's the way you feel about it.' And she turned to go. I felt hot and cold at once.

Ray came to the barn door and shouted, 'Cassidy! Whooser's lame!'

Halfway across the drive, Karen Orbach turned slowly. She smiled at me and I felt like a mouse that has just been dropped in a box with a corn snake.

'I think I'll just wait for you in the barn, *Cassidy*,' she said.

My heart did a nasty little samba.

'No, you won't,' I said. 'I think you should go now.'

Karen softened. She looked at me like I was a scared kid.

'Don't be mad. I knew it was you all along. I recognized you by your hands. I didn't even really drive here. I got here through music – even the car – it's all associational. I only just punched through down there . . .' She pointed down the hill toward the trees where the hunters had died. I don't know what my face looked like, but she made a placating gesture when she read my expression. 'Don't worry, I'm not here to mess you up. I'm not going to *make* you do *anything*. This is my quest. It's my problem.'

'What quest? What are you talking about?'

'I'm looking for something that . . . got lost. I wasn't expecting to find you. I wasn't sure you were real – I mean, I just didn't expect to run into you like this.'

I frowned. 'I thought you said you wanted a horse.'

'I just said that to get you to talk to me. See, it's an awkward situation.'

'You're pulling my cunt,' I said.

Karen's eyes narrowed a little as she considered the topological improbability of that. I found a cherry Lifesaver in my pocket and popped it in my mouth. It was a little fuzzy and I had to resist the urge to spit it right back out again. Then I reached up and wiped nose dribble from my upper lip. I kicked a rock. I tried to think like Ray.

'Look,' she said in a different tone. 'Is there any way we could talk about this inside?'

What the fuck.

Who Isn't A Fiction

We went back to Sally's trailer and opened up a bottle of Hennessey. It was the middle of the afternoon, but I got that feeling of warning you get when you step outside on a really cold night in boxer shorts and fluffy slippers to call the cat, that inner warning that reminds you to make damn sure you don't let the storm door lock behind you because everybody inside has their ears full of Sonic Youth and they'll never hear you beating on the door to get in and you could theoretically freeze to death because of it. Of course, I ignored it.

Karen sat on the bed and I sat on the counter next to the sink holding a box of Ritz crackers between my knees. I offered them to her but she said she was on Jenny Craig. Then she told me to call her Cookie.

She swirled her drink in the big plastic party cup I'd given her. She said, 'I guess you figure you know everything. Or you're the only one who knows anything.'

'So far?' I said, and I heard the petulant rise in my voice at the end of every phrase. 'This whole situation? Has been, like? A bad joke? And I haven't met anybody who can begin to explain it to me. People? Have been *kind of a major letdown for me.*'

I was a little surprised at myself. Cookie's bulk sitting on my bed breathing quietly had a way of resonating back to me my own defensiveness, my childishness, my entrenched thinking. I didn't like the way I sounded. But she was nodding understanding.

'I'll tell you what I know,' she said. 'If you don't like it you can pretend we just got drunk and said stupid things to each other.'

And then she started telling me her story. All about the abstract realm and how when she watched TV she could see it in the form of this entity called the Grid.

How the scientists and marketing people and other intellectuals thought they were getting a grip on it, getting rational control of the underlying structure of reality.

But how the truth was actually the other way around.

How the abstract realm was invading the material world by manipulating people's behavior. She talked about the unknown and unknowable nature of its intelligence, if there was such a thing as an abstract intelligence.

About a guy called Gunther who had probably been just a delusion, possibly a puppet of the Grid, and about her superpower, and a lot of other stuff.

Cookie told me that she didn't see the Grid anymore as such, that the efforts of the intellectual colonists had transformed the wild Grid into a living city, a world of numbers and books and ideas that she called the Synchronicity.

How she had learned to walk into this city and out again, which had enabled her to track the dragon across the boundaries created in the wake of ITs passage through material reality.

I drank more when she talked about this city because she was describing something that I'd already glimpsed. I ended up fighting back nausea, because I don't hold my alcohol well.

Finally Cookie finished. She watched me.

'OK,' I said. 'OK, I think I get it. But I wish you hadn't told me. Because now I have to ask you something, and I'm afraid of what you're going to say.'

'You're going to ask me what it all has to do with you.'

I nodded. I fought the fairly strong urge to run out into the wind.

'Maybe,' Cookie said, 'you already have some idea about that.'

I looked at my hands. Now I knew why she had stared. There had been a band of weird girls in her story and they all had six fingers. And one of them had been nicknamed Cassidy.

'IT just passed through here yesterday,' I said. 'I thought maybe you came because of what I did to the . . . offspring.'

I'd almost said 'babies' but at the last minute my lips turned aside from the word like a horse refusing a jump. I took a swig of Hennessey and shuddered.

'Offspring? It has *offspring*?' There was a hard laugh on the edge of her voice that said, *Don't let this be what I think it's gonna be.*

'Not anymore it doesn't,' I slurred. The room was moving pleasantly. It was nice not to be responsible. I wanted to stay here forever.

'What?' Cookie flew at me. The whole trailer shook from the weight transference. She leaned across the counter. 'How many were they?'

'Eight.'

She was spitting on me, her breath hot with whisky. 'And you *killed* them?'

'Whoa, hey,' I said, jumping off the counter and raising the bottle defensively. 'You can calm down now.'

Cookie stopped dead, her eyes glittering. I could see her pulling her anger tight around herself just like earlier she'd pulled her puffy jacket tight over her big bosoms when she'd felt the glass-hard upstate wind.

'I can calm down now?' she mocked, putting all kinds of big African-diaspora soulpower into her words. 'Are you under the impression you're in charge of something here? In your sad-ass trailer with your shotgun and your whisky? Girl, do you think I can't see how scared you are? Give me that, you stupid baby.'

And she reached out and snatched the bottle out of my hand.

'Let's not get physical,' I warned. I knew I had a knife in the drawer.

'You've had enough to drink,' she said. 'Now you just put your butt back in the sink and forget everything you think you know.'

There was liquid snot shining on Cookie's upper lip as she said this and I saw that she was shivering. My head was pounding. The door must have come unlatched when Cookie charged across the trailer, because now it was flapping and banging against the outside aluminum. Sneakers, huddled behind the heater, meowed in protest.

'Fucking door,' I said, and made to go past Cookie. She blocked me with her body. I said, 'I'm going to close the door. Before we all friggin' freeze. I got a limited supply of propane here.'

She let me go. I shut the door and she went and sat down again. I lit a can of Sterno and put the kettle on. There was a little silence until the water started boiling; then that sound seemed to take over the trailer. Neither of us spoke. At last, as I wrested the lid off the Folgers jar, Cookie let out a frustrated sigh.

'You don't make much of a hardass,' she said. 'But I can see you're trying to do a good thing. Too bad you got it totally wrong. You're not a marksman. You're a dragonsinger.'

I put some Folgers in a Garfield mug and picked up the jar of powdered milk, throwing her a questioning look. She just stared at me.

'Milk?' I said in a hostess voice. 'Sugar?'

Cookie blinked. For a moment I thought she might cry.

'OK, have it black, then.'

I staggered over, wishing I'd filled the mug less because I wasn't too steady.

'What happened is my fault, OK?' I said. 'I know that. I brought IT here. Every time I played, something weird happened. And then IT came. I wanted a sound beyond sound and I got it. So it must be that IT was coming because of me. And I'm dealing with it the best I can, which is not very good so fuck me, whatever.'

Cookie said, 'That's not quite right. You didn't bring the dragon. Yes, it came for you. It wants you. But I'm the one who brought it here. I brought you both. You both come from the Grid. From the realm of the abstract. You come from the place where all structure comes from.'

'The place where all structure comes from?' I said. 'They made us study that stuff freshman year. Plato and shit. The Ideal versus the Real. There is no such thing as the realm of the Ideal, though . . . is there? I mean, isn't the whole point of physics the fact that substance and structure are inseparable?'

'OK, listen up,' Cookie said. 'Do you have a pen?'

I pointed to the wall, where Sally had stuck one of those little whiteboards with an erasable marker to write shopping lists on. Cookie drew a diagram. 'See, what we got here is an imbalance between concept and perception. K(mumbo jumbo)2/m ≠ 1 where k is the cornflakes constant and m is the mass of the universe minus bullshit, located on the time axis at the point before breakfast on the first day of reality, GMT. That's Greenwich Mean Time, so we got to allow for a five-hour time lag. Maybe more, depending on Daylight Savings.'

'Cookie,' I said. 'You know what you are? You are a Trailbreak bar. With extra fruit and nuts.'

'Trailbreak? Ha-ha, that's very funny. If only you knew.'

'Seriously,' and I laughed, because I was slurring my speech, 'what is all that junk? You're kidding, right?'

'I'm kidding but I'm not kidding. Look, I'm trying to explain that I can't write you an equation for what you are, because that's the whole point about you. Cassidy, you're the thing that doesn't fit. You don't make any sense.'

'Thanks, Cookie. I needed that.'

She ignored me. 'The dragon, on the other hand – the MFeel, or IT if you prefer – is looking to process you on ITs own terms. That's what IT has already done to the other eight of you. I brought you here to save you from IT, but I couldn't stop IT from coming through, too. And that means I can't stop the ascension of the abstract. I can't stop the Grid from coming here.' Cookie paused. 'Sorry. I'm talking to you like I'd talk to myself. You know how when you talk to yourself and you say, "you stupid idiot" or whatever? That's what I'm doing. I keep forgetting you aren't . . . I mean, I keep forgetting you don't know me.'

This was utterly true.

Ray was banging on the door.

'You gonna help me with feeds, Cassidy?' he yelled. I knew he was still pissed about the electricity because he was using my full name.

'Coming,' I called. But I didn't move.

'But IT has had many opportunities to get me,' I said. 'Only IT doesn't. IT trashes everybody else, but I'm left standing. How do you explain that?'

Cookie said, 'It's the hair-of-the-dog-that-bit-you phenomenon.'

'The which?'

'CASSIDY!' *Bang, bang, bang.*

'All right already.' I wove my way to the door, pulling my coat on. 'What the hell does that mean?'

'It means a little bit of you – well, eight of your versions –

have gotten inside the dragon, and they've affected IT. The logic it was built on is no longer machine logic. IT has been Grid-infected through the logic bullets, and Cassidy-infected through you. And IT is breaking your world so as to get to you. IT can't help this, and neither can you. IT's trying to communicate. The other eight of you are calling you. Or driving IT. Depending on where you're standing. That's why, when you killed those baby dragons, you were killing yourself, too. Damn it, Cassidy.'

'Well, I wasn't going to make friends with them!'

We were both shouting, now. Cookie railed, 'No, but we might have sent them back, and then you could have been whole. Now I'm afraid you can never be one person. This will never be one world. And, sooner or later, IT will break you down.'

'How do you know that? How can you be so sure?'

'I'm not *sure* of anything. But I'm starting to get it now. I was looking for the tape, but I think the reason the Synchronicity has brought me here is because you, Cassidy, are the key to the whole thing. It was you that made the Synchronicity. It's built of your sound. You've grown from the Grid, but you're not a golem. You believe you're a person, but you're actually part of a set of nine bodies. The others have been assimilated by the MFeel, but not you – so you're not Machine Front, either. I don't know what the hell you are. I only know one thing about you for sure.'

I snorted. 'Yeah? What?'

And Cookie said: 'You're not human.'

'Of course I'm human. Come on. Let's not go overboard.'

'No, you're not. You're just a ghost in the machine.'

I stared at her.

'I'm sorry, but that's the truth.'

Where do you go with this one? I was at, like, a loss. Cookie wasn't stupid; then it would have been easy. No: she was just crazy. And she expected me to be crazy, too.

But I wouldn't succumb. I'd just glide around her craziness on words like rollerblades.

I jammed a hat on my head, dragged out my gloves.

'So I'm a fiction. So what? Who isn't made out of Coke bottles and Saturday-morning cartoons and Barbie accessories? How does that really change things?'

Cookie sat back. I could see the sweat glistening on her dark skin, even though it was cold and drafty in the trailer. I could hear her breathing. When she spoke her voice was low and sandy, and she made me feel that I was underwater.

She said, 'How does it change things? Just look around.'

The door opened and Ray's head came in.

'What the hell are you two doing in here?'

Cookie came out with us and followed us around while we fed the horses and checked water buckets and generally battened down for the night. I introduced Cookie as an 'old friend' and I don't think Ray knew how to take this. I'd once heard him remark that he refused to swim in a public pool in Albany because there were black kids with greasy hair in it. Now, though, he looked forlorn when we left him in the barn and I knew he wanted me to invite him to come back to the trailer with us. He had been hinting all day that I should take his shift on foal-watch as partial compensation for ruining his little 'electricity and movies' business, but I'd already decided not to play up to him. And there was no way I wanted him getting to know Cookie.

'C'mere, Ray,' Cookie said, crooking her finger at him. She opened the trunk of the Sonata and took out a paper bag from A&P and a six-pack. Rummaging a little more, she came up with a navy-blue sweater and a box of CDs. She piled everything in Ray's arms.

'I don't got a CD player,' he said.

'Oh, sorry. I thought I might run into my friend Miles. Well, here.'

She took back the CDs and chucked a box of Russell Stover chocolate at him.

'Have a good night,' she said.

That got rid of Ray. Cookie and I carried some more groceries and stuff back to the trailer. I was still drunk. I felt out of control. I knew I should be freaking right about now. Alcohol or no alcohol, I should be flipping out. The whole situation had gotten way out of hand, I was beyond dealing with it, and I seriously wanted to stay drunk forever and let everything just roll over me.

There was something about Cookie, though.

An air.

She held my attention in a way that nobody else had, not in a long time. Maybe it was her size, or the incongruity of her clothes, or her blackness here in white-on-white rural New York. I don't think it was any of those things, though. There was just something about her that felt solid and true where everything else was up for grabs, metaphysically speaking.

It was really tempting to listen to her. Even if what she said contained substantial elements of hogwash. Maybe it was because, hogwash-wise, I suspected that she sounded to me like I'd sounded to the people I'd tried to talk to.

Meaning, she must have more information than me.

I could drop the rock.

'So what are you doing here?' said Cookie while I made grilled Velveeta Processed Cheese Food on bread. 'Killing baby dragons and shoveling shit. What's that all about?'

I told her. About Bard and how it had seemed to be some kind of epicenter for ITs invasion, how people disappeared and music made things happen and no one could really grasp it. I told her how I was planning to bring the tapes I'd made of IT back there and play them for Ben, try to figure out what was to be done. But the baby dragons had sidetracked me, and now I had to get back across miles of snow.

'And along come I, just in the nick of time,' Cookie said. 'I'm not surprised you're into music. But what do you mean, recordings of IT?'

So then I told her about the manifestations, the library plastic, the miniature city made of toy packages and stuff . . . and then this led to the butt-stapling incident and the dead guy.

I loved talking about it and not being treated like a mental case. It was fun. We ate Betty Crocker chocolate fudge frosting straight out of the jar. We dunked pretzels in it. We drank. Cookie fed Sneakers little strips of packaged Oscar Mayer bologna, and soon she was her best friend.

All this time, we were listening to *Jethro Tull Live: Bursting Out* on Sally's tiny boombox, courtesy of the package of D batteries that Cookie had brought. When I got to the part about the dead guy 'Songs From the Wood' was playing, and I noticed that Cookie had gone very still.

'You OK?' I said. 'You feel sick? Maybe we should stop eating . . .'

She licked her lips. Tried to say something. Finally she sort of whispered, 'What did he look like?'

And when I told her, she just stared at the floor. Sneakers head-butted her in the chest and Cookie stroked her absent-mindedly.

'Where's the body now? Do you know where the police took it? No, what am I saying – they'd have it in an evidence room somewhere, wouldn't they?'

Now she was focusing on me, leaning forward, eyes wide open as if she were trying to read an optometrist's chart printed on my face.

'Think, Cassidy. The stuff he was wearing. Was he carrying anything? His personal effects, you know? Oh my God, we have to get to the police station. Cassidy, you got to help me with this.'

I belched. 'Are you, like, looking for something? Because I found this tape, but—'

Cookie got really overexcited then. She was up on her feet, jumping up and down, hugging me, demanding to know where the tape was, and I had to go into my backpack and pull out the Staples bag with the cassette labelled *Wellspring Process.* Cookie clutched it to her chest and did a little war dance; the trailer swayed.

'Whoa, there,' I said. 'Just a second. I'm pretty sure this tape is what kicked everything off. My boyfriend played it, and that's when IT first came. And all the other tapes sound like IT now. Even when people play live at Bard, IT starts to come into the sound. So I can't give it to you, because if you play it we could be more screwed than we already are.'

Cookie sobered.

'OK,' she said. 'OK, don't worry. I won't play it, at least not right now. Let's just slow down here. We better think this through.'

'Yeah. Yeah. Slow down.'

'We need a plan.'

'Yeah, a plan.'

But . . . we were drunk. So, even after we changed the Jethro Tull to Salt-n-Pepa, we didn't focus too well.

'We have to get back to Bard,' I said. 'I think the whole campus is a kind of boundary. Stuff passes in and out. You can make stuff happen with music, just like the dragons made electricity up here when they sang. It's like . . . you know, down in these really deep parts of the ocean where they have, like, these thermal vents? And there's all kinds of life down there that could never exist any other way? It's a little like that.'

'Hmm,' said Cookie. 'OK, how do we get there? I mean, the Sonata out there, that's just a metaphorical vehicle.'

'I was going to ride.'

'It would make more sense to use the Synchronicity. But I

gotta tell you, Cassidy, if Bard is the place where Gunther took the tape, I haven't been able to get there. I tried. The dragon's got it covered.'

'But my friends are there,' I said weakly. 'I made promises.'

'Well, OK, so we ride there. Which one's going to be my horse? You got a black horse, or something with spots? Those brown ones are so boring, I can never tell them apart . . . hey, do you have a black stallion, by any chance?'

'You are *not* riding the stallion,' I said to Cookie's peals of laughter.

Ray was banging on the door again.

I jerked it open.

'Look, Ray, this is a girl thing, what do you—'

I stopped. His face was covered with soot. Outside, the Sonata was on fire.

'Something came up from . . . down there.' He pointed toward the wooded hollow where the TV screens were. 'I was in the barn and I saw something flash outside. I go out and this *thing* flies right over my head, I don't know what the fuck it was. Fucking *singed* me, man, I thought I was gonna die, and look at the car!' His voice broke on the last word.

Cookie dragged me away from the door. She was already pulling on her big puffy coat. I saw her check to be sure that the dead-guy tape was in the inside pocket. Then she grabbed the boombox.

'IT's coming after me,' I said. 'Because I killed them. I knew this would happen.'

'Maybe it's for the best,' said Cookie. 'I was never a good planner, anyway.'

Your Grandma on Crack

The first thing I thought was that the breeding barn would go up like a torch if it caught fire. I ran past Cookie to get to the barn door and start opening stalls, but by the time I got there I'd realized that there was no sound of IT.

No sound of anything.

The night was still. No cars, no planes, no TV laugh tracks from Hannah's house. No groundlight; just Ray with his flashlight and everything else a study in indigo and silence.

I stopped. Cookie came huffing after me.

'If that car blows, we don't want to be here!' she called. 'Cassidy, come on. We're too close!'

I turned to see where Ray was. He'd headed off toward the house.

'Ray!' I shouted. 'Where you going?'

'Forget him,' said Cookie. She gripped the boombox against her chest like a knight's shield. 'Let's see these TVs you keep talking about. We can get into the Synchronicity.'

But I wasn't paying attention to her.

It was too quiet. As my eyes adjusted to the darkness, I studied Hannah's house. A hurricane lamp sitting in an upstairs window cast a small, weak diamond of light on the snow of the driveway. In the drive was the drama of flame and shadow that had been the brand new Sonata. Beyond that patch of light, the rest of the driveway and the entrance to the road were cast in deep darkness.

I thought I could see something. A silhouette. Some kind of structure, or—

Blazing light stabbed into my eyes. I threw my arms up and turned my face away at the same moment, even as an amplified voice barked out my name.

'CASSIDY WALKER, LAY DOWN AND PUT YOUR HANDS ON YOUR HEAD! BOTH OF YOU – YEAH, I MEAN YOU, YOU FAT BLACK WHALE! DROP THE RADIO! BOTH OF YOU LAY DOWN ON YOUR FACE AND PUT YOUR HANDS BEHIND YOUR HEAD!'

I put my hands up instinctively, and I managed to figure out that the lights were coming from two Monster Trucks blocking the exit. Not only were their headlights blazing but there were racks of high-powered spotlights mounted over both cabs.

'It's fucking Sweeney,' I said to Cookie. Then I shouted, 'Ray, you are such an asshole.'

'And to think I gave him a box of chocolate,' Cookie grouched.

Now it was Ray's voice; if I shaded my eyes, I could make out his silhouette standing on the running board of one of the Monster Trucks.

'DO WHAT SWEENEY SAYS, CASSIDY. HE KNOWS EVERYTHING. HE KNOWS YOU CAN CROSS TO THE OUT-SIDE AND HE KNOWS WHAT YOU DID TO THE ELECTRICITY AND NOW HE KNOWS YOU AND YOUR WEIRD FRIEND ARE UP TO NO GOOD. THEY KNOW ALL ABOUT YOU. IF YOU DON'T COME ON AND COOPERATE, THEY'LL KILL YOU. I CAN TELL YOU THAT FOR SURE.'

I turned to Cookie, 'Put your hands up. This is like a bad joke.'

Cookie put her hands up, one of them still holding the boom-box.

Ray passed the megaphone back to Sweeney. It was like they were taking turns with a new toy.

'DOWN ON YOUR FACE,' said Sweeney's voice. 'YOU DON'T WANT TO GET SHOT NOW.'

I glanced apprehensively at the burning car. In movies, they always explode immediately. They sure had exploded a lot quicker than this when IT had come to the Ravine Houses.

'THIS IS YOUR LAST WARNING.'

I lowered myself into the snow. I was more angry than scared.

Sound of several guys running through snow towards us.

Cookie said, 'You get a horse. I'll deal with these guys.'

'*What?*'

'You heard me.'

'They'll shoot me.'

'Nah. They need you. Now, *go!*'

I rolled over and hurled myself in the general direction of the barn. Out of the corner of my eye I saw Cookie still lying on the ground.

'Don't hurt me!' she was squeaking. 'I'm just a bystander, please don't—'

I pelted into the dark barn and made straight for Patriot's stall. Guys shouted and I heard a couple of shots, but I just kept going. Patriot was only a moving shadow and a series of hot snorts as I shot the bolt on his door, darted in and grabbed his halter before he knew what hit him. His first reaction was to back up right into the far corner of his stall, where his water bucket was mounted on a rack. I was on his right side and he'd probably never been mounted from there, so he was even more surprised when I got my left foot up onto his water bucket, switched my grip from halter to mane, and then swung myself onto his back from there. I knew he was surprised because he just stood there. I was surprised, too – I'm a shit rider and I'd never been on a stallion before. I kicked his ribs and then he went – and boy, did he go. Patriot was about twenty-six years old but the way he was going down the aisle toward the light and confusion outside he'd obviously forgotten that.

Outside the barn a circle of five men were trying to deal with Cookie. One had hold of her ankle and one had her hood and they'd half-lifted her off the ground, but she was writhing and kicking like a crazy person.

'Get to the TVs!' she screamed at me as Patriot charged past. I saw flashes of light and heard guns going off. It was all I could do to stay on Patriot's back. If he had bucked or reared I'd have flown; but he just ran for it and I had no control over his direction.

I glanced behind me and saw that Cookie had gotten hold of a rake, and she was back on her feet and laying about herself with it like your grandma on crack. But she was completely surrounded and in a moment she'd be down and they'd pile on top of her, or start kicking her—

The Sonata exploded.

Patriot spun to the left and skidded.

I shot straight over his head and onto the hood of one of the Monster Trucks.

Pieces of metal flew through the air. Cookie's attackers paused.

I rolled over a couple of times and stopped, winded and kind of stunned.

Impressions:

Ray running toward Patriot, yelling at the other guys to stop shooting.

Other guys, shooting their guns anyway, but not connecting with anything much.

Cookie throwing her rake at one guy and diving at the legs of

*another. She knocked him down in the snow and then managed to
scuttle free. When he reached for her, I saw her whack him on the
skull with the boombox and he backed off.*

*The black and fluorescent green of the hood of the Monster Truck
where I'd landed. It was painted up like the Grim Reaper.*

Patriot screaming and dancing. He didn't know where to go.

Flaming parts of the Sonata, scattered all over the place.

*Sweeney himself running toward me. He had a handgun, but no
shovel.*

I turned around and looked inside the truck.

Nobody there.

But the lights were on, so the keys were in the ignition, so—

I scrambled over the hood and swung my legs through the
window. Started the engine.

Sweeney skidded to a stop, raised his hands to shield his
eyes from the headlights and probably also in the hope that I
would stop. I gunned it.

Patriot knocked Ray down and bolted. Sweeney threw himself out of my way in the nick of time. Cookie chucked the
boombox through the truck's open window and got on the
running board.

I fumbled for reverse. Guys scattered as I threw the thing
into second gear and smashed into the side of the other Monster
Truck in passing. We roared out the driveway and through the
snow, down the hill toward the trees.

'Go, go, go!' screamed Cookie. She looked like she was having
the time of her life. I jerked the wheel and took us offroad and
into the tire tracks of the Isuzu.

'I think they'll kill us,' I told her.

'First they have to catch us,' Cookie said.

That would be all too easy, I thought: I could see the headlights of the second truck bobbing up and down in my rearview
mirror. Sweeney would be pissed off for real now. I didn't think
they'd kill us right away. I thought they'd probably tie us up

and rape us and then maybe kill us later, or see what else we were good for.

It's what I would have done if I were them.

We careered down the hill and I stopped by the TVs. Like security monitors in a gas station covering every angle, every one of them was showing Cookie's abstract city. Cookie jumped out.

'Hurry! Here they come!'

The monster truck rammed us from behind and Sweeney's guys started firing. I saw Cookie clambering through the snow in her big purple jacket with the boombox over her head. She turned and beckoned to me. When I reached her, she grabbed my hand.

Then she pulled me into the nearest TV.

Ghost in the Machine

Everybody knows the difference between reality and TV.

Until now.

Because the world's been parsed in some other way, by some other paradigm.

The world's fucked sideways, and I'm in it.

And speaking of IT:

ITs body sines through all aspects, or is perhaps implied by them as if this world were merely ITs jet trail. Down through tunnels and across levels, connectivity more spooky than any fiber optics or radio waves or other linear shit masquerading as magic. This shit's bent and twisted, Calabi Yau out the butt and maybe then some.

'Cookie,' I said. 'What are we standing on? What are these buildings made of?'

'Don't look too closely,' she said. 'You might find out.'

'What?'

'Remember, you're a fiction. And it takes one to know one. You can see through it.'

'I can?'

'You can tell the difference. Most people can't. Not since IT came.'

'Is that why I can walk where other people can't go?'

'I guess.'

I looked at my feet. We were up on some roof, but the Synchronicity stretched in all directions, including over our heads. Our roof was tar with a thin coating of pebbles. Little chimneys spiked from it at intervals, just gray sections of pipe, some of them spewing warm fumes.

I had never taken acid. A lot of my friends at Bard tripped on Halloween. I didn't.

But I saw the reality like the answer to a math problem in front of me: there was no difference between the fumes and the building. The building wasn't solid. There was nothing beneath my feet.

I took a few gasping breaths but Cookie wasn't paying attention to me. She seemed to be scanning for something across the rooftops and bridges.

'I see clouds!' I managed to choke out at last. I sounded wild and scared. I kept looking down. My hands groped the air around me, seeking something to hold on to. My stomach pitched. 'You never said it was a cloud city.'

'Clouds are like people,' said Cookie absently. 'Same types of behaviors.'

I could only stare. How could a place come from inside you; surely the whole idea was the grossest inversion of the way the world really is? We live in the environment. It shapes us. Not the other way around.

Right?

Yet sure as shootin' I knew this place. It was some internal representation, not of the physical world but of some other kind of organization.

I could move through it at will; and it could move through me. There were diagonal buildings, irregular waterfalls flowing through vertical parking lots where the cars stuck to buildings like magnets. People walked on the undersides of bridges.

Down deep under the manhole covers there was the glimmer of something like mercury.

There were shadow animals, like the terrified deer who found themselves bounding through the TV from one slice of ITland to another, only to be shot by hunters watching *Trapper John, MD*. There were stranded cars and lost people and missing addresses, all jumbled in with fire escapes and geraniums in pots.

Distance was no object. A person could be a tiny shadow far away, but when you focused on them they were in your face in glorious 2D. And then they were gone, trailing banners of information about their own perceptions like coattails.

I turned on Cookie in accusation.

'This is a crazy . . . can you even call it a place?'

'What else would you like to call it?'

I didn't answer. I mean, what kind of a thing builds itself? Agglomerates, pulls itself into being by its own bootstraps? The world, that's what kind of thing. And here we go, because it's happening again. It's happening every moment. I feel all verbed-out with the unwillingness of this shit to fix itself and just *be*.

'I've been spending a lot of time here lately, and I've noticed a few things,' Cookie said. 'These city architectures are simple. They seem to represent the structures of human rational thought. But if you were to look beneath them, you'd see they're built on Grid. And the Grid is more complex than you or me – we're at the same level as maybe a cloud, or a storm. The Grid is more complex than that. That's why we can't perceive its structure. It's simply beyond us.'

'I don't like this,' I said. 'I don't want to see this.'

'So don't see it,' Cookie answered in a weary voice. 'And for God's sake don't try to go any deeper. Pull back and focus on the surface.'

And I did. Like being on a train at night and looking at the mixture of exterior lights and reflected interior images through the dark windows, for a second I could see the Synchronicity's architecture and its underlying chaos, and in that mix I knew there were the pre-Columbian tax records of Peru and the 1963 sales records of Allstate Insurance and the needle count on HIV-prevention programs in Holland arranged in a weird amalgam that also conspired to suggest the very surface I was standing on.

But I didn't have to see it all. I could see the roof if I wanted to.

I walked to the edge of the roof and looked down. The effects of this new vision lingered. Threaded through the shapes of the Synchronicity now I could see the rivers of causality and acausality too, the way the world passes through itself, concrete to abstract and back again, plastic as an emotion slipping under the blood-brain barrier. I could see the topology of causal relationships as wild as any Calabi Yau space that Miles could dream up – and no, this wasn't about strings or vibrating universes, but this place could hold those ideas like little incidental flowers sprouting from the cracks of its pavement.

Causal relationships had built this place, and acausal ones meant that the Synchronicity kept changing out from underneath itself. Strange juxtapositions: see the Wall Street trader quaffing Alka Seltzer and fixing his bleary eyes on the monitor with its numbercrawl. See the flies walking in and out of the brown child's mouth faraway, walking with mincing sixlegs because that's what they do. And see what, precisely, these two images had to do with each other – how they would inflect and infect one another and where those consequences, in turn, were going – I could see that, too, even if I couldn't quite frame it in words.

I felt full to gagging with this awareness.

From here I could see also the dream towers of the developers and the factories of children who imagine the world through their animate dump trucks and helicopters. I could see the spirits and the ghosts, the voodoo and the fear sculptures wrought in imaginations of old ladies conjuring in their minds the Bigcity with its terrors. I could see all these things and depending on how I focused my eyes I could perceive their connections and interdependencies.

In a very few places a specific nudge or effort could create a dramatic result. One girl being five minutes late for school in Albuquerque could ruin the fortunes of a Filipino jeweler: the consequences stood ready to fall like dominoes. The old butterfly effect, maybe – or maybe just a little cosmic acupuncture. I could see these concatenations of possibilities, these conspiracies, like circumstantial G-spots in the webbing of the world system. Needles in haystacks of determinism. Monkey/Magna Carta events, that type of thing. The perfect opening chess move. These nexuses were like that, elusive like that. Elusive, but visible to me. And in seeing them, through some lovely synesthesia, I smelled voltage. Like the ionic charge off an old electric train set. I smelled power.

We all have a belief in a world of absolutes. We are all big time into control. This is our age.

But we're all wrong, and we sense this about ourselves; hence the desire for talismans and distractions. Hence the whispered hope that real understanding will never come, not for us. Hence the eyes-closed, headlong-rushing-through-existence, fingers-crossed yearning that we will never be shattered by any killer realizations. Just get us safely to the grave, please.

IT capitalizes on this very fear. IT is like an express train. Get on board and be safe. The metal exoskeleton and groovy beats of IT will protect you from gaps and anomalies in the surface of things. The fact that the world doesn't make sense won't penetrate the skin of IT, not to where you will be riding deep in its gut. And with you inside, IT will penetrate deeper and deeper into the mystery of human existence, and render that mystery calculable, servile and, above all, clean.

Again: by 'you' I mean me, of course.

Because I know deep down that I haven't been brought here so that we can avoid riding horseback to Bard.

I know it's not just to get away from the Monster Truck Boys.

I'm here because this is where I'm supposed to be.

And I don't think I can deal with that.

Cookie was looking at me.

'I know what you're thinking,' she said. 'But it's going to be all right.'

I made a noise that was half-laugh, half-sob. I wasn't up to anything more.

'I propose a trade,' said Cookie. 'An exchange. Me for you. See, I think I worked it out. I brought you through and I disturbed the ecosystem between the concrete and the abstract. I brought you through, and that brought IT, too, because of your other selves being all wrapped up inside IT. Now, logically speaking, I could send you back, but if I did that I'd be a real pig. And there are so many cracks letting the abstract come through that I think somebody needs to be here on the inside to make sure the whole thing doesn't get out of hand. So I figure, I'll stay here and deal with IT, and you go. I'll make sure IT can't get out again.'

I could feel a helpless hope swelling at her words. She was talking about saving me. Sacrificing herself to IT – for me.

A light and grateful buoyancy, and then the hammer of guilt.

'No, Cookie,' I said weakly.

'I don't mind,' Cookie said. 'I practically live here anyway. It's no big deal.'

Liar. It *was* a big deal.

'Cookie,' I said, 'I can't let you do this.'

Cookie snorted. 'That's what you say when somebody gives you a Christmas present you know they spent too much on. That's "*Aw, you shouldn't have.*"'

'I mean it,' I said. 'This sacrificing yourself is a crazy idea. It won't work. Anyway, I need you. You understand this place. I don't. I can't lose you now.'

Cookie clambered to her feet. She took me by the shoulders like people do when they're intending to give you a real talking-to, but in my limited experience that has always been bullshit. I didn't like what I was seeing in her face. To start with, she was crying.

'You are so lucky,' she said. 'How many people get to fight their dragon? How many people even know what it is they have to do? Do you have any idea how it feels to stumble through life knowing this world is supposed to be your . . . your . . . inheritance, your place, your purpose? And it's a total mismatch. You don't know what it is. You don't know how to use it so you let it use you. And you know you could do better in a different world, but you can't reset the game and start again. You can't put the book down and pick up another one, by a different author. You're stuck with what you got. Do you have any idea how that feels?'

She actually expected an answer. I didn't think that was fair, or the point. I stammered, 'No, but . . .'

'No, but!' She was spitting in my face. I was uncomfortably aware that Cookie, when angry, tended to trash people and places. She was a lot bigger than me and she had mentioned something about karate. She whispered, 'Most of us have no chance in this life. Nobody tells us jackshit about what we're doing here. Or if they do, it's lies. I brought you here. I brought you here as best as I could out of what I knew and I've told you all I can and now it's up to fucking you.'

She stepped back and let me go.

'We're only animals. We're supposed to be living in huts on

the savannah,' Cookie said. 'We're supposed to have babies and lose our teeth and die. But that's not what's happening. We made up this other weird shit. We live half in the spirit world. And it's coming here, through stories and through Gunther's marketing plans and God knows how else, it's infiltrating us and we have no defences. Most of us. Humans. Have no defences. But you. *You come from that place.* I know because I've seen you there. I didn't bring you here to be a victim. So get your shit together and do what you do.'

I felt like a beach that's just been swept clean by a big wave. I couldn't even think. But I heard myself say, quietly, 'What about you?'

'I know what I've got to do,' Cookie said. 'Don't you worry about me. I know where I'll be standing when the lightning falls.'

Her face was set. She was determined.

'OK,' I said. I took a big, dramatic breath. 'OK, let's play the fucking tape.'

At first the so-called Wellspring Process was just noises, really genuinely unpremeditated as far as I could tell. Then a little bit of steady synthesizer sound started laying down a backdrop, sort of like a wash laid down on watercolor paper in preparation for painting.

'You hear that?' said Cookie. 'Turn it up.'

It was a man's voice, so soft as to be subliminal. The occasional syllable came through, muffled.

'It's kind of boring,' I said.

Cookie snorted. 'That's the whole idea. We're going under.'

I didn't know what she meant.

But I could hear the beginnings of a soft beat like a hummingbird behind everything. And listening got easier.

And easier.

Until:

This was a place of pure thought. My body hummed, a thought experiment, messy and incomplete. The substance around me: less a substance than a glimmering crystalline wind driving its needles always inward.

The sound had more power than I thought.

Too late, I realized that I would be taken apart, stripped like a piece of old furniture.

I couldn't stay here.

I couldn't last.

Every instinct was telling me to get out.

And with every moment I was less able to resist the pressure. Crushing. Breathless. Disoriented.

I couldn't do anything.

I could hear the little gasps of my own breaths, a bit of vocalization coloring the exhalations. Small whimpers of the kind you wake yourself with while dreaming.

And then IT came. This was ITs place anyway. The lair of the dragon.

Cookie's dragon was not what you could call animalian. It wasn't Chinese, either: no flags, kites, bright-primary-color dance factory. Cookie's dragon was nothing less and nothing more than my IT. IT, as in, *you're it*. IT, as in, *not he or she but*. IT was the kind of pronoun you use when all else fails, so profuse and sprawling in meaning and at the same time so minimally descriptive as to make ITself scary: all inference. If words are just placeholders for experiential baggage, then IT had the same kind of paradoxical quality as zero. IT was everything, rendered to nothing. Reduced to zero, and nothing pretty about IT.

Here IT comes, all the order-making principle you can imagine in one seething mass. The brainwash anthem, the be-one-of-us exploitation, the chain-mail or is it chain-link fence of individuals welded together in compliance with the Law. The dragon, a devouring monster with a series of codas that come lashing after it, whip-like, ensuring obedience.

Hear ITs hypnotic jingle-jangle quickstep. Boogie.

The purpose of IT is to get to the bottom of you. The purpose of IT is to render you into a form of food. This is done largely by streamlining your mind and making you predictable.

IT would like to use you as a place to live and reproduce. IT would like to avail itself of your natural resources. IT would like to tame you and make you happy if possible; but if not, just tame is OK too.

'*Cassidy!*'

I must have fallen over. Cookie was dragging me to my feet. We were still on the roof, and the tape was still turning its spools but all we could hear was Cookie's dragon.

IT came roaring over our heads, trailing absurd quanta of sound, discrete moments rendered senseless by their decon-textualization. IT stank of dismemberment. IT was senseless. IT rammed that fact home again and again and again. I tried to grasp how this was possible. How something meant to uncover truth could only kill truth. I groped for meaning, but that was like trying to climb a greased pole. Every time I thought I had a point of leverage, of understanding, I slid back down, defeated. And the way in which this happened told me that the whole notion of finding meaning was all over for me. IT had crunched this very possibility into ludicrousness in ITs big monster jaws.

All those careful abstractions and gently built cardhouses of human experience and knowledge, rent by incomprehension. Unprocessed by the mind, anyone's mind, all that thought had become junk, the effluvia of information culture bursting forth in a gibberish that threatened to annihilate me by association. Because IT had already annihilated all other creations, all other fashionings, denatured them. Decoded them. And I was next.

'*Listen,*' whispered Cookie. '*Don't believe your own assumptions. Listen.*'

I rallied. After all, Ben had shown me that music was one way of experiencing the unbearable, and yet surviving it. Music was one way of going where it was otherwise impossible to go, and yet returning. If I took IT at face value, IT was winning.

I had to find something in IT. Anything in IT.

Cookie would find an order. That's the beauty of being a schizophrenic. If she was a schizophrenic. She could find the patterns, even if there weren't any patterns, and make them work for her.

But I didn't want to live in a fantasy. I didn't want to concoct a world in which I would be safe, only to have it let me down. Not again. No.

So: *listen*. But how?

Bring everything. Bring everything that you are to it, and be in the room with it, and find out what it is. That's listening, right?

Even if it wants to kill you.

Especially if it wants to kill you.

IT came up over the edge of the building. ITs tail lashed against the Synchronicity with a death-ringing clang so all-involving that I thought I'd pass out. Where it struck the roof I could see chunks of material come away revealing what lay beneath, blobs of numerical construction splintering into thin air. Layer on layer of data floated in the exposed area, a wound in the fabric of the Synchronicity. I felt sick. I felt like IT had struck me. Had damaged all my carefully constructed correspondences and interpretations. I knew then the specific and razorish intention behind all ITs behaviors: IT meant me harm. IT would eat my senses and everything specific about me, if IT could. Then *me* would be nothing but mouth and asshole stumbling headless in the world to the sound of ITs laughing groove.

That was ITs express intent.

Cookie waggled her finger at IT.

'I don't think so,' she said.

She began to walk toward IT. There was no wind. The air wavered like a mirage, but I think that was the heat off the chimneys leading up to the roof. Or maybe there was something wrong with my eyes. I wouldn't have been surprised if they'd started to crack like raw eggs.

Cookie's chunky silhouette waggled back and forth as she walked. She had short legs and a big muscular butt. She was still wearing her silly purple shiny jacket. She had riding boots on and that made her legs taper at the bottom like sausages.

'Cookie, please don't!'

But she did. ITs mouth cranked open, huge and disjointed like a snake's. Down ITs gullet I could see the light and music of video-game arcades and television, endless laugh tracks piled on top of one another in an ocean of entertainment. Demigods and goddesses of screens large and small cavorted in ITs gullet. Soundtracks bleated inanities to each other until they became textureless, a seething mass of common denominators.

Cookie walked into it all like a game-show host making an exit. And as she entered, ITs body spasmed and began to thrash. I saw ITs claws scrabble for purchase on the edge of the building. ITs wings fanned the air as it fought for balance. IT threw ITs head back and I couldn't see Cookie anymore, only the bulge in ITs throat. And in that moment I realized that, like a gourmand on a wishbone, IT was choking.

This was my cue to run. I couldn't seem to do it. Instead I moved forward until I was under ITs thrashing body. No white underbelly. No soft spots. No fleas. No: everything contoured to anticipate attack. Everything logically perfect.

And I grabbed the edge of ITs wing and was carried up.

Wake

Still choking, IT fell backward off the roof, caught itself, and then turned in midair and began to flap away with awkward pelican strokes. I clung to IT with my arms and legs until, with a downbeat, ITs wing threw me in the air. I tumbled onto ITs back, spun, clamped my legs on and gripped with my fingers like a rock climber.

Even as I clung to thrumming scales and sculpted metal, ITs body began to break up like water spread on plastic. Within a few seconds, the dragon had evaporated.

The sound kept coming at me edge on: no matter what I did I couldn't get a hold of its substance, so that as I whirled through the sky with all avenues of the Synchronicity stretching away from me I became aware of the diagonal spaces between spaces; streets between streets; windows reflecting on windows reflecting on puddles. I became aware of all kinds of unconscious algorithms in the relations of things. I got the falling sensation of deep sky, like seeing the stars in the absence of groundlight. Deep sky makes you feel insignificant. Here I had the opposite feeling. This place, this sound pointed lances at me. The sky was flat like a dead computer screen.

Cookie had sacrificed herself, but I was still here. IT was still here, all around me, dragging me through the Synchronicity.

The claustrophobic towers with their walls crumbling endless testimony to abandonment. The carpeted streets and the somnambulistic people. The flatlands where nothing much moved but a seethe of words and their filthy byproducts; and the howling dark surround where commercial images flashed like laughter, relentless and obscene. The mountains that turned out to be made of boxes, that held other mountains which were bigger.

And the remapping of New Jersey, with all natural phenomena arranged in a moat around a castle built entirely of television actors and retail packaging, and all the living people stowed neatly in a round library on top of a hill in the form of paperback books. The dead were more active, swarming through the air as memory-inducing scents. Sentient garbage trucks and songbirds warred on the edges of the moat, competing for crusts that had fallen in the water.

I knew this place at once. It was a drain going down, a sinking feeling; it was the limit of my understanding and as such it kept stretching itself away from me and changing the terms so that I felt alone and insecure.

The whole experience was like digging for diamonds with a stick.

IT rendered the 'city more orderly everywhere it went. IT edited, simplified, forced together paradigms that had no desire to be near each other.

I felt pain and bled inside when IT did this.

IT sliced off heads and rammed walls together. IT grafted children's faces to chainsaw blades and arranged traffic on roads in accordance with license-plate numbers.

And, in time, the sense of altitude changed to confusion. The 'city sucked me down, parted, admitted me.

And still IT sounded.

A sightless place. IT curled around me, a muscle that could move any way and right now it was squeezing me out of me. IT worked up and down my body. Not metaphor. Not music. Not words. Not imagination. Talking real ribs, cracking. And the heat and strangeness of blood pooling in calves because IT won't let blood come back to brain. Brain losing out. Every finger working for leverage, keep IT off my lungs long enough to take another breath.

Too late to get skills for how to deal with a giant musical abstraction squeezing you to death.

Too late for singing lessons, dragon- or otherwise.

Too late for weight lifting.

Why did I assume that getting killed by IT would be straight-forward – as in, now you're alive, then you'll be dead, no worries? Why did I not think about what this would really be like?

My feet were kicking. So many moments crammed inside other moments, I'd never have guessed until they started unpacking themselves and I knew how much I could think in between heartbeats. My feet were kicking without me really being attached to them. The bottom of one boot hit something solid, something not-IT. Scuffed. Caught. Traction. Then the other.

Bracing, my whole body now had a point of orientation. I was upside down in an undefined space except for what I believed was a brick wall.

I was totally fucked.

I felt childish and alone and stupid.

I felt like apologizing to someone, I wasn't sure who, for wasting my life when I didn't even know what it was.

But then I heard my own breath go in and I realized I could move. And all thinking was off. I gasped, wriggled, panted. Breathing was a big drama but I didn't dare focus on that because I had to get my legs free. I reached up towards them: I could still feel the brick wall. It was my only point of reference, sliding against the soles of my boots, and because it was above me if I got free from IT I'd be falling away from that wall and into who knows what void. Fuck. Wish I had a gun.

'*Too bad you got it all wrong. You're not a marksman, you're a dragonsinger.*'

Very funny. Just the kind of wasted brain function I needed at a time like this.

But. Maybe I could make another wall. If I could just get some sound out of myself that had a purpose other than oxygenating my brain. No surplus air, yet – crazy to try to sing but—

I did. I meant it to be something primal and defiant like early Dead Can Dance but it came out more of a guttural moan. My boots squeaked across the brick; something wet, here. IT flipped and slapped me against the wall. First I felt the impact, air shuddering out of me in an involuntary shout, solid even wall in reliable two dimensions colliding with my back. The pain came scampering after, but I was using my hands in desperation now, trying to untangle myself from the claw. I knew I was bleeding because I could hear the blood like a chorus of insects, dripping onto the wall, and now ITs wing was beating against me.

IT didn't like being trapped in here. With my voice I bit at IT, and IT loosened a little more. Thrashed again, and I hit another wall.

So there was another wall.

You made the Synchronicity.

That was what she'd said. And I knew I had a choice. I could sing a whole city around this thing, a cage, you name it.

I'll stay here with you forever, I told it. *You and me, here forever, you can eat me if you want but I won't let you out.*

I said it because it was the closest thing to defiance I had, but it wasn't my idea of a good outcome. Too noble. I should have stayed at Moonshadow and raised horses. I'd have been rich, after a fashion. In the kingdom of the blind and all that. I could have had Hannah's house. I could have watched *Foul Play*. Why be here? Why fight this fight?

Create an environment.

Ben's music-workshop assignment came back to me. Create an environment for sound. Or, create an environment *of* sound.

Singing. The turning point at which music becomes word and the other way around. Mouth sounds, both, same. Music has the quality of sculpting you. You enter it like an ontological carwash in which it can rebuild your engine. Of course this is a cooperative act. Like hypnosis: no passengers, no prisoners. It's the sound of somebody's thought and all that implies. To hear yourself in the act of uttering, to hear yourself in the presence of others and to hear them with you, there, in that space together. Unlike talking, the purpose is not to deliver information. The purpose is to deliver your self.

IT was the sound of ultimate annihilation. IT was a missile aimed to destroy me. IT couldn't literally destroy me but IT could destroy the integrity of my world and remake me according to the machine logic of IT. And the only way for me to get that back was by music, as far as I could tell.

Music is numinous, the breath of thought, the membrane or skin that connects inside and outside, self to other, past, present, future – the integrity and integument of being finds its form in musical expression, musical impression. And if there is a way to survive then that way will be found by, in and of sound, because only sound has the flexibility to shape itself like water and to fling itself into the unknown like a starfish arm groping toward that which does not exist, in the future or otherwise.

Something happens in the mind. Fiction becomes reality, and vice versa. The stew of being human is irreducible to constituent parts. We live in a world of our own making. It has to be. We are products of the systems we make. We make systems based on what we can perceive. We're locked in a spiral.

I took a new breath, and IT didn't like that. I made a space with my voice. The space of me started out small and timid, but it grew. Leaping by intervals I sang out boundaries and then broke them. I breathed and sang and now I had a little room to move.

The wall moved away. IT loosened its coils just a little.

I unfolded.

And more.

I was in a space of my own.

Here is the place: the cobbled street of an old city; scrap of cloud glaring bluish light on the wet pavement; walls of buildings pixilated and aglow with layer on layer of moving images. Dog races and beer commercials and soft porn; men in suits; old movies and breakfast cereal and aerobics and basketball games.

There are figures slumped against the walls and on the ground. Some lie face down, corpselike; others seem to be in a hypnagogic fug as they observe the images.

I count eight of these motionless bodies, and as I do this a realization tickles.

All of them look precisely like me.

I tried to stand up. I was unsteady like a baby deer and, in addition, for some reason I was leaning off to the left, so that everything came at me on an angle.

I could feel IT breathing, behind me.

I staggered a few steps forward and caught hold of a

lamppost for support. The lamppost had been heavily papered with what at first I took to be prostitutes' ads but then turned out to be equations and formulas in which the Greek alphabet held its usual pride of place.

My voice faltered. I picked at the paper. Underneath the first layer there was not steel but crumbling stone incised with hieroglyphics that featured not ibises and Pharaohs but tennis players and race cars.

Underneath the stone was a paste of dead bugs, their exoskeletons flattened and smashed, their juices gone.

But what are you doing? screamed my fear. *Quit messing around and get away from the friggin' dragon!*

Easier thought than done. ITs wings were spreading across the space above me. ITsound whirled with hatred that pierced and penetrated and dug out my veins from within.

IT did not like anomalies.

IT wanted a sleek, futuristic design. Aerodynamic, fuel-efficient, sexy.

I was ruining the pretty picture. It had to flatten me.

You can't do that.
You're against the rules.
You don't make sense.
You don't fit with the plan.
You aren't allowed to be.

I staggered forward. The rest of me were dead or empty: they were part of IT now.

I came to the nearest one of me and dropped to my knees, looked into my own face. She wasn't dead or sleeping but she wasn't conscious, either.

'Wake up, stupid!' I shrieked. I slapped her. I dragged at her hands, tried to pull her to her feet; but I was weak and unstable myself. I fell on my ass, still holding my own hands.

Sing.

It's not performance, this kind of thing. It's not for entertainment value (or in my case lack thereof). Singing like this is the lifeline.

Closer to grunting, anyway, barking out little puffs of almost-baritone imperatives, trying to pump her up like a bicycle tire and make her come alive.

She closed her eyes and opened her mouth.

ITsound slithered over me.

I countered IT. Sang against IT. Tugged at her hands again.

She blinked.

She coughed.

And she started to hum a sour harmony to my wavering half-ass song.

We both got up.

IT dragged the ground from beneath our feet and threw us on our faces. This only galvanized us. We both winced at our skinned knees, bruised arms. Then we crawled.

We each went to another one of us and did the business. We slapped and coddled, we sang the sense back into ourselves. Until all of us were on our feet, defiant, in the abstract city.

We moved in a pack. Staggered, actually, and it was disorienting because now we were sharing eyes, ears, proprioceptors . . . we were in nine places at once and IT was after us.

Ninefold, I looked around. ITs sound was so total, I swear the air had become particulate and I could see ITs constituent elements shaking, molecules going berserk like dancers in a mosh pit.

This is all so physical in a way I never counted on. Makes me realize how little I use or even know my own body.

*

There is a point at which thought feels physical. Every contour and detail, every little twitch and linking reference acts like a coordinated motor event, a dance. And soundmaking really does put you right on that thought/action boundary and keep you there.

I wasn't just singing for my supper. I was singing for my life.

Go swimming in the sea and it's almost all sea with only a little you in the equation.

That's what my singing sounded like in the context of IT.

But go swimming in the sea and you feel every part of your body in a way you'll never know on land. You'll become more alive, guaranteed.

It was like that, too.

The first razor slices of fear proved survivable. IT was around, in and through me, and I was still there. Barely.

Because perfection isn't natural.

The superimposition of systems upon one another leaves fault lines. Gaps. There are places where the paradigms just don't line up. Shoddy carpentry.

These holes are where people can fall through.

I am a product of this gap, or fault, or well. But it's all in the vocab. You see, if it's a fault, then it's bad and dangerous. If it's a well, it's good and bountiful. What's in a name?

My name is Cassidy Walker. I can cross the boundaries between systems. I can steal from one realm and give to another. I'm pure invention. I'm in this world, but not of it.

I thought I was trying to build a world, but on second thought this little song isn't really about architecture, is it? A building is someplace to shelter, or to contain, or to in some way blot out natural design in favor of something front-end heavy, something big-snoutedly mathematical. Isn't it?

But a fight is something else. A fight is messy and scrappy

and not much fun. A fight is about dropping all pretensions and getting on with it. You and me. You being IT and me being me.

And anyway, isn't IT time you came out from behind that pretending-to-be-a-dragon-a-planet-a-city-an-idea curtain?

My body is salty water and minerals arranging themselves in a fragile and temporary process.

But what is IT? An idea.

One blast of IT will pulverize me.

One bite will devour me.

So why don't you? Go on, just do IT.

Just quit fucking up my world and come and get me. If I'm what you really want.

Unless maybe you can't handle me, after all.

OK: here's my song.

My song is blue-fingered ancestresses singing their babies to sleep, fur and rawhide, withies woven for shelter.

My song is barking in the face of a blizzard to clear the lungs. My song is ankle-deep in a thawing brook, tickling a trout between numb fingers.

My song is the desperate sweat and vomit of labor going wrong, and the eyes and hands of the women around me telling me so even when their mouths say otherwise.

My song is the stink of an industrial city and my bleached fingers working cheap cloth and the roar of the sewing machines, and the clawed feeling where my upper back has cramped into a permanent hunch of concentration and subjection so that I become folded like a bat.

My song is performing all the parts of my play on a summer afternoon with only goats for an audience.

My song is gravity and ice and a well-oiled sled on a Sunday morning in the park. My song is planting things and going to watch them grow, every day, and apologizing to the seedlings that I must thin as I pull their roots from the ground because I am young enough to know that I am but one of those seedlings: a lucky one.

My song is peat smoke and packing all our belongings into a rough sack before I carry the younger ones across the back field to hide in the heather because our men have been killed; and my song is also seeing the strong intelligence in the eyes of my oldest who understands what the boots coming up the road mean – and therefore my song is my heart breaking.

My song is hiding in the outhouse in a game of hide and seek and then almost passing out from the smell.

My song is sex like animals that hurts because he goes so deep, so hard, so long, and as his weight grinds my face into the grass I think how beautiful he is anyway.

My song is spending all my money on candy.

My song is how I will punch you in the face if you look at me the wrong way and, if that doesn't work, I'll bite you.

My song is making paper boats and then chucking rocks at them to sink them.

My song is a newborn baby, breathing.

My song is out of tune, off-rhythm, faltering.

Are you sure you want this song? It's nothing much, but it's more than nothing.

You might break me down. Or I might just break you, period.

You won't quantify me like you do everything else, not finally.

And fuck transcendence, by the way.

IT is literally the belief that the world can be deciphered. And all that results of IT being unleashed on the world is that the world has been rendered senseless. Because the world isn't *some other truth* written in invisible ink. The world is its own explanation.

*

IT started to separate. As though my voice were flaying ITs body, IT broke up into strings and strips. These curled and spiraled fragments then fell away from each other with a sound like a ruined harp falling into broken glass. They began to slither away in many directions.

IT was only an idea, after all. IT was an idea that had no place in my sound. For there could be no single governing principle for me, no way to make the world simple, any more than there could be One Great God whether Ra or Yhwh or any other.

No one was in charge of my world.

The executive function was a myth.

Even in consciousness. Especially in consciousness. I did not exist, and that was a fact I was bound to rail against all my life. From that friction, from that fiction of my self, came the very spark of my being.

Life was a session. Anyone could play.

And this simple assertion in my sound was to be the undoing of IT, the Machine Front Animate Logic-Slicer, conceived to arrange world into packageable shapes. Square tomatoes and orderly thought, making minions of us all.

'You don't exist,' I sang to IT. And IT didn't. The logic bullets had been a big fake from the get-go. A joke on the part of the Grid. IT unraveled, gorgeously, disgorging scraps of sound like so much junk.

Little ITs wriggled around, nipping at my ankles, a sea of them, denuded of content, dispersing into the Synchronicity. Leaving me, finally, alone.

All nine of me.

I shut my mouth. Silence rose up like a soft tide.

The Synchronicity percolated beneath my feet: eighteen soles and, beneath them, the fizz of change. There was no sound. I breathed. I looked at myself. My multiplicity was oddly reassuring: safety in numbers?

IT was gone, but there was something left in my throat. There was something left in my head, some fragment of melody, maybe, or something still unfinished. Or maybe it wasn't something left over so much as something becoming possible for the first time. *What happens after*, as Ben would say.

I began to hum, first one of me, then another and another, until all of me were singing. But not in unison: all different.

I was singing nine codas, nine tails that were the wake of IT, and as I sang I walked into myself. My nine bodies walked into one another and for a moment there was a contact point for all of me: there, one body, one mind, one place, one sound.

Then – being Cassidy Walker – I kept walking out through the other side of myself. Nine of me sang nine codas and walked nine ways, and I passed through my self and out the other side into the unknown.

Coda Nine

'There you are,' I said. 'The last time I saw you, you were dead.'

'Don't worry about that.'

When you really looked at him, Gunther was suprisingly slight. There was nothing prepossessing about him; he'd vanish in a crowd or even a crowded elevator. But I detected a certain note of domination in his voice. He expected people to go along with him, and they did.

He pointed to a leather armchair, something that Vincent Price would have sat in – or maybe, these days, Diana Rigg.

'Don't upset yourself too much, Cookie,' he said, and reminded me of my mother. 'IT can't be destroyed as long as you are alive, because your very existence implies IT.'

Ooh, the guy had a way about him; I'm not sure what it was. He seemed so sure of himself – almost to the point of obstinacy. He was square-edged, and he knew his own limits. And it was sad, in a way; but mostly, here and now, it was menacing.

'But I threw myself down ITs throat. To save her.'

Gunther shrugged. 'That was a dumb thing to do. Didn't you realize you were already there? Didn't you know you were her and she was you?'

'I wish you were really dead,' I said.

'I know you do. But if I were really dead, you wouldn't really exist, would you?'

'I still say you're a delusion.'

'Maybe, but I'm yours, honey. Or you're mine.'

I looked around. Nice room. Panneled oak. Parody of seriousness.

'It's pretty civilized in here,' I said.

And my words seemed to bring Grid out of the walls. Gunther himself was turning into a web of connections and disjunctions. I blinked, but it didn't help.

'The less you think,' he said cheerfully, 'the safer you are.'

I stood up.

'Just show me where the TV is,' I said. 'I've got to go to work.'

And Gunther said:

'Everybody on TV works for me.'

He crossed his legs like the devil he is.

Coda Eight

I have swallowed IT, somewhere along the line. As long as I exist, so will IT, because it is made of the stuff of me and vice versa. So: I have swallowed IT and I am inside IT now, in the neverspace that lines the walls and ceilings of the Abstract.

Inside ITs skeleton everything is streamlined and perfect. The answers come easily. Like living inside a pocket calculator. Oh, to be a part of a solvable world. Happy little number in the equation. Everything plays out. Everything comes good.

Order grows, builds, clicks into place as perfection is achieved. Then, even when it all falls apart, the disorder is welcome because a new and better order will come. Joy in patterns.

Choir music; appeasement; death.

I am smiling, beatific. I don't ever want to leave.

Let me stay in the machine forever, and keep your ugly indefinite planet.

Coda Seven

My guitar lies in my lap like a sleeping child. Each string a dragon of possibility; each moment of stroking its chords a lovemaking with the unseen. All my fingers splayed across the neck – some people would think it looks obscene, they'd look away, but I am not ashamed. One extra finger, one extra note, and my hand spidercrawling up the frets in search of some conceptual companionship.

I don't have to pretend to be whole.

I don't have to remember to breathe.

The guitar does that for me. Audible solace.

Gladly I'd lose myself for this.

Music is not narrative. Music is self-embedded, alinear, a waveform comprised of other waveforms, all of them equally identifiable as particles if frozen just so.

That's why musicians are fascinated with mandalas: because we all conceptualize music in terms of object, a 'piece' of music – damn that language again. And yet music is anything, everything, but object. The mandala is not the prayer, the map is not the territory, the score is not the piece.

Or is it?

The traveler is not the journey?

I am walking and I can never stop. It is not the case that if I stop I will die, or the world will end, or anything like that. Literally, I cannot stop. Some people cannot pass through the mist between realms. Pigs cannot fly. And I can't stop.

I want to say that somewhere the other eight of me are also walking and singing or at least mumbling or humming; that one day the music of our diverse experience will knit together, that there will be a line drawn under things that is more satisfying than just a last cup of broth before dying – although, who can say, maybe that is the most satisfying thing of all? I mean, I don't want to fall into one of those Eastern kill-your-ego enlightenment-seeking patterns. I believe in chalky fingers and coffee and work, so I keep walking and spinning out time, and hoping (that's the work part), however diminishingly, for something golden and indefinite to blow my mind. And with or without hope, I walk through systems like cloudy nights.

When I run my fingers through the numbers of the world they feel like fish.

When I close my eyes I could be walking up the wall of the sky.

Could be.

Could be is the only deal in town.

Coda Six

I am on a street called Martha Place. I am wandering downhill.
I know this street vaguely; grew up near here. Lots of trees.
Quiet. I am trying to remember how far it is to Dairy Queen. I
think I will get blisters.

The world is broken forever. Colonization of the thought
realm – can't go back on that one. Why is it so surprising that
the thought realm should retaliate?

The abstract realm, formerly wild, now footholded by us.
Which version of the world will eat whom in the end? Jury
out. No simple answers in nature, anyway: consumption
always a mutual affair.

Cookie: 'You have become more real than any of us.'

Yeah, right. What a comfort.

There is ice on the road. Snowplows have been through, but
they didn't lay enough salt down. My boots are slipping. I
can see my breath. My nose runs.

I have to live in the world, knowing it is fractured, knowing that I am a created thing and do not even belong to
myself.

Not an appealing prospect. There are too many surfaces in
the modern world, too many machine-made details. Too many

dead things. All those right angles and predictable curves, they hurt your head.

I will go into the rain forest and live on fried tarantula.

I will work at Burger King.

I will throw myself under the wheels of something in hope of finally being flattened.

No, little witches, I will not. I will walk down this road with dead squirrels in the middle of it and radio waves all jumbled in my head, the cars will go around me, their drivers listening to WQXR unheeding of its soaring pretentiousness quotient and they will think I am merely taking the air. And when I come to the boundaries beyond which real people can't go I'll hear IT and I'll sing right back in ITs face with every out-of-tune uncool variation of vocal abnormality I can muster.

And I'll cross over, into some other slice of the Brain Salad Surgery aka Synchronicity aka Grid, and be somewhere else again.

A lonely proposition. In one of these places or other I will need to find a boyfriend.

Ouch. Craig.

Maybe not a boyfriend, not yet.

It wouldn't really be fair to the guy, would it?

Coda Five

The Grid seethes as if I am flexing my muscles, and I am as large as a planet or whatever this place is. Scurrying intelligences vie for control, try to figure out how to work my lights and sounds and action figures. I want to say I understand now. Gossamer was a fragment, an envoy of me sent out and then called back.

But I am still here. Always will be. A peeled onion: nothing left of me but scent messages.

I'm the very stuff of the well. Transforming, disgorging, reproducing in slippery amniotic darkshine: keep your babies. I can change in ways they never will.

My nostrils are full of cast-off words, blueprints, binary.

I ruminate on numbers.

I will lie beneath the surface and draw thoughts to me like food.

Coda Four

Always in the Synchronicity, and always running. Whether toward or away from something, always running. Boots clanging as I lope across metal grates pursued by mysterious animalian entities, and the deep spaces of the Synchronicity echo beneath me. Or hurrying on my way to drink the poison in a black hotel, poison administered by someone claiming to be my friend. Looking for a different friend, whose name I can't remember, hoping to find her in crowds of strangers just by recognizing the Peruvian woven shoulder bag she always carries. Searching, searching. And fleeing, fleeing. The two become the same.

Sometimes I think that if I could gather myself in this place maybe I would be strong enough to turn and confront IT where it lurks in the interstices of things. Maybe I could face IT in all its lissome Chanel No. 5 commercial limbs, ITs breath of prosperity and hope, ITs electrodes sunk deep into the parts of my brain that will give forth on command memories of a childhood in which the world was sharp and I saw things as they are, not as I was to be willed to see them by ITs machine consciousness.

But this kind of cowboy confrontation is impossible. Sound

is not image. You can't take IT and stand back off IT. You can't objectify sound because, being made of time, sound changes by nature. Therefore the identity of anything made of sound would seem suspect, wouldn't it? How do you know you're listening to IT when IT is never the same – we're into neverputyourfootinthesamerivertwice philosophical mumbo-jumbo territory here, aren't we? After all: IT sounds like white noise. IT sounds like my voice. IT sounds like music that breaks the identity of music.

So in what sense can IT be a formula to decode *anything*?

In what sense can IT be said to even exist as an 'it'?

The fundamental nature of the world is acausal. Hence the Synchronicity: a self-constructing reality.

So there can be no such thing as Cookie's Machine Front – not in any way that presents a physical threat to the real world, anyway.

There can be no such thing as IT – right?

Except, if there were such a thing as a worldmind, human consciousness increasingly becomes the dominant paradigm. The human mind produces abstract thought. So it is that the realm of the abstract can break through, using us. The Grid can come here. And so can IT, that bastard of Grid and human and mech all rolled up into one big joystick.

Fuck me:

We have created IT, through our own thinking.

And – let's face it – we're pretty simple-minded in the end. We're just a piece of gut with self-perpetuating add-ons.

So what can we make of IT?

IT is a concept of control – thought control, behavior control, physical control – through manipulation of patterns.

That's Gunther: manipulate first, understand later – if at all.

And by association you can get out of this:

Universal consciousness.

Belief in the power of causality.

Belief in time.

Belief in science having *the* answers.

The domination of the rational.

OK, so far as it goes. But IT is only a concept. IT isn't real unless rendered so.

Just by having another idea, you can defy IT. Maybe even change IT.

I wonder what other idea you could have?

Oops. I don't know.

But I can tell you this: when the thing's chasing you around with bared teeth, showing every intention of gobbling you up, you have every incentive to think of something to save your self.

And if you can't think of anything, you better run for your life.

Forever.

Which brings us back to why I'm running.

Coda Three

I am young again, squatting on the ground playing a game of marbles. I know how to play even though 'I' have never played before.

It is a village, I guess East Africa judging by the red soil and the look of the people. I am black too: I look at my six skinny fingers and find that I like this. It feels like coming home.

I am allowed to be happy. The ghosts are everywhere. Animals move inside us.

It is a dream. I know this and I don't mind. I can smell the gasoline as a man fills the tank of his motorcycle. The radio crackles with indecipherable news. The sky to the west is incandescent, and my friends are beating me soundly at this game. I am not paying attention. I am too busy being happy.

There is noplace to go, nothing much to do. But I am inherently happy.

There is no such place as this.

No happy African freedom, no matter how I wish it.

This is only a slice, only the sweet part of the picture: romantic Africa.

It's just a wish. A fantasy concoction. A mighthavebeen, if only.

Did they have a room full of his stuff at home, or had he been wiped out as though he'd never been born? And if he had never been born, what about the lives of the people who should have been his parents? The whole fabric of the world had been altered, and yet somehow all the threads seemed to be hanging together. In pure spite.

I went back to Music Program Zero, but the sound sessions were no longer popular. That brief uniting of everybody on campus to play for their lives had been reduced to the status of half-remembered dream. No longer charged with the responsibility of weaving the fabric of reality with our very sound, we went on with our tiny classes, our Styrofoam cups of Kline Commons coffee, and our strenuous efforts to make meaning from things that disappeared as soon as you touched them.

The library was being rebuilt and there was a lot of new housing going up. Nobody thought this had anything to do with anything except an increasing student body.

Nobody mentioned the burn marks.

On the up side, I got my memory back. It happened like this: I was in the Rhinebeck Grand Union buying Ritz crackers and Nestlé Quik, and I saw this guy in a black trench coat and Doc Martens bent double, scrutinizing the label on a can of soup. He was kind of familiar.

'Gary?' I heard myself say. 'Is that you?'

He straightened and blinked. He recognized me.

'Hey!' he said. 'Cassidy, what are you doing here?'

And it all came apart, like when you pull the bakery string on a cake box and it all unravels and the cardboard falls open and there's a big Boston cream pie inside. I remembered everything. Gary was the older brother of my friend Donna from middle school. They'd moved to Virginia seven years ago. That had happened *before* the *Golden Dragon* episode.

And I remembered him. The last time I'd seen Gary, he'd been a preppy with short feathery hair. Now he looked scruffy and pale and malcontent enough to be a Bard student.

'I go to school here,' I said, a little breathless. 'Bard.'

'You're kidding! I'm visiting Donna – did you know she goes to Marist? And I'm taking a look at Bard while I'm up here. I applied to do an MFA in drama here in the summers. Hey, does this have meat in it?'

I looked at the soup. Minestrone.

'Are you a *vegetarian*?' I said. 'God, you've changed.'

He laughed. 'Do you still play guitar?'

'Yeah,' I said. I could feel a great big smile opening the muscles of my face. I must have looked like I was on drugs. I was being dazzled by all the memories that were breeding ferociously in the background of my mind, springing up huge and animate like Instant Martians, newly sprinkled with water, in a Bugs Bunny cartoon. 'Yeah, I still play.'

We headed over to Bard together and reminisced for half an hour before he had to go to his interview and I had class. As I watched him walk up the hill toward the Registrar's office I could hear my heart thudding. My insides were rearranging themselves to make room for the recovered life that Gary had handed me without even knowing it. My real life, from now on.

Some things were lost, some were found.

Epilogue

I didn't watch any TV for a long time. I wasn't deliberately avoiding it. But I was back at Bard, and you don't need TV at Bard because real life is interesting enough. I don't think I had occasion to watch TV until summer vacation when, dulled-out and hot and at a loose end after a day of packing boxes at a factory that made novelty ashtrays, I sat glassy-eyed in front of the screen and gave myself over.

And in the middle of an *LA Law* rerun, while Jimmy Smits was cross-examining a witness, Cookie appeared in shot over Jimmy's left shoulder. She was sitting in the jury box. She had braided her hair in cornrows, which threw me at first, but it was definitely her. As I sat there, slack-jawed, she even inclined her head ever so slightly in my direction. Regally.

I watched the rest of the episode but she didn't reappear. That was it. Just a glimpse. When I realized this, my throat went hard. My chin crumpled. I went outside, into the cricket-thick backyard and the warm June gloaming. I could hear my mother's feet pounding the treadmill, upstairs. A plane passed overhead. I sat on the squeaky old swing set, the one my dad keeps threatening to get rid of but doesn't. I slapped at mosquitoes.

There was no solution. I didn't know what world I belonged in.

Just live. Bottom line. But how?

An infinity of ways. A city of endless possibilities. A wilderness of choices.

I had turned my back on that. I had exchanged it for TV and a swing set. Seeing Cookie, alive in there in the crazy mix of the numinous, made me feel unsure about this choice.

Did I dare enter that place, ever ever again? Fracture myself on purpose?

Let's be real: would anyone go there on purpose, unless chased by IT?

Seriously: who would?

I might, though. I might, one day.

But tonight I sat on the swing set until it got really dark. Then I went inside and dug the Yellow Pages out of the kitchen drawer. Looked up *Trade Schools*, then *Plumbing*. Wrote down some phone numbers to call, tomorrow.

Tuned the guitar. Too shit-scared to play, though.

Instead fell asleep to the sound of tree frogs and crickets.

Sleep, like the silence between tracks: not the end. Just a significant pause.

I still see her sometimes. Actually, watching TV can be like a *Where's Waldo?* picture book. I just never know where I'll find Cookie. She'll be the hand opening the cat-food package in the occasional Tender Vittles commercial. She is sometimes an extra in romantic comedies, and she always seems to be in the crowd in fictitious baseball games. Once she even caught a home run. That time, she looked right at the camera and gave a huge, smug smile. Just like a chubby black elf.

I think she's there to be a thorn in ITs side. A bug up ITs ass.

I think she's guarding the world.

I think she's still trying to save us, in our fuzzy finite mortality, from being overrun by our own creations.

And maybe I'm just pulling the wool over my own eyes so that I'll feel better. But I hope not.

I hope she's finally home.

MAUL

Tricia Sullivan

In a mall like any other, two gangs of teenaged girls are about to embark on an orgy of shopping and designer violence. In the battleground of cool, they'll fight for their lives to prove that image is Everything. And in another place, within a sealed room, a lone man fights an equally desperate war against a new virus and the scientists who have developed it.

If anyone gets out alive, it will be a small miracle.

SINGULARITY SKY

Charles Stross

In the twenty-first century man created the Eschaton, a sentient artificial intelligence. It pushed Earth through the greatest technological evolution ever known, while warning that time travel is forbidden, and transgressors will be eliminated.

One far-flung colony, the New Republic, exists in self-imposed isolation. Founded by men and women suffering from an acute case of future shock, the member-planets want no part of the Eschaton or the technological advances that followed its creation. But their backward ways are about to be severely compromised in an attack from an information plague that calls itself The Festival. And as advanced technologies suppressed for generations begin literally to fall from the sky, the New Republic is in danger of slipping into revolutionary turmoil.

The colony's only hope lies with a battle fleet from Earth. But secret plans, hidden agendas and ulterior motives abound.